FOR MILTON BASS AND THE "BENNY FREEDMAN" NOVELS

"Benny Freedman is a likeable hero, wise and often funny, and Bass knows how to trigger the reader's emotions."
—*Chicago Tribune*

"A CORKING GOOD THRILLER . . . AND A RICH NOVEL FILLED WITH EXCITEMENT!"
—George V. Higgins

"Bass succeeds from first page to last in giving new twists to familiar characters and situations."
—*New York Newsday*

"THOROUGHLY ENTERTAINING . . . an engaging caper."
—*Publishers Weekly*

"I like this Benny Freedman, soft-guy, hard-guy, who'd clearly rather lose his life than his humor."
—Gregory Mcdonald, author of *Fletch*

"Bass . . . makes you remember Hammett."
—Charles McCarry, author of *The Last Supper*

"TOUGH, COGENT, SHARP . . . UNFLAGGINGLY READABLE!" —*Kirkus Reviews*

Ⓢ SIGNET (0451)

DIRTY DEALINGS...

☐ **THE BELFAST CONNECTION by Milton Bass.** Benny Freedman, the wily and charismatic half-Irish, half-Jewish street-smart police detective is better than ever when he goes to Ireland in search of his roots and finds himself in the middle of a religious war. "Thoroughly entertaining." —*Publishers Weekly* (162307—$3.95)

☐ **THE MOVING FINGER by Milton Bass.** Half-Jewish, half-Irish, Benny Freedman is not Everyman's image of a cop: A poetry-reading martial-arts disciple with a great appreciation for beautiful language and beautiful women. Now he's got to crack a case involving a murdered used-car mogul with a missing finger, a gorgeous widow, and a religious cult that worships money and makes a sacrament of slaughter....
(141105—$3.50)

☐ **DIRTY MONEY by Milton Bass.** Benny Freedman liked having six million bucks in the bank. But now he was caught between the Mafia, who claimed it was theirs and wanted to write out their claim in his blood, and an overheated lady of the family who wanted to use him to make her sexual fantasies come true ... Now with six million dollars worth of *tsouris*, Benny's life wasn't worth two cents.... (144805—$3.50)

☐ **THE BANDINI AFFAIR by Milton Bass.** Benny Freedman is up against the Mob and a no-good beauty as kissable as she is killable. The Mob wanted to bleed Freedman white with fear. But they only make him mad enough to give the masters of terror a stomachful of their own deadly medicine ... as he waded into an underworld swamp of steamy sex and savage slaughter, and where he had to be crazy as a fox to survive....
(148045—$3.50)

Price slightly higher in Canada.

Buy them at your local bookstore or use this convenient coupon for ordering.

NEW AMERICAN LIBRARY
P.O. Box 999, Bergenfield, New Jersey 07621

Please send me the books I have checked above. I am enclosing $_____
(please add $1.00 to this order to cover postage and handling). Send check or money order—no cash or C.O.D.'s. Prices and numbers are subject to change without notice.

Name_____

Address_____

City _____ State _____ Zip Code _____

Allow 4-6 weeks for delivery.
This offer, prices and numbers are subject to change without notice.

The Belfast Connection

Milton Bass

A SIGNET BOOK

NEW AMERICAN LIBRARY

A DIVISION OF PENGUIN BOOKS USA INC.

PUBLISHER'S NOTE

This book is a work of fiction. Names, characters, places, and incidents either are the product of the author's imagination or are used fictitiously, and any resemblance to actual persons, living or dead, events, or locales is entirely coincidental.

NAL BOOKS ARE AVAILABLE AT QUANTITY DISCOUNTS WHEN USED TO PROMOTE PRODUCTS OR SERVICES. FOR INFORMATION PLEASE WRITE TO PREMIUM MARKETING DIVISION, NEW AMERICAN LIBRARY, 1633 BROADWAY, NEW YORK, NEW YORK 10019.

Copyright © 1988 by Milton Bass

All rights reserved

This book previously appeared in a hardcover edition published by New American Library, a division of Penguin Books USA Inc., and simultaneously in Canada by The New American Library of Canada (now Penguin Books Canada Limited).

SIGNET TRADEMARK REG. U.S. PAT. OFF. AND FOREIGN COUNTRIES
REGISTERED TRADEMARK—MARCA REGISTRADA
HECHO EN DRESDEN, TN, U.S.A.

SIGNET, SIGNET CLASSIC, MENTOR, ONYX, PLUME, MERIDIAN and NAL BOOKS are published by New American Library, a division of Penguin Books USA Inc., 1633 Broadway, New York, New York 10019.

First Signet Printing, November, 1989

1 2 3 4 5 6 7 8 9

PRINTED IN THE UNITED STATES OF AMERICA

For
EVVIE and GEORGE
and
LEITA and PORGE
and
VATCH

I

1

IT ALL STARTED WITH THE SHOEBOX. NO, that's not right. A lieutenant in the homicide division of the San Diego police force should have his facts right. It began with the suitcase. The shoebox was in the suitcase. When I went back to Boston to check out whatever my father had left behind when he committed suicide, the only thing I brought back was the suitcase. I didn't know it at the time, but the box was in the suitcase. Everything else I dumped.

It's an easy thing to do. There are people who will come, check over the apartment and make you a bid for every single thing in it right down to a bent spoon. Mr. Latke. The Yellow Pages found me Mr. Latke, one of those Jews who specialize in stereotypes. He barely seemed to glance at anything as he wandered through the rooms, peering into cupboards briefly, checking one or two drawers, putting his hand into the freezer compartment of the refrigerator. However, I could tell from his eyes that nothing had been missed. Nothing. I wished that I could emulate him at a murder scene. My solved ratio would be improved by at least fifty percent.

He finished his inspection in my father's bedroom.

"So," he said, "how much of this do you want to get rid of?"

Get rid of. That was very good. He didn't ask which of your valuable pieces you wished to part with or how much you considered your precious heirlooms to be worth. *Get rid of* implied junk that he might take off your hands if the price was low enough. Not that it wasn't that far from junk. My father and mother's possessions hadn't been that good when they were new.

I looked around the room and just as I was about

to say "everything," I spied the suitcase in the corner. Outside of his violins, there was nothing my father prized more than that suitcase. It was made of real leather and it was the one he took with him when he went on tour with the Boston Symphony Orchestra. As I looked at it, I could picture him sitting in the kitchen with his mink oils and pastes and soft cloths, rubbing the surfaces until they gleamed richly in the light. There was something about owning that expensive suitcase that struck a chord in him as strong as anything Beethoven ever wrote.

But when his fingers twisted and curled up and he had to take a disability retirement, he substituted booze for the music and eventually sold the violins to pay for the seemingly endless stream of bottles that came into the house. But he hadn't sold the suitcase. He had kept the suitcase.

"Everything but that suitcase," I said to Mr. Latke.

He nodded. To him a suitcase was a suitcase.

"Look, Mr. Freedman," he said, "we're both Jewish and the holy days are just around the corner, so I'm going to make you an offer that anyone else in my business would consider foolish. I'll give you four hundred dollars for everything, *shmates* and all."

I didn't know what *shmates* meant, but I could tell they were nothing good. His features had set in the preparatory look for a reaction of outrage or at the least a counteroffer.

"Okay," I told him.

I couldn't tell whether the facial response was joyful at his steal or disappointed that there wasn't going to be a haggle. It probably was a mixture of both. He pulled a paper from his jacket pocket, which I signed, and then he peeled off four hundred dollars from an impressive roll of bills that he fished out of his right pants pocket. I picked up the suitcase and returned to California.

Whenever I moved to a new place, the suitcase went with my other stuff, but I never used it to carry anything. Opening it would have been like opening a door to the past, and that was the last thing I wanted to go through again. So it came along like an albatross hanging around my memories, but at the same time it was like the emperor's clothes—it wasn't there.

Why did I open it? It had something to do with my frame of mind. I was on the thirty-fifth day of the twelve-week sick leave I was forced to take when Del Bramini hired sharpshooters to wing me in the arm and the ass as a warning that I should return the five million dollars my wife Cathy had left me. Dirty money. Cathy hadn't even been a Mafia princess, only the daughter of a mob bookkeeper, and he was still able to scam five million bucks from the mother lode before they caught up with him. And when the cancer took her, she left it all to me. What was it with me and women? Loving me was like kissing death. Bandini. She had skimmed twenty million with Cathy's father, built it up into forty-four million and willed it all to me when the munitions factory she had in her cellar blew her into part of the Boston atmosphere. In less than a year, I had loved and lost two women, two incomparable women, each one unique in her own way. The only thing they had in common was that they left me millions of dollars, dollars that I didn't want and didn't need. A police lieutenant's salary is not what you would call munificent, but it munificed everything I wanted out of life.

So there I was stuck for another forty-nine days with nothing to do, nowhere to go, nobody I wanted to see. I could afford to do any damn thing I wanted, anything, and yet all I could do was punish my body by running ten miles every morning, performing innumerable sit-ups and push-ups, and showering about every four hours in the attempt to wash something off or out of me. Orange juice and English muffins for breakfast, a tuna fish sandwich for lunch and a frozen dinner at night. Twice I had gone out to restaurants when do-gooding people wouldn't take no for an answer, but both times I had spoiled their evenings by being terribly polite and nothing more, and after that I was left alone. What I wanted was to go back to work, to sink my whole body into the routine of police rules and regulations, but they wouldn't let me. Six weeks off for a wound, no matter how serious; two wounds, twelve weeks. I was like the spirit in the bottle in one of the Greek legends, who, when they asked her what she wanted, said, "I want to die."

I didn't want to die. I knew that eventually time would take me through what had happened to a new life of some kind, but whatever it was going to be seemed forever and a day away. Which explains as much as anything why I opened the suitcase.

It was down in our cellar storage area, and when I went down to get a book I wanted out of one of the boxes, I noticed the dusty suitcase. Was I trying to establish something with my dead father that I had never established with him when he was alive? I felt my face crack in a smile as that thought flashed through my head. No, I told myself, I just want to polish the goddamned thing, bring it back to the magnificence it had once enjoyed. Maybe I wasn't a shining example of anything, but that was no reason why the suitcase had to suffer.

So I brought it upstairs, and dug out what polishes and cloths I found in the cabinet under the sink and went at it. I went at it with such fury that inside of ten minutes I had worked up a hard sweat and when I dropped the cloth an hour later, it was as if I had run my ten miles. It made me feel good to see it standing there with the light reflecting off its rich brown hide, and without thinking about it, I unsnapped the clasps and pulled the two sides apart. Inside was the shoebox.

Enna Jettick. The name on the cover of the shoebox was Enna Jettick. One of my mother's few extravagances had been shoes, and the top of the line to her was Enna Jettick. But it wasn't until that very moment, twenty-two years after her death, that I made the connection. Enna Jettick. *Energetic*. I had always thought that Enna Jettick was the name of the woman who either made the shoes or owned the company. I sat there smiling as I wondered what my mother had thought the name meant, but even as I wondered, I knew. Enna Jettick to her had to have been a tall, blond society belle who wore a fur coat no matter what the month of the year, and who had more shoes than Imelda Marcos. Some comedian had commented that with all those shoes, Imelda had

THE BELFAST CONNECTION 11

only one pair of stockings, and I knew that my mother had two pairs because the spare was always hanging up to dry in our kitchen.

The piece of twine that circled the box fell apart as my finger pried at it, and I slowly lifted off the cover, almost in the manner in which a painting or a sculpture is unveiled. For some reason, I had expected a pair of black shoes, so I was quite unprepared for what the cardboard carton actually contained. Letters. One . . . two . . . three . . . four . . . five . . . six letters. All addressed to my mother. All with foreign stamps. With two different kinds of cramped handwriting among them. Six letters. I had two audio cassettes of my father playing the violin, and now I had six letters that had been the property of my mother. These were the physical part of my legacy. How many ounces did they comprise? It was the weight of the memories that suddenly started to pull me down.

All of the envelopes had yellowed over the years, but only one of them looked the worse for wear. It was as if this one had been read innumerable times, the letter being slipped in and out of the envelope by fingers that had either grease or dirt on them, enough so that a good technician could have lifted prints off it. I put this letter at the bottom of the pile.

The top envelope had only one thin sheet of paper in it, and the handwriting was close to that of a childish scrawl.

Dear sister Deirdre,
   Thank you for the ten dollars. Mother is still feeling poorly, and the boys have not been able to find work anywhere. Timmy Walton has been taken to prison for fighting with a British soldier, and him with his da so close to death that you can smell it. Father Delavar preached on Sunday that we should all learn to love our neighbors whether they be Catholic or Protestant, and nearly all the men in the church stood up and walked out, including your four brothers. We are planning to get a bit of nice meat

today, and cook a hearty broth for mother. John
says he hopes you earn enough money soon to
get him to America too so he can make his fortune and none of us will be in want. Meanwhile it is you and the dole that keeps us alive
and it would be nice if you could send a few
more dollars than you have been. Mother says
you should be a good girl and stay out of trouble and go to church as you should. Please send
more money as we need it desperate.

> Your sister,
>
> Margaret

The next four letters were approximately the same, spread over two years—sad recounts of poverty and need, urgent requests for more money than was being sent, news of Catholics who were beaten or jailed for going against British authority, and admonitions to be a good girl. The last letter, the smudged one, had a different scrawl delineating the address, and as I pulled the sheet from the envelope, I could tell right away that a male had written this one, and that the words had been jabbed into the paper with a fierceness that made it feel like I was holding an iron anvil in my hands.

Deirdre—
We received the fifty dollars along with
the news that you are marrying a Jew. Did you
think that fifty dollars would take the curse off
it? Needless to say, our mother is now at death's
door and this news will push her all the way
through. Your brothers and sister have gone to
church to pray for your soul, but we all know
it is in vain. You always were the one to go your
own way no matter who you hurt. When you
scraped together enough money to go to America, we hoped that you would be the salvation
of your family rather than the destroyer. Father
Delavar says you are not the first Irish girl who
has fallen in with bad companions in America,

but that he never expected that you would be one of them. He asked if you are with child. He is saying a special prayer that God will show you the light and that you will turn your back on evil and at the least bring the baby up as a Catholic. Know this then. If you go through with this marriage, from then on you have no family in Ireland, no mother, brothers, sister or other loved ones. You are an outcast, a shamed thing. We never want to see or hear from you again. As far as we are concerned you are dead but not buried in hallowed ground. May you rot in hell for this terrible thing you are about to do.

William

The first thing that occurred to me, being half Jewish, of course, was that nothing was said about returning the fifty dollars. And then a rage began to build in me, an anger so strong that I flung the box and letters from me, fell down on the floor and did push-ups until I collapsed in exhaustion onto the carpet. My body was covered with perspiration and my eyes were wet, but I couldn't tell if it was tears or sweat. No wonder my mother was a such a sad, silent lady, one whose alcoholism had not been caused entirely by my father's own burden. Working as a barmaid, she had obviously sent what she could to the old country, money that was almost certainly vital for her own needs. God knew what it took for her to write them that she had fallen in love with a Jew and was about to marry him. There was no baby coming. I wasn't born until two years later, and I was so difficult even in birth that the doctor told her she could never have another child. I wondered what it would be like if I had a brother or a sister instead of nobody at all. Nobody at all. Except for these sons-of-bitches somewhere in Ireland. I turned the envelopes over until I could make out the postmark on one of them—Belfast. Northern Ireland. Only one of the letters had a return address on it, and I wasn't sure I could make out what it was even with a magnifying glass. The handwriting expert down at the station could probably do it for me. God knew he had few opportunities to use his specialty. I kept thinking of what I would say if I ever confronted these people, these brothers and a sister who had cut off my mother like she was a cancer. Where were they? Were they alive? Were they in the same place? What were they like today, after all these years?

The telephone rang. It was the captain.

"Benny," he said, "I did what I could, but they went back on their word. They won't budge a day. You've got to stay out for the whole shmear."

"That's okay," I told him.

"What?"

"That's okay. I have some things to do and I can use the time."

"Jesus Christ," he yelled, "here you been driving me nuts with your whining that you had to come back to work and now you say it's okay. I been breaking my ass all the way up to the chief when there's a lot more important things I should be doing, and you say it's okay."

"Yeah, it's okay," I repeated.

I was thinking of so many things that he caught me by surprise. Usually I know what's coming and pull my ear a foot away from the receiver. But this time the bang was right in the eardrum, and it was loud enough and sharp enough to knock my head sideways.

I put the letters back in the box and placed the box in the suitcase. But just as I was shoving the two halves together, I stopped still and opened them up again. If I was going to visit my mother's side of the family, what could be more appropriate than to do it with my father's suitcase?

2

THE INDIAN WAS ALMOST SHORT ENOUGH to be a figurine. Black suit and shoes, dark beard, mustache, white shirt with black tie, a black turban wound in a perfect spiral, black edges to his fingernails.

I noticed the fingernails because he had taken the top off a large brown bottle, poked his finger through the protective cardboard covering and was rummaging around inside it.

"Those are vitamins" (she pronounced it "viitamiins"), protested the lady whose suitcase was being methodically ravaged. "They are vitamin-C tablets for my mother."

She turned to me, her dudgeon obviously approaching high. "I shall have to throw away all the top tablets," she said. "This is totally unnecessary."

The tiny Indian proceeded as though nobody else was present, and when he came to my suitcase, he was just as thorough in fingering every bit of clothing, in taking the head off the electric razor, in pawing through the toilet kit, before nodding pleasantly and going to the next victim. Sikh and ye may find. I wasn't sure if only the Sikhs wore turbans or all Indians did. I wondered if they all wound them each morning or if they had the equivalent of clip-on ties. There was plenty of time to ruminate about all of the above because the security at this end of Heathrow for those flying to Belfast was bothersome as well as reassuring. It would take a hell of a terrorist to slip through the nets.

By the time I had filled out the forms and gone through another screening by pleasant, pudgy, pink-faced English ladies who were just as thorough as the Indian had been, I would not have been surprised if someone had instructed me to go behind a screen, take off all my clothes and wait for a person wearing a rubber glove on his hand. We were told that we could take only one piece of carry-on luggage on the plane, and when a lady argued that she needed both her flight bag and her pocketbook, she received only bureaucratic smiles and the repeated declaration that "only one bag is allowed."

The flight seemed short after the long one from San Diego over the pole, but after the intense security at the London end, I wasn't sure what to expect when we landed in Belfast. Would they make us lie down on the moving belt and roll us through the X-ray machine? The only thing out of the ordinary that I could see was that the entrance road had irregularly placed concrete blocks set up so a vehicle with explosives couldn't ram right through the door, and there were barbed-wire entanglements at the sides and guardhouses scattered along the way.

The taxi driver was so affable and the scenery so green and pleasant that I was halfway into a doze when the brakes were slammed on so hard that I was bounced off the back of the front seat and down to the floor. It took me a few moments to remember who I was and where I was, and by the time I slid myself up and into my seat again, the cabby had his window down and was talking to a really big man dressed in khakis and with a red beret on his head.

The soldier leaned a little further through the window and turned his head toward me.

"Would you please get out of the car, sir?" he directed.

This was a voice of authority speaking, the kind I used when I was doing highway patrol in my early days in Northern California, so I unlatched the door and stepped out on the road. There were only a few cars on the highway, but they drove past as though we weren't even there. I noticed the others immediately. There was a soldier with a rifle squatting in the ditch on our side of the road, and across the intersection there were two of them in their own hole, manning a light machine gun. The taxi driver was not asked to get out of the car. He just sat there and looked straight ahead through the window.

"Do you have identification, sir?" asked the soldier, who was wearing sergeant stripes on his shirt sleeve.

I pulled out my passport and handed it over.

"And what might you be doing here, sir?" he asked.

"Visiting relatives."

"Do you have any baggage?"

"It's in the trunk."

Without anything being said, the cabby held his keys out the window, and the sergeant unlocked the trunk where my father's suitcase had been stashed.

"Would you open it please, sir?" asked the sergeant.

I opened the clasps and pulled the sides apart. The sergeant had stepped back and to the side while I was doing it, and I wondered if he thought I might be carrying a bomb. I almost mentioned how thorough the Indian had been at Heathrow and how the nice ladies had double-checked, but the best thing is to keep quiet during security searches. The nervous babblers are almost always innocent, but they sometimes say things that opens new avenues that have to be investigated.

The sergeant drew close to look at my jumbled packing, but just as his hand was reaching in to poke under some shirts, a shot rang out from the left and a bullet screamed between our two heads with maybe two inches to spare on either side. We both dropped to the ground at the same instant, showing that our training was not that dissimilar, and I rolled to the right, vainly seeking where the attack had come from. The sergeant was already on his feet, while I was still trying to haul myself up by means of the rear bumper, and by the time I made it, he was standing over the pimply young man who had been kneeling in the ditch to the side of us, and was pouring obscenities down on his head like he had a bucket full of them in his hands.

"Welch, you dumb son-of-a-bitch," he roared. "What in the name of hell did you think you were doing?"

"My finger slipped," the young man whined.

"Slipped, did it, you fucking sod! Why in Christ's name was there a live bullet in there in the first place? This is a training mission, you poor miserable bastard, and I ought to rip off your bloody head and stuff it up your bum."

"My finger slipped," the young man repeated.

"Get the hell to the car," the sergeant said, and he waved his hand at the two others in the ditch on the other side, who immediately started gathering their equipment together.

The sergeant never even looked at me again, but started heading for a small grove of trees on the other side of the road, where I noticed a car had been tucked in between two trees. I stood there, not quite knowing what to do, then I pulled my suitcase together, shut the trunk and returned the key to the cabby, who was still sitting behind the wheel and whose face was as impassive as ever. I got in the back seat again and we started off. As we passed the car with the soldiers, I saw the sergeant standing by the side of the road waiting for the men with the machine gun to stow their equipment. The one whose rifle had gone off was already sitting in the back of the vehicle, which had no markings on it to indicate any official status.

The cabby was obviously not going to continue his conversation about whether this was my first trip to Northern Ireland, so as soon as my heart resumed a fairly normal rate, I took the initiative.

"What the hell was all that?" I asked. For a moment I thought he wasn't going to answer.

"It was just the boys out doing their job," he said.

"What boys?"

"What's that?"

"Are they Army, police, British, Irish? Who the hell were they?" My fear was turning into rage.

"They're from the UDR," he said.

"What the hell is that?"

"It's the Ulster Defense Regiment," he explained, in the tone reserved for children or the mentally deficient. "They was just doing their job."

"Well, they don't seem to be doing their job too well."

"They do it well enough."

The goddamned bullet hadn't whistled past his head, the son-of-a-bitch. I hoped the sergeant was holding the kid's balls aloft in the air somewhere in this benighted land.

The taxi driver gave me one more piece of pertinent information as we reached the center of Belfast.

"Nice hotel, the Forum," he said as we waited for the street barrier to lift to allow us to pull up to the front of the place. "Been bombed thirty times in the last nineteen years."

I looked at the barrier gate and at the security house which everyone going into or out of the hotel had to pass through, and I wondered what life was like for the bomb squad of the Belfast police department. I wondered what life was like for every police officer in Belfast. Just across the street I could see two of them walking, both with slung rifles, and they also looked bulky enough to be wearing bullet-proof vests. A policeman's lot was not an easy one in Northern Ireland. For the first time in my life, I did not tip a cabby.

The hotel was anything but fancy, but the travel agent had informed me that accommodations in Belfast were neither extensive nor luxurious. The room was clean, had a bed that looked slightly smaller than single, and there was a thirteen-inch color television set. I have worked up a set of standards over the years. Motels are judged by whether or not they have a box of facial tissue in the bathroom and if the towels are more suitable for drying dishes than bodies. The status of hotels was determined by amenities like small bottles of shampoo and lotion and suchlike on the back of the washbasin. I had once rented the best suite in a luxury hotel in Boston, and the bathroom contained a basket of expensive soaps and shampoos, a hair dryer, a telephone extension, a scale, and a nine-inch television set. The bathtub had a

Jacuzzi in it. It cost five hundred bucks a night, and for that there should have been hot and cold running maids, so you really paid for more than you got. We had only tissue and small soaps and fair-sized towels at the Forum, but the color TV and the telephone by the bed had to up its listing by about two grades.

It was eleven A.M., their time, and I hadn't slept in something like twenty-six hours. There are two theories about what to do when you change time zones. Some say you should nap, shower, eat and go back to bed. Others maintain you should fight it through and stay up until it's the accustomed bedtime wherever the hell you might be.

There was no debate possible in my case. I was too hyped up to go to sleep, the airline food had solidified in my stomach to the point where I wondered if I would ever be hungry again, and I couldn't wait to confront whatever relatives might be left me after all those years.

I looked in the telephone directory but there was page after page of Callaghans. There were even more Callahans than Callaghans, but my burden was too heavy as it was for this to provide any solace. The name on my mother's kiss-off letter, and my face burned as I thought on that for a minute, had been William. I checked through the William Callaghans and there were enough of those to man a battalion. The one address I had was on the letter from sister Margaret, who had obviously married because the name written above the street and number was O'Malley. I tried to match one of the myriads of O'Malleys in the book with the address Sergeant Jenks had deciphered for me in San Diego, but I had the same luck the third time I tried it as I did the first. As with all investigations, it was going to be necessary to visit the scene of the crime.

When I showed the address I had to the driver waiting at the taxi stand outside the hotel, he pursed his lips, furrowed his brow and stared off into space for what had to be a minute. I figured he didn't know the street and was trying to get some bearings.

"I can't take you there," he said finally.

"You don't know where it is?"

"Oh, I know where it is all right," he said, "but it's in the Falls, and there isn't no driver who will take you in. I will take you four streets away, and you can walk in from there if you want."

"Why the hell can't you . . . ?" I began, but the stolid look on his face told me the answer. Enemy territory. He wasn't going to cross the line. I've never been in a war, but I worked with a detective named Moran who was in Vietnam, and he would tell me sometimes when we were on stakeouts about what it was like to be in combat in the jungle. You only went into enemy territory because you were ordered to, and nobody had the power to order this cabby to go into the bush.

Although the dropoff point had to be in territory he considered fairly safe, he still looked nervous as he watched me get out, took the money and pointed in the direction I was to go before he drove off with a slight squeal of tires. I looked around. There was no jungle here, only drab brick houses which had all kinds of slogans painted on their walls, mostly having to do with the IRA. IRA. What's in a name, Juliet asked the dark sky. In the United States, IRA stood for Individual Retirement Account, something to take care of you in your twilight years. Here it was quite different, quite, quite different.

I started to walk in the direction the cabby had pointed, but within a block was totally bewildered not only as to whether I was going right, but also where the hell I was. There were surly-looking young men sucking on cigarettes and leaning against buildings all over the place, and I finally went over to a trio that had been staring at me since I had crossed the street.

I held the slip of paper in front of me almost like a virgin holds the cross before a vampire, and they all looked at it without saying anything.

"Can you tell me where I might find this address?" I asked them.

"Are you an American?" one of them wanted to know.

"Yes."

"Why do you want to find this place?" the tallest one asked. Their accents were so strong that I had to work at understanding what was being said to me. It seemed like a mixture of brogue and cockney and Brooklynese, or it might have been pidgin Swahili for all I could make out.

"An aunt of mine lived there many years ago, and I'm over here to try to get in touch with her," I told them. It was none of their business, but I was lost and alone and in no position to mount a righteous stand.

"You go up two streets and take a right, and it's halfway down on the left-hand side," the tallest one said.

"Do you know what family is living there now?" I asked, but they just stared back at me, and after a few seconds I muttered "Thanks" and went on my way. If this had been San Diego, I might have rousted them against the wall just because of their attitude, but I was a stranger in a strange land and even though my badge was pinned to the inside of my wallet, I didn't have the gun that would have been necessary to forge my position. There were some small kids chasing each other down the block, their whoops of laughter no different from those where I lived, but even these children were an unknown quantity to me, and I kept my eyes on their location as well as on everything else. What the hell are you afraid of? I asked myself. The unknown, I concluded. The incident on the highway was still sticking in my gut.

I went two streets up, hung a right and walked what I considered halfway down. There were odd numbers on the houses on my side and the one I was looking for was an even, so I crossed the road but had to go back two sets of stairs to find it.

There it was, the one I was looking for. It stood out from the others only because there was a black wreath hung on the door, the kind that betokens death. Jesus, I thought to myself, if you want a symbol, Benny, here it is. Turn around and run like a deer. But even as I was thinking it, I was walking up the stairs.

Before I had to decide whether or not to knock, the door opened and a man and a woman stared at me for a moment before stepping back to allow me space to enter. The only thing to do was nod at them and go into the vestibule as they went out and closed the door behind them. On my left were stairs going up to the second floor, and on my right was a half-open door which also had a black wreath hanging from it. Which of the three floors, if any, did my aunt live on? Should I go up the stairs and inquire there or poke my head into the place where death was already visiting?

Once again the choice was made for me. The door opened all the way and an elderly man's rosy-spotted face peered out at me. He had a shock of white hair that blended perfectly with his rotund, chalk-white skin, and the red veins running down and across his generous nose indicated that alcoholic beverages were not unknown to him. He was looking at me inquiringly, the kind of look that solicited speech, so I bit the bullet and said:

"I'm looking for the home of Margaret O'Malley."

"Then you've found it," he answered.

"Would you be so kind as to tell me on which floor it is located?" I asked. Here the guy had thrown one short sentence at me, and I was already falling into the rhythm of their speech. In another day I would probably be saying "begorrah" after every other word.

"Well, it's this very one," he said, opening the door wide to disclose a myriad of people standing in a cloud of cigarette smoke so thick that it looked like you could lean on it.

"Come in, come in," he ordered, waving his hand in a way that brooked no denial. As I went through the door, he whispered, almost like there was a conspiracy of some sort, "Sean is in the parlor."

He took me by the arm and led me through the people, each one of whom stopped his or her chatter to stare until I had passed by, and then resumed it at what seemed double the decibels.

If I had thought the first room to be crowded, the second had to be close to the slave holds on the wooden ships. There were more people and chairs crowded into the room than seemed possible, and you had to thread your way through to get to the front, where the casket was situated. I looked down at the young man lying in it, clad in a cheap black suit and with a rosary draped through his folded hands. His head looked so peculiar that I gawked at it as though I were all alone in the room and there was no time limit imposed. It seemed larger than any skull I had ever seen, and its shape was way off center. The body, although thin and puny, seemed normal, but the head was that of someone suffering the so-called "elephant" disease. I wondered what terrible plague had struck this young man down, and I caught myself in time as I started to turn to ask the question.

Rather than to just stand there with my mouth open, I continued the turn until I was facing the rest of the room. It was divided into two sections of folding funeral chairs, one on each side of me, and there seemed to be two quite different groups of people sitting in them. The one on my right was a mixture of males and females of all ages and sizes. The women were talking to each other, often over the fronts of the men sitting in between them, and as they talked they wiped their eyes with small handkerchiefs.

The other group had only two women, one young and the other just right to be her mother both in age and looks. On the other side of her was a man old enough to be her father, but every other chair in the group was occupied by a young man. The only one crying was the young girl. The rest of them sat there carved out of stone.

"Is Margaret O'Malley here?" I asked the man who had brought me in.

"That's her over there," he said, nodding at a middle-aged woman sitting in the front row on the right side, gazing at the coffin and crying her eyes out, every once in a while uttering a low keen as the women on each side of her held her arms and wept along with her. I looked for resemblance to my own mother but found none.

"And who might you be?" asked the man in a voice loud enough to command the attention of those nearby.

"My name is Benjamin Freedman," I said, "and my mother was Deirdre Callaghan."

"Ah," said the man, his eyebrows arching in surprise, "then you are the son of the Jew. I am your Uncle William, and that's your cousin Sean stretched out in the box."

3

"How's your mother?" asked my Uncle William, speaking as though he had seen her only a day or two before. He wasn't asking about his sister Deirdre; he was asking about this woman who had married a Jew.

"She's dead," I told him, as the blood made my face feel all hot.

"Is she now?" he said, his voice flat. Since he had told her she was "dead" some thirty-three years before, the news didn't seem to surprise him now. "Do you have a wife?"

"She's dead too," I told him.

"What was she?"

"What was she what?"

"Was she Jewish too?"

"Half."

"What was the other half?"

"Italian."

"Go on with you," he said. "Do you have any kids?"

"No."

"Well at least that's something," he said. "Their Irish blood would be so thin that they'd piss pink. Are you a Communist?"

"No."

"What are you then?"

"A policeman."

"A policeman? I never heard of a Jew being a policeman."

"My father's dead too," I told this dinosaur. Whether he wanted to or not, he was also going to know about the only one-hundred-percent Jew in his family. My stomach was churning so hard that I feared something might burst through it, a creature like the one in the movie *Alien*. I looked at the "creature" in front of me. This guy went beyond bigotry. The stuff he was spouting merited a Ten Commandments of its own. What had made me come all those thousands of miles for this? What had made me think that there could be a social connection as well as a blood one? Did I want anything to do with these people? Better to have stayed at home licking my wounds than to have sought out another source of sorrow. The twenty-seven hours without sleep suddenly fell down on me, and I closed my eyes for a moment in the vain hope that when they opened again I would be anywhere but where I was. But that's exactly where I was.

"Come meet your Aunt Margaret," he said, taking me by the arm and pulling me toward the front row, where the frothy hats were bobbing as the mourners dabbed at their eyes. We stopped in front of the woman he had pointed out before, who gazed up at us through her tears.

"Margaret," he said, "this is . . . this is . . ." (the son-of-a-bitch couldn't remember my name) "Deirdre's son, who has come from the States to visit with us."

"Deirdre's son?" she asked, her mind trying to break through her present tragedy to one of the past. "Is Deirdre with him?"

"Deirdre's dead," said William.

"She's dead?" she repeated, still looking at William. Then her eyes shifted to me, the messenger who had brought her word of another loss. "My sister's dead? My Deirdre's dead?"

I nodded at her because all the weeping in the room had ceased as though a higher being had waved a wand, and I didn't want my voice to be crying out in that wilderness.

"And you're her son?"

I nodded again.

She stood up and threw her arms around me, buried her head in my right shoulder and began her wailing louder than ever.

"The Lord taketh and the Lord giveth in return," she cried. Lifting her head from my shoulder, she addressed the room:

"They have murthered my son, my baby son, but He has sent another to take his place."

Then she buried her face in my shoulder again and began her wailing anew. Her grasp was such that I could not remove her arms without the use of force, and as I looked through the ribbons on her hat, I could see that every eye in the place was locked on my face tighter even than the arms around me. I was stealing the scene from the corpse. This woman (I was not able to think of her as Aunt Margaret) was so befuddled by what had happened that she was reading heavenly intents into my appearance, and the rest of them seemed ready to believe it.

After a while, I began to think that maybe this was purgatory, and we were going to be standing like that forever. But a slight young man walked over from the side of the room, pulled the pudgy arms loose and sat the lady down carefully in her chair.

"Ma," he said, "you can't be tiring yourself out so. There's still a way to go."

Then he turned to me and said, "If you're my Aunt Deirdre's son, then I'm your cousin Brendan. Would you like to get a breath of fresh air?"

He turned and I followed, past the chairs, through the people in the other room, out the doors and onto the outside stairs. I blew out before I breathed in, wanting to clear whatever crap was in my lungs rather than sucking it all through my system. If the Surgeon General of the United States was right, everybody at the wake might as well have crawled in with Sean.

"Your mother said murdered?" was out of my mouth before we had even completely turned to face each other.

"What?"

"Your mother said your brother was murdered."

"That he was," he acknowledged.

"What were the circumstances?"

He looked at me quickly, and for a moment I

thought he was going to tell me it was none of my goddamned business.

"Did you see the girl sitting with the bunch at the other side of the room?" he asked.

I nodded.

"Her name is Molly Peters and she's a Protestant," he bit off. "She claims she and Sean had been seeing each other secretly for the past year, and that they were engaged, and that he was coming from meeting with her when he was shot down in the street. If what she says is true about her and Sean, then we think somebody from her family found out about it and took my poor brother's life. Did you see her in there? We told her not to come, but she said she was going to be here if the whole IRA stood in the way. And then she brings all those UDA bastards with her as a bodyguard."

"What's a UDA?" I asked.

"It's the Ulster Defense Association, the toy soldiers of the Brits."

"Do you have any evidence that they murdered your brother?"

His eyes swept up to meet mine again.

"What are you? A policeman?" he asked.

"That's right. Lieutenant Benjamin Freedman, Homicide Division, San Diego, California."

"And did you come six thousand miles just to find out who murdered my baby brother Sean?"

"Right now I don't know why I came," I told him. "I found some old letters of my mother's, and I had the urge to meet some blood relatives, people I might clasp to my bosom and who would give me the feeling of having a family."

He was quick to note the bitter tinge in my voice.

"We're not a very notable lot, are we?" he asked, his own irony coming through. "I'm the only one who has ever been to university, and for sure my poems haven't been published in the United States. But if you're a Catholic over here, you don't get a chance at the work that doesn't strain your back and bow your legs, you don't get a chance at the decent housing, you don't get to be elected Lord Mayor of Belfast, and you don't find the police trying very hard to find out who killed your brother. I will admit though that Uncle William is the pick of the lot. Come on back in and meet the rest of the family. You might find some of them not so bad."

He turned without waiting to see if I was following, and left me with two choices. I could walk down the stairs, find a cab, return to the hotel and be on my way home on the first available flight. Or I could go in and meet the rest of the family.

Which I did. In spades. Uncles and aunts and cousins. Seemingly dozens of them. Their names, a litany of Hibernia, ran over me like rain off a duck's back. With the exception of one, I might have been meeting the people political candidates shake hands with at the gates of the factories. The one was Catherine, William's daughter, a girl pretty enough to have made her stand out on her own, but also the only one of the whole bunch who seemed genuinely interested in making my acquaintance, in greeting me as a relative as well as a person.

"I never knew my Aunt Deirdre," she said, "and I feel so much the less for that."

"Well," said Brendan, "that's the lot, the whole crew. Where are you staying?"

I turned and looked at the people across the room, the girl still crying and the men seemingly ready to attack upon order.

"What did you say her name was?" I asked Brendan.

"Molly Peters," he practically spat out.

I weaved my way through the aisles and crossed the room to stand in front of the girl. My presence seemed to make the tears in her eyes hold still for a moment before jumping.

"Miss Peters," I said, "my name is Benjamin Freedman, and I'm just in from America. Sean was my cousin and I just wanted to tell you how sorry I am for your loss."

She, on her part, was at a loss for words, and the man sitting next to her, the one I presumed was her father, stood up and extended his hand.

"John Peters," he said, "and I thank you for your good wishes on this doleful occasion."

He then introduced me to his wife, whose name I didn't catch, and his two sons, whose names didn't register, and to every other of the young men sitting there with them, none of whose names got past my outer ear.

"What was your name again?" Mr. Peters asked. He had obviously been paying as much attention to mine as I had been to theirs.

"Benjamin Freedman."

"And you say you're a relative of Sean's."

I nodded.

"Begging your pardon, but Freedman is a long way from both O'Malley and Callaghan."

"My late mother was Deirdre Callaghan," I told him.

"Ah, so," he said. "Well, it was decent of you to come over and try to comfort our poor daughter. Those people over there have been whispering that we done poor Sean in, but it was none of us. We knew what was going on between the two of them, and we weren't happy about it, but Molly had set her mind and that tipped the weight over everything else."

"I'm sorry to have met you under such circumstances," I said, moving my head to include all of them.

"Will you be long in Belfast?" asked Mr. Peters.

I thought about that for a second.

"I'm not sure," I said. "Right now it's up in the air."

I then patted the girl on the shoulder, releasing the stream of tears again, and went back to join my "family," who were looking at me peculiarly, not exactly sure of my actions and definitely unsure about my motives. Brendan was standing there with what looked to be a wry grin on his face.

"Well, aren't you the one," he said.

"Someone from the family had to do the right thing," I told him, reflecting his grin. "You're all acting like a bad road company of *Romeo and Juliet.*"

"If Sean hadn't taken up with that girl, he

wouldn't be lying there dead now," said Brendan. "Only death can come of mixing with Protestants. They won't be happy until we're all dead or driven over the border and maybe all the way to the sea."

"I'd like to read your poetry sometime," I said.

"That you will. And once we get this Christly business over with, maybe we can find out just how thick the Callaghan blood runs in your veins."

"When's the funeral?" I asked.

"It's supposed to be tomorrow," he replied, "but I see Uncle William is having a bit of a do with Mr. Perkins over there, and I'm sure it's about money that I'm just as sure the family doesn't have."

I looked over in the corner and a red-faced man in a dark suit seemed to be having a lively conversation with Uncle William, whose pasty face had also turned an interesting shade of red. I walked over and stood beside the two of them.

"What's the problem?" I asked.

"Nothing," said William. "It's a family matter."

"I'm family," I said.

You could have knocked him over with a nightstick. He stood there staring at me as though I were a Communist ghost.

"All right, then," he said. "Perkins here said that the funeral Meg wants will cost eight hundred pounds and she hasn't got eighty to scrape together."

"I'll pay the cost," I told the man.

"I beg your pardon?" he said in that universal tone of funeral directors.

"I'll pay the eight hundred pounds for the funeral."

"But who are you, sir?"

"I'm a cousin of the deceased."

"And where will the money come from?"

"Do you take traveler's checks?"

That gave him pause for the moment as he considered. I had the feeling he had never been paid in traveler's checks before.

"What kind?" he asked.

"American Express."

"Yes," he said. "That would do it."

I pulled one of the slim black books out of my breast pocket, asked him how he wanted it made out, and then signed eight of the green slips.

"Thank you very much, sir," said Perkins. He turned to William. "The funeral will go on at ten as scheduled." And he was out the door.

"Well," said William, "you're not only a Jew, but you're a rich Jew."

There had to be a touch of admiration, almost pride, in his voice. At least *his* Jew had the right stuff.

I didn't know how to answer his expression of gratitude so I just went out the doors to the outside and down the stairs and down the streets until I finally came to one that had taxicabs available.

As I rode back to the hotel, I thought on the past hour. I had found my Irish roots all right, but only God knew what kind of plants they fed.

4

I WAS BEYOND TIRED, BEYOND SLEEP, SO I took off my jacket and tie, slipped off the shoes and fell back on the bed, my gritty eyes staring up but not really seeing the ceiling. It was like looking into a void where there were no colors, no solidity, no way in or out.

What had brought me here to this godforsaken country? What was I running away from and what did I think I was running to? Murder? A homicide cop can't run away from murder no matter how far he travels. Whose idea of a joke was it that had me flying thousands of miles to walk into a wake where my cousin Sean was laid out with a bullet in his skull?

My total worth was something over forty-four million dollars, according to the most recent bank report, and I could have bought any goddamned castle I wanted in Ireland. The way their economy was going, I could have bought Ireland. Instead, I had bought myself a gang of ignorant anti-Semites who looked on me as something that belonged in the sideshow of a cheap circus.

Once the funeral was over, I would . . . *The funeral!* I didn't know where the funeral was going to take place. Ten o'clock, the man had said, but he hadn't said where. It had to be in a church. But they would be leaving from the house, and all I had to do was get there at something like half-past eight to make sure they didn't go without me.

I was starting to feel drowsy but at the same time I was beginning to feel hungry, and I knew that I wouldn't sleep until I had given my stomach something to chew on while I was doing it. The light in the window was fading and even the noises from the street were muffled.

Sleep or eat? Just as I was about to let sleep take over, there was a knock on the door.

I couldn't move. There just wasn't enough strength in my body so I called out, "Yes?"

There was no answer for a moment, and then a very tentative feminine voice said, "Cousin Benny?"

Cousin Benny.

I pushed myself up and off the bed, but I couldn't find a light switch so I staggered over to the door and pulled it open. Standing there, a hopeful little smile on her face, was my pretty cousin, William's daughter . . . William's daughter . . . ? . . . Catherine! It hit me for the first time then that she had the same name as my wife, and I stared at her, trying to find similarities, of face, of body, but this was a delicate flower of a girl while my Cathy had been a full-bosomed beauty in all her glory, a woman in every sense of the word.

"Cousin Benny?" she said again, as though she were not certain that I was the person she was looking for.

"Yes," I said. "Yes, Catherine. Come in. Come in." And when she had done so, I closed the door and we were standing in almost total darkness.

"The light," I said, and went feeling along the wall like a blind man might in a strange room, but no switch was to be found. I blundered along until I hit the bed and then worked my way up to the end table, where I found the lamp and turned the switch. The glare blinded my eyes for a moment, and when I turned, Catherine was still standing by the door, her hand on the knob, poised as though ready to flee into the woods Bambi style.

"I'm sorry," I said. "I've got some jet lag and walking into that wake gave me quite a turn. Just give me a chance to splash some water on my face."

Her hand dropped from the knob so I went into the bathroom and cleaned up a bit. I needed a shower and a shave, but at least a clean face was a step in the right direction. She was still standing by the door when I came out again, but her arms were down by her sides and her feet were flat on the floor. I could tell by her face that she was asking herself why she had come here in the first place so I moved over to the far wall, as far away as I could get from her.

"Why don't you have a seat?" I asked, pointing to the only armchair available. She hesitated a moment and then walked over and sat down, her back straight up and her legs held primly together. A flower was the right thing to compare her to. The deep blue of her eyes and the white pinkness of her skin were framed by jet-black hair that fell softly to her shoulders. She was a skinny thing, and there wasn't the slightest bulge in the front of her sweater, but her legs were good, and there was no doubt that she was going to turn into a beautiful woman when her petals unfolded.

"I'm sorry to be bothering you," she said, her eyes shifting over to the rumpled bed, "when you must be tired from your journey, but I need someone to talk to and there's nowhere else to turn. You see, I was friends with Molly Peters in school, and it was me introduced her to poor Sean. I also know her parents and she is the apple of their eye, and though they had mixed feelings about Molly and Sean, they would never have done nothing that would cause Molly such grief."

"The brothers?" I said. "The friends?"

"No, not the brothers neither, and though I can't be positive about the friends, it all has the wrong feel to it. My cousins are all talking about getting their revenge and neither my father nor my uncles are saying no to it, and it would be worse than a shame if more blood was spilled, especially if the rest of them are all as innocent as Sean was when it came to the troubles."

"Catherine," I said, "I'm a stranger in a strange land. Why do you come to me with this?"

"They said you are a policeman," she answered. "I want you to find out who really killed Sean so that blame can be put in the right quarter and no innocent blood will be shed, and this will help you in your quest."

"Quest?"

"Yes, the reason you came to Ireland."

"And what might that be?"

"Why, 'tis plain as the nose on your face. You

came to embrace Mother Church. You came to fulfill your heritage as a Catholic."

Instinctively my hand went up to my nose. I have a nice nose, not too big, not too small. Just right. With not even the hint of a Semitic hook. No one looking at my nose would think Jewish. But then again, no one looking at my nose would assume that what I wanted most on earth was to adopt my mother's childhood faith. I say childhood faith because she never once went to church in the years I knew her, just as my father never went to the synagogue. They each talked as though they were stalwarts of their race and religions, but it was straight nationalistic rather than religious. The girl was sniffing at the wrong totem pole.

"Do you know a nice place to have dinner, Catherine?" I asked.

She looked at me uncomprehendingly. She was so hyped up on my conversion that only mention of the dividing of the loaves and fishes would have allowed her to follow the train of thought.

"Dinner?" she said. "We don't go out to eat much, except for some fish and chips or a Wimpy. No, I don't really know of any nice places."

"They can probably tell me of one at the desk," I said. "Would you like to have dinner with me and we can talk some more?"

"Yes," she said. "I'd like that. I'd like to do that."

"Do you want to call home and tell them?" I asked, pointing at the telephone.

"No," she said. "We don't have a telephone. Nobody has money for a telephone."

"Shouldn't we get word to your folks where you are so they don't worry?"

"No, that's no problem," she said, "as long as I'm home before eleven."

These people are more liberal with their daughters than I would have given them credit for, I thought. I had expected chastity belts and twilight curfews.

"I have to take a shower and shave," I told her.

"I can wait in the hall," she said.

"No, I'll take all my things into the bathroom with me," I said, "and you can sit here and watch television."

So there we were forty-five minutes later, ensconced in a cozy restaurant whose menu was printed in French, surrounded by what seemed to be the Irish equivalent of yuppies, whose loud voices and laughter showed that their aims and desires were exactly the same as those in the States. It didn't make me feel at home, but then again, lately I hadn't felt at home when I was at home.

5

FUNERALS ARE NEAR THE BOTTOM ON the list of events I like to attend, just above Super Bowls. Not everybody feels the same way. We have a deputy inspector in San Diego who seems to enjoy nothing more than parading bodies out of this world. There are usually just under a hundred police officers killed in the line of duty each year in the United States, and I would bet that he attends ninety-eight percent of the funerals no matter where they are. He must pay his own expenses to some of them because it is doubtful the department has a very large budget for this kind of thing. Once he even went up to Montreal to participate in the ceremonies for a Mountie who had been gunned down trying to serve a warrant on an Eskimo. I expect the inspector has a whole slew of fancy uniforms to wear to these things, even though I've seen him duded up only three times, twice when we buried men from our own department and once when he was on his way to the airport to fly off to some leave-taking somewhere or other. "Resplendent" is the only way to describe how he looked. When he finally bites the big one himself, and if I'm still around, I'm going to take special care that day with my buttons, shoes and the visor of the cap of my dress blues. It's the least I can do.

My mother's funeral was my baptism, and I didn't really understand what was going on. It wasn't just that I was only eleven years old, although that had to be part of it. My father never told me why she had been wasting away like that, and by the time she died she wasn't my mother anymore. I saw that there was a woman in that casket, but she couldn't have been anybody I knew.

The only ones who came to my father's funeral were four of his friends who had played with him in the

Boston Symphony and one of his former students who had seen the small notice in the newspaper. That time I was more grateful that my father was out of his misery than I was sorry he was dead. It was only when his friend Meyer reached into the casket and tried to untwist the diseased fingers that had deprived him of his beloved violin playing that I had started to cry, because it was the first time I had truly realized why my father had become an alcoholic and had taken his own life.

The only other two funerals were those of Moran and Mrs. Dienben, both of whom lost their lives while saving mine when I had been taken prisoner the year before by the fanatics of the Church of the Holy Avenger. Moran, the quintessential Vietnam vet, was a fellow cop who was operating according to the code of honor, and she was a Vietnamese refugee who knew the price you had to pay for freedom. Both of them paid for my freedom. I was still in such a state of shock when I attended their funerals that it was like I wasn't there even as I was there. But they counted; they etched their little marks on my soul.

Bandini, who made me fall in love again even as I was still grieving over the death of my wife, Cathy, never had a funeral, although they must have done something with the piece of hand that was left after she blew the rest of herself into vapor. I almost went to the Boston police department to claim the remains, but I didn't have the strength to answer any questions about why this person with a Mafia background had such an arsenal in the cellar of her house, and how I might be involved in the matter. I kept telling myself that I wanted to remember the whole Bandini rather than the little bit that remained, but I knew in my guts that I didn't have the guts to involve myself in what could only prove to be a disaster in my personal life. I preferred being known as a hero rather than a scumbag, which was only human, I suppose, but it still stuck in my craw, and I knew it was something I would never be able to swallow.

I could feel my body shivering as I lay there in the bed in the Forum Hotel in Belfast, Northern Ireland,

and thought on all the funerals and non-funerals I had attended and non-attended before the one I was about to attend that morning, and I started shouting obscenities at the TV set because that was the only other thing in the room that could speak.

The night before, when I had returned from having dinner with my cousin, Catherine, I had felt almost warm inside because this sweet, nice, pretty girl was flesh of part of my flesh, blood of part of my blood. There was something comforting about having a cousin, a real cousin, like this. There was no fooling myself that I now had a family, an honest-to-Jesus family, because all of the rest I had met seemed like louts, and that included the women. But Catherine had reached me with her chatter about her father and her brothers, and how her mother had died the year before, and how her older sister now took care of them all, and how her younger sister was planning to be a nun, and how she would love to go to art school if she had the money, and how she would give anything to visit the United States, and how she'd never eaten in a place like the one we were in, and wasn't sure of what she was eating while she was eating it. It was like listening to soft rain on the roof or the wind blowing through a field of hay or little children playing nicely in a sandbox. If some seeker after truth had asked me what innocence is, I would have replied "my young cousin Catherine."

That all changed over the double chocolate cake when I asked her what she thought about who had murdered Sean. It seemed to catch her by surprise, as though the original question was mine rather than hers. She was halfway to her mouth with a big chunk of cake, but she held the fork in front of her for a moment and then carefully replaced it on the plate.

"The women here don't really know what is going on with the men," she said. "It's like those American films on the Mafia that we see on the telly. The wives and daughters keep their mouths shut and go to church and pray and cook and clean and have babies, but they aren't allowed to ask any questions, and they're told nothing about the true nature of the things the men do. The women are like a flock of sheep, and the shepherds are wearing coats of wolfskins."

"Your cousin Brendan isn't the only poet in the family," I told her. "You have a way of describing things that gets to the heart of the matter without using a lot of words."

"Och," she said, "Brendan is a one, isn't he? Went to university on scholarship because he said that the British taxpayers were footing the bill, and he was going to make sure the English paid for their tyranny over the Irish. The only one of us who ever went to university. He's a deep one, he's a dark one. He'll disappear for a time and then show up like he'd only gone to the pub for a beer. And he stays clear of politics. While everyone else is ranting and raving about this and that, he just sits there and smokes and sips his malt and has a little smile on his face. Sean was just the opposite. Sean loved to march in the parades, and compete in the races and have as good a time as you could with whatever there was. He used to joke about running for Parliament on the Sinn Fein ticket one day, and he was popular enough with the crowd, but he was not what you would call political. He said to me only two weeks ago though that even if he had been the head of the IRA, he would have given it all up for Molly. I asked Father Delavar if it was a sin that I had brought the two of them together, and he didn't really answer me. Just told me to do the stations and be a good girl. I lay in bed at night and wonder if it is my fault that Sean is dead. Was it me that made him a target for the Protestants, like the rest of them are saying? It wasn't Molly's family did him in, I'm sure of that. Her brother Albert used to race against Sean, and if things hadn't been like they are, I think they would have been friends too."

"If I were a Belfast policeman," I said, "all that you have said would be enough for me to investigate potential Protestant retaliation. Who else is there who would do a thing like that?"

"Well, there are the toughs that run the blocks," she said, "but they all liked Sean because he won the races for our people. I don't think they would have done a thing like that."

"What toughs are you talking about?"

"The toughs. The gangs. Did you ever see that beautiful movie *West Side Story?*"

"Yes."

"Well, that's who the toughs are. They run the blocks over here just like they do in New York. You give them what they want. But they all liked Sean. I know they liked Sean."

"How would they have felt about his being engaged to a Protestant girl?"

"Oh, they wouldn't have liked that. They wouldn't have liked that at all. But they didn't know about it. Only Molly's family and me knew about it."

"That brings us back to the Protestants. Or you."

"Me? Are you saying that I killed Sean?"

There were tears in her eyes, and she was looking like she was about to bolt from me, the table and the restaurant.

"No, I'm not saying that. All I'm saying is that a policeman can only go on the facts he knows. And if Molly's family and you were the only ones who knew about the engagement, then that is where a policeman would start looking."

She chewed on that for a moment in lieu of the cake.

"Suppose the IRA found out that Sean was engaged to a Protestant girl," I said. "Would that be enough for them to kill him?"

"Oh, God, no. They'd never do a thing like that."

"How do you know?"

"I just know. They wouldn't do a thing like that."

"How do you feel about the IRA?"

Her face went into that set look I have seen so many times on people who have no other way to turn. It's the last refuge. My country right or wrong. My religion right or wrong. My race right or wrong. Whether they be criminals or law-abiding citizens, they all have something *right or wrong*.

"They're all we have," she said finally. "There

are politicians who talk and priests who preach and people who say don't bring worse on our heads than is already sitting there, but the IRA are the only ones who are doing.''

"Doing what besides blowing up police stations and blowing away people?"

"They're keeping the world's attention on what injustices are being done to the Catholics of Northern Ireland."

"There is no other way?"

"If you have brought a magic way from America, Cousin Benny," she said, picking up the fork and holding it once more in front of her mouth, "then tell it to me and I'll tell it to everybody else."

I watched her eat three good-sized chunks of cake.

"What about the police?" I asked her as she washed the crumbs down with a slurp of coffee.

"They came, they asked a few questions, and they left, just as they always do when a Catholic has been done in."

"Are you saying they don't do their job?"

"I'm saying that the only way we'll ever know who murdered poor Sean is if you find out who did it, Cousin Benny."

"Catherine, I'm a lone American in a foreign country. I solve few enough cases in San Diego, where I have a full department behind me. Most of the ones we solve have to do with a husband killing his wife, or vice versa, or a guy stabbing his girlfriend, or vice versa, or young kids robbing their first liquor store. Outside of those, our record isn't that inspiring. If you don't think the police are doing their job, you should go to their superiors and complain until something further is undertaken."

"Nearly one hundred percent of the police are Protestants," she said, "and to them another dead Catholic is one less to bother with."

I thought on how the Germans had looked at the Jews, on the German doctor who said that the Jews were a cancer, and as a medical man it was his job to separate the disease from the body. But this wasn't Nazi Germany, for God's sake. Sure enough, the Catholics lived in ghettos, couldn't get their share of jobs or education or political representation, but they weren't being herded into concentration camps and gassed and cremated. I looked at Catherine as she concentrated on finishing off her cake. In South Africa, her pinkish white skin would make her one of the anointed. The same in the states of Georgia and Mississippi, or any one of the country clubs in less segregated territories. She could also sit in this restaurant and eat her chocolate cake without fear or prejudice strictly because it was impossible to tell from her physical appearance what her religion might be. But God help her if she tried to move out of her environment. And what about me? How hard did I push a case when it involved a Mexican or a black? I was pretty sure I gave it the same attention and energy as I did a case involving a San Diego yuppie, but I knew cops who did little more than ask a few questions, fill in the forms and forget about it.

However, that was more than I could do for my cousin Sean. My hands were tied in so many ways that Houdini would have asked for a knife. Would it do any good for me to call on the Belfast police and inquire as to how the investigation was going? Brother officer to brother officer? Hands across the sea? They would probably hand me a rubber duck and explain what I could do with it. But Sean was blood. Maybe I owed him that little bit.

"Catherine . . ." I began.

"Everyone calls me Cathy," she said.

I don't know what look appeared on my face, but it was enough to startle and alarm her. In addition to everything else, some presumably higher being thought it amusing to suddenly stick another Cathy into my life. One Cathy was all I needed or would ever need. There wasn't room for another one. It was possible that someday I would meet a woman who would fill a different niche, just as Bandini had, but never another Cathy, superficial as the rule might be. I tried to thaw my face into something resembling a smile, but I could see that she was still unsure of what had happened.

"I'd like to keep calling you Catherine," I said.
"Why is that?"

Why indeed? There must always be truth between us.

"My wife's name was Catherine, but I always called her Cathy," I said. "She is dead, but the name will always be there, and every time I hear it or say it, there is only one person who will occupy my mind. Even though I have become very fond of you in the short time we have known each other, I can't move you in beside her. You will be my special Catherine and have your own place in my heart and mind."

Jesus! If this was how my Irish blood was going to affect me, I had better go out first thing in the morning and buy a lyre and some pointy elves' shoes. In a strange way it relaxed me to let my emotions go like this, and somehow it had to do with having uncles and aunts and cousins, no matter how opposite they were from everything I believed and stood for. Or maybe it was the lilt of the language; it made you feel like you were performing in an operetta set in Never-Never-Land. Or maybe it was because this beautiful girl was almost young enough, or I was almost old enough, for her to be my daughter. She reached out her right hand, which felt a little sticky from the cake frosting she had wiped off her lips, and covered the back of mine.

"There is nothing I would like better than to be your Catherine, Cousin Benny," she said, and I felt the warm fingers press down my cold flesh.

I insisted on taking her home by taxi, and this time the driver drove right to her door without any questions. It could be he was a Catholic, or it could be he just wanted the two-way fare, or it could be that he didn't give a damn either way.

"If you'll be here at nine o'clock," she said as we stood at the bottom of the stairs, "then we'll have the whole family together."

"Pretty lass," said the cabby as I stood by the barrier in front of the hotel to pay him off.

"She's my young cousin Catherine," I explained

to him, even as I knew it was none of his goddamned business.

There was a lot to think about, but the jet lag hit as I was crawling into bed. I can't recall whether the last word in my mind was "funeral" or "Catherine." Maybe both.

6

EVEN AS I KNEW THAT I HAD COME TO the right place, I was telling myself that this had to be the wrong place. It wasn't a funeral; it was a parade. There seemed to be more than a hundred people milling around in the slight mist that bathed your face with coolness. This included drummers, brass players, giant youths holding flags and banners, and men, women and children chatting and laughing and seemingly having a wonderful time. There were also police, lots and lots of uniformed police, standing off to the sides, several feet away from the edges of the crowd, bulky in their bullet-proof vests, some with slung rifles and a few with automatic weapons. I spotted the plainclothesmen right off because even though they weren't in uniform, they stood out from the regular participants like a boil on the tip of a nose, their eyes always moving, their bodies turning this way and that as they perpetually weaved their way through the mass that parted for them as the Red Sea supposedly did for Moses.

I, too, picked a path, but more carefully, not quite sure of either myself or my goal, but eventually I reached the bottom of the stairs and started up them to go through the door. Just as I reached the threshold, two burly young men stepped before me and thrust their bellies against mine, their hands half-raised to grab me if I tried to continue any further progress.

"What might you be wanting here?" one of them demanded.

"I've come for the funeral," I told him.

"It's only family in there now," the other one said.

"I'm family."

They turned their heads to look each other in the

eyes, taking the time to fill their faces with contempt before they came back to me.

"We know everyone in Sean's family down to the cats they keep," said the first one, "and you've never been among 'em."

"I'm a cousin from the United States."

"Oh? And what might your name be?"

"Freedman." I figured, what the hell, go all the way. "Benjamin Freedman."

They did their Tweedledum-Tweedledee act again, only this time when their faces returned to me, there was what you might have called almost a sly grin on them.

"Go on with you now, whoever you are and whatever you want," said the first one. "This is a solemn occasion and no time to have your head broke in pieces. Go on with you."

"Go in and tell my Uncle William that his sister's son is here," I told them. "Go get my Cousin Brendan. Or my cousin Catherine. Or my Uncle Barney or Frank or Jack. Or any of their sons or daughters. Or go tell my Aunt Margaret that you won't let me in for my cousin Sean's funeral."

This time I enjoyed the looks on their faces. I edged forward slightly and they parted to let me through, their hands still slightly raised as though they might let me go halfway before they grabbed and hurled me back down the stairs.

The coffin lid had been closed and members of the family, some of whose faces I remembered and some I didn't, were standing there silently except for one or two who were exchanging sporadic words. Several of the chairs had been removed, and those that were left were scattered haphazardly around the room. Neither my Aunt Margaret nor my cousin Catherine was visible, but Brendan came across to greet me as soon as I entered.

"I thought you might have packed up your bags and left," he said, putting out his hand to shake mine. "I was thinking last night that your walking in on something like this would make a good beginning for a play. It has all the elements required for a grand drama."

"What of the ending, Brendan?" I asked. "I'd

like to know where everybody stands when the curtain goes down."

"If I knew something like that," he said, "I'd be at the betting parlor rather than here. Would you like a drop of something to go against the chill out there?"

"No, thank you. I haven't had my breakfast, and I don't drink much at any time of day."

"You say that, now? Are you sure you have the Callaghan blood running in your veins, or are you an impostor? All of your uncles are already half to the wind, and your cousins, including me, will be well out to sea by nightfall. What you do at home is your business, but while you're over here you must follow the custom unless you have a certificate from your doctor."

"My mother, your Aunt Deirdre, and my father, your Uncle Isaac, were both alcoholics," I told him, "so it's a tradition I'm very familiar with. It's also one I don't intend to follow."

"Would you believe it?" said Brendan, and I could see that he was already half to the wind himself. "I not only have a cousin named Benjamin, but I also have, or at the least had, an uncle named Isaac. You'll have us all going to synagogue before you leave here."

"You may be going," I told him, "but I have never been myself and I have no intention of starting the practice in Belfast, Northern Ireland. The whole world would start spinning in their graves."

"In any case . . ." he began, but just then my Aunt Margaret came out of one of the other rooms on the arm of a priest, an old man, whose frailty had to come from a serious illness rather than just his age. His skin had that translucent quality that seemed to put an aura around his head like you see in the paintings of Jesus and the saints, and he walked as though he was uncertain just where his foot might contact floor.

"Ah, Benjamin," she said as soon as she caught sight of me, "come over and meet Father Delavar. I've told him how God has sent you to comfort us in our loss."

I walked over and stood before them, the chubby little lady whose face was wet from the tears that seemed to have glued themselves to her cheeks, and the frail little man whose white collar looked more natural than the color of his skin.

"You're Deirdre's boy, are you?" he said, squinting up at me. "Catherine has told me of your mission over here, so we'll get to know each other well before you return to the States."

My mission? My mission? Oh Jesus Christ, I thought, and there was as much prayer in the plea as there was blasphemy, she's told the old fart that I have come over to embrace Mother Church. But this was neither the time nor the place to begin a debate, so I just nodded gravely and touched the free hand that he waved at me vaguely.

"It's time we started," said the priest, speaking to everyone in the room. "It's going to be a long morning as it is, and we dast not be late getting to the church."

Raincoats of all types and colors were immediately donned by the women and a few of the men, and umbrellas were distributed to those who wanted them. Since I didn't have a hat and it seemed to be raining more insistently than it had been, I almost took one myself until I noticed that none of the men had availed themselves of the pile in the corner. It wouldn't do for the American cousin to show he was not as impermeable as his Irish kin so I passed them by as I went out the door. Six brawny young men had preceded us with the casket, and by the time I reached the outside it had been laid on a flat wagon that was drawn by two black horses with black feathers jutting up from their bridles. The family, and I was amazed by how many of them there were when they were mustered in one bunch, stood directly behind the wagon, followed by the musicians, and strung out behind them was the crowd in loose but orderly fashion. The priest was handed up to sit beside the driver of the wagon, and one of the women walked over and insisted he take her umbrella, which happened to be pink, but no one seemed to mind this piece of fashion daring. Brendan saw me standing on the steps and motioned for me to join him in the family throng.

"Are all your funerals like this?" I asked.

"Oh no," he said. "If you die peacefully, you're put away quietly. But if you're murdered in a war, you get the full honors accorded to a hero."

"But you don't know why Sean was killed, nor who did it."

"The first we know," said Brendan, "and the second we'll find out."

"Let the police handle it, Brendan," I said. "This kind of thinking just piles one body on top of another, and too often some of the bodies are innocent ones."

The look on his face was no longer that of a blood relative welcoming kin from across the sea. His blue eyes stared at me like he was assessing my whole being for judgment day.

"If you were all Irish, Benjamin," he said, "if you were one of us, then you would know better than to depend on Protestant police to see that justice is done. It could be that ten bodies will have to be placed on the scale to even up for Sean. Maybe a hundred. Maybe a thousand. But whatever weight is needed, that is the weight that will be secured. And maybe one extra for luck."

He stared a few seconds more and then his face broke into a grin. *And maybe one extra for luck.* Had he said that to show that the bloody promise that preceded it was said in jest? Was the whole thing a joke? No, it wasn't a joke. The joke, if anything, was on me, just as it would be on whoever else became involved. I felt the rain penetrating my hair right into the scalp and shivered as if that would shake it off. But as I was trying to think of something to say, the drums began.

The funeral in San Diego for Moran had been as formal as any military ceremony could be with public officials, hundreds of police in their dress blues, rifle shots by a Vietnam honor squad over the grave, taps, folded flag and speeches by the mayor and commissioner. It was a hazy time for me, but I could still remember how it made me feel part of a wholeness, a cog in a perpetual wheel. It was comforting in many ways.

But as the drums banged and the bugles blared in a song I could not recognize, as the horses' hooves clopped and the wagon wheels squeaked and the marchers' feet slopped on the wet pavement, I felt an alienation that had nothing to do with my being a stranger in a strange land. This was not a celebration of death, but rather a declaration of war. As we marched along, the bystanders on the sidewalks applauded as though we were troops setting out for battle rather than mourners on a sad journey.

I think it was six blocks to the church, and by the time we reached there the rain was coming down with some ferocity, and I could feel the wet on the shoulders of my jacket underneath the raincoat as well as the bottom of my pants and shoes and socks. The church was one of those large stone buildings of indeterminate architecture, the walls blackened by the soot of scores of years. It seemed colder inside than it had been outside, and you could almost feel thin patches of ice forming on your wet spots.

We sat there for some minutes before Father Delavar appeared, this time with a white lace surplice over his cassock, about to cook up a sermon. I couldn't see Catherine anywhere among the multitude of heads. I had meant to seek her out and walk beside her to the church, but Brendan had distracted me with his diatribe, and then it was look straight ahead and walk with your eyes half-closed against the rain. I would have liked to get to know her better, but even she wasn't worth trying to balance out the others on the scale. Here I was using the same metaphor that Brendan had, but mine was not as deadly. The only deadly thing as far as I was concerned was that they were deadly bores, ignorant, uneducated boozers who would spend their pigeonholed lives whining about their lot.

I felt my face flush as I thought on what I had just thought. Prejudice. Bigotry. It wasn't that easy to rise above yourself when you were an oppressed minority. Black and white. Jew and Christian. Israeli and Palestinian. South African and African. Here it was Catholic and Protestant. It was true that they could vote and emigrate and perhaps amass a good living among their own kind, but the unfair barriers made it difficult, if not impossible. What the hell was I doing in a church? In a minute, I'd go up there and knock the little priest aside and deliver my own sermon.

Except that he had already started his, and the coughs and throat-clearings of the audience had ceased. The cold and wet were such that I tried to squeeze myself into myself, seeking inward warmth to try to make up for what was being lost externally. Consequently, my attention was sporadic and the hollow sound of the little priest's voice over the crackling sound system echoed within my head without penetrating the brain. There had been the ritual, of course, but to me it was a dumb show as the priest and the sexton and the altar boys moved about the platform, kneeling and bowing and passing silver bowls around. A chill wind from the north brought the smell of incense to my nose, and I breathed deeply, as though I might get some warmth from the originating flame somewhere on the platform.

I tried to pay attention as the priest started his talk, but it was all about the family and the tragic circumstances of their loss, and my eyes closed all the way. There had to be a great deal of jet lag still screwing up my biological clock, and I wasn't sure where I would have been or what I would have been doing if I were back in San Diego. Only bits and pieces of the sentences registered on my brain.

"It only shows you," said the priest, "how you can't outrun God. Sean was probably the fastest runner in all of Northern Ireland, and there were those who talked Olympics when his name was mentioned, but his speed could not prevent his being overtaken when his time had come to run on God's track."

It always gets me when public speakers, clergy or laymen, talk as though they had just hung up the phone on a private conversation with God. They always use metaphors that make your teeth grate. The rabbi at my father's funeral said that my father was "now playing the violin for God," and the priest at Moran's funeral had stated that this homicide sergeant was now "directing traffic in heaven." This guy, this Father Delavar, whose name had been burned into my memory by reference to him in one of the letters to my mother, was now implying that someone had taken the starting gun for the race and used it as a finishing gun in Sean's head. That wasn't what he was actually saying, but that was what was going through my own head when he threw the stone into my unplacid pool.

There was more, much more, as the man droned on and on, but I was starting to shiver from the cold wet that encompassed me, and I concentrated solely on keeping my teeth from chattering. I became so numb that I was five seconds behind everybody else when they stood for the final part of the ritual.

Then the young men wheeled the casket out of the church, and we peeled off in formation, the rows emptying slowly enough for me to finally catch sight of Catherine, who flashed me a wan smile as she went by holding the arm of a very old lady.

The rain was coming down in the proverbial buckets when we grouped again outside the church, but nobody seemed to be leaving the stadium early, and at the sound of the drums we started off again, marching to what seemed nowhere. I don't know exactly how long it took us to get there, but we finally reached the large iron gate of a cemetery and straggled on through. The road worked its way upward in a slightly circular way, but as we came to the top of the ridge, there was a collective gasp from the people in front of us, and everybody stopped right in his tracks, some bumping into those in front of them.

You could hear the voices on all sides as people asked what the problem was, and finally, after a couple of minutes we moved forward again, but this time the rhythm of the drums did not lead us, and we walked in silence. When my line crossed the crest of the hill and we were able to look down, I realized what had caused such a commotion in the front and at the same time a flash of apprehension went through me. For there before us, standing in a solid block, was a group of maybe thirty people, lined up like a platoon of soldiers, all wearing derby hats, black raincoats and orange sashes across their chests. They were stationed on the other side of a gaping grave that had a mound of soaked dirt piled beside it, what had to be the final resting place of Sean O'Malley.

It took me a moment to realize what was before us, and that was only because of the three figures standing in front of the massed men. In the middle of the three was the tiny form of Molly Peters, and on each side were her mother and father. The fiancée had come to see her loved one laid away, and to protect her, the Protestants had sent along a Praetorian Guard. I looked around quickly but could see no policemen; they were probably on the bottom of the other side of the hill, thinking that all the problems had been left behind on the streets, and not realizing what an explosive confrontation was looming here. I almost turned to run down and get them, but stood fixed, held fast by the realization that I was there only by half a bloodline, and that I was just another civilian soaked to the skin in an alien environment.

The family acted as though there was nothing there on the other side of the hole. They moved the casket to the side of the grave, and helped the priest from the wagon, practically carrying him to the customary spot. He recited the conclusion of the mass for the dead and the casket was lowered into the hole. The family moved forward, one or two at a time, to throw either a handful of mud or a flower down on the box below. I wasn't going to participate, but Brendan took me by the arm and brought me forward, so I added my few bits of mud to the growing pile. That's when it happened. Since I was one of the last ones and all the others had stepped back a few paces, it was I who was standing there when Molly Peters moved forward with a bouquet of flowers in her arms. The crowd behind me made a noise, almost like that of an unfriendly dog who sees a stranger approaching. I could see the front line of the Protestants tensing for attack.

Without even thinking about it, I moved around the grave and walked up to Molly Peters, taking her elbow and guiding her forward until she was close enough to throw her flowers down into the hole. She was crying loudly, her tears matching the intensity of the rain. I turned her around and led her back to her group, stopping three steps before reaching her parents. Then I moved slowly to the side and came back toward my own group. The silence was so thick that it seemed as though no one was even breathing.

But breathing they were because a collective whoosh came out of the group in front of me, and I turned quickly, thinking the Protestants were making a move forward. But all of the Protestants were looking to their right, and as my eyes followed them, I saw four men in khaki, all with ski masks and all with rifles held at port arms, coming out from behind one of the concrete mausoleums that the richer families build to house their ancestors. They were marching in step and all they had to do was lower their rifles six inches to have them pointing straight at the Protestants.

Instead, they moved up to the grave site and took their places, two on each side. At a soft command from one of them, they raised their rifles in the sky and pulled the triggers. But instead of the volley that I had instinctively braced for, there were only the four clicks from the empty rifles. They cocked and clicked again. And a third time.

There was another soft command, the rifles returned to port arms, they turned and marched slowly back to the mausoleum, where they disappeared behind the concrete wall. I waited to see if they appeared further along, but they were staying put for the moment. The Protestant group went back to rigid attention, and as I turned to look, the Catholics were also frozen into place. Only I remained outside the bulwarks, alone in no-man's-land. I looked once again at Molly Peters, and then I turned and walked back to my own group. They were in a solid phalanx, and for a moment I feared there was going to be no room for me at that inn.

But Brendan moved out to meet me, and we worked our way through the first line of family and friends, back up the hill and over the rise with all the others following in turn. Behind us I could hear the shovels of dirt being thrown on top of the casket. The gravediggers weren't going to bother with the niceties on a day as wet as this one. The Protestants were going to stay where they were until they were sure the cemetery was cleared. They obviously hadn't come looking for a confrontation or a fight, but in a way they held the field.

On the bottom of the hill were the police, including what seemed to be an armored car. They were still unaware of what had gone on a few hundred feet away from them, thinking what the hell could happen at a grave site and why walk all the way up a muddy rise? If I had been in charge of the detail, some people would have had their asses kicked.

"Well, Cousin Benjamin," said Brendan, "you become more interesting by the minute. A couple more antics like this, and I'm going to start wishing my own blood ran half Yiddish."

7

THE PROCESSION BROKE INTO INDIVIDual groups once we passed through the gate to the open street again. The rain was coming down so hard that you could not distinguish individual drops, and nature had baptized us all to the point where the wet clothes hung on our bodies like bags of sand that have been dumped on a levee. Brendan had stayed by my side, and every once in a while his fingers attached themselves to the sleeve of my coat for a few seconds as though to continually reestablish a bond between us. Perhaps he was showing everybody that although this Jew was crazy and didn't know how to behave in public, he was still one of the family.

Quite a few people came back to the apartment, most of whom, I assumed, were kin. Upon entering, we all shook ourselves as dogs do when they wish to rid their fur of the elements, and then we helped each other with our coats because they were stuck to whatever layer was under them. I was wondering how long before it would be proper to return to the hotel, take a hot bath and reincarnate myself in dry clothes.

Bottles of whiskey, seemingly dozens of bottles, magically appeared with real glass tumblers beside them. There was to be no plastic attached to this commemoration. Brendan poured half a glass and thrust it into my hand.

"This is not drinking, man," he said. "This is self-preservation."

The whiskey felt as though it had been warmed beforehand, and as it slid down the throat, it left a trail of heat behind it, stopping in the stomach in the exact spot where coldness often laid its heavy hand on me.

Brendan refilled the glass despite my attempt to remove it from the target area.

"Look, man," he said, "you've got to heat your body to the point where your piss raises steam or else you'll get your death. I've already lost a brother this week; I can't afford to have a newfound cousin give up the ghost too."

There were so many things wrong with the entire situation—me, them, us—that it didn't take much persuasion to allow everybody who passed by to continually replenish my glass. I wanted out of there one way or another, and there must have been at the back of my mind the desperate idea of passing out. The O'Malleys might not have been able to raise the money for the funeral, but unless they had knocked off a distillery, they had come up with enough to make everybody forget the wet and the rain and why all this was happening in the first place.

Brendan was the only one who did more than pour me drinks; the rest of the cousins and aunts and uncles were busy with their own little gabfests, laughing louder and louder as the day went on. I wondered if I went up and asked them about Sean, whether they would look at me blankly or remember why they were present at such a "sad" occasion.

"Is there anything to eat?" I asked Brendan, as he filled my glass again. "I haven't had anything to eat today and it's almost two o'clock."

"There might be some food somewhere," he said, "or we can get in some fish and chips. However, that's a full meal you've got in your glass now and that includes the vitamins. He pronounced it "viitamiins," just as had the woman who was outraged by the little Indian poking his dirty fingernails into the bottle she was bringing for her mother. What the hell was I doing in a country where they said "viitamiins," and at the same time blew your bloody head off?

"Benjamin," said Brendan, "twice you have gone over to the enemy side and come back with your pecker still intact. Third times can prove unlucky."

"Who am I to worry about?" I asked. "The IRA or the Protestants?"

"You have nothing to fear from the IRA," he said. "They take care of their own."

"Why would they take care of me? I'm only half Irish and I'm not Catholic. They didn't seem to take care of Sean, and he was one of them."

"Sean was not IRA, Benjamin," said Brendan. "That I can guarantee you."

I looked at him through the haze that was beginning to glaze my eyes. I hadn't been this drunk since I was twenty-one years old and had tried to match boilermakers with my friend Gallagher, another pure-blooded Irishman who was probably the toughest police sergeant in Boston. At least I thought he was my friend until he tried to beat me to death because he thought I was having an affair with his wife, and then he turned out to be an out-and-out enemy. What about the young pure-blooded Irishman in front of me? Was he my friend as well as my cousin, or would he also turn out to be an out-and-out enemy? To hell with it. Time to put some cards on the table.

"I know you can guarantee me that, Brendan," I said, "because you are with the IRA."

"And how would you know that?"

"I'm a policeman, for Christ's sake."

"Ah, you have made a deduction. And what would that deduction be based on? I'm a poor university student, a poet, a voice of reason among the unreasonable, the one who stuck by you when you stuck your neck out. Do you add all that together and get IRA? Tell me what gave me away?"

I seriously thought about throwing up, and took another swallow of whiskey to wash the feeling down.

"Well," I said, "detectives, good detectives, have to have a little of the poet in them too. We get a gut feeling about who might be what in a given situation. I have a gut feeling that there's a whole layer of you that would have to be peeled off to find the real Brendan. Where are you, Brendan, when you disappear for days at a time? Are you shacking up with some colleen? Are you visiting friends in the country?"

"I have done both on occasion." He smiled. "And who told you I disappear for days at a time? Cathy?"

"Or are you off somewhere on a mission?" I continued, sliding over the Catherine question. Christ, I didn't want to bring her any problems from the New World. I could feel my hands shake a bit as I thought how I would like to get this grinning pretty boy into an interrogation room where we would wipe the smile off his face. I felt the vomit creep up my throat again and took another swallow. Brendan refilled my glass.

Why was I suddenly so antagonistic toward him? He was the only one who had treated me in a civilized manner. He was the one who had stuck by me. What if he was IRA? What business was it of mine if the Catholics and Protestants of Northern Ireland wiped each other out? All I would have to do was get Catherine out of there, and the rest of them could chop themselves into stew meat. Where was Catherine?

"My mission," said Brendan, "is to keep my people from being wiped off the face of the earth. As a Jew, you should know what a problem that can be sometimes."

"Your brother was wiped off the earth, Brendan. As a Catholic, that should show you that you're not doing a very good job of it. You need help and this half-Jew is going to give it to you."

"In what way?"

"In what way?" I echoed. "In the way I've been trained. I don't know this town or the people but you do. If we can work together, maybe my police training can combine with your knowledge of who's who and where's where to find out who murdered Sean and why it was done."

"All we have to do is find out which one among all the Protestants out there did the actual bloody deed," said Brendan, "and we have as much chance of getting in among them as they would with us. I'm basically a man of peace, Benjamin, but we're moving fast toward a day of mass slaughter rather than the few at a time we have now."

"No more slaughter," I said, and I could feel the tears forming in my eyes. "We can't have any more slaughter because . . . because . . . Is there a place here where I can throw up?"

He took me by the arm and led me through the room into the kitchen, where a group of women was milling around a table. I could sense their curious looks, but I was concentrating so hard on fighting my gorge that I wasn't seeing clearly enough to make out anyone's actual face. Brendan rapped on a closed door before us.

"Aunt Flora's in there," some woman said.

"Aunt Flora," said Brendan, "we have an emergency out here."

The door opened and a little old lady flustered her way past us. Brendan pushed me through and closed the door with a slam. I fell to my knees and stuck my head into the toilet bowl. My God! The old lady had obviously been so upset by Brendan's command that she hadn't taken time to flush. If ever there was a sign from on high, this was it. God didn't want me to drink whiskey, to be an alcoholic like my parents, to become as one with my new "family." I stared down into the bowl as though I could read my future in what was floating there. I tried to induce retching but it didn't work. The courage wasn't there to put my finger down my throat. This was going to be purgatory rather than purgation. I pushed myself to my feet, reached up and pulled the chain. The water in the tank made a lovely whoosh as it raced past my head into the bowl, and I saw all my sins disappear and be replaced by clear water. I had now been double-baptized, once by the rain and now by the toilet. It was time to rise from the dead.

I returned to the kitchen, where the women were still shuffling around the table, and though I vaguely remembered all their faces, the names were beyond me. I moved in among them, thinking that I might eat a little of the food and that would make me feel better, but all that was there were more bottles and more glasses. They were having their own little party in the harem quarters.

I looked at them and they looked at me, but nobody said a word, so I turned and went back into the living room. Peering through the smoke, I sought out Brendan, but he was nowhere to be found. Where the hell was my coat? I didn't see any coats anywhere so I went through the door and outside into the rain, which seemed to be letting up a bit. I don't know how many blocks I walked before I found a taxi that would stop for me. I had hailed several but they had gone right by me. You could never find a taxi in the rain no matter what part of the world you were in.

My wallet was so soggy that I had trouble pulling it from my pocket, but I finally removed the wad in it and put all the bills in the hand of the cabby. He looked at me for a long moment, removed two bills for himself and stuck the rest in my shirt pocket.

"You got an early start on the rest of us, eh, mate?" he said, and drove off.

The clerk who handed me my key didn't seem fazed by my appearance, and none of the other guests in the lobby gave me a second glance as I walked into the elevator and sought out the button for four. Somehow, perhaps because of the rain on my face as I had wandered looking for a cab or because I hadn't had a drink in about forty minutes, my head seemed a bit clearer, but I was still having trouble putting one foot down in front of the other. It also took a few extra moments to get the key fitted correctly into the lock, not helped by my impatience to rush into the room and strip off the clothes that were beginning to chafe the sensitive spots of my body.

All of this, plus the jet-lag excuse, may have accounted for my not immediately sensing the situation I was walking into, and it took my nose about four seconds before it sensed the sweet aroma of pipe tobacco. My hand slipped under my jacket as I quickly looked up, but of course there was no gun there to reassure me in my moment of dangerous need.

Not that there was any danger or need present. He was sitting in my one armchair, his trench coat unbuttoned, his felt hat pushed back a ways on his head, right hand holding the pipe up to his mouth, left hand prominently displayed on the upholstered arm. He was showing that although he could get into my room with ease, there was no threat in his presence. My nose finally broke through the pipe smoke to the essence; it smelled cop.

"Lieutenant Freedman," he said, "forgive me for presuming to wait for you in your room, but there was such a bustle in the lobby."

"What's your name?" I asked. He knew that I knew he was a cop so there wasn't any need to say "Who are you?"

"Simmons," he replied "Inspector Kenneth Simmons."

"Is it usual practice for the police in this country to break into a room without a warrant?" I asked.

He took a puff on his pipe and smiled.

"I'm afraid there are all kinds of practices we have in Northern Ireland that are not usual," he said.

"Well, let me start changing one of them," I said. "Put out your goddamned pipe."

8

HE LOOKED AT ME FOR A LONG MOment, pushed himself to his feet, stuck the pipe in the right-hand pocket of his trench coat, and put his hand out for a formal shake.

"I'm terribly sorry," he said, "and I must apologize for my intrusion. I was sitting in the lobby surrounded by the Russian orchestra that's in residence for the festival, and I sought refuge here to sort out my thoughts in quiet."

"This is bush-league stuff, inspector," I said, ignoring his hand, which he dropped as naturally as he could to his side again. He had started to slip it into his pocket to retrieve his pipe but remembered my edict in time. "They don't even do this kind of thing in the movies anymore. It went out with Sydney Greenstreet and Peter Lorre. Or are you just getting those movies over here now?"

He didn't know what the hell I was talking about and neither did I. I was still sodden from the whiskey and the rain, inside and out, and, God help me, I was homesick for San Diego. Not just for the people I worked with and the few friends I had, but for the whole blooming San Diego area, Tijuana sewage and all. Instead of basking in the warm sunlight, I was standing and shivering in front of a show-off cop who thought he could wow me by getting the manager to open the door for him. I had the feeling that the guy was as good at policework as he was at impressing me.

"I'm going to take a bath and change my clothes," I said, and without looking at him again, I rummaged through the bureau drawers and the closet until I had what I needed, and took it all into the bathroom.

While I was soaking in the tub, I looked at my

suit and shirt and socks lumped in the corner, and wondered about cleaning and laundry at the hotel. There was just this one dark suit that I had worn to the funeral, and now I was down to my sport coat and slacks and a sweater. I could always buy what I needed, but why bother if I was about to get the hell out of there altogether.

He was back sitting in the armchair when I came out some thirty minutes later, but the pipe was still in his pocket. I had thought he might just leave after our little standoff, but he obviously had things to talk about that he felt needed talking about.

"What do you want?" I asked. "Why are you here?"

"Well," he said, "it could be that I'm just paying a courtesy call on a fellow officer from the United States, extending him a welcome to our country and inquiring if there is anything we might do to make his stay more pleasant."

"Yeah, it could be, but it isn't. And why do you know that I'm a policeman and how do you know that I'm a lieutenant?"

"Oh, we have our ways, lieutenant, just as you do."

"Do you flag everybody who comes here," I asked, "or just suspicious-looking characters like me?"

"Well, we do tend to judge people by the company they keep," he said, "and you seem to have some interesting friends here."

"I have no friends here," I said, "just relatives."

His eyebrows rose half an inch.

"Relatives? You don't seem to have called on anyone named Freedman."

"Callaghan. My relatives are the Callaghans."

"And how might that be?"

"My mother was a Callaghan," I said, "Deirdre Callaghan, who emigrated from here some thirty-six years ago. If you're as good a policeman as you say you are, why didn't you come up with that little gem?"

His face reflected his annoyance. My surprise was bigger than his surprise.

"And why might you be visiting these *relatives* at this particular time? Did you know that a murder was about to be committed, and you wanted to be here for the funeral?"

At least I had cracked his veneer. He had given away a little more than was professional.

"Are you making some kind of formal complaint, inspector?" I asked. "Because if you are, then either show me some papers or take me in. I know that things are pretty rigid over here, but I happen to be a citizen of the United States and a police officer to boot, and I don't have to put up with this kind of crap."

He raised his hand in what seemed to be a conciliatory gesture and then made a halfhearted stab toward his pipe when I didn't relent immediately. I had a feeling that this pipe was as important a tool to this guy as his pecker. Maybe more important.

"We know your record, Lieutenant Freedman," he said, "and we're not about to give any trouble to a policeman with your heroic background. But your captain told me about your doings with that church group, and you know that we face the same kind of fanaticism over here."

"My captain? You don't waste time or expense, do you?"

"We do our job."

"And how would that account for your hassling me?"

"A great many Americans, especially those with Catholic connections, don't understand the situation over here, and they foolishly support and sometimes take an active part in obtaining weapons for terrorist groups in Northern Ireland. We have to check everything out."

"Since you didn't know I had Callaghan blood in me, and you did know that my name was Benjamin Freedman, how come I was checked out so quickly and so thoroughly?"

"First of all, you are associating with people who are being monitored, and second, the Israelis are among the top arms dealers in the world."

I almost couldn't believe what I was hearing. Either I was in the presence of one of the stupidest cops I had ever encountered, and I had met some beauties, or he was trying to get me to deny something that would give him a lead on what he thought I might be up to. Arms smuggling? Israelis? Who wrote this guy's scripts?

"Are you telling me that my family, the Callaghans, are suspected of illegal activities? And are you further telling me that I, an American police officer, am under suspicion of being an arms dealer for the Israelis? What the hell were you smoking in that pipe, inspector?"

His face flushed and his hand instinctively started to move toward the pocket. This guy was as bad off as a junkie. In an interrogation, all you would have to do was take his pipe away and he'd confess to anything.

"The Callaghans are only peripherally involved in what we're working on," he said. "It's the O'Malley murder I'm concerned with."

"So am I, inspector, so am I. I come over here to meet my relatives for the first time, and I find that one of my young cousins has been murdered. And from what my other cousins tell me, the Protestant police of Belfast don't seem too vigorous in tracking down the murderer."

"There are Catholic members of the police department here," he said, his face flushing, "and one of the detectives on the case happens to be a Catholic."

"You've got a point there," I told him. "In the United States, there always seems to be one black detective where a black person has been murdered, and a Mexican where a Mexican has been done in, et cetera, et cetera. Look, inspector, you and I have started off in the wrong direction, and I would like to turn us around before we are too far apart."

"I've already apologized," he said stiffly.

"I know that and I would also like to apologize for my behavior. I came in here soaked to the skin and without any food in my stomach, and it was quite a shock to find you sitting there. My family seems to feel that the police are dragging their feet in this case because they suspect poor Sean was gunned down by one of the Protestants who was enraged about his relationship with Molly Peters. They asked me to look into it, and though

I have no official status here, I told them I would do what I could to find out what progress has been made in the investigation. You and I are both police officers, both of us specializing in homicide. It would be appreciated by both me and my family if you could bring me up-to-date so that I can relieve their fears and suspicions."

He looked at me for a long moment, as though weighing my intent and then balancing it with what had been accomplished and how much of it could be divulged safely. I had laid it on pretty thickly about the family tie even though Catherine was the only one who had asked me to look into it, and she was basically the only one I really cared about. The jury was still out on Brendan. Maybe it was the way he looked at me sometimes. He was the only one who had taken me under his wing, but I still wasn't sure what kind of bird he might be.

"Since we are both police officers," he mimicked, "and both specialists in homicide, I am sure you well know that we cannot give out information on an investigation that is still in the preliminary phase. There are many leads we are following and as soon as something definite is found, which we expect momentarily, all interested parties will be notified."

"We phrase it almost the same way," I told him.

"Phrase what?"

"The announcement to the people concerned and the press when we don't have one goddamned clue and have no idea where to turn. At the least, could you tell me the circumstances of the murder, how it was discovered and what was on the coroner's report?"

He put that on the scale and weighed how much harm it could do. He pulled a little notebook from his pocket and flipped a couple of pages.

"The victim was supposedly on his way home from visiting with Miss Molly Peters, and seemed to be following what we have been told was his accustomed route. Miss Peters said he left her at eleven-forty-five P.M., and the coroner estimates that he was murdered sometime between twelve-thirty A.M. and one-thirty A.M. Death was instantaneous. The weapon was .22-caliber and the muzzle was held directly against the left side of the victim's head when it was fired. The Brainefield station received an anonymous call at two-forty A.M. saying there was a dead man on the sidewalk halfway down Brattle Street. A car was sent and the body was discovered. There were no people on the street when the car arrived, and when officers questioned the occupants of the surrounding buildings, all of them said they had heard and seen nothing. You realize, of course, that this section of the city has its own laws of procedure, and that the various blocks are controlled by gangs of young thugs. It is possible that the victim was murdered by members of a rival gang. It is possible that the murder was committed in the course of a robbery. It is possible that there might have been a political motive. Various persons are aiding the police in their investigation. All avenues are being diligently pursued, and it is believed that the culprit might soon be in custody."

He looked up from the notebook as though he might have been an unprepared sixth-grade student reciting his assignment and wasn't at all certain of the teacher's reaction. I would have graded him a C, possibly a C-minus. What the report boiled down to was that they didn't know from Shinola.

"Why does the family feel that the police are not pursuing the case as diligently as they should?" I asked.

"I'm sure it has been your experience, lieutenant," he said, "that the families of the victims never feel that the police are pursuing a case as diligently as they should."

He had me there. I don't know how many times a father, mother, sister or brother screamed at me that we weren't lifting a finger to find out who had murdered their so-called loved one. Sometimes it turned out that one of them had murdered their so-called loved one, but you couldn't say nyah-nyah to them when you put them under arrest.

"I appreciate your giving me this information, inspector, and I will tell the family what has been determined so far."

"On your side," he said, "I would appreciate any cooperation you could give me. You might learn things that would be naturally withheld from us." He fished his wallet out of his side pocket and withdrew a card. "I can be reached at this number anytime of day or night. If I am not in the office, they will get hold of me."

"I am not going to spy on my own family," I told him stiffly.

"I don't expect you to," he said. "It's just that I'm sure you want the murderer brought to justice as much as the family and we do."

He held out his hand and this time I both took it and shook it.

"Inspector," I said, "while I am over here, perhaps I could visit your headquarters and see how you operate. We are always looking for ways to improve our own procedures and techniques."

He studied me carefully for a few moments. What, he wanted to ask, is behind that little request?

"Yes," he said, "that might be arranged. We are terribly busy, but we are always ready to cooperate with police departments from throughout the world. It's been a pleasure meeting you, lieutenant, and perhaps we might have a beer before you leave for home."

While I was wondering about that one, there was a knock on the door, and Catherine called out, "Cousin Benny? Are you in there, Cousin Benny?"

The inspector's face looked like that of a husband caught cheating, and I wondered if he was going to run into the closet or under the bed. I gave him time for neither, crossing quickly to the door and opening it wide.

"Cousin Benny," said Catherine, "are you all right? Brendan said you had disappeared on him, and I've been asking everybody. Old Mrs. McClintock insisted on walking in the procession, and it took me forever to get her back home at the end. Then when I . . ."

She caught sight of the inspector and stopped talking with her mouth still open. For a moment I thought she was going to turn and run, but then her face hardened, and she went so far as to take another step into the room. I closed the door and turned to look at the two of them, their eyes locked on each other in the way of two fighters who are taking their instructions from the referee before the bell allows them to go at it.

"Catherine," I said, "this is Inspector—"

"I know who he is," she said. "What is he doing here?"

"That's a good question," I answered, "and one we haven't fully worked out yet. The inspector has been filling me in on what progress has been made into the investigation of Sean's murder, and—"

"I'm sure he's been filling you in," she said. "That's what he's best at—filling in."

"I take it you two have met before," I said, turning to the inspector. He nodded his head and withdrew his pipe from his trench-coat pocket. Little Catherine seemingly had an unnerving effect on the good inspector. Or the bad inspector. It was all a matter of how you sliced it.

"The inspector assures me," I said to Catherine, wanting to get it all down before a witness, "that the investigation is being pursued vigorously, but that there are still some avenues that must be investigated." I had fallen into police jargon naturally, almost as though I were on the case myself, and had to explain to one of the family why it wasn't being solved immediately. The brotherhood of cops.

"He assured you of that, did he?" asked Catherine. This was not the Catherine I knew. There was a hard look on her face, the kind that I had encountered many times in my own career, the kind that shows that this person is capable of doing whatever is considered necessary to achieve the desired end. It started to sink into me even deeper that I was in the middle of a war zone, and that every man, woman and child was in the army. Despite what I had known and the little glimmerings I had noticed in the past few days, the superficial aspect of Belfast was that of any other city with people going around doing their accustomed things. Beirut, at least, had been blown to hell and looked like a battlefield, but here I was in a hotel that had facial tissue in the bathroom and a color TV in the bedroom.

"I must be going," said the inspector, starting to cross over toward the door.

"He assured you of that, did he?" Catherine repeated as he drew near to her. "Did he assure you of why him and one of his thugs roughed Sean up on the morning of the day he was murdered? Did he assure you of that?"

The inspector kept going and was out the door before I could move. What could I have done anyway? Grabbed him and beat the truth out of him? I suddenly realized I was in the middle of something that was beyond my experience and possibly my capability. What was I going to do?

"Catherine," I said, "have you had your dinner?"

"That's why I'm here," she answered. "To bring you home to supper."

9

THE WILLIAM CALLAGHAN DOMICILE turned out to be situated three brick houses down from the O'Malleys', except that the Callaghans were on the third rather than the first floor. I had the feeling that the rest of the brothers didn't live much more than a stone's throw away from where we were at the moment. The gathering of the Callaghan clan, for whatever reason or occasion, would take only a blast on the ram's horn and get out of the way.

Catherine insisted that we ride the bus to her house because taxis were "so expensive."

"I heard about your paying the piper for Sean's funeral," she said, "and we don't want to be sending you home with nothing but memories."

"I've laid by a store of those already," I told her, "and they're worth every penny."

"Well, we know that every American isn't a millionaire," she said, "and everybody doesn't live like on *Dallas* and *Dynasty*."

It caught me by surprise that all these people were so familiar with the hit American television shows that I never watched myself. When you fly six thousand miles from home base, you get the idea that everything will be totally new and different, that neither group will have any idea how the other puts its pants on in the morning. I suppose if you went to the boonies of Pakistan, you would probably find yourself feeling alone and isolated, but I'm also pretty sure that wherever you might go in the world today, there's a TV antenna sticking up out of the thatched roof and reruns of American action dramas flickering on what little electricity is available.

I could picture the expressions on the faces of Catherine and the rest of the family if they learned that although I wasn't as wealthy as the Ewings and the *Dynasty* moguls were supposed to be, I was worth enough to be treated with respect by even a Saudi Arabian sheik. The forty-four million dollars willed me by Bandini was, according to my bankers in Upsala, New York, growing by leaps and bounds every day of the year.

So there I was with all those millions working for me, and I was riding the goddamned bus. What would Catherine say if I told her I could buy her the bus or her own taxi, or that I could pay for the funerals of all her relations, friends and whatever strangers she might like to throw in?

"Go on with you," she'd say, but I wouldn't. For some strange, or maybe not so strange, reason, I wanted to stay right there and get to know these people well enough so that when I finally left, there would be no doubt in my mind how I felt about them. Right then the score was Catherine one, everybody else zero.

We had to walk several blocks after we got off the bus, and I noticed that there were still those small groups of young guys hanging around the corners or leaning against the brick walls. It's amazing how the men in high-unemployment areas look alike no matter where you are. This was my first time out of the United States, but any one of these punks could be slinking around a street corner in San Diego or New York or maybe even Peking for all I knew.

Catherine looked straight ahead, never once acknowledging the presence of any of them, and while I was waiting for a whistle or a catcall after we had passed by, not one of them did more than look at us casually, almost too casually, their eyes focusing in between rather than on us.

It wasn't until we were almost at her house that I had a chance to ask the question that had been nipping at my mind ever since we had left the hotel.

"What was that all about with the inspector roughing up Sean the day he was killed?" I asked.

"I don't want to talk about the man," she answered primly, almost as though I had gotten fresh with her on our first date.

I stopped and turned toward her, putting both my hands on her shoulders. Before I had a chance to say a word, two of the young men we had just passed were standing alongside us, one on each side.

"Is there a problem, Miss Catherine?" one of them asked.

"Problem?" she repeated, not quite sure of what was going on. I knew what was going on, but I kept my hands on her shoulders, ready to let fly in both directions if they came on to me.

"This is my cousin Benjamin from the States," she said. "We're just on our way to my house for some supper."

"Good day to you then," he said, touching his cap, and the two of them moved back to their spot against the building. I took my hands off her shoulders.

"Who were they?" I asked.

"Oh, a couple of boys from the neighborhood," she said. "I don't know their names."

"What do you mean you don't know their names? You all live in each other's pockets here. How would you not know their names? They knew your name."

"Oh, one's Tom, and I can't think of the other one," she said.

She started off walking again, and I watched her for two steps before catching up. Things were getting curiouser and curiouser. Was the dainty prettiness of my cousin Catherine only skin-deep? It was so frustrating to be caught in a situation where I not only had no control over anything, but where I also had no chances of gaining information that would help me work out any solutions. I had the feeling that if I went to the Belfast public library, they wouldn't let me into the reference department or lend me any books. I couldn't blame Inspector Simmons for freezing me out; I would have done the same for him if he had come barging into San Diego to visit his cousins in La Jolla.

There was also no doubt in my mind that the O'Malleys and the Callaghans and the rest of the tribe I had encountered were all living in a tight society that barred outsiders from even breathing the air of their domain. And the biggest factor of all was that I was an outsider. The blood that ran through my body might have some of the same genes that ran through theirs, and we could exchange the words uncle, aunt, nephew and cousin, but that didn't make me any less the outsider as far as both their lives and deaths were concerned. It was the same in every ethnic ghetto in which I had to work. You could feel it tighten up around you until you were practically grabbing at your throat for breath.

I wasn't trapped there, to be sure. I could turn around right then and be on my way back to San Diego on the first plane heading out. Turn my back on Catherine and the rest of them and go home and throw the shoebox with the letters inside it into the trash. Or burn them. But even as I was thinking it, I was knowing that I could never burn them out of my mind, that I was going to stay there and see it through to whatever end it might lead. Not so much the murder of Sean, though I wanted every murderer everywhere caught and punished, but because as far as I knew these were the only people in the world who had any blood connection to me. If I turned my back on them, all I would have left was that empty apartment in San Diego and memories of two women that froze out thoughts of any woman in the future. The last thing I wanted right then was to be alone again.

Catherine had turned to wait for me, and I started toward her.

"You're not acting like you're very hungry," she said, "and Laura makes the best stew in all Ulster."

I almost asked again about Inspector Simmons and the roughing-up of Sean, but she was in a position where she could run away from the question as she had the moment before, so I thought I would chew on that while I chewed on Laura's famous stew.

10

AS FAR AS LAURA'S STEW WAS CONcerned, there was more than chewing involved. The foremost problem was to keep your gorge from rising. If this was the "best" that Ulster had to offer, then the province was doomed for other than its religious differences. This "stew" was toxic enough to be rejected at a hazardous-waste-disposal site.

The first warning signal, CONDITION RED, was the fetid lamb stink that rose from the black pot, which was brought directly to the table. Laura chunked out the portions into heavy soup dishes, piling it up for the men and being less generous for herself and her sisters. For the first time in my life I wished I were female rather than male. We had drunk a few ales while we were waiting to be called, and William and the two brothers, whose names I didn't remember and which were never mentioned during the course of the meal, kept asking when the grub was going to be ready.

My welcome had been somewhat restrained but still cordial with Uncle William extending his hand for a shake, the two boys grinning and offering nods and both Laura and Cissy turning pinker by the moment. Catherine kept the conversation going, asking me questions about California and did I know any movie stars, and had I ever arrested a member of the Mafia, and was I planning to stay long enough to see the whole province because it was said to be so beautiful up north and she'd always wanted to go there herself, and what was my wife like, which gave me a few bad moments as I uttered some banalities or other, and would I be coming to church on Sunday and . . . and . . . and . . . until her father told her to close her gab and let the man eat.

I would have gone on talking forever if it would

have excused me from sticking my salivary toe into the glutinous mass that was not that far beneath my nose. The surface was covered with pools of grease that had formed almost immediately when the glob was transferred from pot to plate. There was a loaf of good wheat bread from which I received a thick slice and from which I nibbled to keep my mouth moving in the semblance of mastication, but finally my Uncle William remarked that I didn't seem to be eating my stew and was something the matter.

The matter was that I had taken one small spoonful and what was in my mouth made the aroma that had bothered me seem ambrosial. The plate was full of chunks of lamb that were more fat than meat, and though there seemed to be bits of potato and carrots and some undefinable vegetable mixed in, they weren't large enough to pick out individually. I had been bold enough to hold onto the knife that had been used to slice the bread and attempt to cut the fat off one of the lamb globules, but the rubberiness was too much for even the serrated blade and it kept slipping off and hitting the plate.

The Callaghan family, Catherine included, were wolfing down their portions with great gusto, fat included, seemingly swallowing the large chunks rather than chewing them, their lips and part of their faces covered with grease, which they occasionally wiped off with the back of their hands even though there were paper napkins that had been ambitiously folded into what had obviously been intended to be something swanlike. I could feel the beads of perspiration trying to pop out on my forehead even though the kitchen was extremely cool, and I finally decided to hell with it. I almost made the mistake of saying I was a vegetarian, but remembered in time that I had eaten veal the night before at the restaurant while Catherine had chunked her way through a Cornish hen.

"I've got a confession to make," I said, and they all stopped to stare at me. "I didn't know I was coming out to dinner here tonight, and just before Catherine arrived I had a big steak with fried potatoes and broccoli and ice cream for dessert. Delicious as this is, I'm afraid that I'm just plain stuffed."

"Come on now," said William, "a man can always find a little more room, and besides, you won't get that many chances at stew like Laura's while you're over here."

If I had been a devout Catholic as they were, I would have crossed myself and prayed to God to make that statement true. But I was too busy embroidering the lie that was needed to save my life.

"I had cake with the ice cream, a big piece of chocolate cake."

"I had a piece of that cake last night," said Catherine, "and it was sweet enough to choke a horse. Let the man be for the time. This isn't the last of his suppers here while he's on his visit."

If I had been a devout Catholic, I would have prayed to Jesus that he take mercy on me because of what had happened to Him, and to make this the last supper I would ever have in this house.

"I'll take it," said one of the brothers, and he scooped up the plate from under me. The other brother insisted that he share, and I could see William gazing somewhat wistfully at the two of them scrabbling for the last portion of Laura's stew. If he hadn't been the father figure, I'm sure he would have joined in the fray to get his due part.

Dessert was Laura's special version of an English trifle, and they all insisted that despite my previous meal, I had to taste a bit, which turned out to be absolutely tasteless even though I could see traces of a red jam swirling through it.

"We've made coffee," said Catherine proudly, and the jar of instant was brought right to the table with the spoon sticking out of it. Ordinarily, I no longer drink coffee, just as I rarely eat red meat, but I had two cups to wash down whatever tastes might still be hiding in the crevices between my teeth.

The only remark from the brothers, Cissy and Laura during the meal had been the request for my plate.

Otherwise, the boys just ate, and the two girls turned a little pink if their names were brought into the conversation. It was all Catherine asking me questions, and my brief answers, and occasional queries from William about something that kindled his interest, mostly having to do with Hollywood or the rich Jews who controlled everything in the United States. I think if I had caught him on a videotape, I could have sold the program to any network that had hopes of duplicating the success of *All in the Family*. William made the original Archie Bunker sound like Mother Teresa.

The television in the living room had never been turned off while we were "eating" in the kitchen, and the men returned immediately to it while the women cleared and cleaned up. Catherine came in with us after a minute, shooed there by Laura, who said that she should help entertain their American cousin. She sounded like they would need an interpreter to make meaningful conversation between the two groups.

Some more bottles of ale were brought forth, one of which I gratefully sipped, and all of them, including Catherine, gave their full attention to the telly. Now that we had exhausted Hollywood and the Mafia, there was nothing more to discuss. Here I had come all these miles to snuggle into the bosom of my family, and they were more interested in watching a musical variety show. They provoked me into making a move. I almost asked William to tell me about my mother's girlhood, but chickened out at the last second. I settled for second best.

"Catherine told me that the police roughed up Sean the morning of the day he was murdered," I said. "Do you know what that was all about?"

I would have bet that nothing short of a nuclear explosion would have pulled their eyes and ears away from whatever nonsense some English comedian was babbling at them, but at least I got the eyes, every eye in the room.

"Now why would you say that?" asked her father, staring straight at her.

"They did give him a bit of a pasting," said the

older brother. "He showed me the mark on the back of his head where they shoved him against the door."

"Were they there to arrest him?" I asked.

"Oh, no," said the brother, "it was Brendan they were looking for. Sean never got mixed up in anything."

"Nobody tells me a thing around here," complained William. "A man has to come from across the ocean for me to find out what's happening three doors down."

"Why were they looking for Brendan?" I asked.

"Oh, they're always looking for Brendan," said the younger brother. "The good Lord knows how many times he's been taken in for questioning."

"Why is that?"

"Why is what?"

"Why should the police keep taking Brendan in for questioning? Do they think he's doing something criminal?"

"Worse than that," said Catherine. "They think he's IRA."

"Is he?"

"He's never said that he is. But then again, he's never said that he isn't."

"They can't arrest him just for being IRA," I said. "You have to do something criminal before they can arrest you. This isn't the Soviet Union, as you well know."

"Ha!" said William. "You're over here a few days and you're already an expert on what they can and can't do. Russia's a picnic compared to Ulster. Let me tell you, Benjamin, that they can do anything they damn please. They take you before the judge and you're gone. And you have to turn over every rock in the province before you find out where they've taken them."

"Why would they rough up Sean?"

"It's that Inspector Simmons," said the older brother. "He's been on Brendan for two years now, and he's mad when you open the door and he gets madder as he goes on."

"Sean opened the door and they just hit him?"

"Oh, no. First they ask is Brendan home, and when you say he isn't, they come in and look, and when they don't find him, they ask where he is, and you say you don't know, and then they ask you two more times and then they knock you against the door."

"Can't you go to a superior officer and complain?"

"That's been tried, but all you get to do is sit on the bench in the front of the building, and nobody ever calls you in."

"I thought Inspector Simmons was in the homicide division. Do they suspect Brendan of being involved in a murder?"

"Inspector Simmons," said Catherine, "is in whatever division he wants as far as Catholics are concerned. He roams the neighborhood like he's the rent collector, and the mothers tell the wee ones that they best be good or they'll turn them over to Inspector Simmons."

"There were all kinds of police at Sean's funeral," I said, "but none of them seemed to take notice of Brendan then."

"Oh," said the older brother, "that would have been a fight they could have heard in London itself if they had tried to snooker Brendan at his own brother's funeral."

"But those were IRA men up on the hill at the cemetery, weren't they?" I asked.

"That they were for sure," said the younger brother proudly.

"Were they there because Sean really was IRA?"

"They were there because one of us was killed by the Protestants," said William, "and they were there to show that the murder would be avenged."

It was weird to hear this ignorant man talking like one of the nobles in *Macbeth,* but the controversy, the war, the "troubles," whatever the hell you wanted to call it, had been going on for so long that certain phrases had to be familiar even to the Williams that were involved.

"Where is Brendan?" I asked.

THE BELFAST CONNECTION 85

"You never know where Brendan is," said the older brother. "He could be at university, he could be at one of the little magazines that puts out his poems, he could be drunk somewhere at a friend's house, or he could be coming up the stairs to see us now."

A silence went over the group as we listened for Brendan's footsteps, but all we heard was some fat lady singing in a high voice on the television. The opera ain't over until the fat lady sings. It was time to end this family reunion.

"Well," I said, "I should be getting back to the hotel. I want to thank you for a lovely evening and a great meal" (with a glance at Laura, who turned pink), "and I would like to take all of you out to dinner one night before I go back."

Nobody said anything but they didn't seem to take the offer amiss, and I was looking forward to observing these animals in a fancy restaurant. Or rather, observing the people at the tables around us.

"I'll walk you to your taxi," said Catherine, jumping up to get her coat. The buses must have all closed down for the night, or I'm sure she would have had me on one of those.

"I can find the way well enough by myself," I told her. "I'm getting to know the neighborhood."

"But you can't tell who'll be roaming this time of night," she said, "and you a stranger among them. Charles, why don't you come with us?"

The older brother looked up from the television at the sound of his name, but it was obvious that he was in no mood to put his glass on the floor, stand, give up the television, and accompany us outdoors on a cool night.

"No, no, no," I said, "I can find my way without any help. It's only the four blocks over and the two up."

"Well," said Catherine, "as long as I've got my coat on, I might as well walk you down the stairs. Come along, then."

There was no invitation from any of them as to when I should come again, or what I was going to be doing for the rest of my stay, or any inquiries about what they might do for me while I was there. They had given me a meal, and now their obligations were over. I felt very much alone at that moment, even with Catherine chirping all around me. As we walked out, I took a quick look, and every one of them was absorbed in what appeared to be a dart game between teams wearing different-colored sweaters.

It was raining just a bit when we came out on the stoop, and Catherine put her arms tight around her as though her thin coat wasn't enough.

"I'd best walk you to the taxi place," she said. "You'll get lost in this dark."

"I will not," I told her. "I'm a grown man. I'm a policeman. I know how to find my way in the dark. And besides, I'd be worried about you coming back here all alone."

"Me!" she exclaimed. "But I live here."

"That may be," I said, "but you don't want me to worry nevertheless."

"Have it your way," she said. "You're stubborn enough to be a Callaghan. When are we going to see you again?"

"Whenever you want. I thought I might take in the Belfast sights tomorrow, and then maybe rent a car and go out into the country for a few days."

"I have a chance at a job tomorrow," said Catherine, "and I don't know when I'll be through with all the questions and the papers to fill out, but I'll call you at the hotel toward the end of day and we can decide on something then. I'll try to get hold of Brendan because he said he wanted to take you around and show you the real Belfast."

"Good enough," I said. "I'll talk to you tomorrow."

"You take care," she said, and turned and ran into the hallway, her arms still tight around her against the cold.

Well, I thought, that was my real family welcome. That was what I had come six thousand miles for. The

THE BELFAST CONNECTION

funeral was more fun than dinner at the Callaghans. What more could there be after that?

And that's when they pulled the cloth bag over my head, and knocked me to the ground.

11

IT'S WEIRD WHAT GOES THROUGH YOUR mind in those split seconds. I had been knocked on the head, held prisoner, punched and shot so many times in the past year that there was more of a "Here we go again" reaction than one of surprise as I went down hard on the sidewalk. The bag felt like one of those big canvas things they use to haul mail or small packages, and they were pretty slick getting it over my head in one shot because the edges could catch on your shoulder or arm or head as they're trying to shove it down over you. But nothing caught, and they pulled it down so hard that the bottom of the bag whacked the top of my skull with enough force to make my knees buckle.

As I hit the concrete, I yelled as loud as I could, as much from surprise as a plea for help, but the noise sounded muffled even inside the bag. At the same moment, what had to be a piece of pipe was whacked against the side of my head with enough force to bring tears to my eyes, and I heard a voice telling me faintly through the cloth that if I made one more sound, the next knock wouldn't be so gentle.

They hauled me to my feet and I felt a belt or a rope tighten around my waist, pinning my arms tight. There seemed to be a lot of swearing going on in the outer world, but then I heard the roar of a car engine close by, and I was lifted and thrown into something narrow enough so that my head and shoulder banged first and then my knees as I came down hard. Something or somebody dropped on top of me, which, from the weight and bony points I figured to be a man.

The vibration told me we were in motion, and, veteran detective that I am, I deduced that we were in the back seat of a car that was proceeding at a fairly fast rate and not slowing down much for the seemingly innumberable corners. After some time had passed, I could hear the sound of voices, but I couldn't make out what they were saying, partly because of the bag but mostly because I was still having trouble translating Northern Irish into English under the best of circumstances.

The air inside my canvas prison was becoming foul, the sweat had broken out over my entire body, and my heartbeat had to be somewhere around one hundred and ten, but I figured that the kidnappers would still be too hyper from the excitement of the snatch to listen to either my protests or pleas with any degree of sympathy. Over it all was the remembrance of the guy who had tapped me with the lead pipe.

This gave me time to ponder on who and why someone might be taking me to where. The only thing you could be sure of was that nothing good was planned. There was the slight stink of creosote in the bag, and I could feel the burning spreading through my eyes, nose and throat. I contemplated for a moment playing them dirty by dying, but since that might have been what they had in mind in the first place, that would not gain me any points in the scorebook. I was so sick and tired of having become the patsy of the various groups who had bandied me about in the past year. It reminded me of the old joke about the decent guy who was having all these terrible things happen to him, and he goes into the cathedral and cries out, "Why me, Lord?" And this booming voice comes back with "Because you piss me off."

My relationship with God had been peripheral because my nonobserving Jewish father and my fallen-away Catholic mother couldn't have cared less about giving me a religious upbringing. They had gone through all the motions of being what they were, but always on a secular basis. And now, when things in San Diego had seemed to quiet down for me, when the Mafia mobs in both New York and Boston had guaranteed that I was off the hook as far as they were concerned, I had to come all this way to become involved in a religious war that was never going to be settled until everybody in the whole damn province intermarried with everybody else and all the children were half-breeds. Fucking was the only thing that could save Northern Ireland from what was plaguing it.

I realized that the lack of air combined with the creosote was making my brain act funny, and I heaved against the weight that was pressing down on me.

There was some muttering and then somebody yelled out, "What's your problem, mate?"

"I can't breathe," I yelled back, but I could tell that my yell wasn't very loud. My heart rate was faster than ever, and I realized I really would die if something wasn't done. I heaved again against the weight that was holding me down. There was some more palavering, the weight went off me, and whatever was tied around my waist was loosened.

"You keep your mouth shut and stay down there on the floor," a voice commanded me from what had to be the front seat, and the bag was pulled up high enough for me to drag some air into my lungs. The canvas came down to just past my ears, but my nose was free and for that much I was grateful enough to just breathe in and out and lie there quietly.

But finally the air gave me enough strength to ask, "Are you people sure you got the right guy?"

There was no answer. There was one man in the back with me, sitting with his feet in the middle of my shoulders, and I was pretty sure there were two in front, the driver and the one who had given me the orders about my behavior. We drove for maybe another fifteen minutes before we pulled into some kind of dirt driveway and stopped. We could have been fifty miles from Belfast, or we could have been two streets away from where they nabbed me if they had done the classic circle maneuver.

I was just about to ask again whether they might have snagged the wrong man when the one in front said, "All right, get the sack down over him and then get him inside."

The bag was pulled down to my knees again, which wasn't easy with me on the floor and the guy above me working from the seat on his knees, and I was hauled out, sustaining one badly bruised shoulder from the side of the door and another knock on the head from the top of the door. But at least they didn't wrap that rope around my waist again. I was wondering how many arms shipments President Reagan would have agreed to send these guys to get me loose.

"Freedman," he would have mused when they woke him from his afternoon nap. "That name doesn't ring a bell. Don't offer them more than an aircraft carrier."

I stumbled over some kind of doorjamb, but because of the bag I couldn't bend to fall on my knees and went straight out flat. I could hear curses as I was yanked to my feet, and then I was taken down a set of stairs with my feet scrambling to keep pace, but the only reason I remained erect was that two of them were holding me by the sides of the bag.

The sweat was soaking right through my clothes, and the stink of me was competing with the creosote. It was one of those times when you think that you would be better off dead even as you know you don't mean it.

I don't know how long they had me standing there, but without warning the bag was stripped off me, and I could breathe in the damp, musky air of what had to be a cellar. It was better than the finest after-shave lotion ever brewed.

The only light came from one small candle, and for a moment I had the sensation of being alone, but then one of the shadows moved, and I could just make out a man in what looked like army fatigues with a black ski mask over his head. IRA. He was dressed the same as the so-called honor guard at Sean's funeral. Then the other two moved, and I saw they were outfitted the same. Only one of them was good-sized, the other two rather slight, so I took one step toward the big guy and launched the toe of my right foot square into his balls. He doubled over and went to the floor with a yell as I turned to face the other two, who had hesitated a moment before coming at me. I tried a karate chop at the one on my right, but he ducked his head at the crucial moment, and the side of my hand cracked into solid bone. It always went so perfectly in the martial-arts class as you struck and grunted at the same time, the strike being simulated and stopping just short of your opponent's vital area, and the grunt being real. But whenever you tried one of those maneuvers in real situations, the son-of-a-bitch against you never cooperated by having his vital area where it was supposed to be. Usually, it was someone who had never studied martial arts so he couldn't be blamed for his lapse, malefactor though he might be in the regular social system. So what I had was a numb hand while two guys swarmed all over me.

Who knows? I have practiced all kinds of hand-to-hand combat, I was in great shape from my gym workouts and running, and I might have taken those two guys with a little luck. But as luck would have it, one of them was still holding the length of lead pipe and while I was preoccupied with the other one, he laid it along the side of my skull, just catching the top of my ear, hard enough to knock me to the floor in a semidaze.

I landed right on top of the one I had taken out earlier with the tip of my shoe. Kicking people in the testicles has become one of my specialties. It is the kind of offensive weapon that is difficult to use initially because as a male, you cringe from the thought, especially if something along that line has ever happened to you. It is going against the grain, violating the code, altering nature's biological edict. Whenever a baseball is fouled so that it hits the ground behind the plate and spins up into the catcher's crotch with supersonic velocity, every man watching, whether right there or as a television spectator, instinctively squeezes his legs together in both sympathy for whatever catcher has had his bell rung and in gratitude that it was not his pair that were put to the test.

Big policemen, like linebackers, don't have to utilize this form of warfare. They either land on the perpetrator, or pick him up and shake whatever brains he has loose in his skull, or belt him one with a ham-sized fist that would take the steam out of anybody. But a guy my size has to resort to whatever tricks are available in the repertoire of dirty pool, and kicking in the balls had become one of my standard techniques.

So who knows what I would have done against those two remaining guys if one of them hadn't still possessed the pipe. As I lay there just this side of consciousness on top of the groaning mass beneath me, the one without the pipe stepped over and kicked me on the side of the head. That put me over the line and I knew no more. I have never kicked anybody in the head. A man has to draw the line somewhere.

12

I WAS IN A VERY SMALL ROOM WITH Catherine. Not my Cathy; young Catherine, Cousin Catherine. We were both talking at the same time, but I couldn't make out what she was saying, and I didn't know what I was saying. All I knew was that she had a look of fear on her face, terrible fear, deadly fear, and that my own face was twisted into something unusual, but I couldn't tell what it looked like because all the walls in the room were black and there wasn't a mirror.

She was wearing a dark skirt and a white blouse, which was unbuttoned halfway down, and hanging between the two sides of the collar was a gold cross on a gold chain, and she was yelling something at me as I came closer and closer, and I shivered in the cold, and I looked down and I was naked, bare-ass naked, with my thing sticking out in front of me, its head red and angry, and I was angry too because Catherine was suddenly holding her cross in front of her, sticking it at me, and I was hollering that it wouldn't help her because I was half Jewish, and she was screaming back and slapping my face with her right hand, harder and harder until I finally yelled, "All right. All right. All right."

"He's coming around," I heard someone say, and the hand stopped hitting me. I tried to lift my arm up to my face to cool the burning on the cheek, but I couldn't move either hand from behind me, and I tugged but the hands wouldn't come apart, and I opened my eyes to see the candle burning on the table across the room and one of the men in the camouflage suits standing in front of me. I was sitting in a chair with my wrists handcuffed behind me, and my legs were tied to something underneath me because I couldn't pull them apart, and the man in front of me, it was the big one, slapped me once more and I felt some blood drip out of the bottom of my nose onto my upper lip, and I licked it because my mouth was so dry, but the salt taste didn't help my thirst at all. He hit me again.

"That's enough, Ahmed," one of the others said out of the dark.

Ahmed? Ahmed! What the hell kind of Irish name was Ahmed? I remembered the joke about the Jew walking through Belfast at night when he's grabbed from behind and the edge of a knife is pressed against the front of his throat.

"Catholic or Protestant?" a voice hisses.

"Oh, thank God," says the man. "I'm neither. I'm a Jew."

"Well, friend," says the voice, "you just bumped into the luckiest Arab in all Ireland."

It was typical of my life that the joke seemed all too true. He hit me again.

"This pig has not only physically damaged me," said the alleged Ahmed, "but he has insulted me."

"Well, you can settle all that later on after we find out what we want to know," said the voice out of the darkness. "Let me handle it for a start."

He stepped in front of me, nudging aside the big guy, who gave up his position reluctantly. The accent of the big one was definitely not Irish. It was some native tongue with an English overlay. Ahmed. What the hell was an Ahmed doing in this nightmare?

"Who are you?" asked the man in front of me.

I had nothing to hide. I would tell the truth in response to every question they asked me. But even as I was making that decision, I knew that this would not be enough. I was mixed up in something that had nothing to do with me, and whatever I said was going to be wrong.

"My name is Benjamin Freedman," I told him, "and I am a lieutenant in the homicide division of the San Diego police department. That's in California. In the United States."

"What's your real name? Who do you really work for?"

My heart sank. The truth was definitely not going to work with whatever these people were after.

"That's it. Just what I told you. My passport is back in my hotel room, but if you'll take my wallet out, you will find my identification and my badge and my gun permit and my driving licence and—"

"We have already gone through all that," he said. "We don't give a fook about the forgeries. We can make forgeries as good or better than those. We want to know who you are and what you are doing over here."

"He's an Israeli," said the big guy. "He's Mossad. Let me question him. I'll have him begging to his God in five minutes."

"What are you doing in Ireland?" the man asked, as if the other one had not spoken. I had the feeling I was dealing with the leader of the band.

"I came over to visit my family," I told him. "My mother was Deirdre Callaghan, and the Callaghans and O'Malleys are all related to me."

"Did you bring proof with you?" he asked. "Did you bring papers showing that your mother was Deirdre Callaghan?"

"Well, you can ask any of them," I began, and then I stopped. I had brought nothing, not even the letters, with me when I came over. They had all taken me at my word that I was Deirdre's son. But then, maybe they had second thoughts about it. Not one of them had said that I resembled my mother in any way, and it could be that they had turned me over to one of their interrogation teams to find out if I really was who I said I was. There was my birth certificate in Boston and some former schoolmates who would remember my mother even after all these years, but all that wasn't going to do me any good in a cellar somewhere in Northern Ireland at this particular moment in time. No matter what I said, I was, as the man had so aptly put it, "fooked."

"Who are you and what are you after?" the man said again. "We're not leaving here until we know the truth, and that could make for a very long and painful time. By the time Ahmed gets through with you, even the dogs would turn away from what's left. Tell us what we need to know, and we'll set you loose without the hair being mussed on your head."

Oh, yes. I could just see Ahmed turning me out of there without a haircut. Old-fashioned American Indian style. Come back in the morning and we'll have your scalp fixed up nice and all ready to be replaced.

"Look," I said, "like Popeye, I am what I am and that's what I am. Call my captain in San Diego and he'll tell you it's all true. Or ask Inspector Simmons. He checked me out."

Even as I was saying it, I realized what a booboo I had just made, because the guy's hand was moving toward my face with the word "Simmons," and he racked me a good one by the time I said "out." He hit even harder than the big one, and I could tell he was angry enough to be somewhat out of control.

"*Simmons,*" he yelled. "And what about Simmons? What about Inspector Simmons? What was he doing in your hotel room? Is he the one brought you over here? Are you working for the Brits? Are you British undercover?"

"Jesus Christ," I yelled, "what's the matter with you people? Do I sound British? The only time I've ever been in England was when I went through Heathrow on my way here. And Simmons came up to check on me because he thought I might be working with the IRA. With you people. You're all so paranoid over here that you think everybody else is on the other side. I'm on nobody's side. I just came over here to make contact with the relatives I'd never met. As far as I'm concerned, you can all blow yourselves to hell and back, and the sooner the better. Am I keeping you from blowing up a car full of explosives downtown and killing all kinds of innocent people? Am I keeping you from shooting someone in the back? Shouldn't you be trying to lob mortar shells at a police station somewhere? What the hell do you want from me? I'm one guy, an American, over here to see my relatives, and no matter what you do to me, and I mean no matter, it isn't going to change any of that one bit. You can make me yell and scream and confess to anything you want, but it isn't going to change any of what I've said one goddamned bit."

The hand came around and hit me again. That's how much of an impression I had made on this guy.

"You're a liar," the man said. "You're a bloody fooking liar, and we're going to get the truth out of you no matter what it takes. Now I'm asking you for the last time. Who are you and what are you doing over here?"

I didn't even bother to answer him. I felt very tired. The left side of my face felt swollen, and the handcuffs had cut into my wrists when I yanked my arms apart every time I was slapped, and there was no feeling in my legs because the ropes were so tight, and for the first time in my life I believed there was a God, and he was punishing me for coming over here among these madmen. Not because I pissed him off, but because I was so stupid. I had enough scum to deal with right in San Diego; I didn't have to come six thousand miles looking for new ones. Why was I fooling around with these people when I could have gone right to Beirut to the high rollers? This was a shitty little war in which fringe groups were killing people while the so-called nice citizens were letting it happen. And of all things and in all places, to be under the jurisdiction of a guy named Ahmed.

"All right," said the leader, "but what's about to happen to you is on your own head. I gave you the chance."

It was almost like he was apologizing to me. Was this a decent man who was forced into behaving like an animal? Did he think that he had to do what had to be done because his cause was a just one? I remembered my father ranting about the German torturer who would come back from the concentration camp after a day's work, have a nice dinner with a pretty good wine, listen to some Beethoven, go to bed and make love to his wife, sleep a dreamless sleep, and be fresh and eager to go back to his job in the morning. I had punched or slapped a few people in the interrogation room in my time, but always in the anger of the moment, and always with a sense of shame afterward. Would this guy feel bad after Ahmed had turned me into stew meat? I doubted it.

Ahmed was so eager to get at me that he nudged my questioner out of the way before he was ready to go, and almost knocked him over.

"Listen, Jew," said Ahmed, "I'm not going to put a cloth in your mouth. You're going to scream, but there's no one around here who can hear you. I'm not going to put a cloth in your mouth because I want to hear you scream. Do you understand, Jew? Do you understand what I'm telling you?"

"Blimey," said the third man, who was lost somewhere in the darkness, and you could tell he wasn't looking forward to what he was about to witness. Ahmed moved his hand to the right, and I heard the spring slap a blade into position on a folding knife. It turned out to be some six inches long, and I could see that it had been honed to the finest of edges. I would have screamed before it came near me, I would have begged, told them anything I thought they wanted to hear, but I knew it was so hopeless that I didn't even try to muster the strength to bother. The only hope was that he might miscalculate and finish me off. But you could tell that Ahmed had done this kind of thing before, and he wouldn't make any mistakes. My heart was going so fast that I couldn't make out any individual beats, and I felt the sweat drying off me as it poured from my body in that cold, damp room.

Ahmed was inspecting me like a barber just before he starts to shave, or a butcher just before he starts to chop, or a diamond cutter as he looks for the exact spot where the cut is to be made. I knew he was going to start with my face, and wild thoughts were going through me about ears and noses and eyes and cheeks, and just as he lifted the knife toward me, the door was smashed open, the wind blew out the candle, and we were in total darkness as some people yelling at the top of their lungs crashed into the room.

13

WHOEVER IT WAS THAT CAME BARGing through the door couldn't have wished me worse than those already holding the ground so I yelled out, "The big one's got a knife." While I was shouting it, I shoved as hard as I could with the bottom of my feet and was going over backward when I heard the blade swish past where I had been just a moment before. Now some would say that with the noise of my own heart pounding and the screaming that was going on in the room, I wouldn't have been able to pick out the edge of a knife blade whistling past my chest area, but I did, believe me, I did. Ahmed wanted to cut off at least one slice of half-Jewish salami before he closed down the deli.

When I hit the floor, both the chair and the back of my head seemed to break, and I lay there in a semi-daze amid all the wild shouting and the thrashing of bodies that seemed to go on endlessly. I kept expecting the flash of guns, but it would have been stupid for anybody to shoot in the pitch black. It was impossible to tell how many were up against my three kidnappers, and I wondered how they could tell friend from foe in the darkness, especially when my gang was wearing camouflage clothes in the first place. Twice people stumbled over me, but they kept on going to wherever they ended up. Finally, there was one great last shout, and then complete silence for a few seconds.

"Anybody got a light?" somebody called out. There was no answer for a few more seconds, and then somebody else said, "Let me get my bleeding matches out."

The first match obviously broke up in his fingers,

THE BELFAST CONNECTION 101

which earned it a curse, but then there was a distinct scratch and a light flared in the corner by the door.

"There's a candle somewhere," I called out, but the match didn't last long enough for anybody to find it. The next match proved sufficient, and the faint glow from the candle dimly lit the central part of the room.

"All right," said what had to be one of the newcomers, "let's see what the damage is here."

Someone found another candle, and this was placed beside the first one, bringing the light further into the corners. There was one man lying on the floor belly-side-down, and two others sitting up crookedly, one of them moaning a bit and the other one rubbing his thigh in a way that indicated great pain. I tried to count how many there were in the room in the uncertain light, and first came up with eight but then made it nine as a man stepped out from one of the back corners. Six. Six people had busted through that door and saved my ass from Ahmed.

The bizarre thing was that the six newcomers were dressed exactly the same as the three who had been my hosts. Camouflage suits and ski masks. I wondered if there was ever a ski-masked terrorist who actually knew how to ski. Or, had ever seen snow?

Five of the men were walking around freely, and I figured they were from the party of uninvited guests. I couldn't tell who was who without a scorecard, but I knew that the big one stretched out on his belly was my friend Ahmed, and I figured that the one who had hurt his thigh was from the new bunch because two of his buddies were bending over him, and the third guy who had bagged me was the one who had stepped out of the corner because he was being very careful not to make any sudden moves.

"Who clobbered this one?" asked one of the men who had been checking his buddy, walking over to Ahmed and trying unsuccessfully to turn him over. One of the others moved over to help him, and they both heaved at the same time to flip him right-side-up.

"Jaysus," said the first one as he straightened up

and stepped back a pace, peering down at Ahmed through the slits of the eyeholes in his hat. They all were looking at the same spot, but nobody said anything else. They were standing there like they were in some sort of tableau, and it wasn't time to go on to the next pose.

"Excuse me," I said, trying to roll off the remnants of the chair. Only two of them looked over at the sound of my voice. Whatever the hell was holding the attention of the rest of them was really holding their attention.

"Oh my goodness," said the first one who had tried to move Ahmed, "there is Benjamin Freedman himself. A little the worse for wear but still himself."

I had thought I had caught a certain familiarity in the sound of the voice in that it had a recognizable lilt to it that made the words easier to understand than the others. But the last sentence cinched it for me.

"Cousin," I said, "would you be so good as to loose me from durance vile." If you were going to request something from a poet, it was right that you did it in poetic terms.

He pulled the ski mask off his head, and there stood Brendan O'Malley resplendent in his state-of-the-art IRA uniform. There was no question now about whether he was or wasn't, did or didn't, as the commercial says. Besides his hairdresser, I now definitely knew. Which led me to ask myself: since Brendan was IRA, who might the original sons-of-bitches be?

"It would be my pleasure," he said, walking over toward me. Just then the one in the corner tried to make a break for the door, and two of Brendan's people grabbed him and slammed him to the floor so hard that he seemed to bounce once before he lay still. Brendan hadn't even glanced around, which indicated either perfect faith in his comrades, bad hearing, or inexperience. Satchel Paige once advised that people should never look back because that way they wouldn't know who might be chasing them, but if you want to stay alive in the killing business, you have to keep your eyes peeled three hundred and sixty degrees and your ears peeled to the slightest tinkle of the bell.

"What have we here?" asked Brendan, as he bent over to inspect the situation.

"Those are handcuffs behind my back," I said. "I hope one of those buggers has the key."

"Charley," said Brendan to one of the masked figures behind him, "look in Brent's pockets. It's most likely to be there."

Charley leaned over the guy who had tried to dash out the door, and started rifling his pockets. Meanwhile, Brendan was trying to untie the ropes around my legs, but the knots had been pulled so tight that he couldn't undo them with his fingers. He stood up and looked around.

"Oh, well," he said, "you have to do what you have to do." He walked over to the guy who was still moaning on the floor, pulled the glove off his right hand and slipped it on his own. Then he moved over to Ahmed, uttered a very audible sigh, leaned down and pulled out a bloody knife from wherever it was lodged. He looked around the room at his people. "Which one of you came in here with a knife in his hand?" he asked.

"That knife belongs to the man it was stuck in," I said. "He was about to carve up my face when you busted through the door."

"Well," said Brendan, "that sounds like just deserts. Undone by his own petard."

He bent down again and wiped the blade clean on some part of Ahmed's clothes, then came over and sliced cleanly through the ropes holding my legs together.

"I think I've got it," said the man going through Brent's pockets, and he came over with the small key in his hand. Brendan took it from him and after some fumbling around in the dark in back of my body, achieved the double click that set me free. I started to stand up but fell right down again. Brendan laughed, pulled me to my feet and held me steady until the blood returned to the proper spots in my legs.

The failed escapee moaned and sat up, holding his head in both hands. Brendan walked over and yanked the ski mask off him. It had concealed a pug-faced Irishman who reminded me of one of those pit bulls that never let go once they get a death grip.

"Well, Brent," said Brendan, "I hope there's a reasonable explanation of why you kidnapped my American cousin after he left my uncle's house last night."

"An explanation you want, do ya?" the man said with a snort that solidified the dog metaphor. "You're the one has the explaining to do. Bringing a spy into the midst of us. Betraying the brotherhood. Murdering one of your own." His left hand went out in the direction of Ahmed.

"Murdering one of our own," said Brendan with a laugh. "Since when has a Libyan been one of our own? Since when has the INLA been our own? When you people pulled out of the movement to go on your murdering rampage, you stopped being our own. Since when do men who take orders from the Soviets and the Libyans and the Iranians, who line their pockets by robbing banks in the name of freedom, who delight in taking credit for the murder of women and children, since when do such scum deserve to be included among our own?"

"I know who all of you are," said Brent. "You can all take your masks off as far as that is concerned. I know who all of you are and you'll pay for following this traitor to the cause. You're doing the work of the Protestants for them. You might as well be in the UDR for what you're doing to Ireland, and you're all going to pay."

"I like your nerve, Brent," said Brendan, "even if I don't like you. Here you are sitting on the floor next to a dead Libyan with Murphy over there groaning his head off, and you're threatening us. What difference would it make to us if we left here with three dead men on the floor instead of just one? In the long run it would be better for the cause of Ireland, and the only one who would miss you would be the keeper of the pub where you buy your beer."

"You wouldn't kill us now, would you?" said Brent, and there was just the faintest hint of fear behind his bravado. "Say what you want about the differences we have in how it is to be done, but we all still want the same thing, don't we? We all want to be free of Protestant tyranny and be part of the United Ireland and have the Catholics come into their own."

"You can skip the speeches," said Brendan. "I not only know them all, but I can deliver them better. No, we're not going to kill you this time. Which is the opposite of what you would have done for us if the situation had been reversed. But I'm giving you fair warning. You do your dirty deeds out of our territory. Stay down by the border and away from Belfast. And most of all, stay away from my family because when you come near one of us, you come near all of us."

As he said the last part, he reached out and put his hand on my shoulder, and right then I knew I had come all those miles for just such a moment as this. The feeling that went through me was so strong that my knees got a little weak again, but I stood straight and as tall as I could. The Callaghans were showing the flag, and I was part of the parade.

"We're going to leave now," said Brendan, "and we're taking your guns with us as souvenirs of the occasion. I know you've got plenty more stashed away, but we've been running a bit short lately. Pass the word to your other cells what I've just told you. We've got enough people to fight without adding each other to the party. You serve the cause your way if you want, and we'll do it our way, but never forget what the cause is and that it comes first."

"What about Ahmed?" asked Brent.

"What about him?"

"What are we going to do with him?"

"You can eat him for dinner for all we care," said Brendan. "Let's go."

It was just breaking dawn when we came outside what appeared to be an old cottage set among some scraggly trees. There were three cars in the yard, one of which I assumed was my chariot from the night before.

"Do something to their motor," said Brendan to one of the men, and the hood was lifted on the Ford Escort that was closest to the door, and the guy twisted off a few things and yanked some wires.

"All right, you people," said Brendan, "we'll

meet tomorrow night at nine at the usual place. Make sure you stow the gear well and drive back careful. And me and my cousin say well done to all hands."

Brendan stripped off the camouflage suit to show his regular pants and shirt underneath. Then he opened the trunk of the car, unhooked something and stowed his gear, including his gun, in the opening, closed it down so that it looked like it was plain flooring and slammed the door.

"Come, Cousin Benjamin," he said, indicating that I should get in the front passenger seat. When we started off, the others were peeling off their camouflage suits, but they still had their ski hats on. For all I knew, they could be the rest of my cousins or strangers, but it was obvious that it was none of my business and was going to stay none of my business.

"Well, Cousin Benjamin," said Brendan, as we turned off the dirt road onto a paved one that seemed barely wide enough for two cars, "you've become quite a celebrity in the few days you've been in Ireland, what with both Inspector Simmons and the Brent bunch wanting your company as much as possible."

"What the hell is the INLA?" I asked.

"The INLA," mused Brendan, "what is it? Well, the initials stand for Irish National Liberation Army, and it broke away on its own while I was still a little boy, sometime in the middle of the 1970's, give or take a year. There was said to be about two hundred of them to begin with, and they tied themselves in with the so-called Marxists, which means that they deal with the Russians and the scud like that dead one back there. There are some bad ones and some good ones, but their groups are very small, rarely more than four, so we have the devil of a time keeping up with them. I doubt there's more than a hundred of them left now since they spend as much time killing each other off as they do the so-called enemies of the cause. 'Mad dogs' is as good as any way of describing them. To me they're like the gangsters you had in the States during Prohibition. They are a wicked lot who steal from the poor as well as the rich, but every once in a while we find it necessary to work with them."

"How did you know they had me? How did you know where to find me?" I asked. "I don't think I've ever been more scared in my life, and you would be amazed to know what my life has been like the past year."

"We've got one or two lads inside a few of their cells who report things they think we ought to know," said Brendan, "and I was lucky enough to be in the right place at the right time to get the word. You see, it wasn't you they were really after."

"I kept trying to tell them that, but they wouldn't listen."

Brendan laughed and I smiled. It felt good to know that I could smile again.

"There's a bit of what you might call internecine warfare going on right now," he said, "and quite a bit of uncertainty about who is who and what is what. The INLA has been trying to make a special arrangement with my group, and somehow became paranoid when you appeared on the scene. Especially after they found out about Inspector Simmons visiting you in your hotel room."

"But he was there because he suspected me of being part of your group," I said.

"Aye. But Brent's bunch didn't know that."

"They asked me for proof that Deirdre Callaghan was my mother," I said, "and I, of course, didn't have any. But it made me realize that you people didn't ask me for any proof. I just walked in and you took me at my word."

Brendan laughed again, but this time I didn't smile.

"Inspector Simmons was very thorough in his inquiries about you in the States," he said. "He even spoke to someone in Boston about your birth certificate. And Deirdre Callaghan was listed as your mother."

"But how do you know all this?"

"Oh," he said, "not everybody who works in the police department is Protestant. There are even a few who say they're Protestant and have to go to confession each week to be pardoned for the lie."

"But you didn't know any of this when I walked in on all of you at the wake."

"I'll admit you caught us by surprise with that," said Brendan, "but it was no time to go through your britches. So we just played it as it lay until something more definite came along."

"What's about to come along now?" I asked. "Are they going to come for me again? Should I get the hell out of Ireland?"

"Do you want to?"

I thought about it for a few seconds.

"No," I concluded, "I really don't. Not right now. I came over here to find my blood relatives and I have. I came over here in anger, and there's still some in me, but there's also something else trying to crowd in, and I want to find out exactly what that is. If it's not going to get me killed, I'd like to stay on awhile longer."

"We've got some finding out to do," said Brendan, "and that will take a few days. I have to reach the man who controls Brent's group, and find out what all this circus has been about. The first thing we . . ."

He stopped the sentence short and applied the brakes at the same time. I quickly turned my head to look through the windshield, and there in the road was a big guy in a khaki uniform holding his hand up for us to stop. The Ulster Defense Regiment was doing its thing, and my heart, which had slowed down to normal during the ride, went back into tom-tom rhythm.

14

BRENDAN DIDN'T SAY ANYTHING, BUT his knuckles around the steering wheel were white. The burly soldier came toward us and the first thing I noticed was the sergeant's stripes on his arm. I was just thinking that fate wouldn't have the nerve to be playing tricks like this on me when he stuck his beefy face in the window, and sure enough it was my old buddy who had stopped the taxi on my way in from the airport and almost had me stopped forever. He looked at the two of us, but there was no sign of recognition as he paused a moment on each face.

"Would you please get out of the car?" he asked, an order rather than an invitation.

We both complied and I came around from my side to stand beside Brendan. The rest of them had to be somewhere, and I looked around as casually as was possible, and spotted them in approximately the same positions they were in when I was hauled over the first time. The light-machine-gun duo was across the road in a ditch, and a little behind us was what appeared to be the same pimply son-of-a-bitch who had almost killed one of us with his loose trigger finger. Or rather, tight trigger finger. I wondered if there was live ammunition in his rifle and where his trigger finger might be.

The sergeant was checking Brendan's papers, and then he held out his hand to me.

"This is my cousin visiting from the United States," said Brendan.

"My passport's at the hotel," I told him.

"Do you have any other identification on you?" he asked.

I took out my wallet and flashed driving license, credit cards and a few other things, but I didn't go as far as where my badge was pinned or show my police identification card. No need to pinpoint me in his mind. He didn't seem that interested, barely glancing at my cards while his eyes moved around the car.

"And where would you be coming from this early in the morning?" he asked.

"We stayed overnight with our cousins in Glenarie," said Brendan, "and I have to be back at my job at half after eight."

"Was there a fight at the pub?" asked the sergeant.

"No, it was a quiet evening," said Brendan.

"Then what happened to this one?" asked the sergeant, pointing to the swollen half of my face and the mussed-up clothes.

"He was going outside to the back in the dark to spend himself of several pints when he took a header right into the fence. We didn't miss him for a half-hour and then it took another one to find him."

Brendan sounded as though he'd never been to high school, let alone college, and I tried a look that indicated a terrible hangover. It wasn't good but it was good enough.

"Would you open the back, please?" asked the sergeant.

Brendan removed the key from the ignition, and we all walked around to the rear, where he unlocked the trunk and lifted the lid. There were various empty cans and bottles in there, and—my heart gave a bump that almost lifted me upon my toes—a piece of the camouflage material was sticking out of the corner of the alleged secret trunk within the trunk. The sergeant was moving his hand down among the debris, and all he had to do was shift his eyes six inches to the left to spot the edge of the uniform.

I looked over at Brendan, and saw that he was aware of the piece of cloth too. He leaned slightly forward to the right as though he was going to make a dash for it. That machine gun would cut him in half before he got twenty paces. At the least, the big sergeant would catch him and pummel him senseless before dragging the two of us off to jail. We had maybe another five seconds. You couldn't miss the damn thing sticking up there in the corner all by itself.

"Is his rifle loaded this time?" I asked the sergeant, pointing over to where the acne case was slumped over his gun.

"What's that?" he said, straightening up and looking back along the line of my finger.

"Does that soldier have live bullets in his rifle?"

"And what business would that be of yours?"

"The last time you inspected a vehicle I was in, he shot a bullet between our heads that almost killed one of us. I was coming in a taxi from the airport, and he—"

"I remember it well," said the sergeant. "I even remember you now."

"When I get home to California," I said, "I'm going to tell everybody that the most dangerous thing in Northern Ireland is the untrained soldiers who stop you on the road to search your car. I'm going to call the newspaper and have them write a story about it. And when we get back to Belfast, I'm going to go to the American consulate and tell them what happened when I came in and when I go to visit cousins."

"He don't have no bullets in his rifle this time," said the sergeant, slamming down the trunk door so hard that the whole car shifted a bit. It was as if the memory of the event had placed the hapless soldier where the slam would cut him in half and close the door on his memory. The sergeant's face was as red as a baboon's ass, and he was even having a little trouble breathing. I had the feeling that the private was in for a long day's journey into night.

"That won't ever happen again," said the sergeant. "We've a good group, a professional one, and something like that will never happen again. You can tell that to your American consul and all your newspapers in California. We're a good group. Now, go on your way with you."

There's an old, old joke about being calm under pressure. When caught robbing a delicatessen, it says, smoke a herring. You never saw anything so cool and collected as me and Brendan strolling back to our seats in the car and slowly driving off while the sergeant stood over the private and gave him what-for again. I wanted to turn my head to see if he was making him open the chamber of the rifle to show what he had in it, but we weren't that cool and collected. We went around a curve in the road.

"Holy Mother of God, Cousin Benny," said Brendan, "what was that all about?"

I told him what had happened in the taxi on my first day, making it all sound hilarious rather than frightening, and interrupting myself with huge blasts of laughter in between sentences. I was so high that I didn't need a vehicle to get me to Belfast. Although the little car was doing close to sixty on a very bumpy road, I could have run to the city and back before it turned the next corner.

"You lead a charmed life, Cousin Benny," said Brendan, laughing uproariously at nothing in particular. "It was only by luck that we found out about Brent and where he was taking you, and it was only by luck that you were shot at on the way in from the airport so that you could save our bacon back there. There may be some Jew mixed in there, but you've got a hundred percent of the luck of the Irish."

That stopped my laughing, that brought my high down to low. How many more times could I cheat death before the statistics caught up with me? In the past year I had been so close so many times that you'd think I'd be used to it by now. But only a person who had never experienced it would think anything like that. Once is once too many.

"What would have happened back there if he'd seen the suit?" I asked.

"Because of the suit and the guns, I would have disappeared for a while," said Brendan, "and it would not have been a pleasant experience while they were interrogating me. It's better now that we have the treaty, although God knows why that has made a difference. But it would still have been bad enough, and when I did surface again, it would be for a long prison term. It wouldn't be as bad for you, but it would be bad enough, and at best they would have thrown you out of the country forever. Never to see your dear Irish relatives again," he finished with a laugh. "Would you miss us, Cousin Benny?"

"I'd miss you, Brendan," I said seriously. "And Catherine. The jury's still out on the rest of the bunch."

"Well, you're going to be seeing more of Catherine and less of me for the next few days. We've got to ship you out of town until we can get word to McGlindon and find out what the problem is between us."

"Who's he?"

"He's the grand panjandrum of the INLA. He's serving sixty years in durance vile for murders proved and unproved, but he's still running the show from wherever they've got him at the moment."

"You don't know what prison he's in?"

"They move him from here to there and then back again."

"How does he run his show that way, and how do you get word to him?"

"He has ways and we have ways, but it isn't all that easy. So I'm going to have Catherine take you on a tour of the North while we get it sorted out."

"You've got things a little mixed up, Brendan," I said. "You're trying to turn my world upside down. I'm a cop. I'm not the one who's supposed to go on the lam."

"You'll likely be a lamb going to slaughter if you don't," he replied.

"But I don't want to place Catherine in any danger. I can rent a car and go by myself. Besides, her father would never let her travel with me."

"I'll answer your doubts in order," said Brendan. "First off, Catherine will be in less danger in the North than she would walking the streets of Belfast. Second, Lord knows what you might blunder into on your own. Although there aren't many of them, the INLA has friends throughout the province, and if word is out on you, they might finish you off before we can do anything about it. This is a small country, and Americans stick out like sore thumbs. And finally, Bill Callaghan will think that Catherine is off visiting her friend Anne up near Limavady. Since Laura does all the cooking and the washing and the cleaning in the Callaghan house, Catherine's presence is not essential. She likes you and will welcome the chance to get to know you better."

"I really like Catherine," I said. "I like her about as much as any woman I've met, let alone cousins."

"Ah, she is one, isn't she?" said Brendan. "When I decide to settle down, it's going to be Catherine or one just like her for me."

"Catherine?" I said in surprise. "She's a lovely girl, Brendan, but she's not an intellectual."

"I don't want an intellectual," he said. "I want someone who will have the tea hot when I get home at night, and who can't wait to get the clothes off me."

"Catherine?" I repeated, as shocked as a man of my age and experience could be. "Are we talking about the same Catherine?"

"Aye," he said. "That's the real Catherine. It's just that she doesn't know it yet."

"But you're first cousins," I said, seeking desperately for negative reasons.

"Oh, I'm sure we could jolly Father Delavar into working out something with Rome on that score."

The idea of Brendan marrying Catherine was so repugnant to me that I felt the rage rising from my belly to my head, and I wasn't sure of what was going to happen when it thunked against the top of the skull. What the hell was I so upset about? I liked the girl, yes, but only because she was my cousin and because she was pretty and innocent and had been so nice to me. Christ, I was fourteen years older than she was. Not that far from twice her age. What was it with me? But even as I was trying to think of other reasons against it, we were going down the main drag of Belfast, and Brendan was pulling into a parking space.

"Look," he said, "I have to get this car back to where it belongs. Your hotel's just down the street. Go to your room and get cleaned up a bit, pack some essentials in a small bag, and at eleven o'clock you're to leave the hotel by a door in the back of the kitchen. Just walk through it like you belong there, and then stroll out the gate in the fence. Make sure nobody is following you, and then go to the corner of Malvern and Haughey streets, where Catherine will meet you. Do you have a map of Belfast?"

"Yes, I got one from the desk clerk."

"Then you'll be able to find your way. Do you have any money?"

"Yes, I have plenty of money."

"Good. Because we've got none to give you. Catherine will take you to where you can rent a car. I'd advise you to go to a bank and change to Irish pounds so you won't have to be signing your name on any traveler's checks anywhere. Catherine will know where to call each day to find out what the situation is. Have yourself a good time and don't worry about anything. Do you want to carry a gun on you?"

I thought about that for a long minute.

"No," I said, "I don't want to have a gun."

"If you change your mind, Catherine will know where to get you one. There will be people along the way to help you as they can. Now go off with you."

I was thinking so hard about what was happening that I just got out of the car and started to walk toward the hotel.

"Cousin Benny," I heard, and turned around, Brendan had rolled down his window and was peeking his head out. I went back and stood beside him.

"Thank you for saving the bacon," he said. "I'd die before I'd let them put me inside." The window rolled up and I went back to the sidewalk.

As I walked through the security shed to the hotel, I nodded at the guard, who was smiling at me. It was amazing how they got to know you after the first few times. I wondered how secure the security really was. I was thinking about Catherine as I got my key and rode up in the elevator. She seemed to be part of whatever the hell apparatus Brendan was operating in. Was she just the innocent little beauty I had considered her, or was she head of the IRA's Women's Auxiliary? Why didn't I just pack my bags and go home? As I was asking myself that question, I pushed open the door and smelled that sweetish pipe tobacco.

15

"YOU SEEM TO HAVE QUITE A FANTASY life, inspector," I said, even before I turned my head to look at him after retrieving the key from the door.

"What?"

"I get the impression that you envision yourself as some kind of Sherlock Holmes who sits there puffing his pipe and then comes up with a brilliant solution to the mystery. I think it might be illuminating to check your record and see how many cases you have solved and how many are marked pending or still under investigation."

"I'll stack my record against any man's," he said, knocking his pipe into the ashtray and standing up. He was wearing the same coat, same hat, but not quite the same expression on his face. I had obviously annoyed him with my Sherlock Holmes comparison. How would he be feeling if I had tagged him with Dr. Watson? I slipped off my jacket and threw it on the bed. My "funeral suit" had been cleaned and was hanging in the closet, and I would have to make my getaway in that, but Catherine would know where I could buy an Irish tweed jacket if we needed to look more informal on the road.

"Where've you been?" asked the inspector.

"With my relatives."

"Your bed hasn't been slept in," he said, indicating its unruffled quality with his hand. "You've been out all night."

"See," I said, "Sherlock Holmes couldn't have done any better with a clue like that." I looked over at the bed and indicated surprise. "You're right, the bed hasn't been slept in."

"Then where did you sleep? And what happened to your face? And why are your clothes so mussed up?"

"That's all my business."

"No, you're wrong. It's my business and I'm going to get the answer to all my questions or we'll go to the Yard and see if we can come up with some answers there."

I held out my hands close together, ready for cuffing, just as a pimp had done to me once when he knew I had very little evidence in the case that was being investigated. I had almost punched the son-of-a-bitch for his effrontery, and I must admit that I braced a little as I weighed the inspector's reaction. As far as he was concerned, there were no hands in front of him.

"What kind of law do you have in the States?" he asked. "How can a policeman come over here, throw himself in with the criminal element and refuse to cooperate with the legitimate authorities?"

"Let's get some things straight," I said, and I could feel the heat rising in my battered cheek. "Justice in the States is a lot more even-handed than it seems to be over here with your kangaroo courts and your Royal Ulster Constabulary shooting unarmed people in the back. Things like that sometimes happen in the States but not as a matter of official policy. Second, I am over here to visit my family, and since I've been here, not one of them has been arrested on a criminal complaint. And finally, my encounters with you have yet to show me that I am dealing with any 'legitimate authorities.' All you've been, inspector, is a pain in the ass."

That almost got him. He leaned forward and there was the look on his face that indicated some part of his body was about to go into action. But he caught himself. I'll say that for him. He was able to control himself if not the situation.

"All right, then," he said, taking his notebook from his pocket, "this is now an official inquiry."

"Let me see your credentials and a warrant," I said, as formally as I could with half a swollen face and smudged clothes.

"I don't have to show you anything," he said, a

grim smile on his own face. "Now where were you last night?"

"I had dinner at my uncle's house."

"Which uncle was that?"

"I can't rightly remember," I said. "They're all so Irish-looking that I get them confused."

"You weren't at the O'Malleys'," he said. "At least we know that for sure."

"Ah, that's the only one under full surveillance, then?" I said.

His face got as red as my cheek. He'd let loose more than he should have.

"Who can verify your story?" he asked.

"All of them," I told him.

"All of who?"

"All of my uncles and my aunts and my cousins. They'll account for every minute of my time."

We both knew that he would be lucky to get their names out of them, let alone where I might have been at any time. I was beginning to enjoy the benefits of criminal conspiracy.

Simmons snapped his notebook shut and stuffed it in his pocket.

"I can see I am going to make no headway against this attitude," he said. "It is quite possible that later today we will continue the questioning under more formal circumstances."

"Why don't we have tea together?" I asked.

"Oh," he said, "we may be having more than you'll want to swallow. When are you planning to leave the country?"

"I haven't decided yet."

"Well, as long as you're here, I want you to stay put in Belfast and report to me if there is any change in domicile. I want to be able to reach you at all times of day or night."

I gave him what I hoped was a beatific smile.

He left without a by-your-leave, but since this was the way he had also arrived, it evened out.

It was eight-thirty in the morning and there was plenty of time so I stripped down and took a long, hot shower, holding my battered face up to the spray. I felt the little indentations in the shoulder, arm and right cheek of my ass where people had put bullets through me. It had become a kind of ritual with me every time I took a shower, like the way Catholics made the sign of the cross. I remembered a little Jewish ditty my father used to incant whenever my mother, from force of habit, made the sign to either ask for or ward off something.

"Kopf und schmeckel und tzitzke tzitzke," he would intone, rhyming the words to her hand movements.

"What does that mean?" I would ask each time he did it, and one day he gave me the translation. I was maybe nine years old, and he thought for a moment before he supplied the answer.

"It means," he said, "head and pee-pee-maker and tit and tit."

I didn't understand what he was saying, but I knew it wasn't complimentary to what he considered my mother's so-called religion. However, even to this day, whenever I see anybody make the sign of the cross, I can hear my father's mocking voice accompanying them in my mind's ear. Unfortunately, I didn't know more than an occasional Jewish word so I couldn't make up a ditty for my own religious, or at least superstitious, triad of bullet-wound movements.

I put on my suit, dug out the map of the city and started to figure out where I was to meet Catherine. I was somewhat unsure about going off with her like that, and thought that maybe she would balk at the idea when Brendan told her about it, but inside I knew that I was excited about the trip. It wasn't because the INLA had supposedly put out a contract on me; that threat seemed very faint and hard to take seriously. It was exciting to think of traveling through the green countryside with this lovely girl, of having her all to myself away from her boorish family and, yes, from Brendan, who had much more than cousinly ideas about her.

I pinpointed the intersection, which was quite a ways from the hotel. There had to be buses but since I was sneaking out of the hotel, I couldn't ask directions at the desk, nor would it be smart to stop someone in the street and inquire about it. It would be just my luck to pick a plainclothesman for my guide. No, the best thing would be to hoof it. There was just under an hour and a half to get there, and if I didn't faint from hunger, I should make it easily.

I packed my flight bag with the essentials, walked to the door, stopped, turned, came back and sat down on the bed.

"Let's just go over the situation as it is," I said to the television screen, "and bring everything up-to-date. First of all, your name is Benny Freedman and you're a cop. Second of all, you've tied yourself in with a bunch of Irish Catholics who make Archie Bunker seem like Robert Redford. Third, you are involved as an accessory with the IRA, which operates against legal authority. Fourth, you have been fingered by the INLA for reasons unknown to you, and must take it on the lam. Fifth, you are in the shit as far as Inspector Simmons and presumably the rest of the police department are concerned. Sixth, you are really looking forward to taking this idyllic trip to the countryside with your pretty, innocent nineteen-year-old cousin Catherine. Seventh, you haven't had carnal relations with a woman in God knows how long, and there is a disturbing stirring in your loins that may be associated with said Catherine. Eight, if you don't get going, you're going to miss your appointment."

"Do you have any comments on any of the above?" I asked the TV screen. "Might you be more responsive if I turned the set on?" I asked, rising to do so. My hand was on the switch when I pulled myself out of it. Bemused was one thing; nuts was another.

I looked out the door and saw nobody in the hall. There was also no one in the elevator that took me to the basement. Following Brendan's instructions, which had been most explicit, I found the door to the outside. It opened easily, as did the door in the back gate, and I was out somewhere on a rear street. So much for security. I paralleled the main street for a few blocks, checking back to see if anybody was following me, before venturing out, and then found my spot on the map before proceeding. At the first little café, I got myself two muffins and a cup of hot tea. This relieved me of much of my giddiness. I then stopped at what looked like a big bank and went to the exchange window.

"Yes, sir?" said the sober-looking young man behind the cage. He was also dressed in his funeral suit.

"I would like to exchange some money."

"How much, sir?"

"One thousand. No, two thousand dollars."

He looked at me but didn't seem fazed by my request. Would he remember the American who asked for more than the usual couple of hundred? I pulled out one of my black-covered books, endorsed four five-hundred-dollar checks and slid them under the grate. He just looked at me, not bothering to pick them up. What the hell was going on? He shook his head as though he had been dreaming of a pastoral landscape or a girl lying naked with her legs spread.

"What denominations would you like, sir?" he asked, picking up the checks.

"Nothing too big," I said. "My wife and I are going out to the country to see if we can pick up some antiques at the local markets."

He did some calculating on his machine, then counted out a fair-size stack of bills and a few coins.

"Thank you, sir," he said, as I stuffed bills into three different pockets.

"Thank you," I answered as anonymously as I could.

There were dark clouds in the sky and a slight drizzle coming down when I walked out of the bank and resumed my pilgrimage. Perfect Sherlock Holmes weather.

16

AT FIFTEEN MINUTES PAST ELEVEN, I decided I couldn't stand on that corner so conspicuously so I moved halfway down the block and became very interested in the display window of a camera store. I hadn't brought a camera with me and after about ten minutes, was actually thinking of buying one so that I could take pictures of all the members of the family and also some scenic views on the trip with Catherine. But then reality set in and I could see myself sitting in my comfortable chair at home and reminiscing over a photograph of Uncle William. All these people were burned deep enough into my mind's eye to make a color photo unnecessary. And the trip with Catherine, if she ever showed up, might not be that memorable.

At eleven-thirty, I thought the clerk in the store was staring curiously at me through the glass and I moved back to the corner. I had no sooner reached there than Catherine appeared, the strap of a small duffel bag slung over her shoulder.

"Where've you been?" she asked excitedly, looking wildly in all directions.

"I was here at eleven," I said, "and when you didn't show up, I moved down the street a way so as not to attract attention."

"I was here at eleven on the dot," she said, "and you were nowhere to be seen. I finally called the hotel but they said there was no answer in your room."

"Did you leave a message?" I asked, my heart sinking at the thought of being under the tutelage of this master spy for the next few days.

"No. The clerk rang off without a by-your-leave.

When you go back, tell them that they are very rude there."

"We're late," I said, "and better get going. Where are we going?"

"We're going to a car-rental place. We'll have to take the bus. Brendan said you shouldn't use your real name."

I thought of a taxi, but a bus would be more anonymous. And how did Brendan expect me to use a false name when I would have to show my driver's license to get the car?

"Did he give you any papers for me?" I asked.

"No."

"Let's go," I told her.

Twenty minutes later we got off the bus and there was a whole string of car-rental agencies down the block.

"Did he say which place we should go to?" I asked.

"No."

Brendan was as good at this as she was. No wonder they kept blowing each other away. They didn't know any other technique.

I had to show the woman both my driver's license and my passport, the details of which she noted down, and I had to leave a fairly hefty deposit in order for them to trust me with their vehicle.

"Would you be needing any maps?" the nice lady asked.

"We're going down into Ireland," I said, "but a nice general map would be fine."

"Do you know where we're supposed to go?" I asked, once we had settled into the car and I had ruefully contemplated the steering wheel being on the wrong side.

"Brendan said we should head up to the Causeway Coast," she said, "and enjoy the scenery."

"How long is this excursion supposed to last?" I asked her.

"I'm to call in every day from wherever we are, and Brendan will give us the word," she said. She was sitting there like a little kid on her way to the circus, looking around at everything as though we were moving through a fairy kingdom rather than the parking lot of a rental-car agency.

"Do you know which way to go to get us started?" I asked. "Once we're on the highway I can follow the map, but right here I don't know any more than if we were in Afghanistan."

"I'm not sure," she said, "but I think we go off that way."

"That way" was not the right way, but eventually we came across the M2 highway, and I followed the arrow that pointed to the North. At a tourist-information booth I secured maps that were about four miles to the inch, and then I asked Catherine if there was anyplace special she wanted to visit.

"No," she said cheerfully, gazing out the windows as enthusiastically as she had in the parking lot, "as long as we drive north as Brendan said. We're going to be at least three days, according to him, so we're our own masters as far as that is concerned."

Just past Randalstown we went off the turnpike to the A6 road and stopped in a homey-looking town named Maghera for what turned out to be a most substantial lunch with soup and roast chicken and browned potatoes and overcooked brussels sprouts and a trifle for dessert. Catherine drank two beers along with me, and I wondered what the Irish would do if the vogue of designated driver ever reached the Emerald Isle. I could see Paddy pointing to his friend and saying to the cop that "Mike is the designated driver because he's only had nine Jameson's and eleven beers."

Catherine insisted she wanted to look through the shops before we left, and was ecstatic when I bought her a gold bracelet that she had admired in the tiny jewelry store. She didn't even make one token protestation, but just slipped it on her wrist and danced out of the place. Even the crusty-looking old jeweler had a smile on his face as I paid him off.

It was near dusk by the time we got on the road again, and just as the dark was setting in we reached a sign that said we were in Aghadoway.

"Let's find us a place to stay before we get lost,"

I said. "We don't want to be wandering the highways where we can be stopped by a roving patrol." I had been somewhat apprehensive about this all the while we had been driving. Suppose Inspector Simmons had put out an APB on us not only to the police but also to the so-called soldiers who roamed the roads and stopped your car on whim so that pizza face could shoot a bullet past your skull.

"There's a petrol station down there," said Catherine. "They'll probably know where we can get a room."

Since we needed gas anyway, I pulled into the station and told the young man to fill it up. While he was doing it, Catherine engaged him in conversation, and though I could understand what she was asking, I could barely make out three words of his mumbled replies.

"Thank you very much," she said, as we took off again. "You've been most helpful."

"Was he Irish?" I asked.

"Of course he was," she replied, looking at me strangely. "What did you think he was?"

"Some kind of Serbo-Croatian," I said. "Did he know of anyplace and did it sound like one where human beings could stay?"

"We go three miles down this road," she answered, "and take a right on a dirt road for two miles, and then take a left on a smaller road, where we go for one mile, and then there is a guesthouse named Dinwiddie's where they also serve food. He said it was frightful expensive, but we'd have to go all the way up to Coleraine if we wanted to find anything else. Shall we look for something cheaper?"

"No, it sounds fine," I said, wondering how the hell she had gotten such specific directions from the gas jockey back there. If I were alone in this country, I would have to roam the roads forever and would probably starve to death.

The directions were not quite as exact as she had told me, but eventually we came across the place, and it looked most enticing as its lights glittered in the blackness of the wild country around us. Catherine said she would pop in to see if they had a room available, and by the time I had the car parked beside the other three vehicles in the yard, she was back with a young man who shouldered our two light bags and led us in to the cozy warmth of what appeared to be a most charming inn.

It was a big old house that had been completely redone within the past few years by someone with taste as well as money. As we stood in the entrance hall looking up the curved banister to the second floor, a fairly young woman with a pleasant face came out of one of the doors to the side to greet us with a welcoming smile.

"Dinner will be in an hour," she said, "but if you'd like some tea before that, we can bring it up to your room in five minutes."

I was still fairly stuffed from our chicken dinner, so I stood there while Catherine looked questioningly at me and then said that we would be quite comfortable waiting for the meal.

"There's a nice fire in the library," said the woman, "and you can just help yourself to whatever drinks you want. We use the honor system here, and you tell us what you've had when you're settling up."

"I would just like a hot bath for now," said Catherine, and the woman smiled as we followed the young man up the stairs.

The huge bedroom was done in pinks and blues with what looked like a queen-size bed with a canopy over it, and all kinds of sofas and chairs with plump pillows scattered over them. The young man put down the bags and stood there expectantly until I handed him two pounds.

"If there's anything you need," he said, "just call down to me or my mother. I'm Alfred." And he was out the door before I could open my mouth.

"Oh, Cousin Benny," said Catherine, leaping backward onto the bed for a gentle bounce, "I've never been in a palace like this before. We're going to have lots of fun here."

"I think a hot bath is a good idea," I said. "But Alfred forgot to show me where my room is." I walked over to pick up my flight bag.

"This is our room, Cousin Benny," said Catherine, sitting up on the bed. "This is where we're both staying."

"Was this the only room available?"

"I don't know about that," she said, "But this is the only room I took."

"But we can't stay together in the same room," I said, my face getting pinker as I strove to maintain both dignity and command. "Why would we stay in the same room?"

"Brendan said we were to pass ourselves off as married," she said, "and an Irishwoman would be shamed if she didn't stay in the same room with her husband."

"He meant that we should look like we're married when we're on the road," I said, "because if they're trying to find me, they'll have their minds set on a man traveling alone. But Brendan couldn't have meant sharing the same room at night. For God's sake, you're a girl, not a woman. I'm old enough to be your father. And besides, we're cousins. We're first cousins. I'll go see if they've got another room."

"I tell you that will put the suspicions in their minds, and we'll end up explaining it all to a policeman. You can't do that."

"Then we'll leave and find another place where they won't think we're married. We'll say that you're my sister, or the truth, my cousin, and we'll get separate rooms."

"I'm tired and I'm not going," she said, falling back on the bed again. "Why do you have to spoil things, Cousin Benny? This has been the best time of my life so far, and now you're trying to spoil it. I just want to keep you from getting killed. That's what we're all trying to do, save your life, and you're acting like you were a cardinal with the pope."

There was a little sob in her voice as she got the final ridiculous metaphor out, and I walked over to the bed and looked at her. Sure enough, there were tears crawling out of her closed eyes and down her cheeks. I gazed around the room. One of the sofas looked big enough to sleep on if I twisted my body in a few challenging ways. And it was true that we were safer traveling as a married couple. Whoever the group was that was supposedly after me, they would be spreading the word about a lone American on the run rather than a married couple on vacation. If I kept my mouth shut, or mumbled like the kid at the gas station, I might even be able to pass as a native son.

"All right," I said, "we'll do it your way for this one night. But from now on we make sure that we have a two-room suite or adjoining rooms or whatever the hell we can find wherever we're going."

Her eyes popped open and she leapt up from the bed, throwing her arms around my neck and kissing me hard on the lips. No young bride could have been more enthusiastic.

"Oh, Cousin Benny," she said, "you won't regret it. We're going to have the best time ever. Do you want to take your bath first or shall I?"

"You go," I said. "I don't think I'm going to bathe tonight."

She went scurrying over to her bag to pull out clean panties and whatever, carried it all to the bathroom, where she started filling the tub. She didn't close the door all the way, and I could see her moving back and forth as she unbuttoned her blouse. It would be embarrassing for me to walk over and slam the door shut. All I had to do was turn my head or move out of the line of sight.

"They've got bubble bath here," she squealed, unzipping her skirt and letting it drop. Did she know how visible she was through the two-inch gap between the door and jamb? Did she know I was standing there watching her, nailed to the post by . . . What? What was keeping me from moving my head or my body? I thought of Cathy and then I thought of Bandini, both so different from what the Irish would call this slip of a girl. I had loved and lost the two of them barely in the past year. What the hell was I looking for now? There was a splash as Catherine plopped into the tub, and a little "eek" as the hot water reached her sensitive areas.

I turned and went to the door, let myself out of the room and walked down the stairs to the library, where a fire was burning cheerfully in the grate. I went over to the buffet and poured myself a splash of Scotch and a bit of branch water. Sipping it in front of the fire, I mused on the condition of the world and my small part in it. I held the glass up before the flickering flames. It was going to be all right. In this house, the lady had said, you were on your honor.

17

"I'M SORRY," SAID THE NICE LADY, AS WE came down the stairs into a brown-paneled basement room that housed five tables with four chairs at each of them. She stood there in a white apron with a contrite look on her face. What the hell had she done that was so naughty?

"I'm sorry," she repeated, "but the fish didn't look good at the market this morning, so we have only one main course tonight."

The one other couple in the room, a middle-aged pair, nodded understandingly, and both Catherine and I smiled at her to show that there were no hard feelings on our part.

"It's roast lamb," she said, and my heart sank as I immediately attached it to Laura's stew, "the most famous stew in all Ulster." Everything had been so nice up to that point, Catherine still flushed from her hot bath and my own belly warmed by the small Scotch. Even though we had devoured the huge lunch, I was hungry again, perhaps from the Irish country air through which we had driven, perhaps from the excitement of being on the lam, perhaps from Catherine's predinner strip-tease, perhaps from all or none of the above. But whatever anticipation had been stirring my cilia now turned to a mild nausea even before I was faced with the meat itself. Why couldn't Saint Patrick have rid the isle of sheep instead of snakes?

How wrong can you be? The thin slices of meat, slightly pink in the middle, were as tender and tasty as Laura's concoction had been tough and terrible. There were also tiny new potatoes and fresh green beans that had apparently been soaked in butter, and for dessert a chocolate mousse that made every pore in your body feel that it had chocolate coming out of it. Catherine asked if we could have some wine with the lamb so we had a bottle of a French red that was good but not great. When we retired to the library after dinner, the hostess offered us brandies on the house, and both Catherine and I accepted along with the other couple, who turned out to be on holiday, as they put it, from somewhere near Manchester.

As I sipped the brandy, I totted up my drinks for the day and wondered if the curse of the family was about to descend on me. When I was in high school and junior college, I had imbibed pretty heavily despite my disgust at my parents' alcoholism. I hung with people who drank and I didn't want to stand out from the crowd. But when I had run away to California to get away from both my parents' curse and my frightening experience when Jack Gallagher had wrongfully accused me of having sexual relations with his wife, I had gone cold turkey for something over three years. But then I had started socializing again and since it was mostly with other cops, it was again drink or stand out from the crowd. Cathy and I would have wine when we went out to dinner, and except for that I was pretty dry the rest of the time. But here I had drunk two beers for lunch, a Scotch before dinner, half a bottle of wine and now I was slurping down a brandy. Despite all the food, I was feeling a little woozy. In fact, quite a lot woozy. But I kept on drinking until the glass was empty. After all, I was a Callaghan, wasn't I?

"I think it's time we went up to our room," said Catherine, setting her empty glass on the coffee table.

"Ah, you young brides," said the Englishwoman unexpectedly. "I can remember when I was that eager to get this big lunk into bed." She gave her husband an affectionate tap on the arm, which he received with a small smile of affection. You got the feeling that they were still pretty good in bed.

Catherine stood up and extended her hand to me, which I clasped gratefully because I didn't seem to have the energy to push up by myself. She was strong despite her slight build, and I wondered if it had something to do with Laura's stew. We met the owner-chef coming down the stairs as we reached the bottom step.

"Breakfast starts at seven-thirty," she said cheerfully, "but you can sleep in as late as you want and we'll still have something to eat for you."

Catherine put her arm around my waist and we went up the stairs slowly, one careful step at a time, almost as though we were deep in some kind of philosophical discussion that had to be conducted at a perfectly even pace. Except that we weren't exchanging a word, and I was concentrating solely on keeping my balance. I hoped I wasn't going to be sick. That would be just great. Big bad Benny puking in front of his kid cousin.

Catherine pushed the door shut behind us and led me over to the bed, where she gently sat me down. I looked up at her appraisingly. She had matched me drink for drink that day, and if anything, she had put down more of the bottle of wine than I had. The Irish. God bless the Irish. The room felt cold despite the fire blazing away merrily on the grate.

She dropped to her knees in front of me and I had a moment of panic before I realized she was removing both my shoes and my socks. Then she stood and slipped off my jacket, all the while crooning a barely discernible tune. She was starting to undo the buttons on my shirt when I yelled "Stop!"

"What's the matter?" she asked, concern on her face.

"I've got to brush my teeth."

"Och," she said, "I've forgotten my own toothbrush. I'll have to use yours."

This seemed reasonable at the moment, but as I fumbled in my bag for the brush and the paste, I said, "I'll buy you one of your own tomorrow. And some clothes. We both need more clothes than this."

I looked at the paste on the brush with some trepidation before I ventured it into my mouth, but there was no problem despite the amount of foam that was generated. When I returned to the bedroom, Catherine was standing in just her bra and skimpy panties, and while I was wondering whether I should say anything about this, I noticed how long and slender her legs were, and how her rear end curved better than Sandy Koufax could in his prime. Catherine pulled her nightgown out of her bag and retired with it to the bathroom, where this time she closed the door firmly behind her.

I went over to my own case and rummaged before remembering that there hadn't been room for my pajamas, and I would have to sleep in my undershorts. I was starting to move pillows around on the sofa when I heard the toilet flush and Catherine returned in what could only be described as a nightie, a skimpy sleeveless thing that hung just below her vital area. My Cathy had a couple of those. She also had a long flannel thing that she wore to bed when she wanted to play colonial housewife. Bandini never wore anything to bed but that special look on her face. God damn, but this girl was attractive.

"What are you doing?" she asked, after she had watched me for a few seconds.

"I'm fixing up my bed," I said.

"Silly," she said. "There's the bed."

"That's your bed," I told her. "This is going to be my bed."

She came around and took the pillow out of my hand.

"Cousin Benny," she said, "why are you being so difficult? That bed is big enough to fit the whole Callaghan family, let alone the two of us. It will be the same as you being in your hotel and me in my own bed at home."

I looked down at the curves and bumps in the love seat. By morning I would be a pretzel. I was so tired that I knew I would be asleep as soon as my head touched the proverbial pillow, so I let her lead me over to the bed and tuck me in. I thought for a moment she was going to lean over and give me a good-night kiss, but she turned away and started putting out lamps until there was just the flickering light and shadows from the fireplace. When

I closed my eyes, there was just enough reflection for me to see pink rather than black. The bed was beginning to warm up under me as I heard Catherine lift the covers and slide into her own side.

Except that she kept on sliding and in a moment was snuggled into me, her flat chest against my right shoulder and her nose pushed into the side of my face.

"Cousin Benny," she said, and I could feel her warm breath against my skin, "I love you."

I didn't panic. I didn't panic because so many different emotions were going through my body and my brain that I was totally confused as to what I wanted to do, and in what order I wanted to do them. One definite possibility was moving up on my own side and consummating the lust I had been feeling since the second glass of wine. I shivered as I thought what it would be like to take this young, unspoiled creature, and cleave my body to hers for the moments it would take to forget everything else in the world and just concentrate on the sheer passion of what was happening. Jesus, I thought to myself, we're getting pretty poetic about a plain old fuck, aren't we?

But even as I was thinking it, I knew that I was not going to let it happen. The kind of tenderness I had for this girl had nothing in common with the love that had consumed me with Cathy and Bandini. My feelings for Catherine had to do with family ties rather than soul-sharing or even her physical attributes. I realized at that moment that it was exactly the same way I had been attracted to Sophia, Cathy's cousin, when I had been trying to track down where my wife's millions had come from. Sophia was as ugly as Catherine was beautiful, but my feelings toward both of them were exactly the same. I don't know how you would describe it. Maybe you could call it love-once-removed. It was more like a desire to protect and cherish someone rather than merge your whole being into hers.

"I love you, too, Catherine," I said, "but right now we've got to get some sleep."

She wasn't buying any kind of that nonsense. She

buried her nose deeper into my cheek, and shook her head in exasperation. It was the kind of thing that could drive a celibate man crazy.

"No!" she said. "No, no, no. Don't you understand what I'm saying? I love you. I want to marry you and go back to the States with you and be your wife forever and ever."

"Catherine," I said, moving my head a little to the left to relieve the pressure of that nicely tilted nose, "you know we can't ever get married."

"Why not?" she asked, in the voice of a little girl who has been told that she cannot visit her friend Melissa. She put her warm hand on my belly, covering the navel, and I felt the muscles try to tense away from the sensation.

"There are all kinds of reasons why not," I said, my mind trying to work against the alcohol. "For one thing, we're first cousins."

"You can get a dispensation for that," she said.

"Second, I'm so much older than you."

"My friend Fiona married a man forty years old, and they're happy as larks."

"Your father wouldn't permit it."

She snorted her answer. Drastic action was needed.

I went for the big one.

"I'm not a Catholic," I said.

"Father Delavar could fix you up with that in a jiffy," she said. "That's why God brought you over here. To return you to the true faith so that you will go to heaven when you die, and so you and I could be married. I knew it the first time I saw you. I've already discussed it with Father Delavar."

"And what did he say?"

"He gave me all the reasons against it that you just did, but when I told him I would have it no other way, he said he'd do what he could if you would embrace the faith."

I thought of the old joke about the cripple going to Lourdes, dropping his crutches and falling right on his ass. That summed up my faith pretty well.

"I like you, Catherine," I said. "I love you as one does somebody who is the same flesh and blood. But I don't love you as I did my wife or . . . as I did my wife."

"You don't find me attractive?" she asked, and there was enough hurt in the voice to make my belly squirm under the warmth of her hand.

"You're one of the most attractive girls I have ever met," I told her. I had almost said "women" to make her feel better, but it was necessary to keep in her mind the difference in our ages.

"You wouldn't want to do it with me?"

Christ! *Do it with me.* This was going to be a tough one to work around. I needed a few moments to think of a reply that would get me off the hook but allow her to keep her pride.

"Do what?"

"Do it. You know. Do it."

"Catherine," I said gravely, "someone with your faith in God and with all you have to offer should remain a virgin until you marry."

"Well, if that's all that's bothering you," she said, "you can ease your mind. I've already done it. Twice!"

I was so surprised that I spoke without thinking.

"You've done it twice? Who with?"

"With Dennis Raftery," she said, defiance in her words. "Three years ago when his mother was visiting her sister in Londonderry. We did it twice."

"And those are the only times?"

"Yes."

"Three years ago?"

"Yes."

"And how come you haven't done it since?"

There was a pause and the nose was withdrawn all the way from my cheek.

"I didn't like it."

"Why not?"

"It hurt. There was maybe five seconds of pain, and then Dennis huffed for three seconds and then he rolled off me."

"How about the second time?"

"There was just the three seconds of Dennis huffing."

"And you never did it again?"

"Never. Dennis kept bothering me until I told him I would tell my brothers, and he crosses the street when he sees me coming now."

"If it was so bad both times, why do you want to try it again?"

"Because my girlfriend Sarah told me it can be like magic with the right man. You're the right man, Cousin Benny; you can show me magic. You do it to me. And if it isn't magic, then I'll leave you be. But I know it's going to be magic."

In the mood she was in, I knew damn well that it was going to be magic no matter how lousy I might be.

"We can't do it," I said.

"Why not?"

"I don't have any condoms."

"Neither did Dennis."

"But in the United States nobody does it without condoms anymore."

"Why not?"

"Because of AIDS. You know about AIDS. You've seen the commercials on the television."

"But you haven't got it, have you?"

"You never know. Before I was married, I had several sexual partners. And you never know. Be reasonable, girl. You don't want to die. You've got too much to live for. And think how I would feel if I gave you a fatal disease."

There was another fairly long silence as she digested all this. The hand was withdrawn from my stomach, and the spot felt cold where it had been so lovingly caressed. I held my breath. If she had moved her hand three inches below where it had rested, she would have destroyed both my arguments and my resistance.

"You can't get it from kissing," she said. "Everybody says that."

"That's right."

"Then I'll settle for some kissing tonight," she said. "And tomorrow we'll get some condoms."

"Why don't we just kiss each other good night and then get some sleep," I suggested.

"No, I want some real kissing. You can't deny me that."

So for what seemed to be at least a half-hour we kissed. Fortunately, all she knew about kissing was holding your lips together and pressing them against someone else's. At least there was this much innocence in Belfast. There were a couple of times when I pulled my head back and then kissed her on the eyes and the cheeks and the nose, but that was as far as I would let myself go. All the girl had to do was open her lips just a little so that the tip of her tongue pushed against mine, and the night would have been lost. My conscience would have been so stricken that I probably would have turned Catholic and married her. But she didn't and neither did I.

Finally, she pulled herself away a bit, apparently all kissed out.

"I love you, Cousin Benny," she said, and within seconds was sound asleep.

"I love you, too, Catherine," I said softly, and lay there for I don't know how long, contemplating in the dim light from the fire the tent I had erected in the town of Aghadoway in Northern Ireland. I thought about how both Cathy and Bandini would have laughed if they could have witnessed this little scene. My ache for both of them was so bad that I could feel the tears pushing at my eyes, and I crumpled into sleep along with my tent.

18

"TELL ME ABOUT SEAN," I SAID, AS WE headed north again toward what the sign said was Portstewart.

There is truth to the axiom about being in the right place at the right time. Shortly after dawn my head was situated in the only position on the pillow that enabled the sun biting through the slight crack in the draperies to shine directly on my eyes. I turned slightly so I wouldn't open them into full glare, and was just a tiny bit startled to see Catherine's perfect profile some two feet away. I remembered everything instantly, including having too much to drink, my first "necking" session in fifteen years, and that I was dealing with a girl who had romanticized me into the Lochinvar who was going to gallop off with her to the paradise in the west.

She was sleeping the sleep of the young, completely relaxed and capable of continuing until some outside force intervened. Grow old along with me, the best is yet to be. She was right. Fourteen years' difference didn't mean that much when you came right down to it. I knew of plenty of couples with a big age spread who seemed happy. I kept myself in pretty good shape and would be able to at least stay even with her physically for many years to come. When I was seventy, she would be fifty-six, and everybody would say what a lucky bastard I was to have such a beautiful wife who would take care of me right through senility. Then she could be one of the richest widows in the world and get herself a really young guy to balance the seesaw she had been on. Cathy had been my age and Bandini somewhat older, although it was impossible to tell the age of a woman as beautiful as Bandini. But I knew the age of the kid beside me—

NINETEEN—and I smiled as I slid out of the cradle and onto my feet. The head felt good—no hangover.

I smiled again as I looked at all the girlish paraphernalia scattered around the bathroom. I realized I had missed all the comfortable little annoyances that come from moving hair dryers and combs and bottles and jars so that I could find my own workable spot to wash my face and shave and brush my teeth. There was just enough space on the floor for me to do sufficient push-ups to work up a good sweat, which was all the real exercise I had been able to manage since coming to the Emerald Isle. People had been working out on me, to be sure, but that was not a healthy exercise program to follow.

The water in the shower was rather sporadic, varying between burning hot and icy cold, but there were plenty of soft, fluffy towels, and I felt real good when I came out of the bathroom. Cathy was awake and looking at me.

"Come here and give me a kiss," she ordered.

"No."

"Why not?"

"You got enough last night to keep you until you're an old woman. Now let's get dressed and on our way."

She flounced out of the bed, and as some sort of gesture, she pulled her nightie over her head and was stark naked three steps before she went into the bathroom. The vixen. A girl as innocent as this could only be called a vixen. Any other term would be too harsh.

After we had downed a hearty Irish breakfast, Catherine was horrified when she witnessed my transference of a hundred and thirty-six pounds for our night's lodging, dinner and drinks. Once we got in the car, she started carrying on about how outrageous it was, and how that night we would stay in a bed-and-breakfast somewhere and eat fish and chips for supper.

"I've got plenty of money," I reassured her, but she would not calm down about it, which was when I asked her about Sean.

"Sean," she echoed, needing a moment to transfer her thoughts from money to mayhem. Her summing-up was not what one would call a definitive description of a person, a cousin, or even a human being, but there was enough to give me pause once or twice.

"Sean was a good lad," she decided. "He was just the opposite of Brendan, but then again, nearly everybody is just the opposite of Brendan. He's one of a kind. Sean was more like everybody else except for his running. He could run like the very wind, and even the Protestants cheered him on when the race was against an outsider. Tommy O'Toole, who was a grand runner on his own when he was a young man, Tommy was always trying to get Sean to join up with a club, to get some real coaching as he put it, but all Sean ever did about his training was change into his shorts and then beat everybody else by a mile. It was something to see him flying down the track with his hair streaming behind him, looking so frail that you'd think the wind would blow him away, but nothing could stop him, nothing."

I couldn't see her face because I was watching the road so carefully with everybody driving on the wrong side and passing on blind curves, but I could sense the change in her as she realized that something had stopped Sean in his tracks, that he would run no more.

"Was he mixed up in the IRA as Brendan is?" I asked.

"No, I'm pretty sure not," she said, "no more than any of us."

"What does that mean?"

"What?"

"You said no more than any of us. Are you all mixed up in the IRA?"

She thought about that a bit.

"You might say that," she concluded. "We do things that we're asked if the need arises. We don't carry guns or shoot people, but nearly all of us are ready to lend a hand where a hand is needed."

"You said you didn't think the Protestants killed Sean," I reminded her. "If not, then who?"

"That wasn't what I said. I said I didn't think Molly's family had anything to do with the killing. They not only wouldn't do anything to hurt Molly, but her uncle who lives in Belcoo said he would hire Sean after him and Molly was married so they could live apart from the troubles.''

"What about IRA people?"

"What about them?"

"Might they have killed Sean to keep him from marrying Molly?"

She snorted, one of her habits that I was growing accustomed to, and which I also found somewhat charming.

"Even if one of them had wanted to," she said, "he wouldn't of dared having to account to Brendan. No matter who it might be, Protestant or one of our own, Brendan's going to catch up with him someday by one way or another, and then devil take the soul of whoever it might be because he's going straight to hell in a hurry."

"Do you know anything about what happened that night?"

"Which night would that be?"

"The night Sean was shot. Do you know what he did that day? What time he went to Molly's house? How he got there and how he was getting back? Who he might have seen and who might have seen him? Did you see him?"

"No, I didn't see him at all that day. Aunt Meg said there was rumors of jobs at the steel mills and he had gone up there in the morning, but if there were openings, no Catholic got one that day. Or any other day. Molly said he came to her house around seven, just after she and her mother had finished cleaning up from supper. And they had watched telly for a bit and then went for a walk. I'm pretty sure they were . . . they were . . . doing it, and they probably had someplace they went to, and she said he left there a little later than usual but not that much."

"About how far is it from Sean's house to Molly's?"

That took a bit of figuring.

"Somewhere between three and four miles, I would say," she ventured.

"And how did he go there and back?"

"The way he went everywhere. He ran."

"Both ways?"

"I presume so. He probably never had the money for the bus. Sean didn't know any other way but to run. No one could catch him. No one. The only thing that could stop him was that bullet. That's the only thing that is faster than he was. I'm the one introduced them, you know."

"Yes, you told me."

"I curse the day that I did. He'd be alive if it wasn't for me."

"I'm sure he thanked you every day for bringing him together with Molly Peters. You mustn't blame yourself for a murder that might not even have had anything to do with Molly Peters. All the blame lies with the murderer, whoever it was. You obviously brought him some happiness in the few years he had. Just concentrate on the happiness he had because of you."

"I was never that close to Sean," she said. "Brendan's the one took me under his wing. Sean and I were good friends, good schoolmates, good cousins, but even though Sean won all the racing trophies, Brendan was the champion in our family."

There was a fork in the road and the sign indicated we should take the right one, but it took me a moment to figure out which side of the highway we should be on when I moved over, and the truck behind us seemed to miss us by two inches as it swept by with horn blaring. At least some things are the same no matter where you go in the world.

A few miles later we could smell the sea, and then we pulled into one of the prettiest little towns I have ever been in, the small white houses along the sea walk looking like they were painted on a screen rather than places where people flushed toilets. It was obviously a summer tourist area because there were more shops than seemed sufficient for a town this size, but since we were pushing into fall, the streets were fairly empty and "Closing Out Sale" signs were in most of the windows. There was a space in front of one of the larger stores so I pulled in behind a khaki-colored vehicle that had camouflage stripes along its sides and on its roof.

"There's time before lunch," I told Catherine, "to buy you a toothbrush and some clothes and whatever else you need."

"You don't have to buy me any clothes, Cousin Benny," she said. "I have sufficient to last until we get home again."

"I don't," I told her. "And since everything seems to be on sale, we might as well take advantage of it."

Once she got into the spirit of things, Catherine went as wild as any shopper could go. Nearly all of the clothes were for summer wear rather than for cooler weather, and in most of the stores the stock had been pretty well picked over, but she oohed and aahed enough to build up quite a wardrobe before we were through. We would come out of a store and load the packages in the back of the car, and then sally forth to check another. I bought enough things for myself to get me through the trip, but I didn't find the nice tweed jacket I was looking for.

When we had finished buying Catherine a yellow slicker and seaman's hat to match, she came out of the store and said, "That's enough, Cousin Benny. The back seat is almost full and you must have spent all of your money."

"I've got a little left," I told her. "Why don't we spend it on lunch?"

"This sea air is making me hungry," she admitted. "Have you ever seen a place as beautiful as this one? I would love to take my sisters here on holiday."

"That might be arranged," I said. "Why don't we see what kind of restaurants they have around here?"

"Fine," she said, tucking in the last package and slamming the door on her treasures. "I could go in and ask one of the shopkeepers, and then . . ."

She stopped talking abruptly and stared at something behind me. I turned quickly but there was no one in sight except for a man walking a tiny dog.

"What's the matter?" I asked.

"I've got to call Brendan," she said, and I turned again and noticed the public phone booth situated near the corner. "I forgot to do it yesterday, what with all that was going on, and he'll think me a glunterpake. Do you have any coins, Cousin Benny?"

I was being weighed down to the point of hernia by two pockets full of change because I didn't know one from the other so I gave bills for each purchase and took many coins in return. I pulled out a handful and poured them into her cupped hands. We walked over to the phone booth and she said "I'll only be a sec" before she closed the door. Obviously I was not supposed to be privy to whatever the master plan might be.

I moved past the booth to the corner and turned so that I could look at the sea beyond the phone booth. Two soldiers, one an officer, came out of one of the buildings and approached the car in front of ours. Ready for maneuvers. The officer had one of those magnificent walrus mustaches, and as he laughed at something while he waited for the other to unlock the vehicle, I could see the flash of his teeth underneath the red bristle above his lip. Toothbrush. We'd bought everything but a toothbrush, and although I wasn't repelled by the thought of Catherine using mine, she should still have her very own. There had to be a drugstore somewhere in the town. We could ask when we checked on restaurants.

Catherine was talking animatedly to Brendan or whoever, and I noticed what a big ass the officer had as he climbed into the seat beside the driver. I thought a British officer would be more formal and sit in the back. Maybe the class system was disintegrating.

Catherine's face suddenly changed into one of some kind of fear or horror, and as she slammed down the receiver, she pulled open the door and started moving toward me just as I was on my way to find out what the problem might be.

"Benny," she said, breaking into a run, "we've got to get out of this town right away. We've got to—"

I didn't hear the rest of the sentence because just then the explosion blinded me for a moment and shoved me backward. Catherine was knocked off her feet and lay on the sidewalk to the left of me, her skirt hiked above her knees, a bloody gash where a piece of glass or metal had sliced through her.

Past her I could see where the military vehicle had been but now there was just a mass of metal. The blast had been so powerful that there were no flames, only smoke pouring out of the twisted wreckage. The front end of our own car had been totally destroyed and the roof had been blown out, with the packages burning in the back seat. The BMW that had been in front of the army car had been catapulted down the street maybe twenty feet and was lying on its roof.

I saw all this as I was moving toward Catherine, who was so still on the pavement that I feared a piece of metal had hit her in the head, but as I reached her, she started to move both her hands and her legs, and her eyes were wide open as I bent down.

"We've got to get out of here," she said, speaking to the air as much as to me. "Brendan says we have to get out of here."

I pulled her skirt down and checked the gash, which was just a superficial cut and wouldn't require stitches. Then I moved my hands over her body slowly and carefully to see if anything was broken or whether there might be any other cuts or bruises. She seemed all right except for that one spot on the leg.

"Can you stand up?" I asked her, moving my hands under her arms. She got to her feet, swayed for just a moment and then seemed capable of supporting herself. I kept a hand on her arm just in case she needed a bit of help.

"We've got to get out of here," she said again. "We've got to get in our car and drive out of here."

"The car's gone," I said, pointing toward it with my hand. "The whole thing's wrecked."

A couple of people appeared from inside the stores, all of whose plate-glass windows had been smashed in by the explosion. Even though I knew it was hopeless, I felt I had to do something about the military car, and I told Catherine to stand right there while I ran toward it. The amount of explosive had to be gigantic because the damage extended more than two hundred feet in every direction. There was something lying on the sidewalk, and as I came close, I could see it was a human leg, from the knee down, the khaki strip of pants, socks and shoes all attached. It was as if a cleaver had chopped it off cleanly. There wasn't any blood because the force of the blast must have closed off the veins and arteries, and I couldn't tell if it was from the officer or the driver. What difference did it make? Probably the families of the two men would have been better off if there weren't this piece to bury somewhere. For the rest of their lives they would wonder if it had been the leg of their loved one, as the minister would put it, or the other one.

There was nothing else to be seen in what little there was left of the car. Not another scrap of flesh.

There was the weird hoot-hoot of the European emergency vehicles on their way to the spot, and more and more people began to arrive on the scene as I went back to where Catherine was standing. All her leg would need was to be washed off and cauterized, but from the vacant look in her eyes, I could tell that much more was going to have to be done about the shock that had temporarily short-circuited her nervous system. I put my arm around her and could feel the shiver that was going up and down her body.

"Brendan said we shouldn't have been here," she repeated again. "We shouldn't have been here."

If our car had been parked somewhere safe, I would have led her off and driven away from this horror before the authorities had their wits about them to begin the investigation. But what was left of our car was sitting behind the death vehicle, stranding us for the moment as completely as if we were on an uninhabited island in the far reaches of the Pacific Ocean. Some police and some soldiers had arrived and were surrounding the damage area, moving the crowd back. I wondered if there was a car-rental agency in a town as small as this. If we could just drift away and get lost, then we wouldn't be noticed and could go on our way again.

"Excuse me, sir," said a voice beside me. I

turned and there was a policeman standing there. "Did you witness the explosion?" he asked.

"We weren't looking that way," I told him.

"But you were here when it happened," he stated. "I see that the young lady has been hurt. We must get that attended to and then you can answer some questions."

"It's only a minor cut," I said, "and we know nothing about what happened. We are just taking a little vacation and were traveling through the town."

"You are an American, sir?"

"Yes, I am."

"This won't take long. We'll have a doctor look at the young lady and take your statement, and then you can be on your way again. Which is your automobile, sir?"

"The one behind . . . the one behind . . . where it happened."

"Oh my." Young as he was, he actually clucked. "Then there will be much that the inspector will want to ask you."

He took Catherine by the arm and started to move toward where the ambulance had stopped on the road. He was leading her to medical help, but he was also making sure we didn't go away. It's strange what your mind does in situations like this. I almost said to him, "We're not the ones you want to talk to. Brendan's the one you want to talk to."

19

"LET US GO THROUGH IT AGAIN RIGHT from the very beginning," said Inspector Simmons.

Déjà vu, as Mork used to say to Mindy. How many times had I pulled that routine with some creep during an interrogation? You do it in shifts with each detective making the suspect go through the story at least three times, and if you have maybe five detectives available to pull the routine and at the same time hammer at any seeming inconsistencies, you quite often have someone break down from sheer exhaustion, or maybe even boredom, and tell you what you want to know. It may not be the truth, but it is at the least what the prisoner thinks you want to know. Usually a lawyer who cares enough can straighten it out so that too much injustice isn't done, but it would be interesting to see the figures on how many people have been convicted because they were forced to repeat their story an interminable number of times.

Whoever pulled the strings on humans must have been chuckling away to see me sitting in this plain white interrogation room that contained only three chairs. Standing over me was my good buddy Inspector Simmons, who this time around had his pipe firmly in hand and I could damn well lump it if I didn't like it. But since I was personally innocent of any wrongdoing, I had the equivalent of my own pipe.

The problem was that I knew that Brendan was not innocent in the matter of the car being blown up. Even if he had not taken an active part in what had happened, he had probably been involved enough to put blood on his hands. Christ, why did I have to be tied up with the Northern Ireland Catholics? Things would have been much more simple if my family ties were Protestant, and I could be dealing with the confident majority instead of these beleaguered souls. But then again, my father could have married a black from South Africa or Mississippi, or a West Bank Arab. The trick was to think about everything but what Simmons was trying to get out of me.

"Inspector," I said, "I've used this method of interrogation too many times myself to fall for any of its tricks. Next you'll be telling me that my cousin Catherine has confessed to the whole shmear, and it will make it easier on both of us if I come clean on my part. Give it up, man. I've told the story four times now to you and your buddy from the military, and it's been exactly the same each time because that is the truth of what happened."

"Start from where you left the Forum Hotel," he said indomitably, "and tell me how you got out of there without being spotted."

"I went out the front door," I said. "You can check with the guard in the little house or with whoever you had on my tail."

"Nobody saw you go out the front door," he repeated for the fifth time. "How did you know about going out the rear employees' entrance? Who is in on this with you? What kind of mission are you on? Have you anything to do with supplying illegal arms to Irish criminals? What is your relationship besides that of alleged blood to Brendan O'Malley? Why were you here in Portstewart? What did you have to do with the other four bombings that took place in the province at approximately the same time?"

That brought me up short. Nobody had mentioned other bombings until that very moment.

"What other bombings?"

He gave me a contemptuous look and took time to stuff his pipe anew.

"What other bombings?" I repeated. The sight of that leg on the sidewalk would be with me for the rest of my life.

He had to pull and puff hard to get the tobacco going, but he finally had enough steam to blow some of the sweet stink my way. He sat down on the chair opposite me.

"I'll tell you," he said, "even though I'm sure that you know what they are as well as I do. The blood from them is on your hands as much as this one. A car exploded in the middle of Belfast with three killed and sixty-seven wounded, five of them gravely. Mines were set off on the roads leading from two police stations near the border, and a fire bomb destroyed the house of Desmond Moriarty. Luckily, here and Belfast were the only places where lives were lost. But it's all on your head as much as it is on the rest of them."

"Who's Desmond Moriarty?" I asked.

He looked at me in disbelief.

"Desmond is in the leadership of the DUP," he answered.

"What's the DUP?"

"The Democratic Unionist Party, man," he answered irritably. "Don't try to be playing games with me. Now start with when you left the hotel."

"Look, inspector," I said, "it's dark outside and I didn't even get to eat lunch. I hope to hell you're treating Catherine better than what's been going on here. I've told you everything that happened from when we hired the car and what we did on the way up here. I was interested in seeing the country while I was here, and Catherine was kind enough to act as my guide and escort."

"Just a cousinly jaunt, eh?" he said, and I could tell by his voice that he was about to pounce on something that was out of line.

I nodded, not wanting to use any words that could tilt the situation any further.

"You stayed in Aghadoway last night, didn't you?"

I nodded again.

"The innkeeper says that she had no Benjamin Freedman or Catherine O'Malley last night. There were two couples staying there, one named Williams from Manchester, and the other one named Mr. and Mrs. Frank Shaughnessy of Belfast. The descriptions of the Shaughnessys fit that of you and Miss O'Malley pretty well. If you want to deny it, we can bring the owner here to verify the identification."

The vixen. She had planned all along to get us in one room. I had been parking the car while she went in to inquire and register. I may not have fornicated with her, but she sure had fornicated us. It was not a situation that could be explained at all to Simmons or to anybody for that matter. Better just to look lewd and lascivious and let it go at that.

"You've got me, inspector," I said. "I'm a dirty old man. Sightseeing was not the main object of this trip. But that's as guilty as we are of anything."

He just looked at me, waiting for me to fill the conversational gap. An old trick but one I had to go along with at the moment.

"If we had anything to do with what happened," I said, "why would we have parked directly behind the army vehicle? Two more minutes and we would have been getting in our own car to look for a place to eat lunch. Think about it, man. It doesn't make sense. If we had anything to do with what happened, we would have parked someplace safe. We would have been well out of town before the damn thing went off. When could the bomb have been placed in the car? Where would we have been when it was? And how the hell did you manage to come here so fast and try to pin it on me?"

"I happened to be looking at the telex when your name came over it," he said almost reflectively, thinking about something else as he was saying it. "There's too much coincidence where you're concerned, boyo. Just too much coincidence."

"When can I see Catherine?" I asked. "When can I make a phone call? Where can I get a lawyer? How long are you allowed to hold us without pressing charges?"

"In answer to all your questions," he answered, pointing the end of the pipe at me, "when I'm damned good and ready."

The officer from military intelligence came back into the room. I couldn't tell his rank from the markings he wore, but he did carry one of those riding-crop things under his arm, a British tradition that probably started when they used to beat natives out of the way just as a machete clears jungle brush. He had been very meticulous in his questions to me, never changing expression or tone of voice no matter what my answer. There was no way of telling whether he was smart or dumb.

"Any progress at your end, inspector?" he inquired.

"No, major," said Simmons. "He's still withholding the truth on all matters."

"Well, at least he was telling the truth about where he drove the car since he rented it," said the major. "The agency mileage card tallies with the number of miles driven by the vehicle to get to here. If he had sneaked off from Aghadoway during the night and then gone back there, there would have been another forty miles on the marker."

Simmons winced as all this was revealed in open court as it were. Not bad policework as far as I was concerned. It was lucky that the speedometer had survived the blast.

"They'd been leaving that car in the same spot all week while they were assigned here," said the major. "Fairly bad security that. But you get careless when you're in what you consider a safe area until you find out there are no safe areas. Good lesson for all of us, but too bad for those two. Faversham was a particular friend of mine. We'll all miss him in the unit. Well, we've done all we can. The rest is up to you chaps."

He touched his riding crop to the tip of his visor, did a rather smart about-face and left. It was a good thing that the midnight ride Catherine had in mind for us didn't involve the use of the car. If we'd gone out for pizza and nobody had noticed, we could have been somewhat in the sauce.

Simmons was looking at me noncommittally, drawing slowly on his pipe and twitching his eyebrows every few moments as though they were a lighthouse on a rockbound shore on a foggy night. Either he was putting two and four together for a total of seven, or he had no idea where to take it from where it was now. In either case, I felt better about our personal situation. Unless they had worn Catherine down to the point where she was now confessing to our having had a hand in the attempted assassination of the pope by that crazy Turk. I doubted that, however. Those either in the IRA or on the fringe seemed to be steeled against pressures from either the police or the Protestants. They had the ghetto stoicism, and though she seemed a fragile slip of a girl, there was steel as well as determination beneath the surface.

"Tell me what happened after you left the hotel," said Simmons.

He got me. He reached me. I turned from an experienced cop to an enraged citizen.

"Jesus Christ," I exploded, standing up from my chair so hard that it fell over. "Just what the hell kind of a cop are you? Can't you tell that you're barking up the wrong suspect, that this well is dry, that it's time to quit here and go after whoever is really guilty of the crime? How anyone could think me capable of rigging a car bomb on two guys I never knew for whatever reason there may be is beyond reason! You're either a dumb shit, inspector, who doesn't know which way to turn in this case and consequently is hanging on grimly to the ridiculous bit there is, or else you have some personal problem with me that might be anti-Semitic or anti-Callaghan or both. Give it up, man. You're wasting valuable time that you might be using elsewhere. When I'm finally allowed a phone call, it's going to be to the American ambassador. I am not without reputation in the United States, and I can fan a fire that will burn your ass right up to your high command."

"Your ambassador has been informed of your helping us in the investigation," said Simmons equably, knocking the ashes from his pipe on the back of the adjoining chair so that the ashes fell on the floor. That seemed very un-British to me. Or very un-Irish. It was strange. I tended to think of my family and the Catholics as a whole as Irish, while Simmons and the Protestants were seemingly British.

"Now tell me about what you did after you left the hotel in Belfast," he said, cramming tobacco from his pouch into the bowl of the pipe.

I made a game out of it. What I tried to do was remember what I had said the time before and repeat each word exactly, including the "thes" and the "ands" and all the rest. Tired as I was, it became intriguing and soon I convinced myself that I had total recall. I hadn't bothered to pick up the chair so I stood there as though I were reciting a piece in elementary school. There were times when I would be stuck for a few moments as I lost the thread, but then there would be other ones where the words would gush out of me as I became caught up in the rhythm in which they had been delivered originally, and the brain would go into fifth gear as I drove along. I don't know how close I came to repeating the story word for word, but it felt good all the way, and that was the main thing that mattered at the moment.

Simmons never broke in or tried to stop me in any way. He sat there puffing on his pipe and looking at me almost as though I were a TV program he wasn't that interested in. When I finished, I was hoping he would ask me to do it again because there were a few places where I wasn't sure of my recall, and I wanted to see if I could dredge it up better this time. The task I had set myself fueled my body with new energy, and my stomach started rumbling to remind me that fuel was needed if I was to keep going.

"Is there any chance of getting a sandwich and a mug of tea?" I asked, hoping that I wasn't sounding pitiful or begging.

He stood up without saying a word and left the room. I sat still in the chair, not knowing whether or not they had some kind of a viewing monitor on me. This was a small town, however, and the best they could have managed was a tiny peephole somewhere. In any case, I was going to sit there like a lump on a log rather than pace around and indicate nervousness of any kind.

Something like ten minutes later the young policeman who had singled us out at the explosion came into the room. He still looked so neat and clean that I rubbed the stubble on my chin reflexively. There was a smile on his face, which was the opposite of what I had been experiencing the past several hours.

"Well, sir," he said, "it seems as though you are free to go."

"What about Catherine?" I asked. "What about the young lady?"

"I don't know about that, sir. I was only told to fetch you to the sergeant."

As I stood up, I could feel the sweat under my arms, and it was as if there was a fine layer of dirt over my entire body. I had looked forward to changing into my new-bought clothes and forgetting everything but wandering along the coastline. Catherine had been all excited about really seeing the Giant's Causeway to match it with the picture on her calendar at home, and we had been about to roam the Glens of Antrim, which the lady at the information center had told me was one of the most beautiful parts of the province. I wondered if the police had notified the car-rental agency that their vehicle had been totaled. The lady had pushed me into paying the few extra pounds for insurance coverage, and at least I was off the hook on that.

The sergeant was sitting behind his desk with what looked like all my possessions stacked in front of him.

"That's quite a stack of money you're carrying," he observed as I stood before him.

"I happen to be a very rich American," I told him.

"You're all rich over there," he said smilingly. "Next time just send your dollars instead of yourself."

"Where's Catherine?" I asked.

"Who?"

"The young lady I'm with. My cousin. Catherine Callaghan. Where is she?"

"She'll be along in a moment. They're just waiting to have her statement typed out so she can sign it. Have you done so?"

"Yes," I told him. "Quite a while ago. Where's Inspector Simmons?"

"I wouldn't be knowing nothing about that," said

the experienced sergeant. "The Belfast people go their own way."

"Is there a car-rental agency in town?" I asked.

"No," he said. "We'd be having nothing like that."

"Then how do you get out of here?"

"There's buses. And there are two taxis. They'll get you started on your way."

"Is there a place where you can stay overnight?" I asked. "Is there somewhere you can get something to eat?"

"Oh, yes. The Bull and Bear Tavern has a few rooms and they can always scare you up a bite of something no matter what the time. You turn right as you go out the door, and it's maybe five minutes from here. Ah, here's your young lady now."

Catherine looked tired and a bit sad but none the worse for wear. I looked down at her leg and could barely see the thin red line where she had been cut. She walked right up and put her arms around me and squeezed pretty hard for someone who didn't work out with weights.

"Oh, Cousin Benny," she said. "They wouldn't tell me anything about you except to say that you had confessed to everything and I better do the same if I knew what was good for me."

"What was good for you, Catherine?" I asked.

"Telling the truth just as it was," she replied, "and just as my mother and the priest always told me."

I was so disappointed that the inspector wasn't there to hear her. She was a vixen, this girl, a goddamned vixen.

20

THE BULL AND THE BEAR WAS ONE OF those dim, musty pubs that look like George III became very annoyed when told he could sleep there. Just as in a Hitchcock movie, all conversation ceased when we stepped through the creaking door into the taproom.

The faces of the customers could only have been cast by whoever did the early Guinness films, and I wondered what stars should be playing our parts as I carried my movie metaphor to its illogical conclusion. Pee Wee Herman for me and Shelley Long for Catherine.

I walked up to the man behind the bar and in a voice as low as possible, said: "We were told we could get a room here for the night."

"You were told you could get a room here for the night?" he bellowed back in case the people down the road hadn't heard me.

"Yes."

"We do have a room, that's for sure," he said, "and you're welcome to it. Do you need any help with your satchels?"

"We don't have any," I told him. What the hell, I said to myself, use the orphans-in-the-storm gambit. "Our car was behind the one that blew up this morning," I continued my tale, "and all our luggage went with it. We also haven't had anything to eat since breakfast this morning, and the sergeant said we could probably get something here."

It worked. God, how it worked. They all started babbling at once, and we had two offers of drinks, and the manager's wife came out of the kitchen to find out what was going on, and within minutes we were seated at a table with big bowls of steaming soup before us and four half-pints waiting for our attention, and a whole loaf of bread, and bacon and eggs to be prepared whenever we were ready for them.

The cook supervised our eating of the food as well as the preparing of it.

"You poor dears," she said, clucking like a whole hen house, "you poor, poor dears. Another minute and you could have been sitting in your own car to be blown to glory along with them soldiers."

I had no way of knowing whether we were among Catholics or Protestants, whether they were rejoicing in the deaths of the soldiers or lamenting them. All you got was the excitement of people who were near somebody involved in a cataclysmic event. Since nobody there had witnessed the incident, they had to make do with what they had heard, and every once in a while they would turn to us and ask, "Is that how it was? Was that what it was?"

I would nod every time whether that's how it was or not because they didn't need more than that to carry them forward with their own tales, and I was sure that within a week each one of them would have turned into an eyewitness of the whole event. Catherine ate silently, her head bent just enough to avoid anyone's eyes.

When we had filled ourselves with the soup and eggs and bacon and bread and refused a slice of cake, I told the cook that we were very tired and would appreciate being shown to our room. She bustled about energetically until she had us upstairs in a garret that was tiny but unexpectedly most clean and comfortable.

"The loo is right next door," she said, "and since the other room is vacant, you have it all to yourselves. There's more blankets in the closet, and would you like to wear one of my nightgowns, dear?"

"No, thank you," said Catherine, "I'll do just fine."

"Ah, I'm sure you will," said the woman, eyeing me appraisingly. "You won't be cold with this one around," and she gave me a departing nudge with her elbow. Change Pee Wee Herman to Bruce Willis.

Catherine sat down on the bed, spread her hands for support and let her head droop to shoulder height. My watch indicated twenty-five minutes past eight. Tired as we were, it was too early to go to bed, but there was no radio and no television, the town was shut down, and drinking with the boys downstairs held no enticement.

I sat down beside her and put my arm around her shoulders. She leaned her head so that it rested against me, her hair tickling the side of my face.

"We don't even have a toothbrush to share tonight," I said. "Tomorrow we'll have to get new stuff all over again. But at least we're going to be alive enough to do it."

She didn't say anything but her hand moved around my waist and pulled me a millimeter closer.

"What did Brendan say to you on the telephone, Catherine?"

Her hand pulled a little tighter but we were already as close as flesh and bone could get. I waited what had to be a whole minute, but there was still no answer.

"What did he say, Catherine? Tell me what he said right from the beginning. What he said had something to do with those two men being blown to hell and gone, and I want to know what he said."

"I can't tell you," she mumbled.

"Catherine," I said, "even if you're a member of the IRA Auxiliary, you owe it to me to tell me. You people have involved me in one hell of a mess since I came over. It's true I could have stayed home and avoided the whole thing, and it's true that I can go back to Belfast tomorrow and fly out of there by the afternoon, and that would be the end of it for me. But it's not that simple or easy. I've met you and I've met Brendan, and I don't want to let the two of you go now that I've found you. But I'm a police officer and a decent human being, I hope, and I can't just stand by while the two of you are involved in blowing people into small pieces and killing and wounding any innocent bystander who happens to be there by chance. What was accomplished by all those killings and maimings?"

"It focuses the world's attention on the injustices that are being done the Catholics in Northern Ireland," she delivered by rote. "Brendan says we are at war, and when our lives are at stake, we must do whatever is necessary."

"Catherine, that's not the real you talking. Somebody poured that sentence into your ear, and it flows out of your mouth. The British lost two men here, and they'll send six to take their place. The headlines in the British newspapers will be screaming about the murderous IRA and how they must be stamped out. The Protestants will be shaking their heads and saying that the IRA must be annihilated and maybe it would be a good idea to blow some Catholics up to even the score. What happened will only make things worse rather than better."

"Then you tell us what to do," she said, releasing her arm and pulling her head away from me. "Should we just sit still and let them keep us forever caged in the Falls like we were animals in a zoo? Are my brothers to be forever on the dole? And their children after them? The Protestants will never give an inch. At least we can keep reminding them from time to time that we're real people, that we can kick as well as be kicked."

She was trembling and the tears were running down her cheeks.

"What did the inspector say to you when they had you in there?" I asked.

"He said that Brendan was going to hang and I was going to be sent to prison until I was an old woman, and that he had almost all the evidence he needed, but he would do what he could for me with the judge if I just confessed to the whole thing."

"What whole thing?"

"He didn't tell me."

"That's because he doesn't have a damn thing. Did he say anything about me?"

"He said that your own government was going to be arresting you and deporting you back to the States, where you would go on trial for furnishing illegal arms to the IRA. He also said that you hadn't fooled them a bit about being related to the Callaghans, and he was certain that it would turn out that you were a Jew agent sent over to cause trouble among the Christians."

"That's a whole thing all right. Did you believe any of this?" I asked her.

"Oh, Cousin Benny," she said, the tears running full-tilt down her cheeks, "it can't be true that you aren't my real cousin, can it? I couldn't be feeling this way for a stranger. I'd know if you weren't flesh and blood. I don't want to go to jail, Cousin Benny. The men are taken off with their heads high and shouting that the cause will never die, but I don't know what would happen to me in prison, living in a cage, away from my brothers and sisters, getting older and older and never seeing my family again."

This time she put both arms around me and stuck her face into my chest, both our bodies straining in the awkward position to the point where I finally lifted her up and turned her so that she was sitting in my lap. I began covering her face with comforting kisses, but this time when our lips came together, I pushed her mouth apart with the tip of my tongue and tasted the saltiness of the bacon along with the sweetness of her breath. I could feel the burn between my legs.

But then my hand slipped down to her chest and when my fingers encountered only the slight protuberance of the nipples through the thin material without any fleshiness behind it, I stopped short, pulled my head away and then nestled her into my chest again. This was my cousin, my young, young cousin, in her last year as a teenager before going into the roaring twenties. But though she might have been young in years and worldly experience, her birthright in the ghetto had cursed her with a tough softness and a matching soft toughness. Simmons would have had to put her to the Nazi tortures in order to break her code of silence, and she would keep forever silent about the blowing apart of two men while at the same time she would confess to her priest about doing it twice with Dennis Raftery.

"What did Brendan tell you on the phone?" I asked again.

"He said that things were still muddled and we

should stay out for a few more days," she replied, speaking softly into the side of my neck. There was a long silence, but I waited it out.

"Then he asked where we were," she continued. There was another long silence. "When I told him, he became quite upset. 'Get out of there!' he yelled at me. I didn't understand what he was talking about, and I started asking him what he meant, but he just kept yelling, 'Get out of there! Get out of that town right now. Don't talk anymore. You and Benny must get out of that town right now.' So I hung up the phone and started to come toward you when I was knocked down. That's all we said to each other. I wanted to tell him what a good time we've been having, but he didn't let me. He just kept yelling, 'Get out of there.' "

"We're not having a very good time now, are we?" I asked her. "You can't have a good time when you know that you've been a part of killing people."

As I was saying it, I couldn't understand why I was being so cruel to this child. Was I talking to her or to myself? What was the question I was asking? My country right or wrong? My so-called family right or wrong? Was the situation as hopeless as most observers believed it was, or could the pumping in of money by the United States create job opportunities for both Catholics and Protestants that would give them incentives to live in peace? I thought of all the news stories I had casually perused about the situation over the past years, rarely reading one to the end. How different it was to be suddenly thrown in the trenches among the whole lot of them. She didn't answer my question and I really hadn't expected her to.

"Tomorrow we'll go back to Belfast, Catherine," I said. "I'm tired of running. I'm also bored with it. My father brought me up to never run; my police training taught me to never run; and as the spiritual says, I ain't going to run no more."

She pulled her head away from my neck again and looked at me questioningly. It seemed that I wasn't the only one in the room who didn't understand what I was talking about.

"Why don't we go to bed?" I said, nudging her to her feet. "You use the bathroom first."

When I came back from my turn at the "loo," which was one of those old-fashioned lulus where pulling the chain sounded like you were trying to alert the neighborhood to an occurring disaster, Catherine was already in bed. I happened to glance at her clothes piled on the chair and on top were both bra and panties. I sighed, pulled off everything but my undershorts, switched off the tiny lamp and climbed into bed. This one was closer to a single cot than a double so I moved no further in than the absolute edge. I felt her turn toward me and more than my heart gave a lurch in anticipation of what might ensue.

"Would you hold me for a bit, Cousin Benny?" she asked, and I turned and took her into my arms. She put her cheek against mine and squeezed hard, but almost immediately relaxed into a comfortable position and within a minute was breathing softly in deep sleep.

The vixen. I smiled and tried to think about all the things that would have to be done the next day, and what the hell might happen when we returned to Belfast, but I fell asleep within the next minute myself.

I guess that made me an unwily old fox.

21

WE ENDED UP HAVING TO HIRE THE local taxi man to drive us back to Belfast. The ninety-six pounds was obviously way beyond any fare the guy had ever dreamed of, and probably would be the high mark of his professional career. In addition, it brought him into fairly close contact with two who had been involved directly in the tragedy. It made him so hyped up that he couldn't stop talking. First we had to listen to his description of the bombing, which was quite vivid despite his having been home eating his lunch at the time. All I had to do was grunt at appropriate intervals when he asked, "Isn't that the way it was?" and then he would go on again about the soldiers being there on a "secret" mission, and how he had noticed some suspicious strangers scouting the town in the past week, and how he had very close friends in the IRA although he wasn't allowed to divulge any specifics. I inferred from all of the above that he was a Catholic, that he knew no one in the IRA, unless you could count his brief exposure to Catherine, whose exact function in the organization I was as yet unable to pinpoint, and except for me, who was an IRA leader's first cousin, almost once removed.

Catherine matter-of-factly accompanied me up to my room in the Forum Hotel. She hadn't said a word during the whole taxi trip, and I couldn't decipher the look on her face. The only thing you could be sure of was that there was no joy in it. As a matter of fact, with the fur coating on my unbrushed teeth, I wasn't feeling that chipper either.

The room had been tossed in such an obvious way that even the three bears would have caught on instantly. Simmons wanted me to know that I was being turned inside out and that my every move was being monitored. It was one thing for them to leave my shirts disarranged, my other pair of shoes thrown under the bed and the sheets flung down on the rug, but somebody had overstepped his bounds by pulling out the entire roll of toilet paper and streaming it around the bathroom. I wondered if a chambermaid had come in to do her appointed tasks and had fled the place in horror, or whether the police had passed the word that this room was to be left as is until I had gotten the message.

Catherine was mystified enough by the toilet paper to start talking again, and even went so far as to untangle it from whatever it had been draped around and wind it back on the roll. It wasn't as neat as the factory had done it originally, but at least it was back in working order, and Catherine closed the door to try it out.

When she came out again, I asked her what her plans for the day were.

"Whatever you want," she said.

"I have nothing in mind," I said, "and I've lost my taste for sightseeing for a while."

"Then I guess I'll be going home," she said. "I'll tell my sisters that Dixie took sick with the croup, and I couldn't stay there any longer."

"Who's Dixie?"

"She's the friend that I was supposed to be visiting while I was out with you," she said.

"I'll take you back," I said, "but first we have some shopping to do."

"Oh, no," she replied, "you've bought me enough already. And all of those beautiful things gone. At least the memory will be sweet."

"The real thing will be better," I told her, and out we went to the shopping district. This time I insisted on laying it on big, and we not only bought a fancy wardrobe for Catherine but also some blouses and sweaters for her two sisters, and ties for the brothers and Uncle William. If they stopped to count, they would realize that Catherine had the best of it by far, but with their education, I was pretty sure we would be safe. I also thought of getting a cookbook for Laura, but then decided that I didn't want to deny the family the pleasure of eating her food *au naturel*. Or even *oy veh*, as my father used to say while rubbing his stomach after downing too many of my mother's boiled potatoes. From what I remembered of her cooking, it wasn't that much better than my cousin Laura's, but it was rare that we ever had even the semblance of a real meal in our house. Mostly it was fried meats and boiled potatoes or whatever else could be thrown together in as little time as possible. Eventually, the booze became both their food and drink, and anything that required chewing was a rarity. Fast-food joints were my sources of nourishment right through junior college.

What with the number of bundles we had, Catherine didn't argue about taking a taxi this time, and luckily the driver didn't make a fuss about going into the Lower Falls area. While I paid off the cabby, Catherine was busy unloading bundles, and then the two of us gathered them together and started up the stairs.

Just as we reached the top, however, the door opened and there stood Brendan. Both Catherine and I started forward at the same time, expecting him to move out of the way, but he stood still, his hands in his pockets, a strangely solemn look on his face. Unable to stop in time, Catherine bumped into him, dropping two of her boxes to the stone.

"Brendan," she said irritably, "look what you made me do."

"Oh my," he commented, "it looks like our American cousin has purchased half of Belfast. Or is it that the groom has rewarded his *wife* with some presents because she was so good on their wedding night?"

The way he said *wife* was harsh enough to put me on my guard, but with all those boxes clasped in my arms, I was as helpless as a baby white seal in clubbing season. Something very deep was bothering Brendan, and even Inspector Simmons would have deduced that it had to do with me and Catherine.

Catherine, however, was so excited about not only her presents but those for her sisters that she was oblivious to Brendan's anger.

"Get out of the way, Brendan," she said. "I have to show all this to Laura and Cissy."

He stood aside just enough for her to squeeze through, but returned quickly to his original position to block my way. Catherine was clattering up the stairs, all her thoughts concentrated on her sisters' reaction to their gifts, and I could hear her shout as she went through the door. Brendan and I stood there staring into each other's eyes the way fighters do when the referee is giving them instructions before the bout. I turned to the right and carefully piled the packages and bags on top of each other. His look was such that I felt the need to be capable of defending myself.

"You're back early," he finally said. "The honeymoon wasn't all you expected it to be?"

"I didn't expect to see two men blown into jelly in front of my eyes," I told him.

"I read about that in the newspaper this morning," he said. "They'd be alive today if they had been home where they belong rather than over here."

"Brendan, how can you be mixed up in such a thing?" I asked heatedly. "You're not engaged in a real war. You don't have any kind of an army. You're just a scattered bunch of terrorists killing people here and there without any rhyme or reason to it. You're not even one group anymore. You've got all these splinters killing and wounding each other as well as innocent bystanders."

"There are no innocent bystanders in Northern Ireland," he said. "Either you're for us or against us; there's no real 'Peace Lane' for anybody to hide in. I should have let Brent do you in when he had you."

"Why the hell are you acting this way?" I asked. "What has changed so between us that you would want me dead?"

"You took an innocent girl and used her like she was a London whore," he said. "Here I'm sending her off with you to save your life, and you shame her in the eyes of both the world and the church. What will Father Delavar say when she confesses to him about playing the two-backed beast with her Yiddish cousin?"

Was he teasing me with his euphemism for "doing it," and was he serious about soiling her in the eyes of the church? Father Delavar might have known about Dennis Raftery's "huffing and puffing," but it was more than doubtful that Brendan did. Christ, what I had before me was a jealous man, one who felt he'd been betrayed by Judas from the States.

"Nothing happened between me and Catherine on the trip, Brendan," I said. "Except for being part of a horrible event, she's the same now as she was before we went. I've done nothing sexual with the girl. How could you think that of me?"

"Tell me you didn't register as man and wife at Aghadoway," he bit off. "Tell me that you didn't sleep in the same bed."

"But Catherine said that you told her we were to travel as a married couple so the police or Brent wouldn't suspect I was the lone man they were looking for." The *police!* Simmons had been here before me.

"Simmons told you about the way we were registered at Aghadoway, didn't he?" I said. "He's trying to drive a wedge between us."

"It makes no difference who filled me in on it," he said. "I never told Catherine any such thing about the two of you posing as man and wife."

The vixen. The little vixen. Tense as the situation was, I almost smiled in spite of myself. I remembered a story about Napoleon when he was about to be crowned emperor of France and the court officials informed him that they needed thirteen virgins for the ceremony. "In France?" he asked with raised eyebrows. My innocent little "virgin" Catherine was turning out to be as clever a manipulator as Bandini had been. My heart skipped a beat as I thought of Bandini, and the sadness descended on me as though she had disappeared from my life but a moment before.

"Look, Brendan," I said, "Catherine undoubtedly worked out the married routine because she thought she was protecting me. We were registered as man and wife and we did sleep in one bed. But it was a queen-size bed and nothing happened. Absolutely nothing. I lost a woman I loved very deeply some weeks ago, and I find myself incapable of thinking about sex at all, let alone with a kid cousin like Catherine. I find myself drawn to her, but it's like I was her brother or even her father. She is an attractive girl, and I am touched by her sweetness and flattered by her caring and her concern. But that's as far as it has gone and as far as it will ever go. Nothing physical happened between the two of us. You have the word of someone whose life you saved and who owes you the truth at the least.''

Now I was stretching it a bit because we did kiss and sleep naked together, and I did come close to doing exactly what Brendan had suspected. But it was true that I had not invaded her body as the doctors put it whenever they stick a needle into anybody. As far as I was concerned, Catherine was exactly the same as Dennis Raftery had left her. What would Brendan do if I told him about that coupling? He really loved her, I realized. Or at least wanted her for his very own for the rest of their lives. Sometimes possession is confused with love.

The look changed on his face, but you could tell that there were all kinds of doubts still plaguing him. He stepped out of the entryway to stand beside me, but I never found out what he was going to say or maybe do because as I turned to face him, I saw a car speeding down the street toward us, weaving a bit from side to side, and my police instincts went into instant reaction. I leapt forward against Brendan and knocked him down on the stone doorway with me mostly on top of him. In addition to my weight whooshing most of the air out of him, his skull bounced just hard enough to make him passive, and as I turned my head to get as low as possible, I saw the car going by with some kind of machine pistol spraying bullets at us out of the rear window. There was a face there, too, a face so young and contorted with both hatred and fear that it was like one of those gargoyles you see sticking out of the outside corners on old buildings. It was only by chance that my head had turned toward the street rather than away from it, and even as the bullets were spraying above us, the ricochets bouncing everywhere but into our bodies, I was thinking about how I would rather not have that face in my memory to intrude in my future dreams.

It couldn't have lasted more than a few moments, but in that kind of situation each second is forever. I heard tires squeal as the hit car tore around the corner, but I lay there a few more seconds, more out of the inability to move rather than any safety precaution. I lifted my head a bit and looked down at Brendan whose eyes were staring into mine.

"Were they after you or me?" I asked.

"What difference does it make?" he answered. "The important thing is that your knee is in my ballocks and the future of the O'Malley line is in jeopardy."

My heart was racing at Le Mans speed and I could feel the sweat soaking into my shirt. Was this son-of-a-bitch as cool as he was making out to be? I almost grabbed his arm to take his pulse, but instead I rolled off and pushed myself to my knees, ready to fall down again if the damn car came screaming around the corner again for a second try.

Catherine and her sisters came barreling down the stairs and reached the doorway just as Brendan sat up. Cissy, who was obviously the quickest of the three, was shoved by one of the ones behind and fell on top of Brendan, knocking him back to the stone.

"Back off," he yelled, trying to shove the poor girl off him. "Do you want to finish off what those sods couldn't do?"

"Are you all right?" Catherine called from somewhere in the rear. "Are you both all right?"

I didn't answer because I was looking up and down the street, my antennae still waving in the breeze. There was no one to be seen. No one! You could be sure that there were dozens of eyes peeking out from behind their curtains, but not a single soul in this area was going to get involved in something that didn't affect him personally. The human thing was to withdraw into your nest and hope that you were overlooked in the big picture.

"Oh, we're doing just fine," said Brendan, helping Cissy to become vertical before standing up himself. "All we'll need is to brush the dust off."

"When will the police get here?" I asked, my ears trying to pick up the sound of sirens.

"Well," he said, "that's hard to say. Since they only come through here in their armored car and that not too often, it's doubtful that they'll ever know it happened unless there's a supergrasser on the street who's on their payroll, and whoever that might be won't be venturing out for a few hours yet."

"What's a supergrasser?"

"What's a supergrasser?" he repeated. "There's many ways you could define the term. You could use an insect comparison or animal droppings or get fancy and talk in terms of Mata Hari and suchlike, but basically it's a piece of dogshit who takes pay from the Protestants in exchange for information on Catholics who are trying to do something for their people, including weasels like himself. There aren't many telephones in this neighborhood, but if there is a supergrasser with one in his house, it's possible that there will be a police vehicle here within a half-hour, and that we will be questioned about the bullet marks in the walls and we may even be taken to headquarters for more intensive procedures. So I would suggest that you and I depart these premises forthwith, and go somewhere that will not only be safe and warm but also might have a pint or two available to wash the taste of fear out of our mouths."

"Who was it?" asked Catherine. "Who were they after?"

"Och," said Brendan, "you're even beginning to ask the same questions as your cousin Benjamin. Why don't you just pick up the rest of these boxes and take them upstairs? This one on top has two bullet holes in it. I do hope it wasn't somebody's underwear. Come, Benjamin, we must be going."

I walked down the stairs with him, then looked back to see Catherine picking up the last of the boxes. There was an excited look on her face again, no doubt caused by her anticipation of her sisters' reactions to the unopened presents that were left. The fact that Brendan and I could now be lying there on the stoop with blood still pouring out of the bullet holes that were ebbing our lives away was already erased from her mind. If a settlement could ever be made between all these people, how many generations would it take to bring their minds and souls in tune with what they heard in church every Sunday? Was this all in a day's work both for Brendan and for the rest of them? Being a homicide cop in San Diego was going to be child's play if I ever pulled through this ordeal with my own ballocks intact.

When we reached the corner, I stopped, grabbed Brendan by the arm and turned him toward me.

"There's one thing we have to get straight," I told him. He didn't answer, just stood there patiently waiting for what I had to say.

"You saved my life," I said, "which might have been endangered in the first place only because of my relationship to you. And now I have saved yours in a situation where I was only endangered also because of my relationship to you. So we're not even when it comes to owing each other for the saving of our lives. I don't know what the exact percentage should be, but I do know that I have a little more weight on my side of the scale. If anything, you owe me."

"True," he said, slapping me on the back. "The beers are on me."

22

"IT'S EITHER THEM OR US," SAID BRENdan, taking a long swig of whichever Irish potion he had ordered for us. I could never make out the difference among the pints and half-pints and beers and ales and lagers and bitters and all the other crap they lapped up. To me, booze was booze and beer was beer, and they all tasted approximately the same no matter what brand or definition. Since everybody in Ireland, including, I would hope, the lost tribe, is reputedly a king, we were drunk as kings rather than lords. We were quaffing the Hibernian equivalent of boilermakers, but I had no idea what kind of whiskey we were downing or whether it was beer or ale we were cooling it off with.

In one way or another, the Irish were going to be the death of me yet. Jewish alcoholics like my father were a rarity. I had once met the food-and-beverage manager of the Hilton Hotel in Jerusalem while he was on a visit to San Diego, and he had gone on at length about how little alcohol the Israelis consumed.

"We finally put a tab of ten dollars for the first drink in our nightclub," he said, "and nobody complained. But nobody bought a second drink at the regular price either." He was an Englishman and he kept shaking his head in disbelief.

The Irish, on the other hand, are synonymous with drinking. They have been known for their wassailing ever since somebody first noticed that the froth on the malt and hops that had been left too long in the dark corner not only tasted pretty good but made you feel pretty good as well. My first serious drinking took place when I was in junior college in Boston and I became friendly with a cop named John Gallagher. Boilermakers were as mother's milk to him, and I went through a whole year where he got me plastered at least three times a week after our workouts in a neighborhood gym. I think then my drinking had quite a bit to do with how I felt about my father and the memories of my mother because once I left Boston I became almost a teetotaler. I took a drink once in a while, maybe only to prove something to myself, but basically, orange juice, especially fresh-squeezed, was what I got off on.

And here I was drunk in some tiny pub several blocks from Catherine's house where we had gone to recover our spirits after our "little incident" on the stoop. Brendan may have been drinking just to get drunk, but with me it was a case of attempting to soothe nerves that were jumping all over my body and relax muscles that had tightened into knots that no Boy Scout could ever unravel.

I looked around the bar at the three men in there besides us. It was so dark that you could barely make out figures. Woody Allen would have been comfortable there because he once said he never trusted air he couldn't see. Both the bartender and two of the men had nodded briefly at Brendan when we arrived, but we were left alone at our little corner table.

"There's no other way around it," Brendan repeated. "It's them or us. Brent won't quit until I'm laid away and he's tarred you with the same brush."

"Look," I said, "why don't you come visit me in the States for a while? We can leave today and you can stay until the heat cools off over here. Be my guest for the whole thing."

"It's never going to cool off over here," said Brendan, "and they wouldn't let me out of Ireland or into the United States even if the pope said I was clean of heart and true of spirit. My name is on a special government list. Simmons has had me down to the station twice this past week, and that was for nothing at all. I'm a marked man. Besides, I can't go running off from my mates and my responsibilities. If you abandon your post in war, it's treason, and that is punishable by death. Once you join up, you're in it forever."

"That's what the Mafia guys say in the States," I told him, "and from what I've seen, some of your operations aren't that far apart from theirs."

"Oh," said Brendan, "some of the boys are getting into that now. Can you tell me a better or quicker way to raise money for weapons and ammunition than to deal with drugs? From what I've read, that's how your CIA worked it for the Contras in Nicaragua. Guns went down and drugs came back. Brent's into it, I know, and some of his people are using the stuff themselves to keep their peckers up."

"The boy that was shooting at us," I said, "the one in the car. He couldn't have been more than fifteen or sixteen years old. Is that one of the 'them' we're supposed to go out and kill?"

"Anybody who shoots a gun at you," said Brendan, "even if he's still in the cradle, you kill him if need be. I was fourteen years of age when I went on my first mission. I didn't have a gun because there weren't enough guns to go around that night, but if I had one at the time and they had told me to point it at somebody and pull the trigger, I would have done so."

"Would you do anything you had to for the cause, Brendan?" I asked. "Just like the Nazis and the Communists and the Mafia and all the others whose so-called 'causes' have provided so much pain and suffering to the world? How far would you go, Brendan?"

I felt so weak and dizzy that it was all I could do to keep from falling off my chair right on what had to be a filthy floor. It was so dark that you could only tell there was a floor by putting your feet on it, and right then I wasn't sure exactly where my feet were situated. If we were going to get them before they got us, it was going to take us two days of conditioning just to get wherever the hell they were.

Brendan was pondering my question, and by the time he got around to answering it, I had difficulty remembering what I had asked in the first place.

"I have done everything I had to do for the cause, Cousin Benjamin," he said gravely. "I have done the ultimate for the cause. The Nazis and the Communists and your Mafia pale into insignificance when compared to what I have done for the cause."

"And has it been worth it?" I asked him. "What have you achieved by what you have done? If I go with you and we wipe out Brent and whoever the hell else you want, and I go with you and we blow up some British soldiers in a car, and I go with you and we gun down some police and we kill some of the Protestant leaders and maybe we get some innocent bystanders, what will we have accomplished, Brendan? Will it change the situation in Northern Ireland for the better or the worse? Has it changed the situation in Northern Ireland since you took over from whoever came before you? I don't know how high up you are in whatever your group calls itself, but as a leader, do you have a long-range plan or will you be killed or live to pass the baton on to somebody else who will be still running in place the way you are now?"

"You're quite eloquent when you're drunk, Cousin Benjamin," said Brendan, "and you have brilliantly summarized the situation. Now, would you please, from your infinite wisdom and experience, give me a way to bring justice and equality to my people? The Protestants have got the so-called democratic majority, they've got the English soldiers not only backing them up but sometimes leading the way, and they could see us dead in the road and barely bother to lift their feet to walk over us. A hundred years ago there was a poet named William Allingham who wrote an epigraph that said:

Not men and women in an Irish street
But Catholics and Protestants you meet.

That's the way it is and that's the way it will always be if we let them get away with it, and the only way we will get what we want is by fighting for it because they won't give up a millimeter of what they have any other way."

"But your numbers seem to dwindle each day," I said. "From what I read there are less and less of you all the time, and now you're killing each other off, and the people, even those who are for you one hundred percent, are weary of the blood and the terrible waste. Why do you go on?''

"Why? Ask me why the coloreds in your country went on and on even when they were lynched and beaten and set on by dogs. Ask me why the South African blacks keep going when they are shot down like they were pigeons on a pole. Ask me why the Arabs will keep fighting until all of the Middle East blows itself up. Ask me about the Afghans. Then tell me about the Catholics in Northern Ireland. Tell me what we can do other than what we are doing."

I took a sip of the beer and had trouble getting my throat muscle to swallow it. I was beyond hunger, thirst and the ability to go to the bathroom, although only God knew what it was like in a bar like this. Now I would never know either. I don't think the Irish ever have to piss out their beer. Like the ants, they're filled with formic acid, and they burn it away. I was thinking all this as I was considering Brendan's earnest request. What was my personal solution for "the troubles" in Northern Ireland?

"Brendan," I said, trying to push myself to my feet and paraphrasing the sergeant from *Hill Street Blues*, "let's go get them before they get us."

23

I COULD SMELL THE STINK COMING OFF me as I lay there in the dark, beer and whiskey that had rotted their way through the intestines and were now seeking air through every pore in the body. The vague sound of soft voices was coming from somewhere nearby, but my brain was in no condition to make assessments. I put my hand up to my forehead and found it clammy with dried sweat. My whole body felt the same way, but amazingly there were no aches or pains. Where were the aches and pains?

My head jerked as it sank into my consciousness that I could move my hand up to my head without any restraints. I moved my other arm and lifted both my legs as far as my strength would allow. Something was very wrong. I wasn't tied or handcuffed or strapped to the bed. I put both hands to my head and felt every inch, front and back, side and side. There were no new bumps there. Nobody had hit me on the head to knock me out so they could dump me on the bed in this dark room. What the hell was going on? This was against all regular procedure. I couldn't even count how many times it had happened to me in the past year. There was a time when banging me on the head was close to being a national pastime.

Then what had been done to me and how had I ended up where I was? Okay, detective, reconstruct what seemed to be the non-crime. I thought hard. What was the last thing I could remember? Catherine and I had returned to the hotel and gone shopping and then . . . Brendan! I had been drinking with Brendan after those punks had tried to mow us down Chicago style, and I had stood up by the table and said "Let's go get them" and . . . and .. and that's as far as I could remember. Everything after that was darkness.

Did we go get them? Had we gotten them? Or had they gotten me? Was I now being held by Brent in this dark room until he could rustle up another Libyan to work me over? Where was Brendan? Whose voices were those coming through the door?

I moved my legs to the side of the bed so that they could grip the edge and pulled myself up to a sitting position. The dizziness was such that I couldn't decide whether to throw up or lie down again, but I realized that if I vomited in a reclining position, I could choke to death in my own puke. No, it was better to barf semi-erect, and if I had enough strength, I could maybe project it far enough so as not to soil my clothing too much. I was amazed that I could plan ahead so clearly in my condition.

The nausea eased up a bit but the pounding in the skull became fiercer as I moved forward and then stood up as slowly as possible, my hand holding on to the side of the bed as a balancing rod the way the high-wire people use the bamboo pole in the circus. What the hell did they call it when man first stood up and stopped being a monkey? Something *erectus*. I wondered if I would ever have the opportunity to be *erectus* again? Who was out there?

I moved slowly in the dark toward the little bit of light that shone from under the doorway, using my hands the way a blind man probes with his cane, but there was no furniture in the way and finally I reached the door and placed my ear against the wood. The voices were so low that all I could make out was a mumble, but you could tell that more than two people were talking to each other. There would be long pauses in the conversation, but then they would start up again, and I pressed my ear as hard as I could into the door in hopes that I could at least pull one or two words out of the jumble.

Which is why I got such a good crack when somebody on the other side tried to shove his way into the room. It knocked me back a few paces, and there I was weaving around in the dark until the door was pushed open and then I was weaving around in the light.

"Cousin Benjamin," said Brendan, "what in the name of Beelzebub are you trying to do?"

"I'm trying to stand up, you goddamned fool," I answered him as politely as the circumstances would allow.

Brendan put his hands on his hips, tipped back his head and laughed. No, he didn't just laugh; he roared. To me it looked like his interpretation of how an Irish poet should show amusement, or a rather poor imitation of Errol Flynn in *Captain Blood*. I knew I was the source of the merriment, and if I had been physically able, I would have grabbed him around the throat and shaken some sobriety into him. This was a serious medical case he was facing, and he had about as much sympathy as Goebbels mustered when informed that the death rate among Jews at Dachau was far above what had been projected.

"You did fairly well, Cousin Benjamin," said Brendan, "considering that you are obviously not what I would call a drinking man. If you would like to get that taste out of your mouth, we have a few bottles here that would provide a nice contrast."

I looked out into the other room and saw three other men, none of whom I recognized. I checked their bodies to see if I could equate them with the ski-masked crew that had liberated me from durance vile, but that was no more helpful. They were all looking at me with slight grins on their faces but also a touch of sympathy, and I inferred that these were men who also knew what it was like to be racked by a humongous hangover. I walked in to join them once I was sure that my legs would not betray me.

"Fill me in," I instructed Brendan.

"There was no great matter," he said. "You decided to start your morning nap at the pub, and we brought you here to finish it off in comfort."

"Is it time yet for my afternoon nap?" I asked.

"It's almost time for your evening nap," he replied. "Nay. No one would think it too far out of place if you decided to retire for the night."

"Where is the bathroom in this place?" I asked.

"It's out that door and down the hallway to the right," said Brendan, "and if you're going to be needing paper, you had best bring it with you."

"No," I told him, "I don't have the strength for anything that momentous."

The toilet area was surprisingly clean, but there was no washbasin or any of the other amenities that go with the ultimate place of refuge. When I returned to the room, I noticed that two of the men were working on what had to be a pipe bomb. I shivered, thinking back on Bandini and her amateur obsession with pipe bombs as part of the regular arsenal of death. Christ, here I was in a foreign land, hung over to the next decade, and joined with a terrorist group that was planning to blow the hell out of somebody or something. It was like the old joke about the whore being asked by the john how come she was doing what she was doing for a living when she had a Radcliffe diploma hanging on the wall. "Just lucky, I guess," she told him. That was the story of Cousin Benjamin right then—just lucky, I guess.

"What does the future hold in store for us?" I asked Brendan.

"The plan still goes," he answered. "As soon as the guns come, we go looking for Brent."

"What do you mean as soon as the guns come?"

"Surely, Cousin Benjamin, you must realize that we cannot carry guns around on a regular basis with Inspector Simmons or one of his thugs ready to pounce on sight. The guns are brought to us as required by need."

"What about the guy bringing the guns?" I asked. "Is he unpounceable?"

"Nobody is unpounceable down here," said Brendan, "but some are less likely to be pounced on than others. Would you like something to eat? We can bring in some fish and chips."

The one time I had stepped into a fish-and-chips takeout place, the stench of fishy grease had been so strong that I had barely made it out the door again without losing the contents of my stomach all the way back to my fifth birthday party. Even the brief thought of fish and chips at that moment brought such a surge of nausea to me that my knees buckled a bit as I sought to maintain control.

"No, thank you," I finally managed. "Food doesn't appeal to me at this moment."

Brendan laughed again and his three mates chuckled softly, but it was a friendly response and I felt a sense of comradeship. Which immediately turned to horror as I realized that as soon as the gun bearer arrived, we were going out on a murder mission. Why had the fates decided to throw me into these situations in the past year? Evil companions. My feelings for Bandini and my fear of the Bramini mob had almost turned me into a murderer, and now I had enlisted to go out on another murder mission. It was all wrong. The prime reason against it was not just that I was a cop; the crucial point was that I was a human being. It was one thing to wage war against evil, such as with the Germans, or against civilian murderers, such as I dealt with in San Diego. But this was not a war. And even if you allowed them that technical point, it was still not my war. It was true that Brent was a murderous psychopath and the world would be a better place with him out of it, and it was my profession and duty to accomplish such, but I was out of my jurisdiction both as a policeman and as a private citizen. And what of Brendan and his bunch blowing up the English soldiers' car? That was murder. What should I do about them? It was time to bail out, to adhere to basic principles. In short, to haul ass.

"Brendan," I began, just as the fragile outer door exploded inward as the result of someone's heavy boot or a shoulder smashing against it, and four men poured into the room, led by Brent with an automatic pistol in his hand. The three others leapt in after him, including the kid whose contorted face I had seen in the rear window of the murder car. He was holding what had to be the same Uzi in his hands, and it was pointing directly at me. The three men who had been sitting in the chairs in the room sprang to their feet, but no one moved as Brent's men waved their guns menacingly in our direction.

"Brendan," said Brent, "the word is out that you are looking for me. We thought we'd save you some trouble."

He smiled by moving his lips apart, and you could tell that this man was as crazy as the guy who had mowed down John Lennon or the nut that had tried to kill Ronald Reagan. There were demons in his mind that could only be placated by some form of death, and it didn't much matter whether it was that of someone else or his own.

The finger of the kid who had the drop on me seemed to be just a billionth of a squeeze way from activating that trigger, and I could feel the sweat pop out all over my body again. Neither Brendan nor any of the others was saying anything. We had no guns. We had no chance. The only question was whether Brent was going to kill us here or somewhere else.

Whether it was because of the hangover or because I was involved in a situation that was completely alien to all I believed in or stood for, a fatalism came over me that went beyond anything I had ever felt before. There was nothing to lose, nothing at all. But just the instant before I was about to jump at the kid in hopes of catching him by surprise or of diverting his buddies' attention while my own people made a stab at it, a shot rang out from just outside the doorway, and Brent was knocked forward into Brendan, who grabbed the gun out of his hand and then let him slide to the ground.

I continued my jump against the kid and smashed him against the wall so hard that he was instantly unconscious. I dove for his weapon and came up with it trained on the other two who had been standing against us. But they were still so dumbfounded by what had happened to their leader, that pulling triggers was the last thing they had in mind. Brendan stuck his gun into the belly of the guy to the left of him, and two of Brendan's people quickly disarmed the other one. The field was ours.

"Down on your faces," Brendan commanded, and Brent's two joined their leader on the floor. I checked the kid I had slammed into the wall. He was breathing heavily and when I pulled him back a pace, his right arm, the one that had taken the brunt of the impact, hung loosely. His shoulder was twisted peculiarly and when I ran my hand along it, I could feel some kind of break or dislocation. A surge of shame went through me for a moment as I looked down on my adversary, who couldn't have been more than fifteen when you checked him out close up. But then I remembered this retired sergeant I had met at a police picnic who had been decorated three times in World War II. We were talking about street punks, and he told me how toward the end of the war the Germans had put rifles in the hands of kids as young as twelve and had told them to go out and kill as many Allied soldiers as they could.

"When we first came across them," said the sergeant, "we would take their rifles away, give them a kick in the ass, and tell them to go home to mother. But every once in a while one of them would get lucky and kill one of your buddies. So then we started cutting them down just like they were real men. It didn't last long, but I've never regretted doing what I had to do. It's the same with these street kids; you can't think of them as only needing a kick in the ass to straighten them out. If it comes to that, you kill them before they kill you and to hell with the review board."

I turned back to Brendan, who was kneeling by Brent. He looked up at me.

"Gone," he said. "That saves us a bit of trouble."

He stood up and went into the hall. "Everything's all right," he yelled. "There's nothing to be concerned about."

It hit me then that we were in a building filled with apartments, and not one person had come out into the hall to find out what the shooting was about. I had passed three doors on my way to the toilet, and there had to be three more on the other side, plus those on the other floors. But we could have been on a deserted island in the middle of the Pacific Ocean for all the public notice we received. The Catholics in the ghetto made the proverbial monkeys seem like all-seeing chatterboxes. Brendan came back into the room and turned toward the doorway.

"All right," he said. "You better come in now."

It hit me so hard that it made my knees wobble a bit again. We hadn't been saved by the intervention of God. Luckily, one of Brendan's people had been out there behind Brent and his bunch. Or he had someone hidden in one of the other apartments who was riding shotgun on our place. Whichever it was, all of us, especially including me, owed our lives to that person, and if there was anything I could ever do to pay it back, whether it was in money or in services, I was ready.

"Come in," said Brendan. "Come in."

And Catherine walked into the room, a Magnum in her right hand and a cloth shopping bag in her left. Our gun carrier had finally arrived.

24

I HAVE KILLED THREE MEN IN MY LIFE. One was a young hood during an attempted liquor-store holdup; one was a member of the Church of the Holy Avenger that kidnapped me; and the last one was a Mafia hit man for the Pascaglia family when they tried to get back the millions my wife Cathy had left me. The guy in the liquor-store holdup was banging at me with a shotgun, and with one more round he would have blown away the rest of the counter that was providing my only protection. As it was, he came close enough to put three pellets into my shoulder, and if he had aimed the gun three more inches to the right, he would be drinking stolen booze somewhere right now while I was lying in my honorable grave. As it happened, I just emptied my gun in his direction and one of the bullets caught him in the throat.

Even though the liquor shootout was four years ago, I too often think about the anonymous guy lying there on the floor next to the chilled beer cabinet while I had to wait around and be questioned by Internal Affairs about the shooting. He was maybe twenty years old and had a scruffy beard and mustache to go with his dirty denim jacket and jeans, and every cop that was there kept coming over and telling me what a good job I had done to waste a punk like that.

"You did what you had to," they all said in one form or another. "Don't give it another thought."

But I do. I give it lots of other thoughts. I keep thinking that if the muzzle of my gun had been an inch or two another way, I would have only winged him, and then I would have either never thought of him again or at least felt pride in doing my job well in protecting the liquor store and its clerks. But that wasn't the way it went down.

The second guy was a middle-aged church fanatic who was about to shoot me when I was trying to break out of the cave in which they held me prisoner. It happened like a snap of the fingers and I never saw the body after that so somehow it was more like a bad dream than a reality.

Strange as it may seem, whenever I think of the other guy I killed, I feel pretty good about it. He was one of Pascaglia's enforcers, and his nickname was "The Crusher." He was trying to crush the life out of me with his hands when I got him. I can still taste his blood in my mouth, but when I do, I don't try to spit it out—I swallow it. Being a policeman throws you into the killing business even though there are only a handful of cops in the whole country who kill anybody in the course of a year. But it's always on your mind, every day, that this might be the one in which you kill or get killed. It goes with the territory.

The weight of killing was on my soul as I looked at Catherine when she came through the door. In addition to the shock of discovering that she was the one who had saved our lives, there was the concern of how she was reacting to the wasting of a human being, albeit one of Brent's classification. The instant question was whether this was the first one she had ever done, or if it was something that had happened before. She had denied being an IRA member, but she had also said that she would do whatever was needed. There was no doubt that Brent had to be "done" if her cousins and their cohorts were to be saved from their own deaths, but what was her state of mind when she pulled that trigger?

Brendan took the gun out of her hand and one of the other men relieved her of the handbag. You could tell by the awkwardness of the transfer that the bag had more guns in it. When she had come up the stairs and seen Brent through the doorway, she must have reached into the bag, pulled out the first weapon she could grab, and fired. A Magnum can knock you over backward, but there was no indication that it had done it to her. I had felt the wiry strength of her naked body, and now knew that she could hold ground as well. My little cousin Catherine. I smiled inwardly at my naiveté.

Catherine looked around the room at all of us, glanced at Brendan again, then walked over to me, threw her arms around my neck, buried her face under my chin and sobbed, "Oh, Cousin Benny." I knew right then that this was not only the first time she had killed anybody, but probably the first time she had ever fired a gun. I glanced around the room over the top of her head, and stopped for a moment as my eyes reached those of Brendan. The look on his face changed even as he was watching us. The concern for Catherine that had been there the moment before turned into something that twisted his features just a bit. Not much, but enough to put a little shiver through me.

She had come to me instead of him. It was my arms that were around her, and my voice that was comforting and soothing her. The Brendan that had been there all her life, the Brendan that loved her, was passed by for the Jew from the United States whom she had known for barely a week. Of course, he was upset. I would have been the same way if our positions had been reversed. But even if I had wanted to ease the situation, there was nothing I could do about it at the moment. And to be honest, there was nothing I wanted to do but hold her in my arms and breathe in the slight snottiness that accompanies all-out crying.

Brendan's men, meanwhile, were tying the hands of Brent's crew, including the boy, who had been revived with a glass of beer thrown into his face. He started crying from pain and fear but stopped when one of Brendan's guys gave him a slap against the side of his head. I began to open my mouth to protest, but instantly remembered that this was the same kid who had tried to cut me down in my prime, and also what the sergeant had told me. But at the same moment there was a little twinge in me because I knew that one more rock had been placed on top of my wall.

"It's time to be moving out of this place," said

Brendan, picking up a sack and dropping the Brent guns into it. "Cousin Benjamin, you had best go first with Cathy and be clear of the neighborhood."

"What about them?" I asked lifting my hand from Catherine and waving it in the general direction of the men lying on the floor. "And him," pointing to Brent.

"I haven't quite figured that out yet," said Brendan, "but you best not be part of it no matter what it is. You've done your tourist sightseeing for the day, and now you should let the natives take it from there."

He walked over and disengaged Catherine's arms from around my neck and turned them into his own body. I saw the look on his face while he was doing it, and I could tell that it had gone against his grain to be forced into this action. He wanted her to come to him on her own, just as she had to me, but when he realized that was not to be, he swallowed some of his fierce pride so that he could cradle her to him for at least a moment.

"There now, Cathy," he said, "don't go on so. You saved our lives, you did, and for that we should be dancing for joy rather than wailing. What you did here was the same as mopping the muck off the floor for the good of all in the house. It's not even worth going to confession about."

She snapped her head back from his chest and stared into his eyes.

"Oh my sweet Jesus," she said, "what will I tell the father?"

"He's heard worse, Cathy," he answered. "He's heard much, much worse. Now you must be off. It's likely to be a long night for us, but I'll see you first thing in the morning. Cousin Benjamin doesn't know the streets here so it's up to you to guide him until he can find his way back to the hotel. Now off you go."

He held out his hand and I reluctantly gave over the Uzi, feeling that I was stripping myself of the only protection I had known since I had come to Belfast. It was so strange to be without a gun weighing comfortably along my side.

Catherine started for the door but just before she reached it, she stopped short and turned around. She had been very careful all along to keep her eyes from the men on the floor, both the living and the dead, but as she came back, she almost stepped on Brent's right arm.

"The bag," she said.

"What?" asked the bewildered Brendan.

"The bag. I must take the bag with me."

"What bag, girl?"

"The one I brought the guns in. It's Cissy's bag and I have to give it back to her."

Brendan looked around the room with a smile on his face. Women, he was telling us. Women, women, women. He emptied the guns onto the table, and handed over Cissy's bag. Catherine mustered up a small smile of thanks, turned again and went out the door with me after her. As we walked along the hall and then down the stairs, I kept looking for people going in or out of their apartments, but not a soul, not a single soul.

I had no idea where we were when we came out on the narrow street. All these alleyways of North Belfast looked the same to me, and I estimated it would take a million cops to do a door-to-door search of the area. Even then, I was sure, whoever they were looking for would be slipping from warren to warren just ahead of or behind them.

"I don't want to go right home," said Catherine.

"What do you want to do?"

"I want to go to the hotel with you for a bit."

I knew right away that what she wanted and needed was to be held and caressed and kissed and reassured that her soul wasn't going straight to hell. And I also knew that this time I wouldn't be able to restrain myself as I had before. I was still so hyped up from what had happened that it would take every starlet in the world to blunt my lust once I got going. But after what had happened, I couldn't abandon her to go it alone, to return home and try to act as though there had been no Brent, no gunshot, no man falling down dead in front of her. Abandoning her now would be worse than letting Dennis Raftery huff and puff over her again.

We walked something like eight blocks before we came to a thoroughfare that had taxis available, and were driven in silence to the hotel. My room was neatly made up this time, and the first sheet of the new toilet-paper roll had been folded into a triangle by the maid. Catherine just stood by the door after we came into the room, and when I realized that she would remain standing there silently unless an outside force intervened, I took her by the elbow and asked if she would like to lie down on the bed. She obediently walked over, placed herself flat on her back, and then curled up in what could only be described as a fetal position. It was all I could do to keep from gathering her up in my arms, but that is exactly what I didn't do, more for my own peace of mind than for hers.

"I'm going to clean up," I said as I gathered some of my new-bought clothes and took them into the bathroom with me, where I showered, shaved and dressed, enjoying the feel of the unwashed cloth against my skin. The eyes were still a bit bloodshot, but the hangover was gone. I realized there was no danger of my following my father and mother's path down the alcohol trail. Whatever else they had stuck into my genes, at least that curse wasn't there.

Catherine hadn't moved one iota from the position she was holding when I left her, and she looked so young in the dim light from the one lamp that was switched on that I knew I was safe, which meant that she was also safe from me. There was no way that there would be any carnality between this girl, this cousin of mine, and me. The feeling that went through me with the revelation was even better than the one where I became aware that my hangover had gone away.

"Catherine," I said, sitting on the side of the bed and pulling her head and shoulders onto my lap, "would you like to talk or would you feel better if we just sat here like this for a while?"

After a minute had passed, I figured she wasn't going to answer, but then she lifted her head just a bit, and said, "I didn't mean to . . . I didn't want to kill anybody, Cousin Benny. But when I saw him with the gun pointing at Brendan, and the other men with the guns, and you standing there to the side, I did what I did.

What I mean is that I didn't even think about it; I just did it. My eyes were closed, Cousin Benny. My eyes were closed when that gun went off. And when I opened them again, the man was laying on the floor and the rest of you were jumping all around the room. But I didn't mean to . . . Am I going straight to hell, Cousin Benny? Am I going straight to hell?"

I put my hands on her cheeks and turned her face a bit more toward me.

"Catherine," I said, "what Brendan told you is that truth. If you hadn't done what you did, Brendan and I would be dead at this very minute. God sent you there to save your loved ones. For that you go to heaven, not hell."

To me, lying is one of the most despicable things that can poison the relationship between two people. I didn't believe any of the crap that I was handing Catherine. My father had cured me of God at a very early age. I couldn't have been more than four when he started shouting at me about God.

"What kind of a God would allow six million of his Chosen Race to be burned up like trash?" he would yell. "Answer me!" he would command, as if this frightened little boy had the answer. "What kind of God would do that? God knows, the Jews have screwed up plenty over the years. But for that you maybe take away their matzoh. You don't kill them. What kind of God would do that?"

He was always saying "For God's sake" or "God knows" or more likely, "Goddammit," and a little kid found that mighty confusing. Who was this God that was being invoked? Was he good or bad? Bad or good?

But to Catherine, God, and Jesus, and the Holy Ghost were entities with whom to be reckoned. They were as much a part of her as the skin around her body. If she could be convinced that God approved of what she had done, she would be cleansed in both soul and mind. She could walk away from it just as I had been able to wash my hands of what I had done to the Crusher. But if not, she wouldn't just have the problem that I had after killing the kid in the liquor store. She would also have a vise around her heart that would squeeze the blood out of her, that would make her entire life one of misery until her death sentenced her to hell forever. If my lies could serve as protection against all that, then my face was going to be blue and my nose a foot long by the time I finished.

She lifted herself up on the bed so that her face was straight in front of mine, no more than two inches away. The face was different, there was no doubt about that. There was no physical change; the beauty was still there. But there was also a gravity that might never be erased. It was one thing to be a Catholic and a supporter of the IRA, to march in your own parades or shout insults at Protestants in their rallies, to maybe throw a few rocks at policemen, or tell them to go to hell when they questioned you, or even carry a sack of guns that you vaguely knew could shoot and kill people. That kept you on the sidelines no matter how close you came to the actual action.

But to shoot a man in the back and watch him fall dead to the floor while you held the weapon itself in your hand, that was another matter. That put a shadow on a face that might forever block out the sun.

"God does forgive me, Cousin Benny," she said. "I can feel it in my heart. I would have been in hell on earth if I had let that man kill you and Brendan. I did what was right. You are good men, you and Brendan, and the other one was evil. I was doing what Father Delavar is always telling us to do; I was fighting evil at its source. Oh, Cousin Benny, I feel so relieved. I would have died if I'd been deprived of Mother Church. But it's all right now. I know it in my heart."

I was barely listening to her because I was watching her lips as they moved, thinking how I wanted to press my mouth against hers, to feel her pushing against me with all her strength, to take all of her and make her part of me. But I kept the two inches; I didn't move a speck of dust closer than the two inches.

"Would you like to go someplace and have dinner, Catherine?" I said. "I am starving."

She didn't even think about it.

"No," she said, "I'd like to go home. I want to give Cissy her bag. I would just like to go home."

I took her down to the cab stand in front of the hotel, gave the driver five pounds and told him where to take her. She was somewhere within herself already by the time she settled in the seat, and barely remembered to give me a small wave as the taxi drew away. I stood there for a minute, undecided what to do about dinner or anything else. I hadn't eaten in twenty-four hours, but I finally convinced myself that I wasn't really hungry, that I didn't want to enter a restaurant full of people and go through the motions of eating a meal. There had been enough placed on my plate already in the past day to fill me up to the gagging level. So I went up to my room, put the Do Not Disturb sign on the outside knob, undressed and went to bed. The dreams were such that for most of the night I couldn't tell if I was asleep or awake. Which was just as well, because I wasn't happy being either.

25

I LAY IN BED UNTIL ALMOST NOON, ALternately dozing and waking, staring at the ceiling in the dim light that came through the cracks in the drapes, my mind mostly blank, but sometimes with disturbing dreams of Cathy and Bandini and Catherine and Brendan and my father and my mother intertwining in ways that shook me awake with my heart pounding in my chest.

Near noon, I took a shower and went down to the restaurant, where I had a cheese omelet and fried potatoes and toast for brunch, bought the newspaper and went back to the room. The front page was all concerned with the United States and Russia (would they or wouldn't they?), a major medical breakthrough in the treatment of hemorrhoids, and another major break, but this time in a main water line feeding West Belfast. They had not yet quite discovered where the break actually was by the time the paper went to press, and the story was full of complaints from people who feared they would be waterless into the next millennium.

I had no desire to go on to page two and threw the paper on the carpet. I looked around the room for succor from my plight, but the room couldn't have cared less. So, as you usually do in situations like this, I turned on the television.

The camera was focused on what had to be a body somewhere out in an open field. Then the scene switched to an alleyway that definitely had a body spread-eagled among the refuse. Then the camera moved on to an automobile that had a body sprawled grotesquely on the passenger side of the front seat, and finally, the camera zoomed in on a body that was hung over a black picket fence. The commentator had been talking all the while this was going on, but I hadn't taken in a word he had said because by the time the second body was shown I knew who they were and how they had come to be there. I shook my head a little just as a dog does when he wants to rid himself of whatever is enveloping his being. The words took on meaning.

"To sum it up," said the newsman in his perfect, clipped English, "the bodies of four males believed to be members of the Irish Nationalist Liberation Army, because one of them, Seamus Brent, has been an acknowledged leader of the group, were discovered in four different sections of Belfast this morning. Police said that there had been no calls claiming responsibility for the murders, but that there were indications that an internecine warfare was being waged between different factions of the IRA. Mr. Brent had been sought in recent weeks to aid in inquiries in three different murders in the province. There has been no evidence as yet tying Brent to the car explosion in Portstewart last week in which Major Harry Faversham and Sergeant Brian Gladstone were killed, but police said their inquiries would include that incident as well. Only two of the other murdered men have been identified, and one, James Boru, seventeen years of age, appeared to have been tortured before he was shot with a .22-caliber bullet in the back of the neck. His right shoulder was broken and there were contusions on the body that indicated . . ."

I turned his words off again. The words that were echoing in my mind were those of Brendan when I had asked him what he was going to do with Brent's body and the three prisoners.

"You best not be part of it no matter what it is," he had said. "You've done your tourist sightseeing for the day, and now you should let the natives take it from there."

They had taken it from there, all right. Brendan obviously had worried about retaliation if any of the remaining three talked, and so he had seen to it that their mouths were shut forever. The poet. My cousin Brendan. The only male in the whole clan who had gone out of his way to make me feel even a partial member of the family.

The man who had saved my life when I had inadvertently become part of the tangled web that all these lethal spiders were scurrying around. Brendan was a killer, a man who could execute another man in cold blood. The only educated person in the family; the one who wanted control over Catherine for the rest of her life. How long did he think he could keep running before he fell or was knocked off the treadmill of terrorism? Brent's gang would eventually figure out who was behind the murder of their leader either by their own deduction or because one of Brendan's men let the word slip to the wrong person. Then the circle would be repeated and some of my own family would be killed, maybe even Catherine if they tied her in with the mess in any way. According to what I had read, they had no compunction about gunning a woman down while she was giving her two young children their nightly baths. I remembered how I had shivered a bit when I came across that small item in the San Diego *Union*.

I took the phone book from the closet shelf and looked up the number for British Airways. The person who answered the phone recited the daily flights, which I noted down on the pad beside me. After I hung up, I sat there staring at the schedule for the morning and afternoon possibilities. There was still one I could make if they had any openings left. All I had to do was call reservations, pack my bags, get in a taxi and I was gone from this problem that had no solution.

I went and turned off the television which was now showing a tape delay of a soccer game that had been played the week before in West Germany. Just pack the bags and be gone. How many times had I said that in the past few days? No, almost from the first day I had arrived here. I had walked in on a wake and there had been death in the air ever since. Now I was part of it. Although I hadn't pulled any triggers, I was as deeply involved as anyone else. I was an accessory to a capital crime. I could plead that I was only a bystander when Brent was shot and not present when the other three were executed, but a good prosecutor would have me nailed to the cross while the others were being nailed to the wall. After all,

I was the one responsible for that boy's broken shoulder. I was the "torturer." Explaining that away in a courtroom was not going to be that easy even when I claimed I was only trying to save our lives. The best thing was to take off like a big-assed bird and get as far away as possible from what had happened and everybody who had been involved.

But Catherine was involved. Catherine was one of those who had pulled the trigger even though she had done it to save our lives. I could see the prosecutor asking her how she had known that Brent was going to kill us. Shouldn't she have just yelled that she had the drop on them and they had better not make a move? Then their guns could have been taken away and no one would have been the worse. In a courtroom we would come out looking guilty as hell when the whole thing was put out of context.

I pulled my suitcase out of the closet and started transferring shirts from the bureau. Then I put the shirts back in the drawer, closed the suitcase and threw it back in the closet.

Catherine! Catherine was involved as deeply as you could go. "Tell me, Miss Callaghan, why you were carrying guns in your sister's bag. Where were you taking them? And for what purpose? The prosecution rests, your honor."

I couldn't let that happen to Catherine. Even though she had convinced herself for now that she hadn't committed a mortal sin, the burden was going to be there for the rest of her life. She would have the same dreams, the same depressing thoughts that I did about the kid in the liquor store. Even though she would say to herself over and over that Brent was an evil man and she was saving the lives of her blood relatives, the guilt would still be there. I had to see to it that she was kept free from both the police and the burden of her own conscience. If I flew away from that, six thousand or six million miles, I still wouldn't be able to escape it. I had to get Catherine away, take her back to San Diego with me so that she would be free of this unending violence and hatred, and so that she would pay no legal price for killing Brent.

Would she go? Would she leave her family and friends? Would her father let her go? I could just see that son-of-a-bitch when we told him that I wanted to take Catherine to America. He hadn't changed since he had written that letter to my mother all those years ago. He hadn't changed one iota. He would sooner see Catherine dead, or see her in jail for life for killing Brent, rather than have her go off with "the Jew." *That was it!* The very first time I met her, Catherine had startled me by saying I had come to Ireland to embrace Mother Church, and she had also said she wanted to marry me and go to America. That's exactly what she had said. All I had to do was open my arms and give Jesus a big hug. But there was all that crap you had to go through before you could convert, and that Father Delavar looked like we would have to do an exegesis of the whole New Testament just to get our throats cleared. And even if I fooled them into believing that I had seen the light and was born for the first time, let alone again, what then would happen? I didn't want to marry Catherine. I realized that I loved her as a cousin and that I would go to the end of the line to save her from death or life imprisonment or even to get her out of this dangerous environment, but I didn't want to spend the rest of my life with her. I didn't want to use the rhythm method of birth control, and end up with a screaming horde of pug-nosed brats. I didn't want to go to Mass on Sunday, or confess my sins, either mortal or venial, to a guy who dressed in a black skirt and didn't date. If I saved her life that way, I would only be sacrificing mine.

But I couldn't let her die either, or go to jail, or spend the rest of her life in poverty, or marry Dennis Raftery or an unreasonable facsimile. There was something within this girl that deserved more, much more. What I had to do was figure out some way to convince her that she had to get out, and then take her out and set her up in a new environment that would allow her to make her own choices about the future of her life. It was possible that she wouldn't want to leave, that she basically liked living the way she did among her family, and that her ultimate goal was a job in one of the shops or even marrying Dennis Raftery. I had to make her the offer, but I also had to give her the chance to make her own choice. I would go see her and lay it on the line as honestly and objectively as I could, the pros and cons, the possibilities and impossibilities, the whys and wherefores. Then it would be up to her.

But when I slipped on my jacket and started toward the door, I saw the white envelope lying on the floor, in as far as someone could push it through the bottom crack from the other side. Without thinking, I yanked open the door and stuck my head out, but there was no one in the hallway in either direction. Realizing what a stupid move this could have been if someone was waiting to either gun me down or bang me on the head, I jumped back into the room, slammed the door shut, and attached the chain link to the outer jamb. I looked down at my hands, and there seemed to be just the slightest tremor showing. At the age of thirty-three, Detective Lieutenant Benjamin Freedman was beginning to crack. In his eleven years as a cop, he had held his own against some of the toughest there were and remained steady as a rock. But here he was less than a week among the Irish, and they had already started to break him into little pieces. I looked down at my hands again, but this time they seemed to be still. And there at my feet was the white envelope.

I reached down, picked it up and turned it over. There was nothing written on either side. It wasn't even sealed. I slid my thumb inside the flap and pulled out the single sheet of paper. On it was written in capital letters: "THE DOGS ARE LOOSE. STAY PUT AT HOTEL UNTIL CONTACTED. EAT THIS NOTE. WITH SUGAR IF NEED BE."

There was neither greeting nor fond farewell. The dogs are loose. The face of my eighth-grade teacher, Miss Olchowski, flashed in front of me. She made us memorize large chunks of everything we read, even the directions for exodus during fire drills. One of our tasks had been Antony's oration at Caesar's funeral, but while everybody else had taken on "Friends, Romans, Countrymen, lend me your ears," I had opted for the one that began "O pardon me, thou bleeding piece of earth, that I am meek and gentle with these butchers."

The twenty-two lines (we all knew exactly how many lines long the burden was) flashed through my mind as though I had recalled them to a computer screen, and I recited them aloud to the door two feet in front of me.

> O pardon me, thou bleeding piece of earth,
> That I am meek and gentle with these butchers;
> Thou art the ruins of the noblest man
> That ever lived in the tide of times.
> Woe to the hand that shed this costly blood!
> Over thy wounds now do I prophesy—
> Which like dumb mouths do ope their ruby lips,
> To beg the voice and utterance of my tongue—
> A curse shall light upon the limbs of men
> Domestic fury and fierce civil strife
> Shall cumber all the parts of Italy;
> Blood and destruction shall be so in use,
> And dreadful objects so familiar,
> That mothers shall but smile when they behold
> Their infants quarter'd with the hands of war—
> All pity choked with custom of foul deeds;
> And Caesar's spirit, ranging for revenge,
> With Ate by his side come hot from hell,
> Shall in these confines with a monarch's voice
> Cry "Havoc!" and let slip the dogs of war;
> That this foul deed shall smell above the earth
> With carrion men, groaning for burial.

The dogs are loose. My poet cousin was telling me that all hell was about to erupt in Belfast, and I had best sit tight until it blew over. I went back to the bedside table and studied the British Airways schedule again. It was now too late to make that day's flight, but there was one early the next morning. I called the airline and booked myself a seat to London. There! It was done. My feeling of relief was tempered somewhat by my feelings of guilt, but there was no doubt in my mind that I was doing the right thing. Catherine and Brendan would think of me only casually after a month, and the rest of the Callaghans and O'Malleys had already forgotten me right after they had met me. I was taking more with me than I was leaving behind.

I switched on the TV set, and watched the film of the four bodies that had been scattered to the four points of Belfast, including some neighborhoods that had never before been touched so closely by the domestic fury and fierce civil strife. Those bodies would be hanging all day as the television station showed them over and over and over again. Something of this nature would be shown on television screens throughout the world before this was over. This foul deed would smell above the earth, with four carrion men groaning for burial.

I turned off the television and lay down on the bed. It was going to be a long day and night before it was time to go to the airport.

STAY PUT AT HOTEL UNTIL CONTACTED.

They would be in for a surprise when they tried to get hold of old Benny. When the dogs are loose, the smart chickens flee the coop. It was too bad that Brent couldn't know how Brendan had either unmeaningly or most cynically compared him to "the noblest man that ever lived in the tide of times." From what I knew of Brendan, there was nothing unmeaningful about it. Brendan knew exactly what he was doing. If the dogs of war had been let loose, it was Brendan-Cassius who had removed the collars.

26

MAKING UP YOUR MIND TO DO SOMEthing has a soothing effect both on the body and on the brain so I slept much better than I had expected to. The ringing of the phone wake-up call gave me a jolt because it was too early for any light to be seeping through the drapes, and it took me a few moments to become oriented as to where I was and where I was going. The packing was finished in only a few minutes. I picked up the letters I had written the night before to Catherine and Brendan, folded them around the five hundred pounds I had obtained for each of them at the cashier's cage, and stuffed the wads into the envelopes. I had left the letters sitting on the desk after I finished them because I thought there might be something further I wanted to say once morning came, but there was nothing to add to the fact that I was leaving, that I was happy to have found them to be friends as well as cousins, that I hoped things worked out well for the both of them, that it was best for all concerned that I return home, and that I would be in touch in the near future. He who fights and runs away lives to fight another day. What about he who doesn't fight before he runs away?

After I had secured stamps for the letters and given them to the clerk, I paid my bill and asked about a taxi to the airport.

"The airport is closed, sir," said the cashier.

"I have a flight in an hour and a half," I told him.

"The airport is closed until further notice, sir," he repeated.

"Why is that?" I finally had the sense to ask.

"Because of the bombs, sir," he replied.

"What bombs?"

"The bombs that went off in the middle of the night and destroyed a British Airways liner and knocked out a wall in the terminal, sir. They say there will be no flights coming in or going out until the whole airfield has been searched. The latest on the radio is that they hope to reopen by the late afternoon."

"Can I have my old room back?" I asked.

"Certainly, sir," he replied with a small smile. "It's just been vacated."

So there I was a half-hour later sitting in the restaurant and eating breakfast. Just as I was putting a forkful of pancake into my mouth, an explosion shook the building with enough force to break some of the outside windows and knock things like glasses and silverware off the tables.

Women started screaming and people began running to the windows, which was the last thing they should have done. There was a puffy-looking elderly man at the table next to me, a second cousin to Robert Morley perhaps, who didn't lose a bite of food during the whole thing. I could picture him during the blitz of London in World War II, calmly having a drink at the officers' club while German V-2 bombs were turning the city into rubble. Say what you want about the British, they have class when it comes to danger or disaster.

Emulating him, I took the final sip of coffee, wiped my hands on the napkin, and walked out of the restaurant to the street. A huge cloud of black smoke was hanging something like four or five blocks away, and the whine of sirens was already filling the air. People were running in both directions, toward and away from the area where the smoke was rising.

"They bombed the MacIver department store," one man yelled at another in passing. I looked at my watch, which showed it was seven-forty-five, too early for the store to have been open. There might have been maintenance people, but at least the public hadn't been jamming the aisles. An armored police car rumbled by on its way to the disaster area, rifles sticking out of all the portholes. I went back to the room and switched on the television, which was broadcasting a taped delay of an English soccer game of the week before. It was almost a half-hour later before they broke in with a bulletin that the explosion had indeed been at the MacIver department store, and that a janitor inside the building and a man walking his dog on the other side of the street had been slightly injured by flying glass.

I tried calling British Airways, but the lines were busy. There was not even a recording asking me to wait until my call could be taken in turn. I looked at the newspaper I had picked up at the newsstand on my way up to the room, but there was nothing on what had happened at the air terminal the night before. There was, however, a picture of a face I knew.

The body of Dennis Murphy, twenty-eight years old, a resident of Falls Road, had been found in the playground behind St. Joseph's Church. He had been beaten severely and then shot in the head through the left ear. Whoever had done the killing had dipped his finger in Dennis' blood and drawn a cross upon the dead man's forehead. Police were inquiring into the matter.

The picture looked like the kind of police photo that is taken when someone is booked, but even though it was probably a couple of years old and the ultimate in graininess, I recognized the man immediately. He was one of Brendan's people, one of the pair who were making the pipe bomb when Brent and his men burst through the door. Which meant Brent's people knew who had offed their leader and three of their buddies, and were out for revenge. Did they know about Catherine?

I looked at the bottom of the door to see if anyone had slipped another message under it for me, but there was nothing. What about Catherine? Did Brendan have protection around her? Should I take a taxi to her house and stay there until we knew things were going to be all right? Should I get her out of the country? Hell, I couldn't even get myself out of the country.

STAY PUT AT HOTEL UNTIL CONTACTED.

Was Brendan in hiding? Was he able to contact

me or had his apparatus broken down because he was now hunted as well as a hunter? I looked at the door again, but the floor was clear.

The television screen was showing scenes at the airport now. It looked like a 727 had been completely gutted by the flames from the bomb. And there seemed to be more than a wall knocked out inside the terminal. The police and soldiers were standing clear of the whole area, which looked like there could be a total collapse any moment. It had been a busy night. Was Brendan involved in the bombings or were there several different groups working at odds toward the same ends? Where was Catherine?

The commentator came back on to disclose that Brent's wife had said his funeral would be held on the next day with a march to the Milltown cemetery where he would be buried in the IRA plot, and that he would be given full military honors as a soldier in the fight for freedom. Police had announced that they would also be present at the funeral, and that no IRA paramilitary rites would be allowed.

The announcer also reported that Protestant leaders had called for a general strike the next day to protest both the bombings and British Prime Minister Margaret Thatcher's "murder" of democracy in Ulster by allowing Ireland a say in the governance of the province. The Protestant honchos said that since she was a murderer, Mrs. Thatcher should "be sent to the electric chair." Mrs. Thatcher, in turn, had warned that she would not back down on any of her country's commitments, and any attempts to flout the law would be met with all necessary force. Meanwhile, riots had broken out in Londonderry and Portadown, and three policemen had been injured by rocks.

I thought of the riot that had taken place in Watts several years before when it looked like all of California was about to be burned down, and that innocent people would be killed before it ended. Some good had come as a result of the Watts uprising, but the Ulster one had religion mixed into the pot to spice up the age-old battle between the haves and have-nots. I looked at the door again, but the carpet was empty. Where was Catherine? Where was Brendan?

I went down to the newsstand and bought some magazines and paperback books, but when I got back to the room, I threw them down on a chair and never picked them up again. I tried the British Airways number, but it was still busy. I went down and had a sandwich, listening to the people babble as they discussed what was going on, and watching the hotel employees attempt to clean up the rubble and fix the windows. Then I went to the desk and asked if there were any messages, but there were none.

When I opened the door of the room and stepped in, my right foot slipped forward, and I looked down to see a white envelope on the rug. I slammed the door and tore open the seal to find the single sheet of paper: "YOU ARE ON THE LIST. STAY IN ROOM. C. IS SAFE. BEAR IN MIND THESE DEAD."

What the hell did that last line mean? *Bear in mind these dead.* It had to be poetry. The poet had to have given me one line of poetry, his or somebody else's. I tried to think of a quote from Shakespeare but nothing matched. *Stay in room.* I piled the bed pillows against the backboard and lay down against them to watch the television screen, which was showing film of the bombed-out department store. Dire predictions were being made about both the funeral and the general strike the next day. The British had mentioned that they might be flying in a crack parachute battalion as reinforcements. Brent's widow was shown saying that those who had killed her husband would pay for it a hundredfold. A Protestant minister came on to promise hell on earth in the name of Jesus and the Nationalists. A Catholic bishop came on pleading for restraint. The sirens outside the hotel were constant, and as I looked out the window, I saw that the streets were emptying of people.

Stay in room.

I disobeyed the injunction by going downstairs to the restaurant for dinner. The menu was limited way beyond what the printed form promised, but I didn't eat much of what was available. I went back upstairs and continued watching the television, but though I never took my eyes off it until I fell asleep at midnight, not once did it tell me the only thing I wanted to know.

Where was Catherine?

27

THE GUARD GAVE ME HIS USUAL FRIENDly smile when I walked through the security shed in front of the hotel entranceway, but when my hand was on the knob of the outside door, he spoke to me for the first time since my arrival.

"It's not a good day to be taking a stroll, sir," he said.

"I'm going crazy sitting in that room," I told him, "and I can't get through to British Airways."

"I heard on the radio that the airport is open again, sir," he told me, "but they are limiting flights. Some of the tourists are just going out there without reservations and taking their chances. One of the drivers told me that there are hundreds of people waiting to get on any plane they can, and I imagine they'll have things sorted out before the day is done."

I went out to the street and walked toward the city hall. Many shopkeepers were busy putting plywood over their windows, and the pace of the people on the street seemed twice as fast as usual. As a cop, you think you can smell trouble when it is in the air, and I sniffed deeply out of habit. There were several negative factors already weighing down the scale, but the deep breath put the marker all the way over. It's amazing how "experts" bullshit themselves into believing they're experts.

There were policemen everywhere, none of them alone. They were all wearing their bullet-proof vests, and carrying either rifles or automatic weapons in addition to their handguns. I instinctively reached down to where I usually carry my own "special," and came up empty. There should be a rule that policemen can take their guns anywhere they go in the world. Criminals seem to. Why can't cops?

Not knowing where I was going or what I wanted to do, I stopped to window-shop at a sporting-goods store, and, on impulse, went in and bought a six-inch, button-release, folding knife, the kind that is illegal in most major cities in the United States. All my purchase did was prove how uneasy I was. Was I scared? No. "Uneasy" was as far as macho me was willing to go in describing my condition. I wanted something to fold my hand around in case Brent's men came looking for me before I was able to fly out of Belfast. A knife can't do anything against a Uzi, but it can discourage people from laying their bare hands on you.

I walked back to my room and switched on the television to a scene that looked like something out of one of those old Cecil B. DeMille epic movies. It also could have been the escape of the Jews from Egypt, or maybe a half-price sale at one of the big San Diego department stores. There had to be several thousand people clogging the streets with police in riot gear ineffectively trying to surround them. There was a focus to the circle, a spot where the swarm seemed thickest around the queen bee, and the announcer informed us that this was where the coffin of Seamus Brent was being hauled to the cemetery on a wagon by his family and friends. The crush of the crowd, however, had stopped the procession dead (I thought that was a most apt description) in its tracks, and now the family was attempting to turn the wagon around and return the body to the Brent residence.

Several youths on the edges of the mob seemed to be tussling with police, and the camera picked up one incident where a policeman was knocked to the ground and his buddies came rushing in with swinging nightsticks to haul him back to safety. One of the teenagers had been hit so hard that he was lying on the ground with blood gushing out of his nose, but as the camera tried to focus in, a policeman dashed toward the cameraman, there was a sudden blur, and then the screen went blank.

When the picture came on again, we were being shown a tape delay of a soccer game that had been played in Yugoslavia in a time of year other than the one we were experiencing because there seemed to be snow along the sidelines of the field. This lasted about five minutes, and then the announcer came on again to say that Protestant groups were forming on the other side of the city, and that rocks were being thrown against the windows of the stores that had not closed down for the general strike that had been called. I figured that Margaret Thatcher was at that moment on the hot line to the colonel in charge of the parachute battalion. If I were a cop in Belfast, I would be pulling my bullet-proof jock strap out of the closet.

Which convinced me that it was time to take myself out of the closet. He who doesn't fight and runs away. I could just see my father's face in heaven or hell watching my performance in this little contretemps. The sneer would go all the way around to the back of his neck. "Sure, Jew," he would be saying, "run away. Let the Irishers see what Jews do when the *goyim* start a fight. 'Look at the Jew,' they'll holler. 'Look at the Jew run away.' "

But these are not my people, I told myself. These are not really my people. Suppose it was Israel, and Catherine and Brendan, to carry it to the ultimate absurdity, were Jewish cousins? Would I pick up my dolls and run home if they were in trouble, or would I go to help them as much as I could? What kind of Jewish-Irish blood runs in your veins, Benny? What kind of guts curl around in your stomach? What have Catherine and Brendan come to mean to you? If you run away, if you fly home, then you are alone again with no chance ever of having a family, even a family as half-assed as the Callaghans seemed to be. You would be alone again, all, all alone.

I took the knife out of my pocket, then stuck it back in. I checked to see that my detective shield was still in my wallet just in case I had to tune in the old-boy network on a foreign station, and I set out again. There was one taxi at the regular stand in front of the hotel, and I approached the driver and told him where I wanted to go. He looked at me incredulously, his bushy eyebrows wagging up and down as though they were on a pull string.

"You wouldn't catch me going down there right now, governor," he said.

"How close to it would you go?" I asked him.

"I wouldn't go anywhere near it," he replied. "Lives aren't worth tuppence in that section right now. Besides, I hear the police are blocking off everything this side of Chandler Street."

"How close would thirty pounds bring me to where I want to go?" I asked him, pulling some bills out of my pocket.

"Thirty pounds?"

"That's right."

"I don't know, governor. You're tempting me, there's no doubt about that, but thirty pounds ain't no blinking good if you ain't alive to spend it or they burn your taxi up on you."

"Would forty pounds make it worth the chance?" I asked him, adding another bill to the stack.

"Get in," he said, taking the money. "I hope me missus doesn't burn the dinner waiting for me tonight."

Our route was circuitous, to say the least. There were streets that the police wouldn't let us enter; there were streets where the driver thought about entering but changed his mind at the last second; there were streets where we entered and turned around again within a few yards because of something he didn't like or because there was a group of men down at the other end. Finally, after what had to be thirty minutes, he stopped and turned to look at me.

"This is as close as I can take you, governor," he said. "You're going to have to hoof it a bit to get there, but I've got a wife and three kids at home, and they ain't got nobody but me to put bread in their mouths."

After he had given me exact directions on where I was to go, I pulled another ten pounds out of my pocket and handed it to him. He contemplated it gravely for a few moments and then tucked it into his jacket pocket with the rest of it.

"Whatever you're trying to do," he said, "good luck with it."

THE BELFAST CONNECTION 215

As I looked around, I could see black smoke rising from several spots in the vicinity, but I had heard no explosions since the big one at the hotel. Some of the columns of smoke were narrow while others were wide enough to be a house on fire or even a whole apartment block. The light was beginning to fade a little because the clouds had moved in and a faint mist was falling. An elderly woman came walking toward me with a small umbrella guarding her pink hat from the wet. She was the only one visible on that whole street, and she gave me a small nod in return for the one I gave her. I started down the route laid out by the taxi man.

Turning the corner brought me into a new world because in the middle of the intersection of the next block was an overturned car that had all its windows smashed out, and there was broken glass all over the road. The eerie thing was that there were no people anywhere in sight. *And I only am escaped alone to tell thee.* I knew that line from *Moby Dick* rather than the Book of Job, but it was weird to have it pop into my mind as I stood at that intersection with no other human being to look at. It was like one of those movies where after a nuclear explosion, somebody thinks he or she is the only person left in the whole world. Just then some kind of mongrel dog came running out of nowhere, paused briefly to pee on the side of the overturned car, and then went running back to nowhere again before I had time to notice whether he was carrying a small cask of brandy around his neck. My mouth was dry, very, very dry.

My next turn was one block down to the right, and I continued on my way. But I was no more than halfway through it when a group of kids, eight of them, ranging in age from twelve to maybe sixteen, came running out of one of the cellarways and immediately surrounded me. They had those faces that you see in photography books about ghettos, faces that are not washed every day, faces that reflect insufficient diets at worst and unbalanced diets at best, faces that reflect hatred toward a world they don't know and can't understand. They were also faces with menace in them, and in their hands were clubs and iron pipes, and one of them, the biggest one, had to be holding what could only be some kind of ceremonial sword.

"Who are you, mister?" he asked, and only I realized the incongruity of him ending such a foreboding question with the deferential "mister."

"I'm an American cousin of the Callaghans on Fairly Street," I told him, "and I'm on my way there now to see if everything is all right with them."

"Fairly Street is burning," said one of the younger kids, turning and pointing with his finger at a wide column of black smoke rising to the right of us."

"What's going on there?" I asked, quickly toning my voice down from my accustomed harshness in the interrogation of young street toughs.

"We don't know," said one of the very young ones. "They kicked our bums and told us to get the hell out of there."

"The police?" I asked.

They all nodded solemnly.

"It might be a good idea to go home in case your folks need your help," I told them. "It's a shame to leave your mothers all alone while there's trouble in the streets and maybe you the only ones to protect them."

That seemed to strike a major chord and some of them lifted up on their toes in preparation for flight.

"What's the best way to get to Fairly Street from here?" I asked.

"You go down three that way," said the swordbearer, "and then you go left for two. Watch out for the bluecoats."

They were gone as quickly as they had appeared. I should have hired one on as a guide because he would know every nook and cranny of the area—where to hide, where there was a loose board in a fence blocking your way, who would take you in and who would turn you in. I took the knife out of my right pants pocket and transferred it to the left back pocket behind my wallet. It was an awkward fit and somewhat uncomfortable while walking, but if someone gave me a superficial frisk, he might just pat the wallet and let it go at that.

Two men came out of a building halfway down

the street, and ran quickly to another one on the other side. One of them was carrying either a rifle or a stick, and it got me to wondering how many eyes were peeking out at me from the windows, or whether a sniper on one of the roofs had me in his sights at that very moment. The light was getting dimmer and dimmer, and all cats look alike in the dark. The police had to be nervous as hell, and the young Catholics had to be itching to pull that trigger on somebody or something, so it was not a good time to be roaming down unfamiliar streets looking for Callaghans or O'Malleys. Brendan had to be either prowling around or holed up somewhere, but he could take care of himself. It was Catherine I was worried about; I didn't want anything to happen to the new Catherine who had come into my life. I couldn't lose two of them; it was unbearable to think of losing two of them.

I decided to walk down the middle of the road with my hands by my sides so that any and all concerned could see that I wasn't carrying a weapon, and that my intent had to be peaceful. I smelled the smoke before I saw the flames, and as I turned to the left after the three blocks straight down, I saw what looked like the fires of hell burning all around. Two cars seemed like blazing torches on each side of the street, and the stink of burning rubber closed in on your throat and made it hard to breathe. One of the houses was also on fire because flames would suddenly shoot out of windows from the second and even third story. Opening a door in a blazing room is the equivalent of turning on a giant blowtorch, with the window acting as a conduit for the heated air. Nobody was running out of the burning house, however, so it was impossible to tell whether they were empty or people were trapped inside.

There was one small fire truck and two police cars in the street, but it took me a minute to pick out both the firemen and policemen crouching by the sides of their vehicles. Just as I was wondering why the firemen weren't doing their job, a flaming bottle landed on top of the fire truck, and as it landed and broke, the hoses and whatever else was stacked on the top became fuel for the new fires that were started. Every few seconds a shot would ring out, but I couldn't tell if the police were firing or being fired upon. Crazy as it sounds, I kept walking toward the inferno rather than turning and running in the opposite direction.

But I didn't get as far as the corner before a loud voice commanded me to stand still and raise my hands in the air.

"Don't even breathe," said the voice, and under different circumstances I might have smiled, because I wish I had a nickel for every time I have said that to some punk I was rousting or arresting. At least I was in the hands of the law.

An open hand smacked me in the middle of the back just to let me know that the person could hit me a lot harder if he wanted to, or even shoot me if the spirit moved him. It's like the old joke where the guy hit the balky mule in the head with a two-by-four and when asked why he had done it, said that this was how he got its attention. Whoever was behind me had my full attention.

"Who are you and what's your business here?" the gruff voice asked.

"My name is Benjamin Freedman," I said. "I'm an American related to the Callaghan family who live on Fairly Street, and since I am about to return to the States, I came down here to give them some presents and say good-bye."

"I don't see you carrying any presents," said the voice.

"I'm going to give them money," I told him.

"Check him out, Timmy," said a new voice. I can usually sense how many people are behind or around me, but the noise from the fire put blinkers on all my senses, and there could have been ten men there for all I knew.

A right hand patted down the right side of my body, then there was a pause as the gun was shifted from one hand to the next, then the left hand checked my left side. Just as I had hoped, it barely felt the outline of my wallet before passing on. You could tell from the quickness of the shakedown that these guys were nervous and didn't like standing in the middle of the street where they were beautifully outlined by the light from the fires.

"As the man said," reported my checker, "money is the only dangerous thing on him." At least the emergency hadn't taken away all of his sense of humor.

"Which one of the houses do your relations live in?" asked the big burly cop who came out from behind me. I pointed to the place, unable at the moment to remember its number.

"Well," he said, "that one doesn't seem to be on fire and nobody has been shooting at us out of it, so I guess it will be all right for you to bid your farewells. I tell you this. If I was an American tourist, this is the last place in the world where I would want to be. And when you come out of there, if we're still here, come to see me and maybe we can get you a ride to the clear area. You might not be as lucky getting back as you were coming down."

I nodded my thanks, turned to see three more of them standing some feet away from me, skirted the fire truck and the police cars, and headed up the stairs to the Callaghan apartment. It was all so unreal. I remembered the time I had taken the Universal Studios tour, and we had passed a house where they could at the flick of a switch turn the place into what seemed to be a blazing inferno, and then with another flick restore it to its original condition. I wish I had a switch to turn off things like this. God must use a one-way switch.

The smoke was beginning to burn my eyes and I kept rubbing them as I plodded up the steps. I felt very tired. When you're used to working out every day, your body gets slack after a layoff. But my mind was tired as much as my muscles. I had come over to Ireland with a mixture of anger and hope, and I was about to leave with both of those gone and nothing to take their place.

I knocked on the door, which was opened almost immediately. Cissy's frightened stare was my greeting, and Laura's face behind her reflected the same feeling. Cissy reached out and pulled me into the hall before quickly shutting the door. She had to be terribly agitated to have put her hand on my arm. Cissy was born to never touch a man anywhere at any time.

"Where's the rest of the family?" I asked.

"We don't know where Da and the boys are," said Cissy. "They went out early and they haven't come back."

"Where's Catherine?"

"Brendan came and got her last night. Da was beside himself when she didn't come home, and I think they're out looking for her. He didn't know Catherine was going with Brendan, and he was fit to be tied."

"Do you know where Brendan took her?" I asked.

They both shook their heads.

"Do you think they might be at his house?"

"Might be," said Cissy. "That's probably where Da and the boys went. I wish they would all come home. What do we do if the building catches on fire?"

"You go down into the street as quick as you can," I instructed her. "But meanwhile, keep away from the windows and don't open the door again until you know who's there. I'm going to Brendan's house to see if they're all right, and maybe they'll come home soon. If they do, ask Catherine to call me at the hotel so I won't worry about her. I may be going home tomorrow, and I want to say good-bye. And I'll say good-bye to you two now, and thank you for your hospitality."

They nodded back at me, unable to come up with the right cliché from their side. But as my hand was on the knob, Laura spoke.

"Can I give you something to eat before you go?" she asked.

Her well-meant offer heartened me to go back into the maelstrom. Fire and bullets were as nothing when compared to eating Laura's cooking.

28

THE FIRE TRUCK AND THE POLICE CARS were gone by the time I reached the street again, and in their place were five men who either lived in the area or were on the prowl from nearby neighborhoods. A tiny little guy was carrying a .30-caliber rifle, which he displayed in a macho fashion, strutting up and down and uttering long brays of laughter as he described how close he had come "to puttin' one of the *barsterds* away for good."

"Who are you?" one them asked as I came abreast of the group.

"He's kin to the Callaghans," said another. "A Yank. Timmy was telling us all about him."

"Have you seen them?" I asked. "Have you seen any of the men of the family or Catherine Callaghan?"

They considered this for a few moments, looking at each other as if they knew that the answer was among them somewhere.

"Have you been to the house?" asked one.

"Only Cissy and Laura are there," I answered. "Uncle William and the boys are out somewhere, and Catherine went with Brendan last night."

At the mention of Brendan's name their ears pricked up. It wasn't necessary to say that it was Brendan O'Malley I meant. My cousin Brendan was obviously the Brendan who stood out from the crowd.

"The boys must be going about their business," said one who hadn't spoken before, "and Brendan's doing what's needing to be done. Catherine is in good hands, you may be sure of that."

"I must be getting back to work," said the one with the rifle, and started down the street with another accompanying him.

"Let's get some buckets going on the fire at the Nilan place," ordered one of the three remaining. "It seems to me it would have been smarter if Cliff had held off his shooting until the brigade had put out the fire there. Now the O'Rourkes' is burning too. We could lose the whole block if it goes much farther."

While they all looked up at where the flames were coming out of the windows, I started down the street on my journey to Brendan's house. There was a burning car at almost every intersection, and gangs of young men were either gathered around the metallic pyres or running back and forth from house to house. The young ones made me more nervous than the older ones because they didn't know in their own minds what they wanted to do, but they all let me be as I made my way the few blocks I needed to go.

There was no car burning at the final intersection, but there was a scene that was the equivalent as far as death and destruction went. A man in a gray trench coat was lying in the middle of the street with three teenagers circling him, two with tire chains and one with a pistol in his hand. The two with the tire chains were swinging as they were scrambling, but the man was rolling about desperately so that they were catching him only once with every ten swings. What threw them off was when they missed, they banged themselves a good one in the legs, and it took them a few moments each time to recover. The one with the gun was trying to set up a sure shot, but either his buddies knocked against him or the man rolled away before he was set. I was about to be a witness to a murder.

The first thing I thought of was the knife, but there was no chance with a six-inch blade against a gun. I glanced around desperately, but all that was available on the street were garbage cans and . . . Garbage cans! I ran over and pulled the metal lid off one battered container, releasing a stench of putrefaction that would have worked against a bullet if I could have directed it like a laser beam. I stood there holding the lid, unsure of what to do, but just then the gunner found the opening he was waiting for and a shot rang out. With a cry of both rage

THE BELFAST CONNECTION 223

and despair, I held the lid in front of me like a Roman going against the Gaels, and went storming down the street straight at them, expecting a hail of bullets to come crashing through the steel and into my body at any moment.

Either they were stunned somewhat at having shot a human being, or they didn't hear me because of the noise of a city under siege, but I was upon them in a few seconds and crashed into two of them, hitting so hard that the lid twisted out of my hands and fell on the pavement with a rolling crash. It was the kind of noise that the San Diego garbage men specialized in at five o'clock in the morning.

The one holding the gun was knocked to the ground, and the second was shoved back against the third one. When the gunner hit the pavement, the gun was jarred loose from his hand, and I dove for it, skinning both my knees as I came down on the cobbles. But I got the weapon, rolled twice and came to my feet in the classic "Freeze!" position that has become so familiar from the acting of the deadly duo on *Miami Vice*. That was all it took to spur the trio into flying down the street in the dim light, leaving behind a dead man, one set of tire chains, the lid of a garbage pail and me.

Then came the second shock of the episode. As I leaned over the man, I saw it was none other than Inspector Simmons, his eyes wide open and staring at me. He was not only alive, but the wound couldn't have been that bad, or the eyes would have looked different.

"Where are you hit?" I asked.

"In the chest area," he said.

I ripped open his shirt and discovered under it his bulky bullet-proof vest, seemingly undamaged. I ran my hands over the whole front, but could find no hole, or even a burned spot to indicate an impact area.

"You seem all right," I told him. He was making no effort to sit up.

"My chest feels like it's been hit with a sledgehammer and burned with a torch," he said, "but praise be to God he didn't aim too low or too high and take off my ballocks or blow my head to splinters."

"You're a lucky man," I told him.

"I'm lucky that you came along," he said. "A few more seconds and they would have finished me off one way or another. It's probably the first time in the history of the world that a man went against a gun with a garbage cover."

"You would have done the same if you'd seen another policeman in trouble," I assured him.

He looked at me for a long moment. "Let's get to the side of the street," he finally said, "before any people with rifles come poking along."

He pushed himself to his feet before I could help him, and held out his hand to me. At first I thought it was a gesture of gratitude and friendship, but then I realized that he wanted the gun I was carrying in my hand. I hesitated a moment before handing it over because it had been so reassuring to hold it for the few minutes, but I was not at home, I had no license to carry one there.

"Is it your gun?" I asked as we made our way to the side of the street and went down a basement staircase. There might have been a little bit of cruelty in my question because this was still a man I didn't like no matter what the circumstances, but there was also straight curiosity. One of the most shameful things that can happen to a cop is to have his gun taken away from him.

"It's mine," he said curtly. "The snipers split me off from my men, and one of the buggers came up behind me and hit me with the tire chain. That was the bad luck. You were the good luck. What are you doing down here in this hellhole? It's no place for American tourists."

"I may be leaving tomorrow," I told him, "and I wanted to say good-bye to my cousins Catherine and Brendan, but I haven't been able to find them."

"We haven't been able to find them either," he said. "I'd give a week's pay to know what that devil Brendan O'Malley is up to at this minute. You can bet that most of the trouble down here tonight can be laid at his feet."

"Those are pretty serious charges," I said.

"Come, man," he said. "You wouldn't be much of a policeman if you didn't learn since you've been here that Brendan O'Malley is a kingpin in the IRA. Somehow he's been able to cover his tracks this past two years, but one day he's going to make the fatal mistake and then we'll have him. I just hope to God not too many more people are murdered before we catch up with him once and for all."

"And who's going to catch up with you people?" I asked.

"What's that?" he said.

"Since I've been here, I've learned that the Catholics have been much abused by the Protestant majority," I told him, "and the escalation to violence, while deplorable, is somewhat understandable."

"You're daft, man," he said heatedly. "You saw what those thugs did to me. If you hadn't come along, I'd be lying out there dead at this minute."

I looked at him long enough for him to realize why it was that he wasn't lying out there dead at that minute.

"I'm not lumping you with the likes of them," he muttered. "I may have thought at one time that your coming here had more to do with other things than visiting relatives, and that you're judged by the company you keep, but I'm not denying that I'm only alive because of your help. And your courage," he added somewhat lamely.

"There's one thing I want you to understand, inspector," I said. "It might make it easier for you. When I went out to help you there, I had no idea it was you I was helping. I went out there to help anybody who was about to be shot or beaten to death. I feel the same way about what's going on over here. I'm sure there's something to be said on both sides, and I'm against terrorism no matter from which quarter it comes. But I see my relatives not only getting the short side of the stick but also the pointed end, and I can understand why they have become so bitter and even dangerous. Now I'm going to the O'Malley house to find out about my cousin Catherine. If you should hear anything about her, I would appreciate your leaving word for me at my hotel."

Just as I reached the top of the outside stairway,

a shot cracked out from somewhere high on the other side of the street and a bullet whistled past my head, splintered against brick and bounced back with enough pieces to have one of them pierce me in the back of the neck. Both Simmons and I had fallen to the pavement the moment we heard the shot, but you can't outrace a bullet and I had the sliver of steel in me to prove it.

"Are you hit?" I called over to Simmons, who was lying stiff as death.

"No," his muffled voice answered. "Are you?"

"I have a bit of metal in the neck," I told him.

He got up on his knees and crawled over to me.

"Bend your head forward," he said, "and let me see."

I felt his fingers probing around the burning area, but even though he was pushing in with the tips, there was no sharp pain.

"I can't make out anything," he said. "But you can't tell much in this light. As soon as we find my lads, we'll get you to hospital for a proper look-see."

I stood up, forcing apart the fingers that were holding my neck.

"It can wait," I told him. "But first I must go to Brendan's house to make sure Catherine is all right."

"She's not there, I tell you," he said, getting up in turn after looking around anxiously. "We checked before we were pinned down."

"I'm going to check for myself," I said, walking down the street without looking at him.

"You're daft," he shouted. "Go back to American where you belong."

The problem was that I didn't belong even in America. I was as all alone there as if I lived in Antarctica. I didn't belong in Belfast either, but it was the only tiny link I had with other human beings. The only way I would leave this godforsaken place was with the knowledge that Catherine was alive and would have a decent future ahead of her.

I could see shadowy figures at the end of the street, but no one challenged me or fired upon me as I walked up the steps to the O'Malley apartment. I knocked on the door but there was no answer. I knocked again. And again.

"Who is it?" a quavery female voice asked.

"It's Benjamin Freedman," I answered.

"Who are you and what do you want?"

"I'm your nephew, Aunt Meg," I said. "Your nephew Benjamin. Your sister Deirdre's son. From America. You met me at Sean's wake."

I was getting so desperate that I don't know what I would have yelled next if the door hadn't opened slightly. She squinted at me through the crack.

"Who?"

"Benjamin, Aunt Meg. Your sister Deirdre's son."

She opened the door wide enough to me to enter, but I still wasn't sure she knew who I was. She had met me in hysteria and probably hadn't remembered to think about me again. I could smell gin emanating from her.

"I'm looking for Brendan," I said, "and Catherine. Cathy. Are they here?"

"Brendan went out yesterday," she said, her right hand idly stroking the back of her head. "He didn't come home last night and I haven't see him this day. I cooked him some salt beef, but he hasn't been here to eat it."

"Is Catherine here?" I asked, already knowing what the answer would be. "Have you seen Catherine?"

"No," she said gravely. "I haven't seen her since church on Sunday. She's a dear girl."

Before I could speak again, there was a loud noise from the street, and I moved over to the side of the window and peeked out through the edge of the shade. An armored vehicle was wending its way slowly down the street, a loudspeaker blaring from somewhere inside it. The decibels were so high that you could hear the grainy words right through the glass.

"Attention," the disembodied voice was saying. "Attention. This area is under curfew. Anyone found in the streets will be shot on sight. Anyone found in the streets will be shot on sight. The curfew will be lifted at eight in the morning. Eight in the morning. Attention. This area is under curfew. Anyone found . . ."

The armored car went as far as the intersection and stopped, possibly to spend the night there. I wondered how many of the things they had to patrol the Falls that night. Enough so that Benny Freedman would get his ass shot off if he tried to go anywhere else. They would shoot and then ask what you were doing out when they had told you not to go. It didn't make any difference if you were an American or a member of the IRA. Anything that moved was going to be treated with extreme prejudice. I turned back to Mother O'Malley, who was wavering just a bit on her feet.

"Aunt Meg," I said, "I'm going to have to spend the night here."

"Oh, that's nice." She smiled. "Do you like salt beef?"

She had no more idea who I was than if I'd been the man from the moon.

29

IT WAS THE KIND OF DREAM THAT TWISTS your guts into tiny knots and drenches your whole body with sweat. For some inexplicable reason, I was dreaming about Cathy and Bandini together, my dead wife and dead almost-wife. We were sitting cross-legged on a bed, one that seemed to stretch to infinity in all directions, all of us naked, and from my end of the triangle I could take in the beauty of each one in every detail except that their figures kept merging into one another so that even though there were always two of them, they were also at the same time as one.

Both of them were reaching their arms out to me in a pleading, loving manner, and I knew they wanted me to make a choice between them, to show which had been the most important in my life, and just when I thought there was no way in which I could decide, my wife's hand reached just a little farther than Bandini's, touching me on the shoulder, and I covered it with my own, hand, saying, "Cathy, Cathy, Cathy."

The hand pulled itself out from under mine and I woke to ten fingers around my throat, squeezing slightly, and Brendan's voice saying softly, "What happened between you and Cathy, Cousin Benjamin? Why do you reach out for her in bed and call her name?"

The hands tightened just enough to cut off some of my air, and coming out of that deep sleep, that dream, I was disoriented enough to be rendered unable to defend myself. But as the reality superseded the netherworld, I reached up and yanked the hands away from my throat, twisted around in the bed, and had his arms pinned in reverse position with my body as the fulcrum. All I had to do was turn my wrist another inch while leaning forward, and his shoulder sockets would have cracked like walnuts.

"Hey," he said with a small laugh, "it's your cousin Brendan here. Did you take me for a Protestant?"

"I took you for someone sneaking up in the dark and trying to strangle me," I said somewhat heatedly, not at that moment making the connections between my dream and what Brendan had said and done. I loosened my fingers and let his arms slowly pull away.

"It gives a man a start to come home in the middle of the night and find someone in his bed," Brendan said. "You're a lucky soul that I didn't ravish you before I found out what or who you were. My mother's lying on the couch with an empty gin bottle on the table, her mouth wide open and the snores loud enough to bring the Defense Force in with guns blazing. She was unable to tell me that my cousin Benjamin had come to spend the night."

"I was looking for you and Catherine," I said, "and I had just come from her house to here when they made the announcement of the curfew so your mother was kind enough to put me up. Where is Catherine?"

"In your dreams, I guess," said Brendan. "You were patting her hand and calling her name when I woke you."

"No, it wasn't your Catherine," I said. "I was dreaming about my wife, Cathy. It's the first time since she died that I dreamed about her, and she was reaching out her hand to me and I don't know what would have happened if you hadn't touched me. Where is Catherine? Did you bring her home?"

"No," he said, sitting down on the edge of the bed, "Catherine's not home. Brent's men have her. They did bad things to my friend McGillicuddy before they killed him, and he told them about Catherine and the shooting. I had word about them looking for her so I took her to what I thought was a perfect haven. But there is nothing perfect in this world, and when I came back two hours later, she was gone and in her place was a note telling me where I could come get her."

"My God," I said, "they're using her as bait for you."

I could see his head move up and down twice in the dim light coming from the living room, where the snores of Aunt Meg were harmonizing with the sirens in the streets.

"What are your plans?" I asked.

"To pay them a visit," he said.

"How many men have you got?"

"I have none at the moment. The police and the soldiers have done a good job of closing West Belfast down, and I don't know where any of my buckos have gone to ground. They're not at the usual places so either Simmons and his bully boys have picked them up, or they're holed away with families I don't know about. If only someone would kill off old Simmons. He's the only one of that whole bunch who knows every nook and cranny around here so that no man is really safe from him no matter where he tries to hide."

"I'm going with you," I said, slipping out of the bed and stretching my arms behind my back to ease the tension in my body. My right hand moved up to my throat and rubbed where the fingers had been.

"I was hoping to hear those words," said Brendan. "They'll be waiting with everything they've got, and it could be that you and I and Cathy will be in heaven before morning. But if we don't go after her, she'll be going up there on her lonesome."

"They'll kill her if you don't show up?" I said. "Just like that?"

"They'll kill her just like that. You still don't realize what's going on here. It's reached the point where there's no difference between men, women and children. Not even blood makes a difference anymore. The man who puts the bullet in Cathy's head could be her cousin from Buncrana. It's like your Civil War was, brother against brother."

"No," I said. "It isn't the same. I don't know what to call what you people are doing, but it isn't he same. Have you got a gun for me?"

"Not here but we'll go to a place where there'll be more than enough to go around."

"Where have they got Catherine?" I asked.

"It's a house in the very center of the district," he answered. "A big building. A regular rabbit warren that's been falling apart for years with some of the places livable and some not fit even for the rats. A perfect setting for Brent and his savages."

"What time is it?"

"It's near four," he answered, "and the rain is coming down hard."

"We've got four hours then?"

"What?" he asked.

"We've got four hours to wait. The curfew is on until eight A.M."

"She could be dead in four hours, man," said Brendan. "We have no time to waste. We should have been off right away."

"I take it you can get us to where we're going despite the policemen and soldiers in the streets," I said.

"I can get you to hell and back no matter how many policemen and soldiers there are in the streets," he said. "They've tried to cut this fox's tail before."

"I'm not going to wear my necktie," I said, slipping it off.

"It will not be a formal affair," said Brendan. "You'd be best without your jacket, too. Let me get you one of my sweaters. No matter how heavy the rain, my mother's cable-stitch can soak up a barrel while those inside it are completely unaware of what the weather's like outside."

"Do you have a bullet-proof one?" I asked.

"No," he said, "If you get shot when you're with me, the bullet's going to go through you. You've been spoiled by being a policeman."

He led me down to the cellar and took my hand as he guided me through the obstacle course of various hard and pain-inducing objects. A lot of the policemen I worked with were Vietnam veterans, and the few times I've had to go through dark places with them, cellars or warehouses or alleys, they drove me nuts because they were so worried about booby traps. But we went banging through, either knocking over or being bounced back by movable and immovable objects.

"All right," said Brendan, when we reached the door, "keep your hand hooked on the back of me belt, be ready to fall to the ground instantly, and anybody we meet is our enemy, whether he be or not."

I don't know how long that trek through the darkness lasted, but it had to be at least an hour. It consisted mostly of going through alleys, and at least four more cellars, and twice to roofs, and three times to street intersections, where we darted across like rats on an ocean pier, and by the time he led me into a dark apartment, I was soaked through and through with the weight of the vaunted cable-stitch sweater seeming like two hundred pounds.

Brendan had used a key to get us into the place, and I figured us to be alone there. So when a soft girl's voice inquired, "Is that you, love?", I fell to my knees and readied to immobilize whoever had asked the question, whether, as Brendan had pronounced, it was friend or foe.

"Yes, it is," Brendan answered as softly.

I heard the strike of a match and saw it flare through the doorway of another room before it was applied to a candle. Then the small flame was brought carefully toward us, and the bearer turned out to be a very young girl, probably no more than sixteen, with one of those waif's faces that peer out at you from posters asking for donations. I pushed myself to my feet again.

"Lucia," said Brendan, "this is my cousin Benjamin that I've told you about. I need you to fetch me the goods."

Without saying another word, she went to the door, blew out the candle and was gone.

"She'll be a few minutes," said Brendan. "Why don't we sit on the floor while we wait?"

"I'm getting a chill from being so wet," I told him, "and the dark makes it feel colder."

"Don't worry about that," he said. "We'll be hot enough within the hour."

I heard him thump to the floor and I followed suit, clasping my arms around me for a semblance of warmth. I could feel the water being squeezed out of the sweater as I applied pressure.

"Tell me, Cousin Benjamin," said Brendan. "Have you ever killed anybody?"

At first I wasn't going to answer him, but then I did.

"Three," I said.

"Three," he echoed. "Well then, I'm five up on you. Does it bother you?"

"That I've killed three or that you've killed eight?"

"Either. Or both."

"I think about it."

"Does it disturb your sleep?" he asked. "Does it color your life?"

"I think about it," I repeated.

"Oh, I think about it too," he said. "There were the three this week, and the five before them, though those were one at a time. But I have the feeling that the three you did in sit uneasy on your stomach while mine just increase my appetite. Because I am fighting for a cause; I am fighting for justice; I am fighting a holy war. While you, you as a policeman, you are just killing for pay."

I don't know what I would have answered to that if the door hadn't opened and quickly closed again, followed by mouselike sounds coming toward us.

"Here you are, Brendan," said the mite's voice, and a match flared again as Brendan relit the candle.

She had a pouch in her hands, which she laid down on the floor. Brendan unsnapped the catches and pushed back the cover. I could see the soft gleam of black metal in the dim candlelight.

"Here," he said, pulling a cut-down semiautomatic from the inside and handing it to me, "I presume you know how to work this darling. It's Czech."

"I can figure it out," I replied, releasing the twenty-bullet cartridge holder and then snapping it back into place. "I can figure it out."

"Here," he said again, passing over a .32-caliber Beretta, "this will keep your belly warm." He handed me an extra magazine for each of the weapons, and then armed himself from the cache. The Beretta was kind of beat-up, but the grease gun was glistening in its newness. I had missed carrying my own piece, but these two didn't make me feel either good or secure. They were meant to kill rather than protect.

"We'll be going now, love," said Brendan. "Keep the bag under your bed for company until I get back."

"I'd rather have you in the bed for company, Brendan," she said with a sweet smile, and I knew that no matter what her age, she was as old as she had to be.

"That you will," said Brendan. "That you will."

I followed him to the door and just as we reached there, the girl blew out the candle again.

"Hand on to the back of my belt just like before, Cousin Benjamin," said Brendan. "I don't want you to miss the party."

As we went out the door, I was asking myself whether I was on this mission as a terrorist or an antiterrorist. And whether, before the night was over, my kill record was going to equal that of my cousin Brendan.

30

THERE WAS ONLY ONE MAJOR DIFFERence from our previous trip through the dark mazes of West Belfast. This time the gods had thrown policemen and soldiers into the boiling pot. One section we went through seemed to be a staging area because they were gathered in small knots around two armored personnel carriers. And just as we were inching our way around a crucial corner, somebody from one of the houses fired a shot that hit the steel side of one of the vehicles and ricocheted into the air with a scream that sounded almost human. The shot was immediately answered by what seemed to be ten thousand bullets smashing into the brickwork of the buildings all around the square. The light from the muzzle blasts was so bright that you could see people clearly through the red haze and smoke. Luckily, for us, the whole force to a man was looking up instead of down, and we crawled around the corner and into the darkness of an alley.

Brendan sat down on the muck and leaned against the wall of a building.

"That was something, wasn't it," he said rather than asked. "They're not using plastic bullets on this night."

"How much farther are we going to have to crawl?" I inquired. "One of those guys is bound to spot us if we have very far to go."

"There's still a bit of a way," said Brendan, "but we won't be meeting many or probably none at all from here on in. The authorities don't come into this section unless it's daylight and everybody is sitting snug inside an armored car. We're on home ground here."

"With only your own waiting to kill you," I commented.

"They're no longer part of us," said Brendan, somewhat sadly. "They've degenerated into savage beasts who kill for pleasure instead of food."

And what about your eight? I wondered. How many of those were for food?

"Shouldn't we get going?" I asked. "God knows what they're doing to Catherine."

"Oh, don't worry about that," said Brendan. "They might kill her but they won't harm her in any way. This is Ireland and she's a woman."

"Chivalry still reigns among terrorists," I noted ironically.

"We're not terrorists, Cousin Benjamin," Brendan chided. "Even these scum are not terrorists. They went off the track but they're ultimately fighting for the same thing we are."

"That all sounds very pretty," I said, "but I still want to get Catherine the hell out of there before someone forgets the so-called code of honor."

"All right," he said, standing up, "here's the plan. We'd best plan it out now because it would be better not to talk once we get there. There are maybe a hundred living places in that building, but they cut off the water and electricity three years ago when there was a rent strike, and they never hooked them up again. So the people who burrow there now are not what you would call middle class. A lot of them you wouldn't even call people. The good thing is that they are on nobody's side but their own so they will steer clear of any shooting that is going on. But they will bash your head in to get your gun or your money or even your boots. Consequently, any you run into will have to understand that you will kill them if they try anything shifty. I don't know how many of the rooms still have people in them. What they do is stay in a place until the stink of their own offal drives them out. Then they move on to another one. But in the three years there can't be too many rooms left in which people can breathe. Those who are still there have to be the worst and the most dangerous of the lot, the ones Darwin was talking about in his theory about the survival of the shittiest."

"Do you have any idea where Brent's men are holed up?" I asked, pulling the magazine out of the gun and then slamming it back in. I flicked the safety on and then off again.

"I'm pretty sure they're on the second floor somewhere near the middle on the back side," he replied. "The note didn't say anywhere specifically, but I talked to a man who'd visited there once and this was the spot to his recollection."

"What do we do once we get her?"

"She holds on to my belt and you hold on to her . . . you hold on to her something-or-other, and we wend our way back to whatever safe spot we can find."

"We've got to do it before light comes," I said, "and that can't be too far away."

"It will be dark a bit longer with this cloud cover," said Brendan, "but we had best be going. When we get there, I'm going to go slamming through the door and you follow and do what has to be done."

"I'm not a bad door slammer myself," I said.

"I'm sure you are," replied Brendan, "but this is my territory. If we ever have to smash doors in California, then I'll let you do the honors. Grab the belt."

It must have taken us close to half an hour to reach the long three-story building that loomed darkly ahead of us. We had walked through all kinds of burned-out places getting there, and I figured in daylight it must have looked like the middle of Beirut or one of the ghetto sections of the Bronx I had passed through in New York. Darkness had to be its kindest time of day.

"Here we go," said Brendan, and led me into a doorway. The stench was so immediate and so strong that I involuntarily gagged.

"Tie your handkerchief over your face," advised Brendan, which I immediately did. The only difference was that the clean linen smell filtered out only a minute bit of the stink. Whoever lived here was going to find hell a summer resort.

I held Brendan's belt with my left hand and the grease gun with my right. As I did every time I held one, I marveled at the almost weightless destruction available in my hand. They had demonstrated a new type on our police firing range that had computer chips inside it somewhere, and the damn thing seemed to think for itself. That would be the next step in our evolution, where the guns would function on their own. I stumbled up the stairs behind Brendan.

When we reached the second floor, he paused for a moment to get his bearings as best he could in the dark, and then he started to lead me down the corridor, which was strewn with all sorts of objects and slippery with garbage, urine and feces. It was the kind of obstacle course that would gladden a Marine instructor's heart.

Every once in a while Brendan would pause in his slow movement and stick his ear against a door. Once he pulled me close and when I pushed the side of my head to the wood, I could hear the murmuring of voices, but they all seemed to be female, and I doubted that Brent's people would have more than Catherine in their midst. Brendan obviously felt the same way because he dragged me on.

The next time he stopped to listen took longer than the first, and then he turned and yanked me alongside. Even without my ear against the door, I could hear through the thin panel a man's voice going on and on in the local patois that was indecipherable to me. Brendan pulled me to the side and indicated by pressures on my arm that he was going to bust in. I readied myself and as his shoulder smashed against the door, I jumped through the opening and whirled to cover whatever was in the room.

There were three men huddled around a candle in the corner, and one of them was holding a bottle in the air that indicated he was about to take a swig before our interruption. They were so startled that they didn't utter a sound, but as they caught sight of the weapons we were holding on them, one raised his hands in the air while the others froze into position.

They were about as decrepit as humans can get, and it stunned me to realize that none of them was really old despite their appearance of the last stages of life, let alone humanity.

"Cover the door," Brendan hissed, and I moved back against the wall and did a half-turn so that if anybody came through, I would see him before he saw me.

"Now, you three," said Brendan, "whether you live or die depends on what you have to tell me. We're looking for three or four men who are holding a girl here. They're of the brotherhood and they have guns. The girl's been here only a day. Now where would they be hanging their hats?"

At first I thought that none of them would answer, and that the noise we had made busting in on them would have alerted everybody on the floor that outsiders were present. But then one of them did speak, and though I could barely translate because of his accent and lack of teeth, I understood that there might be such a group three places down on the other side. Brendan quizzed them a bit more, but that was all they had to offer.

"I'd blow out that candle," Brendan advised them as he came back to the door. "You don't want to be noticeable for the next few minutes."

The candle went out immediately with three of what had to be the foulest breaths in Ireland blowing simultaneously. I felt my way to the doorjamb and moved around into the hall.

"Stand a minute until our eyes get adjusted again," whispered Brendan. "I hope we've hit it lucky with the directions."

We stood there silently and though it was still black as pitch, my eyes could vaguely make out shapes darker than others. Brendan pulled at my arm, and we moved three doors down the hall until we were opposite the one that the derelict had described. Whoever was in there must have been using something brighter than a candle because there was light seeping out from under the door and along its cracks. Two men were holding a conversation inside with no attempt to keep their voices low. Whoever was in there didn't seem to be expecting or worried about Brendan O'Malley coming to the rescue of his cousin Catherine. Perhaps we'd hit another bunch of bums who were drinking their cheap wine and mumbling to each other about how many angels you could dance on the head of a pin.

Brendan positioned me at the side of the door again, and moved back a couple of paces. Then he burst through the thin paneling with me right behind him, and as I came through I stumbled over what looked like a sleeping bag and went down on the floor hard, which saved my life. As I twisted around, I heard a burst of gunfire and saw Brendan going down on the floor with a bullet in him somewhere. I fired at the man on my left and turned to the right just as the one who had been sitting there was reaching for his rifle against the wall, and I put a hail of bullets into him too. Splinters flew up into my face as some shells struck the wooden floor in front of me, and I rolled quickly to the right and came up on my knees as the young boy holding a weapon just like mine was trying to disengage the magazine so he could slip in the one stuck in his belt. He looked so young that my finger froze on the trigger, which gave him time to pull out the recalcitrant piece of metal, reach down to his waist and start to shove the other one into firing position. I leapt the five steps between us and slammed the short butt of my gun into the side of his head just as he fired off a burst that was misdirected into the body of the one I had hit when we first came in. The boy went down hard with blood spurting out of his nose.

I glanced wildly around the room and there she was, Catherine, crouched on a bunch of filthy blankets, her face all streaked with dirt and her dress torn at the shoulder. You could see where the tears had streaked down the black on her cheeks, and just as I rushed over to check her out, a low moan came out of her and she started rocking back and forth on her knees.

"Are you all right?" I yelled at her. "Have you been hit anywhere?"

She was unable to answer me, just the low moan coming out of her, and I quickly ran my left hand over her body, but there didn't seem to be any wounds that I could see. I leaned over and kissed her on the left cheek. "We're here," I told her. "We're here."

We. We're here. I turned and scrambled to where Brendan was lying on the floor, blood coming out of his right arm up near the shoulder. I tore open the sleeve and saw where the bullet had gone in, lifted the arm and saw where the slug had torn out. There seemed to be no other marks on him, but then I noticed a bloody bruise on the side of his head and also blood on the metal corner of an old wooden trunk that he had to have hit on the way down. I leaned over and listened to his heart, which seemed to be pumping nicely, and put my hand over his nose, which pushed moisture into the palm.

I picked up the oil lamp from the floor and checked the other. The two older men were dead and the boy was breathing hard but was alive and would probably recover. One of the men had to have been holding his gun straight at the door when we had broken through, and had shot Brendan before either of us had been able to draw another breath. Two. Two dead.

The score was now Brendan eight and Benny five.

31

BETWEEN WORRYING THAT SOMEBODY was going to come storming in from the dark hall and blow us away, and how I was going to fix up Brendan and get us out of there to a place of safety, I was practically a basket case. It didn't help that Catherine was still in her corner moaning away like a Jewish mother who had just found out that her son is in love with a gentile boy. The only liquids I could find in the room were three bottles of ale, and I finally used the contents of one of them to splash Brendan's face enough to bring a moan out of him. That was some progress, at least. I now had two moaners instead of just one.

I kept darting to the door and looking down the corridors where all you could see in the darkness was the glow of the stink, but the only thing I was accomplishing with that was to make myself a perfect target for whoever might be out there. I began to get the feeling that instead of coming forth when they heard gunfire, the denizens of this hellhole just dug in a little deeper. I looked at my watch and it was a few minutes past six. No matter how hard the rain or thick the clouds, daylight was on its inevitable way.

"Cousin Benjamin," Brendan called weakly. I returned from my umpteenth trip to the door and looked down at him. "You'd best be getting out of this place," he began, and when he saw me open my mouth to rebut, he continued with, "and you damn well better take me with you."

"I've got to find something to bind up your arm," I told him, "but there isn't even a clean dirty rag in this place."

"The girls don't wear petticoats in these modern times," he said, "which is more the pity." It was becoming apparent that Brendan was going to make it out of there, possibly on his own two feet.

I looked around the room again, but there was nothing for a bandage. I sighed, pulled off my shoes, dropped my pants to the floor and removed my undershorts. They were not the most sterile bandage that was ever going to be applied to a wound, but compared to everything else available, they could have come out of an autoclave. Pulling my pants back up and slipping into my shoes again, I tore the shorts into a long strip, wrapped it tightly around Brendan's arm and tied it with two knots. He sat up by himself, wavered a moment and then seemed to gather some stability.

"Would you hand me one of those flagons of ale?" he requested, and I popped the lid with the opener next to the bottle and handed it to him. He took a deep swallow and then shook his head from side to side as if to clear out the proverbial cobwebs. Looking around the room, he said, "You seem to have handled matters in a most auspicious way, Cousin Benjamin. Why is Cathy keening in the corner like Paddy's pig?"

"I don't know whether it's because of something they did to her, or because she was so scared, or maybe she's just so happy that we came and got her."

"Whatever it is, it's got to stop," said Brendan, standing up carefully and slowly walking over to her. On the way he picked up his grease gun and checked the magazine. Then he leaned over Catherine and awkwardly pulled her to her feet with his good left arm.

"Listen, girl," he said, "your cousin Brendan and your cousin Benjamin are here to take care of you. But what we need is a soldier who can shoot a gun if need be and not a blubbering female. Remember that you're a Callaghan."

She rubbed both eyes with her knuckles and stood there silently. Brendan went over to one of the dead men, picked up the automatic that was lying by his side, pulled out the magazine and replaced it with a full one, then brought it back and handed it to her.

"This is the safety," he pointed out, "and it's off. All you have to do is point the gun at anybody and pull the trigger. But never point it at us because we're your cousins and we love you.''

He then walked over to where the unconscious boy was lying and looked down at him. He switched his gun to single fire and placed a bullet in the boy's heart before I could even cry out. I stood there in shock for a moment, looked over at Catherine, whose head was turned in the other direction, then walked over and grabbed Brendan by his arm, the wounded arm, which made him groan in pain.

"What are you doing?" I yelled. "Just what the hell are you doing?"

"They travel in packs," he said, his face white with the pain I had unwittingly inflicted on him, "in cells. This has to be the end of this one, and now there will be no one to pass the word that Brendan O'Malley nor any of those with him were involved in the death of Brent."

"But he was only a boy," I said.

"Over here," he answered, "there are no boys. No babies. No fathers, no mothers, no sisters, no brothers. Over here there are only those who can deal with death."

Poets are the most dangerous killers of all, I realized. Beware of the poets. It was like all those academics who advised Kennedy and Johnson and Nixon to bomb the shit out of everybody. Instead of ink, they wanted blood.

"We've got to move out of here now," said Brendan, "and get ourselves to a safe spot where we'll have friends to help us. God knows what's been going on while we've been picnicking in this magic glade. They could have razed West Belfast by now."

Brendan moved toward the door and Catherine followed. I took one more look at the boy on the floor, then at the two men on my scorecard and joined my group. Another encounter like this and I would be qualified to write poetry.

"Hang on to Cathy," Brendan instructed me as I came into the pitch-black hall, "and I'll get us out of here."

Which he did after we all fell down twice together; Catherine fell down once and pulled me with her; and I fell down once all by myself. Coming out of the door of that charnel house was like being reprieved from hell itself, and I breathed in greedily to let my body know there was life after death. There was a thin mist in the air, the kind you don't notice until you touch your cheek and hair and find they are wet.

Catherine had also turned her face to the slight breeze, and I wanted to give her a hug to reassure her that she still had her whole life ahead of her. Like me, Brendan took a deep breath and then tumbled to the ground in a heap, his machine pistol clattering on the brick, the magazine bouncing loose and ending up at Catherine's feet. When I knelt down beside him, I saw his eyes were open.

"A bit of a dizzy spell," he said huskily. "Just give me a minute and my pecker will be back up."

"There are two men coming," said Catherine, crouching down beside us. I raised my head and saw two figures scurrying out of the mist toward the building. A quick glance assured me that the safety was off on my gun.

"It's Peter Riley and Brian Hartley," said Catherine.

"Thanks be to God," said Brendan. "It may not be as good as your Green Berets," he told me, "but these lads will do in a pinch."

"They're going to the other side," said Catherine.

"Stand up," commanded Brendan. "Wave. Shout if you have to."

Catherine stood up and waved her hands wildly.

"They're coming," she said excitedly. "They're coming."

Thirty seconds later, two young men, two very young men, dropped down on the stairs beside us. They could have been brothers—a year younger or a year older—to the one Brendan had finished off inside. They looked at me suspiciously, but they obviously knew Catherine well.

"We came as soon as we got your message," said

one to Brendan, "but they almost got us once and we had to sit still for a while. What's wrong with you?"

"I have a bullet hole in my arm," said Brendan, "but that's of no matter."

"It certainly is of a matter," I said heatedly. "We've got to get you to a hospital immediately. You're still bleeding and God knows what infection is cooking in there."

"I can't go to hospital," said Brendan. "Do you realize what would happen to me if I went to hospital? I might as well go straight to jail and be treated there."

He turned his head toward the two boys.

"What we have to do," he said, "is get me to Jim's house where he can fix up my arm and we can see what part we'll play in whatever the hell is going on."

"The Protestants are trying to come in," said one of the boys excitedly. "They want to get hold of Brent's body and carry it off somewhere. They've had to move the casket twice to keep it safe."

"What are you talking, man?" asked Brendan, a frown masking the pain in his face.

"They've got all the soldiers out," said the boy, "but they're facing away from us this time. The Protestants keep breaking in anyway because there's so much ground to cover, and it's worth your head to turn the wrong corner."

"What are our boys doing?" asked Brendan.

"Whatever they can," said the other lad, "but we're all broken up into little pieces with no one to call the shots."

"Why doesn't everybody just stop shooting?" I asked. "Why doesn't everybody just stop the goddamned shooting?"

They all turned their heads to look at me, including Catherine, disbelief covering their faces.

"Cousin Benny," said Brendan, "you can't half-understand what's going on here. Now I'm sorry we've got you knee-deep in the muck, and I'll try to get you out before any damage might be done to you, but this is our business, our fight, and there'll be no end to it until we get what is rightfully ours."

"Jesus, Brendan," I said. "Here we are involved in a bloodbath, stuck God knows where in a city that is blowing up around us, not knowing whether we can get back to a safety zone without having our heads taken off, and you're singing me the national anthem. Well, don't expect me to either salute or stand at attention. If you want to continue this craziness, be my guest. But I want to get Catherine and myself to hell out of here and to hell out of the war zone and then to hell out of the whole country."

"You can do as you please," Brendan said coolly, "but you're not taking Catherine."

"Why the hell am I not taking Catherine? Do you want to get her killed?"

"You can't take her out of the country."

That stopped me for a moment as I tried to think back on what I had said that would cause him to come out with something that had nothing to do with anything. I remembered. I had said "to hell out of the whole country," but I was talking about just me. Why would he think I wanted to take Catherine out of the country? There was what could have been a look of hate on his face as he said it to me. Catherine out of the country. He was in love with her. I had forgotten that he was in love with her. In the midst of all this chaos, he was still able to focus on that one thing.

"I don't intend to take her out of the country," I said more loudly than I had intended. "It's me that wants to get out."

"Ha," he said with a laugh. "You've been saying that since you arrived here. Just like the girl who protests too much. You mark my words, Cousin Benny, you'll be buried here."

The chill that went through me must have shown on my face because Brendan reached out his hand toward me, almost as though he was trying to pull his words back. I don't know what would have happened if one of the young men hadn't said in a loud voice, "There's two militia just came around the corner."

We all ducked down and then raised our heads again almost immediately, like we were in a Three

Stooges comedy. Two figures in uniform were advancing quickly across the square, their rifles in the ready position, their heads swiveling from side to side.

"What in hell's name are they doing down here?" Brendan asked softly. "Things definitely must be upside down when two of them come sniffing all by themselves into this piece of territory. Wait till they get thirty meters closer, lads."

And when they did, when the two soldiers crossed the imaginary line that Brendan had set, he and the other two rose up and sprayed their bullets straight at them, hitting them in various parts of their bodies because of the way they twitched and leapt before they fell to the ground.

"Peter," said Brendan to the one closest to me, "go check them out."

Without hesitation, Peter sprang up the stairs and over to the two militiamen, holding his gun at the ready while Brendan and the other one also trained their weapons in that direction. It took only seconds before he was back.

"Done for," he said, having trouble catching his breath. "They're both done for."

"We've got to get out of here quick," said Brendan. "Where there's two, there's twenty more. I can't understand their coming out alone like that. There has to be some armor somewhere nearby."

He stood up straight to look around, and then fell down again, once more losing his weapon as well as his balance. He was out cold this time, and I hadn't brought the last bottle of ale as our medical kit. So I slapped his face softly from side to side until I got a moan out of him and his eyes blinked open.

"We've got to get you to the hospital, Brendan," I said. "There may be more damage than we know of."

"I'm all right," he said. "We just have to get me to Jim's house, and he'll fix me up proper."

"Then let's get going," I said. "Let's get the hell out of here."

"Wait," he said. "We can't all go together. It would be like having a parade. Peter, you and I will go for Jim's house, and Brian can lead Cathy and Cousin Benjamin out of the Falls."

"I'm not leaving you," said Catherine.

"Nor me either," I told him. "You can barely walk and you could pass out again at any time. We'll all go together."

"That we will not," said Brendan. "To invite death is one thing; to take him to bed with you is quite another. You can't get out without Brian to guide you. Cathy doesn't know this section of town."

"I'm going with you, Brendan," said Brian. "My place is with you." He was looking at me as though I had "Jew" written on my forehead.

"You'll do as you're told," said Brendan.

"I can't carry you alone, Brendan," said Peter. "We need Brian."

"There will be no need to carry me. You'll do as you're told," Brendan repeated, and then passed out cold again, falling against Brian. Rather than trying to revive him, we all just looked at each other.

"Do the two of you think you can get him to that Jim's house?" I asked.

"We can make a good run for it," said Brian.

"Then why don't we all make a good run for it?" I suggested. "I'm bigger than either of you, and I can help carry him."

"Brendan's right," said Peter. "Five would be too many. Me and Brian can handle him and keep our bottoms low to the ground, but five would be too many if someone came up quick."

"We don't know how to get out of here," I said. "Do you know how to go, Catherine?"

"I've never been allowed down here before," she answered. "But Brian can tell me where to go to find someplace I know and then we can make it on our own."

"I still feel it's wrong to separate," I said. "I think it would be best for all of us if we stuck together."

"Brendan said we should go on our own," said Catherine in a voice that indicated that was the end of the debate. The general had spoken. Since Peter and

Brian had already indicated that they would not allow us to accompany them, the case was closed.

"Tell Catherine how we can get out of here," I said to the pair, and then there was a hell of an argument between them about which was the best way. Catherine seemed to be listening closely, but I couldn't be sure that she was unscrambling what they were saying.

"Are you all set, girl?" asked Peter, and Catherine nodded. "Then we'll be off," he finished. It took nearly five minutes to get Brendan positioned on Peter's back, but finally he was ready to go. He turned and started back into the building from which we had just escaped.

"Where are you going?" I yelled. "Why the hell are you taking him in there again?"

"We've got to start out on the other side," he answered. "There's alleys there where we might get some help."

They started off, Brendan balanced precariously on Peter's back. Just before they disappeared inside the building, Brian turned toward us.

"You'd best not carry the guns," he advised. "If they see you with the guns, they'll cut you down right off. A man and a girl without guns, they might wait to ask them a question first."

They disappeared into the black hole. I looked down at the gun in my hand and the one at Catherine's feet. The sounds of explosions in the distance were hitting my ears like a native drumbeat in an unknown jungle. Above the buildings ahead of us you could dimly see black smoke rising from at least twenty different spots. Whoever or whatever we ran into, they would almost certainly have more people and more firepower than we did. The lady or the tiger? I dropped my weapon on the concrete and listened to the echo of its clatter.

"Which way, Catherine?" I asked.

She pointed to the left of where we were standing. I looked to see if any more soldiers were coming around the corner, but the square was still empty. The mist had turned into solid rain again, and I felt a chill shake my entire body. Was nature or fate trying to tell me something? Grabbing her hand firmly, I pulled Catherine up the stairs and started to run in the direction to which she had pointed.

32

MY FANTASY THAT WE WERE ALL ALONE in the world was shattered on the very first street because we were no more than a third of the way down it when three men ran out of a house and surrounded us. Two had rifles and the third a handgun, and all of them were pointed in our general direction.

"Who might you be?" asked the oldest of the three, a pint-sized man with a nose whose veins glowed red even in the dim light of the rain-soaked morning.

"I'm Catherine Callaghan," said Cathy, "cousin to Brendan O'Malley." "Brendan O'Malley" were the magic words because as soon as they were uttered, the weapons were instantly shifted downward.

"What would you be doing here, girl, at this time of the morning and with the town under siege?" asked the old alcoholic, his eyes still suspiciously on me.

"We've been with Brendan down here on a mission," said Cathy, as though she were a soldier responding to a question from an intelligence officer. I wondered anew at just how experienced this seemingly innocent girl had been in "the cause." Perhaps I was the innocent one.

"Brendan's been hurt," she said, "and Peter Riley and Brian Hartley are taking him for care. Brendan told us to make our own way back to home."

All three nodded as though they had been in on the decision.

"And who might this be?" asked the old man, pointing at me.

"This is our cousin from the United States," said Cathy. "He's been helping."

All three nodded again as though they had given references for me when the job was first offered.

"They've closed down the section," said the old man, "with anybody out on the street subject to being shot on sight. It's on the radio and telly every minute. There's no way you can make your way back home in the day. They've made two sweeps through this street already, and they say that seven are dead so far, five of them ours, one of them police and the other militia. They're using the steel bullets instead of the rubber, and they're shooting at the cats as they run across the road. You'd have no chance of getting home without they'd shoot you down like a dog or drag you off to prison. There are gangs of UDA running around both in uniform and without, and there's talk that they took Brent in his casket and burned him to ashes in the square."

"I have no one in this neighborhood," said Catherine. "Do you know where we might stay until the dark?"

"Blood relations of Brendan O'Malley will stay with me," said the little man vehemently, "and we'd best be off the street before the Brits come sweeping through again."

He turned and we followed into one of the beat-up-looking houses in the middle of the street. My relatives did not by any means live in what you would call a fancy neighborhood, but it was La Jolla compared to this row of antiquated brick buildings. The two younger men peeled off at the second floor, but the old guy trudged all the way to the top before he led us into a clean but shabby apartment. An old lady was sitting in a rocking chair by the window, and she looked at us with a squint as we entered. There seemed to be nobody else in the place so I assumed that their children, if they had any to begin with, were long gone.

"Mother," said the little guy, and you could have knocked me over with a wisp of straw, "we're going to have company for a while. I'll put the kettle over."

He had to be somewhere in his sixties at a minimum, which would put her somewhere in the eighties at the least. But if not wife and husband, I would have guessed at sister and brother, with no odds on who might be the older one. Whatever her secret, it should be bottled.

"Who be they?" she asked in a cracked voice. The whole scene was like something out of an early Laurence Olivier film, the kind where he wore period costumes.

"This is Brendan O'Malley's cousin," he said, pointing at Catherine, "and this is their relative from the States. They're trying to get home, but it's best to wait until dark because the militia might come through."

"They're coming through now," she said, leaning forward toward the window. I rushed over and reached it just as the old man cautioned, "Don't stick your head where they can see it." An armored car was going slowly down the street, rifles poking out of the tiny portholes. Straight across from us a man was standing at an open window with a rifle in his hand, barely back from where he could be seen from the street level. I wondered if he would fire a shot at the car, which would be returned with a fusillade by those within it. He looked over at me without expression, a tall, skinny man with a weather-beaten face. Then he stepped back and disappeared. The car went around the corner.

"Where's the tea?" asked the old lady. "And bring some bread and butter with it."

"We've only the half of loaf left," said the man, "and only the Lord knows when they'll let us out to get some more. If they ever do at all."

"Paddy," said his mother reproachfully, "there's always food for our guests. And a bit of whiskey, too, I am sure, on a cold, wet day like this with the bloody Protestants running amok."

Paddy went to a cupboard and brought out half a bottle of whiskey, which he placed on the table beside his mother, fetched four tumblers, filled the glass in front of her right up to the brim and each of the others half-full. The old lady lifted hers in the air.

"Here's to Brendan O'Malley," she said, "and all others like him. It's a privilege to have his blood relations as guests in our home."

Then she knocked back the whole thing as though it was Metamucil, draining the last drop and then licking the rim. Paddy downed his smaller portion in like manner, and Catherine and I took tiny sips as our share. It didn't matter how old this lady was; she was going to outlast the Egyptian mummies.

We had some tea and some bread and butter, and then we listened to the radio and watched the tiny black-and-white television screen for the rest of the day while the rain of words equaled that which was pouring down outside. We were told that the whole of West Belfast had been sealed off by troops and militia, but that roving bands of both Protestants and Catholics were moving "with impunity" throughout the area, and that the death toll was now up to ten. Brent's casket was apparently still safe in Catholic hands. It had not been seized and burned by the Protestants, and nobody except those who held it knew exactly where it might be.

The old lady muttered imprecations against the Protestant "swine" who had cut off Brent's life in his prime.

"Thanks be to God," she said to us, "that there are still men like Brendan O'Malley alive to keep us from being murdered in our beds."

It would have been interesting to see her reaction if we had told her that she was furnishing a haven for the real killers of Brent. I kept staring at Catherine while the old lady was going on about it, but she never took her eyes off the television screen. Her hands clenched and unclenched once, but that was it. I wished I or Brendan had been the one to shoot Brent. Hell, to us it was just another mark on the scoreboard.

All the officials were pleading with the citizenry to remain calm, and there was even a message from Margaret Thatcher saying she would not succumb to pressure from either side, and that all guilty parties involved would pay the legal penalties.

There was also a political representative of the IRA who said that none of his group was involved, but that innocent Catholics were not going to stand still for slaughter. "Hear, hear," said the old lady. The Protestant spokesman was a clergyman who said that none of his group was involved, but all loyal citizens would see to it that Ulster was not devoured by her enemy to the south even if it meant dying to the last man, woman and child. He also attacked the British for selling out to the IRA. "Hear, hear," said the old lady.

I was in some kind of a daze because I spent the day sitting there and staring at the television screen the same way as when I was ten years old and the Saturday-morning cartoons were being shown. When I did think a bit, it was only to tell myself that it was best to stay where Catherine would be safe. And me, I admitted to myself. I didn't want to die because I was somebody's cousin.

Just as the last light was beginning to fade, we had another cup of tea and another slice of bread, which finished the loaf. Since there was no other food, it was time to talk turkey.

"What do you want to do?" I asked Catherine. "This thing can't go on forever. If these good people will have us, we should probably stay here until things are under control again. It would be foolish to try to get to your house while all these crazies are out shooting up the streets."

"My da will be worried," she said, "and we have to find out if Brendan is all right."

"This could be it," said the old lady. "If it comes to a pitched battle this time, they could probably use two more soldiers on the line."

"We're not soldiers," I said, somewhat hotly. "This is a young girl with her whole life ahead of her, and I'm an American who would like my whole life to be still ahead of me."

"Paddy," said the old lady, "go down and see if the Murphys will lend us a bottle of whiskey."

It was as if I were not in the room and had uttered no words. We were all silent until Paddy returned with the news that the Murphys had barely enough for themselves.

"They're liars," said the old lady. "They lie in whatever teeth they have left. Paddy will take you down and show you the way, girl. Tell Brendan O'Malley that Bridget Digney wishes him long life and victory in the cause.''

We had been dismissed. She wanted these two "soldiers" out of her house and back on the line where they could fight alongside the folk hero Brendan O'Malley. I was annoyed enough so that I was ready to go. Not to fight. Just to go. Catherine thanked Mrs. Digney for her hospitality, but I didn't say a word as I followed Paddy out to the hall.

"You can stay with the Murphys or the Lenihans," said Paddy. "I'm sure they'd welcome you until the fuss is over."

"No, thank you," said Catherine sweetly, "but we really have to go home." Christ, it was like we had been there on a social call rather than just trying to stay alive. I gave up. I was more worried about getting soaked again than I was of getting shot by either side that inhabited the madhouse called Ulster.

Paddy gave Catherine very specific instructions on how to reach her section of town, and she kept nodding as he reeled off rights and lefts.

"If you get lost or worse comes to worst," he said, "go into a hallway or a cellar. But be careful about knocking on any doors this night because they might think you're somebody else and shoot before asking."

"Does everybody have guns in his house?" I asked. "I thought they were outlawed over here."

Paddy smiled at me in the dark. I couldn't see his face, but I knew he was smiling at me.

"Go with God," he said, and closed the door on us. The rain hit hard enough to hurt, the cold instantly soaking through the flesh to the bone.

"Okay, God," I said to Catherine, "lead the way."

33

I'VE HAD SOME ROUGH NIGHTS IN MY LIFE, but this one was unique to itself. First of all, it was pitch black and the rain was falling like the world had turned upside down and the lakes and oceans were spilling over us. Either the power had been turned off or the streetlights had been shot out, but in any case, the only light came from cars and rubbish burning at intersections, or houses blazing in the middle of blocks, or the occasional glare from a spotlight on an army vehicle. One of the armored cars put on its headlights on one of the streets we were slinking down, and almost immediately rifle shots rang out from the houses, and both lights were destroyed before the driver could even turn his switch off. The people in the truck fired back randomly because they couldn't see anything either, and Catherine and I flattened ourselves on the pavement, the water pushing up in our noses so that we had to turn our faces sideways in order to breathe.

Once we were jumped by what turned out to be five men, but they let us go after Catherine had given our magic password.

"Have you heard any word of how Brendan is?" she asked, after they took their hands off us. They hadn't even known he was wounded, and after expressing sympathy, the leader gave Catherine instructions on how we could reach her house from where we were. Paddy's directions had lasted about two blocks before we were lost, and now it turned out we had gone backward instead of forward.

"Let us take you into one of our houses," the leader offered, "and perhaps we can rustle up someone to guide you."

"No, thank you," said Catherine, "my da will be worried."

All these guys seemed to understand that perfectly; I was the only one who thought it was crazy. I made one more stab at it.

"Perhaps one of you could take us?" I suggested. It had been on the verge of my tongue to offer money as a reward, but I bit it off just in time.

"We'd do that if we could," said the leader, "but I can't spare the one of us. A bunch of them came through here not more than an hour ago, and shot their guns straight into the windows of the buildings. They didn't care who they killed, woman or child. We drove them off ,smartly, but they could be back at any minute."

"Would you have a gun then that we might borrow?" I asked, cursing myself for letting that Brian scare me into leaving our weapons behind. The next time anyone jumped us, I would have liked some firepower of our own.

"Oh," said the leader, "we've not enough for ourselves. It's our women and children we have to take care of, and there are no guns to spare."

"They're coming back," called out one of the lookouts, and I could hear everyone dropping to the road beside me. I reached out to make sure Catherine was down, and my hand landed right on her ass. She didn't say a word, and I wondered if she knew it was my hand.

I lifted my head but couldn't see a thing through the black. You had to keep brushing your face to keep the water clear of your eyes, but that didn't help at all. Suddenly the five men around us must have risen to their knees at a signal I didn't hear, and fired down the street, their muzzle blasts less than three feet over our bodies. There was one scream from somewhere ahead of us, and then came an answering volley from what had to be at least twenty guns. I could hear the bullets screaming past us, but no one from our team seemed injured because there was only silence.

"You'd best be getting on your way," a voice

whispered in my ear. "We're going to have to be moving around, and you'll be all alone out here if you don't want to go into one of the houses."

I wasn't going to bother asking Catherine that question again. Male ego. I should have just told her that this was what we were going to do, and to hell with her getting home to her "da" so he wouldn't worry. I could have calmly informed her that I was staying no matter what, and she could carry on her quest for her father, the Holy Grail, on her own. But at this stage of the game, I wasn't going to chicken out.

Moving my hand from Catherine's rear to her arm, I pulled her up to her knees, whispered that we were going to make a run for it, and took off in the direction the guy had pointed out as the correct one. I had listened carefully while he had detailed to Catherine the way to go home, and this time I was going to lead.

We were already around the corner when the next fusillade rang out, and it was impossible to tell which side had delivered it. There was a burning car blazing at the next intersection, and I headed toward it on the right side of the street. I was amazed that the car could burn so fiercely in the midst of a rain like that, but I guess the elements have their pride, too, and fire was not going to just give in to water. How could you expect humans to act intelligently when fire and water also battle it out to the bloody end?

Just before we reached the four corners, I spotted the dark hulk of what had to be an armored car on the far side. It was pulled back far enough so that you couldn't make out any details, but there was just enough firelight reflecting off its dark walls to have caught my eye. I pulled Cathy down with me at the side of the building we were next to. Had they seen us and were we about to be shot at? It was doubtful because you could barely make out anything in the open, and they had only narrow slits to peer through.

Did we try to go back and around the next corner, or did we wait to see if they were parked for the night or would move out soon? I was worried about any detours because the blocks were not laid out symmetrically, and we could be thrown off direction or find ourselves in a cul-de-sac from which we would have to try to backtrack. While I was thinking about it, the machine made up its mind on its own. There was the low sound of the motor being started up, partially masked by the wails of the wind and the rain, but loud enough for any straining ears to pick out. I had twice heard helicopters above us when we had first started out, but it would have been foolhardy to keep them in the air in this kind of weather, and everything must have been grounded by now.

The armored vehicle moved close to the burning car and halted for a moment before slowly circling close to it and then stopping again. There must have been some mighty frustrated men in that truck. They were flaunting themselves in hope of drawing shots from somewhere so they could cut loose on their own. Suddenly two figures dashed out from somewhere and threw burning bottles at the armored car, one of which exploded on top and the other by the right front wheel. You couldn't tell which one did the trick, but something was hit right and a burst of flame engulfed the entire vehicle. The door opened from the rear and men seemingly poured out of the flames. Then they got what they had been looking for. Shots boomed out from all sides and one of the men from the truck was hit and went down. Two of his buddies grabbed hold and pulled him into the dark. I couldn't tell where the others had gone, but there were shots being fired at the buildings so I assumed that they had come to ground and were regrouping.

Taking Catherine's arm, I pulled her back with me until we came to the end of the street. Directions or no directions, it was going to be impossible to follow the route laid down by the last guy. We had to take the chance of going around. In situations like this, time as well as people are your enemies. After a while, you get a what-the-hell attitude and do things that are foolhardy. It is almost as though you were wishing to get captured or shot or whatever just to get the thing over with one way or another. This has happened to me many times when I have been on stakeout or when I was with the church people or the Mafia hoods. Afterward, you get the shakes when you realize how stupid you have been, but it is also a part of what makes human beings so human.

What happened was that I gave up slinking slowly down the sides of streets, and moved right out into the middle of the road so we wouldn't be stumbling over barrels or stairways or fire hydrants or all the other crap that had been thrown on the sidewalks. I was holding Catherine firmly by the hand and pulling her along with me, my head down against the wind and rain, the only outside sound being that of the occasional explosions that were rocking the area somewhere.

Which is how we walked right into the middle of them. They had to have been stretched across the street in a long line, the way fishermen loop their nets to drag in what they can. The one who bumped into me hit so hard that I was knocked backward into Catherine. He gave a howl and it seemed like a dozen of them fell on the two of us, them punching and yelling, and me screaming as I fell to the pavement that there was a girl, there was a girl, there was a girl.

One of the blows caught me in the head and I was out of it for whatever seconds it took for them to drag us to the side of the road and then down a stairway somewhere, my head bumping one of the steps with a sharp edge, and I could feel the wet of the blood joining the rainwater that was soaking me.

I was shoved against a wall and a flashlight was shone directly in my eyes. Faces and bodies pushed at me so hard that I was having trouble breathing, as much from fear as from pressure on my chest.

"Who are you?" a voice demanded.

"I'm an American tourist," I started to say, but there was an interruption from the back of the crowd, which surged against me harder as someone pushed at them while he was screaming.

"Let me at him," the voice shouted. "Let me at the barstard."

"Easy, Jamie," a softer voice cautioned. "Easy."

"Don't easy me, John," the voice yelled. "My brother's dead and he was worth ten of these barstards. I'm going to kill me ten before the night is over." I could feel him trying to claw his way toward me.

"Who are you, girl?" another voice yelled from close by. "What's your name? Where do you live?" Time for the magic passwords.

"Leave her alone," I started to yell, but someone punched me right in the mouth, and I could feel my lower lip sinking into one of my teeth.

"Who are you, girl?" the voice yelled again. "Where do you live?"

"I'm Catherine Callaghan," I heard her say somewhere to my left, "and I live on Fairly Street."

"She's one of them," the voice behind the pack yelled again. "She's one of them. They both have to die. You promised me that, Frank. You promised me that." This was the side that didn't believe in magic.

"You're not going to shoot a girl," someone else said. "I don't give a damn what Frank promised. You're not going to shoot a girl like this even if she's the pope's daughter."

"Then him," the voice yelled again. "You promised me the first one we caught, Frank. You said I could do him in just like they did to Bobby. You promised me, Frank. You all promised me."

"I'm an American," I yelled. "Christ, can't you tell that I'm not one of you, whoever the hell you are? Just listen to how I talk."

"He's lying," said the voice, seemingly closer than it had been. "He's with her, ain't he? And we all know where she's from. Let me by."

And there he was in front of me. I couldn't see any of their faces because the light was shining in my eyes, but I could tell that this crazy man was going to do what he said he was, and that although some of them might have ordinarily been against a cold-blooded killing, anything could happen on a night like this.

"He *is* an American," Catherine started to yell,

but someone must have clamped his hand over her mouth because the sound was muffled off. I felt a handgun shoved right against my belly, and I heaved up as hard as I could, but they were holding me too tightly, and I was done for right then. It flashed through my mind that my relatives were going to have a hell of a time deciding where to bury me. Holy ground? Half-holy ground?

"Stop!" somebody yelled from the back of the crowd. "Somebody for Christ's sake stop him. Grab the gun."

"You're not going to stop me, Alan," yelled the guy shoving the piece in my belly. I wondered why he hadn't pulled the trigger already. It's not that easy to put a bullet in a man unless you're of a certain mentality. He was working himself up to do it, but his finger hadn't yet received enough strength from his brain.

"Stop him!" the voice yelled again. "Don't let him shoot."

I could feel the crowd part for someone, and the gun moved a couple of inches as the man shoved in beside the one who was going to kill me. Two hands reached out and cradled my face.

"It's him," the new voice yelled. "It *is* the American."

"What are you talking about, Alan?" he was asked.

"It's the American," the man said excitedly. "It's Sean O'Malley's cousin from America."

"Then he's one of them," the boy with the gun roared. "He's one of them."

"But he's the one I was telling you about," said this Alan. "He's the one came over to us at the wake, and he's the one came over to us at the funeral. He's the American I was telling you about. If only they were all like him. You'll kill him over my dead body," he said to the one holding the gun.

Alan! Alan Peters. It had to be one of Moll Peters' brothers that I had shaken hands with at the wake.

"They killed Bobby," said the one holding the gun, but his voice had softened and the muzzle had tipped upward away from my body.

"I know they did, Jamie," said the first voice I had heard, which had to be that of Frank, the leader. "And you'll get your revenge. We'll all get our revenge. But I remember this man now. You weren't with us, but some of us remember what this man did. He's decent. We don't want the blood of a decent man on our hands. There are enough of the others for us. Let him be."

"What about the girl?" somebody asked from the other side.

"Let her be, too," Frank answered. "They're the ones who kill the women. Not us. Let her be, too."

And they were gone. Just like that into the dark, and we were alone in a cellarway, me and Catherine, bruised but alive. I moved my rear end out from the wall a bit, and something dug into my rear. I put my hand down to the pocket and pulled out the knife. It was good they hadn't found that on me. I pushed the button and heard the blade slap out.

"Are you all right?" I asked into the dark.

"I'm all right," Catherine answered.

I was just about to close the knife and push myself to my feet when a dark shape came through the air in a lunge and hit the wall beside me.

"Barstard," the shape cursed. "You're going to die anyway."

Without thinking, I lunged sideways with the knife and felt it go into the shape, into the dark shape, and I pushed as hard as I could, not knowing what part of the body I had stuck it in.

There was a groan, the kind of mortal sound made by someone who has lost the power to do anything but use his voice. Wherever the knife was stuck, it had done the job for the time being at least. Jamie had come back on his own. But the rest of them would soon be looking for him, and American or not, decent at wakes and funerals notwithstanding, this time they would want revenge. I reached out until I found Catherine, still sitting against the wall, pulled her to her feet and out to the road. As the rain and wind hit us full force again, I thought about the night so far, the night that was never going to end. When I died, if they sent me to hell, I would know the neighborhood.

34

WE MADE IT JUST AS IT BECAME LIGHT enough to distinguish people from light poles and garbage cans. Not that there had been that many people to distinguish. As we slogged and sneaked and crawled and ran and hid and dashed through that interminable night, we occasionally came upon groups of police or soldiers or militia, all of whom seemed to have little interest other than to stay alive and keep as dry and warm as possible. One bunch was difficult to work around because they were somewhat spread out, but the dark, the wind and the rain were our friends as well as our problem.

We once again lost track of our bearings, but kept moving in what I thought was the general direction in which we wanted to go. The break came when we moved into the entry of a store to get out of the rain for a minute, and Catherine started to wail out loud.

"What's the matter?" I asked her, taking her by the shoulders, so I could shake loose the hysteria if need be.

"It's Mr. Smith's," she said, pointing at the door behind her. "It's the greengrocer's. It's Mr. Smith's."

This was where Laura went every day to buy whatever foods she needed to destroy for her family's nourishment. We were three blocks over and one block up from where the Callaghans lived.

"Come on," I said, grabbing her hand. "This is no time to be picked up by the police." I realized as I said it how far away I was from San Diego.

I never thought I would say this, but I was happy to see Uncle William's scowling face when he opened the door for us.

"Where the hell have you been?" he yelled at Catherine, looking past me as though I weren't there.

"We've been with Brendan," she said.

"Oh, is that your story, is it?" he roared. "Out God knows how long with this one and your sisters worrying to death whether you're alive or dead. What if the neighbors hear about your spending the night with this one? What are you going to tell Father Delavar when next you go to confession?"

At least he had acknowledged my presence. But he was more worried that I had deflowered his flowerless one than that we might have been killed out there.

"We were with Brendan," I said hotly. "We were with Brendan the whole time. And when you see him, he will tell you that is the truth."

"Oh," he said triumphantly, "when I see him, is that it? Well I've been seeing him for quite a while now."

"Ah," said Brendan, "I was beginning to worry about you two. Where have you been?"

He had come through the door from the kitchen, beyond which lay the bedrooms, and I had the idea from looking at him that he'd been asleep when we had come in. His face was pale, the combination of gray and white that comes from pain and exhaustion. I looked at his arm where the bullet had gone through, but all I could see was a small bulge under the clean white shirt. He probably should have been wearing a sling, but it was obvious that he didn't want to attract attention to his condition.

"Brendan," said Catherine, running over to him and putting her hands on both his arms, including the wounded one. She had no idea of what she was doing to him, and I thought for a moment he might faint and fall to the floor again. "Brendan," she repeated. "Are you all right?"

He managed a very weak smile.

"Right as rain," he said. I could tell that he was going to be like the little Spartan boy who let the fox eat his innards because he didn't want the other kids in class to call him a sissy.

"How is your arm?" she asked.

"It's all fixed," he said. "Nothing big."

"We were so worried about you," she said, letting go of his arms. I thought then that he was going to fall down, but he stood there, swaying only slightly.

"Difficult time getting back?" he inquired of me over her head.

"Not really," I answered. I could play this game as well as anybody.

"There they are," said Laura, coming out of the living room. We all went to the window and saw a line of British troops in full combat gear walking through the street. They were wearing paratrooper boots, and although they were being careful and were moving their heads to cover all sides, you could tell that these were seasoned troops who were ready to handle anything that might come along.

"The reinforcements arrived last night," Brendan said behind me, "and the curfew is being lifted at ten. You can move freely about until dark, they said on the telly, but then you have to burrow in again."

"I'm going to take a bath and change my clothes," said Catherine. "Do you want to take one, too, Benny?"

"No," I told her, "I think I'll wait until I get back to the hotel so I can change my clothes too."

"They've buried Brent somewhere," said Brendan to me, "and they've shoved the Protestants back where they belong so I'm sure things will have quieted down by tonight. Everybody got all the frustration out of his system the past few days, so they'll be calm for a while."

"Including you?" I asked.

"Especially me," he answered with a laugh. "I want to thank you for the help you gave." There was no smile on his face when he said it.

"It was all because of Catherine, Brendan," I told him. "I think everything else here is a bunch of shit, and that includes what you are doing."

"I tell you again, Cousin Benjamin," said Brendan, "walk away from it. Go home. It's not your fight."

"That's what I'm going to do," I told him. "I've

gotten to know my relations better than I wanted to. I'm ready to go home."

"Then we won't be seeing you again," he said, sticking out his hand.

"Oh, yes," I contradicted him. "As the song goes, one more time. I want to give a farewell party for the family. I want them to know how their American nephew-cousin feels about them."

"A party," he echoed. "A farewell party. Will there be booze?"

"Of course. And food. And music. And favors for the ladies. The works."

"They'll like that," he said. "I'll like that."

"Can I make you something to eat, Cousin Benny?" said Laura, coming from the kitchen and wiping her hands on her apron.

"Oh, no thank you," I said quickly. "We ate before we came."

Brendan was looking at me quizzically. I had the feeling his appreciation of Laura's cooking was the same as mine.

Just before I left, Uncle William came over to say good-bye.

"I ought to break your bones for you," he said. "Stay away from my Catherine and don't be giving her big ideas."

"Thank you for everything, Uncle William," I said, and went out the door.

I hadn't walked one block before five policemen took me into custody. My problem was that I had ventured forth long before the curfew was lifted. They shook me down and checked my papers. I didn't have my passport on me, but everything else confirmed who I said I was. They got into a debate as to what to do with me, and finally it was decided to take me to the main checkpoint.

Who should be there but Inspector Simmons, looking as frazzled as I was. He told the policemen he would handle it from there, and instructed me to get into a nearby police car. Then he personally drove me to the hotel. We didn't say one word to each other on the way.

When I got out, I said "Thank you" as I slammed the door.

"Now we're even," he said, and started to drive off.

"We are like hell, you son-of-a-bitch," I shouted at him. "You don't trade off a man's life against a ride uptown."

I doubt that he heard me. The clerk at the key desk said he hoped I had a nice day. The line should have been delivered by Clint Eastwood instead of a skinny, balding Irishman.

35

IT WAS AMAZING HOW QUICKLY THE CITY went back to being what they called "normal." Nearly all of the damage was in the Catholic section so the center of town, except for the stores that were still boarded up, looked the same the very next day. The soldiers disappeared somewhere that afternoon, presumably in holding areas nearby, and the police patrols didn't look any heavier than they had been when I arrived. The authorities had obviously decided to play it cool, making believe it never happened. The newspapers and television had graphic pictures of the burning cars and houses and the bullet holes in the buildings, but reported that cleanup efforts had removed nearly all the debris, and that repairs were being made to streetlights and ripped-up pavements. The known death toll was twelve, and there were some hundred and thirty-six people who were injured. I was sure there were a hell of a lot more than that, but most of them had probably been treated by someone named "Jim," who didn't report gunshot wounds to the local health authority or police.

I spent two whole days putting myself together again, taking frequent showers, sleeping and napping, eating, watching television. I didn't go near Fairly Street and nobody from there came to see me or called.

When I was feeling rested and my mind was at ease, I placed a call to Giuseppe Montenegro in Rome, the guy who handled all the millions that Bandini had left me. They said he would call back and within an hour he did.

"Lieutenant Freedman," he said, "Giuseppe Montenegro here. I trust you are well and enjoying your visit, although I must say that you are not in the most tranquil area that is available in Europe. You should come to Rome and have some pasta. What can I do for you?"

"I want to buy a business or buy into a business in Belfast," I said.

"But you already have a business in Ulster," he said.

"I do? What's that?"

"You own the Greenmead Horse Farm outside the town of—just let me check the file here—outside the town of Lifford."

"A horse farm?"

"Yes, and a quite successful one at that. I told Bandini when she instructed me to buy it that she was crazy, but, as usual, when it came to business, she was right."

"I'm afraid a horse farm won't do, Mr. Montenegro," I told him. "It must be in Belfast." I spent twenty minutes telling him what was needed, and then he spent twenty minutes telling me that it wouldn't work and a substantial amount of money would be lost, and I spent twenty seconds telling him this was what I wanted, and he spent five seconds telling me that if this was what I really wanted, this was what he would then do, and he would be back to me within a few days.

I took a taxi right to Catherine's house. Only she and Cissy were at home. Brendan was doing fine, Catherine said, and she had quite recovered from what we had been through. I searched her face and eyes to see if she was telling the truth, and found nothing to dispute what she had said. Only Jesus, and perhaps her priest, knew what was going on inside her.

I told her that I wanted to give a farewell party for my relatives, kids and all, the following week, that she and her sisters would do the inviting, and should leave a message for me at the hotel on exactly how many were going to be present.

"How many do you think there will be?" I asked her.

She and Cissy counted on their fingers, but then

had to get a pencil and a piece of paper. As far as they could come up with, there would be approximately eighty people there if I wanted all the cousins to the second and third degree. I wanted them all, I told them, and gave them the address and the time.

"That's too late," said Cissy.

"What's too late?"

"The hour. They'll all be starving by then."

So we set it an hour earlier.

"Will you be at the hotel?" Catherine asked as I was about to leave. She looked like she wanted to ask me something but didn't know how.

"I'm going to the North for a few days," I said. "I have to visit some people there."

"You didn't say anything about knowing people in the North," she said.

"It's a business thing," I told her. "I'll check back with you when I return. But leave a message as to how many will be at the party."

"That I will," she replied. I made small talk for a few more minutes, but whatever it was she wanted to say was stuck in her throat somewhere, and I finally left.

When I returned to the hotel, I called the caterer from whom I had rented the hall and told him there would be approximately eighty people at the affair, but that I would know more definitely within a few days.

"I have to charge you by the number you give me," he said, "whether they are there or not."

"That is no problem," I told him. "You plan for eighty."

"I've been going over the figures for what you want, Mr. Freedman," said the caterer, "and it's going to come to nearly a hundred pounds a person. Now what would you like to cut back on?"

"Nothing," I said. "I want it exactly as we talked about."

"Are you sure you know what you're doing?"

"Look, Mr. Rogers," I said. "I'm a rich American. Take advantage of me."

"Well, I will be laying out a good bit of money in advance," he said, "and . . . and . . ."

"I will send you a check right away, Mr. Rogers," I said, "and you can cash it at the bank before you lay out a penny of your own."

"May the Lord send me more like you, Mr. Freedman," said Rogers. "I hope Belfast is as good to you as you are to it."

I then arranged to rent a car and told the hotel to hold my room until I returned. Montenegro had said he would call the horse farm to let them know that the owner was coming, and I was looking forward to dumb animals, green fields, and people who tugged their forelocks when the master of the estate rode by. I thought for a moment of getting in touch with both Catherine and Brendan and asking them if they wanted to go with me, but decided against it. I wanted to be alone. All, all alone. I had planned the business deal and the party on the spur of the moment, and if any second thoughts occurred to me, I wanted to work them through while there was still time to make changes.

The drive north was uneventful except for being stopped three times by militia. Not knowing if Private Welch was one of the group who went through my car and papers each time, I kept a wary eye all around while the soldier in charge processed me. I was in no mood to be shot at this stage of my visit to the "ould country."

Greenmead Farm turned out to be the kind of paradise that exists only in slick vacation brochures. The natural beauty of the rolling hills, the greenness of the grass and trees, something that was foreign to the brownness of San Diego, the sight of the horses galloping over the meadows and the air of tranquillity that was so different from that of Belfast lulled me into a dream world in which I pictured myself spending the rest of my life.

The manager, Robert Deacon, and his family couldn't have been nicer. My room was comfortable if not fancy, and Mrs. Deacon's cooking, especially her roast chicken, was a far cry from what I had been enduring the past few weeks. The fifteen-year-old daughter,

Marcy, determined that she was going to teach me to ride, and we spent nearly the whole day in the saddle, changing horses as needed. By the third day the aches and pains of the various parts of my body that had never experienced this kind of punishment before began to disappear, and I was beginning to feel that the horse and I were one as we went galloping over the meads. She even started me on little jumps, and I began asking Mr. Deacon about which horses we might race ourselves instead of selling them. No matter how dumb my questions, to either Marcy or Mr. Deacon, they were always polite and friendly, and I wondered what it might be like if I built myself a little house on the place and settled down there after taking early retirement from the force.

The snake slithered into paradise at dinner on the fourth night. We were speaking on various matters, and Marcy asked me how I had come to buy a horse farm in Ulster. Her father frowned a bit at the personal question, but didn't say anything. I explained that it had been left to me as part of an estate.

"So you flew over to see that we had given an honest count of your horses," said the impertinent miss, and this time her father really frowned, but still said nothing. Marcy was their only child, and the look on the Deacons' faces whenever she entered a room gave your heart a little tickle.

"No," I said, "I flew over to make the acquaintance of my relatives in Belfast, and only came up here by chance, for which I am very grateful."

"How many relatives do you have in Belfast?" Mr. Deacon inquired.

"It turns out that I have about eighty."

"I didn't realize there were that many people of your persuasion in Belfast," said Mrs. Deacon. My name had obviously been a matter of discussion when I wasn't present.

"I don't have a real persuasion," I told them. "My mother's name was Callaghan, and all my relatives are either Callaghans or O'Malleys, and I think some are Murphys and some are O'Briens and some are . . ." I couldn't remember the names of any of the other husbands I had been introduced to at the wake.

There was quiet for a moment, and then Mrs. Deacon asked: "And where do these relatives of yours live in Belfast?"

"Mostly in the Falls," I answered, and then you could have cut the silence with a knife.

Protestants. It was like a neon light had gone on in my head. I looked around the table and even Marcy had bent her face over her food as if she must memorize each thing on it before she could take a bite. *Protestants.* East is east and west is west and never the twain shall meet.

"I'll be leaving tomorrow morning," I told them. Nobody said anything. There was such a sense of sadness in me that I could feel tears welling up in my eyes. All I had done was mention some names and tell where people lived, and the whole fucking thing had gone down the drain and into the sewer.

"It's been a wonderful vacation for me," I told them, "and you're doing a superb job with the farm. I can't think of one thing anybody would want changed. You've all been so kind to me, especially my teacher Marcy, that I will never forget either you or Greenmead."

We finished the meal without any more talking except when someone asked somebody else to pass something over. It was difficult for me to chew and swallow each bite, but we got through it. I don't know what their motives were, maybe to hold on to their position at the farm, but mine was straight sadness.

Mrs. Deacon gave me breakfast by myself the next morning, saying they had eaten early, and when it was time to say good-bye, they told me that Marcy had gone off somewhere and they would thank her for me.

As I drove off, I realized I would have to sell the farm because now it was more like a hazardous waste site in my mind than a place of peace and tranquillity and refuge.

But it solidified my wild and crazy idea on what

I wanted to do about the business in Belfast and how much I wanted to have the party. I had come to Greenmead to work things out, and things had worked out with a vengeance.

36

THERE WAS A LONG TELEX FROM MONtenegro and a short note from Catherine waiting on my return to the hotel. The drive south had been depressing, the beauty of the landscape and the green of the fields having an opposite effect this time around. I was stopped only once by the militia, and I didn't even bother to look around for Welch. If he wanted to shoot me, let the dumb son-of-a-bitch shoot me.

The Deacons, my friends—and employees. Why did I feel such a sense of betrayal? Because I thought I had found a Utopia where all souls were treated equally? Where it didn't matter what a horse's religion might be? Since they all looked physically alike, you couldn't tell who were Catholics and who Protestants in this benighted province. So you had to ask their names and where they lived before you could make a judgment on whether they were "good" or "bad" people. I had so liked the Deacons, especially Marcy, and I so liked Catherine and Brendan, wanted to love them, but they all made it impossible. They were so enmeshed in their hate, justified or not, that they had sealed their fates in the foreseeable future. I threw my duffel bag on the bed, pulled off my jacket and did a hundred and fifty push-ups, hard and fast, until the sweat broke out all over my body. Then I showered, unpacked my bag, and picked up the two messages that I had deliberately set aside. Things were drawing to a close, and I was a little bit apprehensive.

Montenegro's message, which was dated the day before, stated that he had bought me fifty-one percent of a trucking business that was seeking to expand. We had been forced to pay a big premium to get the extra two percent for control, but the man who ran it was fairly young and still ambitious and hoped to make a lot of money for all of us. He also understood completely what I wanted to do.

There were instructions as to lawyers I must call, bankers I must see, papers to be signed and a meeting with the chief operating officer of the company. Montenegro concluded by saying that it could end up being a pretty good deal after all, that I should call him if I had any questions, and the offer of pasta in Rome still stood. I made the calls and set up appointments for the next day.

Catherine's note informed me that there would be eighty-three people at the farewell party because she had invited Father Delavar and a few other close friends. Brendan, who had helped with the invitations, had said it would be all right to have the extras, and had even called the caterer about the seating arrangements. I couldn't decide whether or not to be annoyed about Brendan sticking his snub nose in.

Seating arrangements? What seating arrangements? I considered paying a visit to my cousins, but it was already dark out and I was tired. Mostly, I just wanted to be alone.

The next day I visited all the business people, including the head of the company I had bought into, signed all the papers, and learned that there would be many more papers to sign in the future because of government red tape and foreign ownership. But everybody concerned seemed delighted with the deal, including the company CEO, who said he understood exactly what was expected, and he would carry it out to the best of his ability.

I didn't get back to the hotel until eight P.M. I thought again about going down to the Falls to see Catherine and Brendan, but Uncle William's face loomed in my mind so I had a quick supper, watched some television and went to bed. I would see them all at the party the next day, and that would be enough. I had trouble falling asleep so I got up and called British Airways and booked a flight to London and then home the day after next. I looked at my watch and it was past midnight. Now it wasn't the day after next that I was leaving; it was tomorrow. Then I slept.

I arrived at the catering hall early to check out how things were going, but there was already a line of relatives waiting to get in. I didn't recognize one of them, but some of them knew who I was and spoke to me, and I told them I would see if things could be pushed up a bit. Mr. Rogers was running around frantically, and informed me that it was most unusual and most disconcerting to have people arrive an hour and a half early for an affair, but he would see what he could do. It was a full hour before he relented, but there was no fuss from the ever-increasing crowd. They were all as patient as they were excited, and some of them lifted up their kids to shake hands with me.

Finally, the doors were opened and they all surged in. Their gasps of astonishment were worth every penny I had spent. Rogers had festooned the whole hall with flowers, and the appetizer tables covered one whole wall. They were literally groaning tables because there was almost every kind of food you could think of, including caviar, which excited some curiosity from the crowd. There were cooks in chef's hats slicing smoked salmon and fillets of beef and turkeys and hams, there were cheeses of almost every description, and breads and crackers and fresh fruits and nuts.

In addition to the three manned bars, there were five half kegs of beer set up at strategic intervals, and waiters passed through the crowd with trays of champagne glasses filled to the brim. "This group will think they're being cheated if the glasses aren't topped off," I had told Mr. Rogers.

The other two-thirds of the room contained the tables set up for the banquet, with a long head table and several round ones, each of which seated ten. I was surprised to see there were place cards, and Catherine, who had breathlessly arrived that very minute, informed me

THE BELFAST CONNECTION

that she and Brendan considered the cards necessary because it was hoped that this would prevent fistfights among the members of the family who, as she put it, "didn't see eye to eye on everything."

The room was jammed way before the official opening hour, with little kids running around and falling down, and the high-pitched Irish voices creating almost a wail of sound that seemed to hover over your head like something you could reach up and touch. Everybody was dressed in his finest, and they all nodded and smiled at me, but Catherine was the only one who actually talked to me. Uncle William hadn't even bothered to say hello, and Cissy and Laura were among the nodders and smilers.

Finally, even Catherine went off somewhere, and I was standing alone with only a glass of champagne for company when Father Delavar came out from somewhere in the crowd and stood before me, looking more like some kind of Irish gnome than a priest despite his black suit and white collar.

"I've never seen the likes of anything like this," he said, gazing around in wonder, "and I'm sure nobody else has either."

"Do you think it would have been better to have had something simpler and given the extra money to the poor?" I asked him.

"Saints, no!" he exclaimed. "You've provided this family with something to talk about for the rest of their lives. It's as if an angel had come down from heaven and waved a magic wand."

"Jesus was a Jew," I said.

"Aye," he answered, giving me a long look, "but you're half Irish, my boy, which gives you a step up on Him." He smiled up at me, exposing his blackened little teeth. I felt like giving him a hug.

"When Catherine came to me all excited that you had come over here to join Mother Church," he said, "I told her not to set her sights too high. Though I'm sorry to say it, it's best you leave here the way you came. You don't seem the type of man who has much faith in anything. I've been hearing confession so long that I know those who can and those who can't, and you're in the latter category."

"Father," I asked, "what can I do for Catherine that will give her a happy life? I don't want her to be a shopgirl who finally marries whatever is available and bears so many children that she has no room to taste the good things of life, let alone breathe."

"Don't go playing God with Catherine now," said the priest. "She's a good girl who has faith and is best off in the environment she knows and is comfortable with. And by the by, I'd like to commend you for your restraint on the occasions when she tempted you. You're a decent man."

I looked at him in astonishment for a moment before it came to me. Confession. Good Christ, the girl told him everything that happened to her. I was sure he also knew about Dennis Raftery and the two times he huffed and puffed with Catherine. Had she told him about Brent? And had he given her absolution? I looked down at the little man and realized I would never know. Nor would anyone else.

"But I'd like to send her to school or take her to the States for a few months and show her what the rest of the world is like."

"Leave her be," he commanded. "She is what she is and will be what she'll be, and your meddling could only make it worse for her, maybe ruin the rest of her life."

I was about to argue the points when the crowd parted once again, and this time it was Brendan who weaved his way toward us, a glass of what had to be Scotch in one hand and a beer in the other. His face was all red, but it wasn't the color you get from drinking; it was more like that from a fever, and I looked at his arm where the slight bulge still showed. Was "Jim" a real doctor or did Brendan have a festering wound under his bandage? I would have to do something about that before I left.

"Ah," said Brendan, "my holy Father Delavar

and my unholy Cousin Benjamin. All the family I need for every and any purpose."

He was drunk, drunk as you can be. His eyes were red holes in his head, and I reached out and touched him on the neck, which was burning hot and sweaty under my fingers. He should have been in a hospital rather than at a party. I didn't want to mention the wound in front of Father Delavar, but my worry was such that I had to say something.

"Are you all right, Brendan?" I asked stupidly.

"Right as rain," he answered. "Couldn't be better. If the Lord took me right now, He would have a happy man at His right-hand side. How do you like the table?" he asked.

I looked around the room at all the tables.

"No, no," he said impatiently. "The head table. The head table. Did you notice what I did with the head table?"

I looked at it closely, but except for being rectangular instead of round, it wasn't that much different from any of the other tables.

"Count the chairs," he ordered. "Count the chairs."

I tried to count, but it was impossible to make out exactly how many there were. He instantly realized my problem.

"There are thirteen," he said triumphantly. "Thirteen. It's your last supper, Cousin Benjamin, and there are thirteen chairs. One of them belongs to Judas, but which one is a surprise."

"I don't think this is amusing, Brendan," said Father Delavar. "To mock the Lord is not a joke."

"This is no joke, Father," said Brendan, his red face dead serious. He tossed down the glass of Scotch in one gulp and took a long swig of the beer. "This is no joke. Jesus was a Jew, you know."

"The good father and I have already gone through that," I told him. "Why don't we move the odd chair to another table?"

"And which one of the honored guests would you

insult by doing that?" asked Brendan with a smile. "Come now. Don't be superstitious about my little joke. Besides, we're the only ones in on it. You don't want the family thinking that one of them is not good enough to sit at the head table. Shall I move you out, Father?"

"No, no," said the priest, almost too quickly. That would have been something to shove the priest aside at the last moment. He would have liked it least of all.

The discussion was ended by two waiters going among the crowd and softly banging gongs, indicating that it was time for each member of the family to search out the chair that had been designated for him. It took a while for the sorting-out, but finally even the children were set in their places and, as one father could be heard saying, told to "sit still and be goddamned quiet."

I was in the center of the head table with Catherine on one side and Father Delavar on the other. Brendan had placed himself alone around the end of the table where he could look across and see all of our faces in profile. The rest of the group consisted of Uncle William, his two sons and his other two daughters, Aunt Margaret and Aunt Flora, and a little man of indeterminate age whom I had never seen before. As I looked across the room, I realized that not one adult, man or woman, would have been able to pass a sobriety test. So far, my major achievement had been to get every member of the family drunk. Was this some kind of revenge on my part for my father and mother being alcoholics? Was I showing these bigoted bastards how they could be manipulated by a Jew? There was a sinking feeling in my heart as the bowl of cream-of-broccoli soup was placed before me.

I was about to pick up my spoon when Father Delavar stood and gave the invocation. I had forgotten the rites and rituals. He kept it brief and thanked the Lord "for His bounty" and the relative from America who had made "this bounteous feast" possible. I wondered how you went about splitting the bill with the Lord.

Brendan was a jack-in-the box at his seat, jumping up every few seconds to say something in the ear of someone at our table, or sallying forth into the main dining room to a particular table. Whoever he talked to, whether it was one person or a whole group, immediately went into gales of laughter. He didn't come near me once.

There was almost no talk at the head table, everybody noticeably concentrating on his food. I tried a couple of times with Catherine, but she seemed sadly preoccupied and only whispered a few monosyllables in return. Was it because I was leaving?

After the soup came salad, and then huge slabs of roast beef, bone in, with roasted potatoes and carrots and seconds for anyone who could manage them, and finally a giant chocolate ice-cream cake, which drew oohs as it was wheeled in on a table before being sliced and apportioned.

The bars had been kept open during the whole meal, and the traffic was busy on all sides. Even the kids seemed a little high, probably from the amount of sugar in the soft drinks and the general atmosphere of their parents and cousins.

Finally, after the coffee and tea were poured, all the waiters, bartenders and busboys left the room, as had been prearranged, and the doors were closed in on us while the men lighted up the cigars that had been passed among them. The time had come for the speech, and as I stood up, I could feel the butterflies, plus what seemed to be some hornets, fluttering and buzzing in my belly.

"Can you hear me in the back?" I called out, after the crowd had been properly shushed by the women. The answer was a huge belch from one of the rear tables, which brought on a minute of laughter before they all quieted down again.

"Although I haven't had the opportunity to get to know all of you personally," I began, "I have had the chance to experience somewhat what your lives are like and the burdens you bear because of your religion and your background. I have your blood in me, but I also have the blood of another minority people, and this has made it doubly important for me to do for you what I can before I return to the United States."

I then went on to outline what Montenegro had worked out for me as far as they were concerned and affected. I told them that there would be a paper for them to sign before they left the banquet hall, and their names and addresses would then be turned over to the head of the trucking company, and any one of them who wanted a job at this company would only have to apply. They would be given jobs with decent salaries and opportunities for advancement. I said that this offer included women, too, which brought forth a gasp from the crowd.

"I'm not offering you a free ride," I told them. "This is not a charity. Any person who does not carry his weight in his job will lose that job. What you are getting is an opportunity. What you do with it after that will be your own responsibility."

There was a further clatter as they discussed what I had said among themselves for a few moments, but then they quieted down again.

"I never had a family before I came here," I said, "and I don't really know whether or not I have one now. But—"

Brendan jumped up from his chair so abruptly that he knocked it over, and all eyes, including mine, turned to watch him as he came around the table and ran right up to me.

"So you're buying yourself a family, are you, Lord? Well, here's a kiss of thanks from Judas." He grabbed my head with both hands and stuck his burning lips against my cheek. "Remember," he continued, "the one who loves you the most is the most dangerous one of all."

Then he ran back to his place, righted the chair, and sat down. The crowd, who probably thought he was thanking me for my generosity, laughed uproariously, but there was such a sinking feeling in my gut that I thought I would throw up the little I had eaten right square on the table. Because that kiss had brought it all together, all the things that had been said over the days since I had arrived. The bewildered Benny Freedman, trapped in an alien environment, had missed it all, but Lieutenant Benny Freedman of the homicide division of the San Diego, California, police department had stored it at the same time in the back of his head, and now it had come together.

I have done everything I had to for the cause, he had said. *I have done the ultimate for the cause.*

Not even blood makes a difference anymore, he had said. *It's like your Civil War was, brother against brother.*

Over here there are no boys, he had said. *No babies. No fathers, no mothers, no sisters, no brothers. Over here there are only those who can deal with death.*

No brothers.

He wanted me to know. He wanted everybody to know. If he didn't get it out, he was going to explode. But he wouldn't tell. He had to be made to tell. He wanted me to make him tell. If I didn't do it, there was nobody else who could. I was the only one trained to make all the connections.

And such a rage went through me that it was all I could do to keep from running over and smashing away at him until I had destroyed that face forever. Why had he done this to me? Why was I the one that had to pull the trigger? Did he hate me that much? The mixture of anger and sadness that went through me was almost too much to bear, but right then I knew I had to settle this forever or it would haunt me for the rest of my life. If he wanted Judas, if he needed Judas so badly, the Jew would give him Judas.

37

I TURNED AND FACED THE CROWD AGAIN, all of whom had begun to babble excitedly while I was staring at Brendan. If my intent had been to "buy" myself a family, then I had obviously succeeded because there was nothing but friendly faces in front of me. Some of the women looked as if they were crying.

Once more the shushes sounded through the hall, and all eyes concentrated on me. What other bounties were the Lord and I about to dispense?

"There's always a catch to any offer," I said, and some of the smiles turned to frowns as they wondered how they were about to be cheated. These were people who had been given many platitudes over the years, all of which had turned into dust. What was the American, what was the Jew, up to?

"What I would like to do," I said, "is pluck my cousin Catherine Callaghan, who has been my friend and guide while I have been here, from among you and take her back to America. I want to show her California where I live and possibly the rest of the United States. I want her to see the opportunities that are available so she can perhaps relate them to you, and then some of you young people can decide whether you want to try your chances in a new place. I read where the youth of Ireland have been seeking opportunities abroad, and I want my cousins to have the same chances. So with Catherine as your advance scout, perhaps we can—"

"No!" Brendan bellowed, jumping from his chair again and running to the front of our table, where he glared at me, his back to the crowd behind him.

"No!" he yelled again. "I won't permit it. I

stopped Sean from marrying the Protestant, and I'll stop you, Jew, from stealing Catherine from me."

He looked at our table, inspecting each face as though he was going to find some answer to his problem in it. Some of them hadn't comprehended what he was saying, but I could see that Catherine and Father Delavar and a couple of the others had instantly worked it through. What he saw was enough to make Brendan utter a wail of anguish.

"It was an accident," he yelled, weaving a few inches from side to side, his face so red that it didn't look human. "I only meant to scare him. He was running down the street and I stepped out and stopped him. I was the only one who could have stopped him, he ran so fast. No one else could have done it. And I told him he had to call it off, and he told me to go to blazes. And I held the gun to his head, only to scare him, and he jerked against it and it went off. It went off. And if I had to do it again, I would. And if you try to steal my Catherine, Cousin Benjamin, my cousin Benjamin, I'll do the same for you."

He fell to his knees, his legs unable to bear the burden of his body any longer. The combination of the fever and the whiskey had sapped him of all strength, and he looked up at us pleadingly, begging to be taken down from the cross on which he had nailed himself. How many hints had he given me every time he spoke about the cause and what must be done? If you have to kill your brother, he had said, then you have to kill your brother. Except that he hadn't wanted to kill his brother, hadn't meant to kill his brother. And now, for revenge, he was trying to get his brother to kill him.

Only the ones in the front tables behind him had heard any of what Brendan had said, and the rest of the crowd was moving forward to find out what they had missed. It would take a while, but finally the truth would be worked out among them, and all would know what had happened that fateful night when Sean O'Malley had made his last run against everything that his brother Brendan had dedicated his life to.

The two Callaghan boys worked their way around the table and lifted Brendan between them.

"We've got to get him to Jim's," I heard one of them say. "The wound has gone bad." They heaved him up and carried him through the crowd, shouting at another cousin that they would need his car. I could tell by the way that Brendan's head was hanging that he was unconscious. It was possible that he was dead. If he wasn't, if they saved him, it would be the cruelest thing that could have happened.

Father Delavar turned to look at me, his face so horror-stricken that I almost reached out my hand to keep him from falling. Only God knew what this little man had heard in all his years in the confessional, but now he had been hit with something that even he couldn't handle.

Catherine was behind him, her beautiful face set into a mask which I realized would always be set against me. She was the one who had given me the assignment. *"I want you to find out who really killed Sean so that blame can be put in the right quarter,"* she had said. I wondered if I had spoken about taking her to America because I knew it was the only way to force Brendan into some kind of action, or if, deep down, I had wanted to take her for myself, to hold that innocence in my hand, to spend the rest of my life at her side.

"Catherine," I said, but she turned and made her way through the crowd and then went out the door that Brendan had been carried through. When push came to shove, she was one of them, and I was one of me. Had Brendan known that? Was this the price he was willing to pay in order to break her off from me? "Leave her be," Father Delavar had commanded. "She is what she is and will be what she'll be." It was the same for all of them in this accursed place. None of them could change.

As I stood there, relatives kept coming up and thanking me for the "grand party" and for the chance to get some "daycent" jobs. I nodded back at all of them, unable to smile, but that didn't seem to be necessary.

My uncle William was the last one to approach.

Although he hadn't bothered to say hello, at least he was going to say good-bye.

"Well, you've certainly done the damage here," he grated. "Best you'd been stillborn in your mother's womb."

Although he had lost, Brendan had won. The family would never turn him in for the murder. And after a while, once the shock wore off, they would excuse it by saying he had only tried to do it to keep Sean from the Protestants. The gun had misfired, they would say. A terrible accident, but one that God would forgive. After all, they were fighting in a war, with Brendan one of their leaders, and things happen in a war. Brendan would never forgive himself, but the rest of them, including Catherine, would be more charitable. Would they marry? Would Brendan and Catherine marry? More than likely, I realized. More than likely.

I was still standing there all alone five minutes later when the caterer came over. His people had started to clean up the place, and the clatter of dishes and their cheerful shouts to each other only heightened my aloneness.

"Was everything all right, Mr. Freedman?" he asked. "Did it go well? I've never done one this fancy before, and I doubt that I'll ever have a chance to do one like it again."

"It went as well as could be expected," I told him, "It went as well as it could go. And I hope you're right. I hope there never is another one like this again."

He nodded and smiled as though he understood what I was saying and agreed with it completely. After all, he was the one who had received the thirty pieces of silver.

38

IT WAS NINE P.M. WHEN I RETURNED TO the hotel and though I didn't want to go up to my room, there was no other place to hide. My flight was at eight A.M., and I pulled my bag from the closet and carefully placed in it the clothes from the drawers and hangers, leaving only what I would need for the night and the morning.

I thought of going down to Fairly Street to find out about Brendan's condition and maybe to see if I could crack the concrete on Catherine's face. My mind was in such a turmoil as I thought of her that I had to keep walking around the room while the thoughts bounced off each other like lasers. What could I say? What could any of them say to me? Uncle William had said it all. I dropped to the floor and started to do push-ups, but neither my heart nor my arms were in it, and I stopped before I had reached a dozen.

I took a shower but that didn't wash off anything. The room was hot so I didn't put any clothes on, just walked around naked, holding myself stiff so I didn't pound my fists into the walls. The television stood there impassively, waiting to do what it could to occupy the mind, but I didn't have the strength to turn the switch. I did have enough to flick the overhead light off, and then I stood there in the dark, the only light coming as a faint glow through the drapes on the window.

I dropped into the armchair and sat rigidly, my legs together, my arms by my side. And that's where I spent the night, the entire night, until the glow from outside turned from streetlights to daylight. All night I kept seeing Brendan in that street, his brother running toward him. I was sure there had been plenty to drink, partly because Brendan drank a lot anyway and partly because he needed to nerve himself up to approach his brother. Deep down he had to have known that Sean would not give up Molly. Was it accident or the subconscious that had pulled that trigger? Twice in my career I had put my gun against a man's head and threatened to blow it off if he didn't do what I said or didn't tell me what I wanted to know. Once I had almost squeezed too hard out of sheer frustration and anger. You didn't think about consequences then; you weren't really in control of your mind or your body. Had Brendan been in control? Had he meant only to frighten Sean? How many nights had he sat like I had and gone over the whole thing in his mind? Over and over and over and over again. Like the fox gnawing at your entrails. I hoped he was dead. I hoped he was alive. I wanted to see Catherine and talk to her. I didn't want to see Catherine. I didn't want to see that look in her eyes. Brendan had known what he was doing when he forced me into being the one who exposed him. He knew Catherine better than I did. I cursed my mother for putting that blood into me. I cursed myself for being a good cop.

At five-thirty A.M., I couldn't wait any longer; I had to get out of that room. It would be better to sit in the middle of an airport's bustle than to keep bouncing off those walls. I left a tip for the maid under a glass in the bathroom, and took the elevator to the lobby.

She was there, of course, sitting primly in one of the individual fake leather chairs, her hands folded across her lap, her legs tight together from the knees down. No nun could have done it better. I wondered how many nuns had Dennis Rafterys in their backgrounds. I felt my mouth twist as his name passed through my mind. Did I hate or envy him for deflowering my young cousin Catherine?

Her face didn't change and her body didn't move when she saw me, so I went over to her, as though she were Queen Victoria and I a general reporting on a losing battle in India. I stood before her and dropped my suitcase on the floor. She jumped a bit when the bag hit the imitation marble.

"Why do you have your satchel?" she asked. "Where are you going?"

"I'm going home."

Her eyes instantly filled with tears, and she pushed herself out of the chair, flung her arms around my neck and shoved her head under my chin.

"Oh, Cousin Benny," she mumbled, "why did you come here? Why did you come here?"

Was she requesting information or bemoaning my presence? Why had I come there? There was certainly anger over how they had treated my mother. Had I come to wreak vengeance on them? Had I come to hit somebody with my fist? Had I come to destroy their lives? No, it couldn't have been that because once I had arrived there had been no desire on my part to do any of those things.

On the contrary, I had wanted to become part of them. I was looking for a family to take me in, to embrace and maybe love me. Catherine had said she loved me, Brendan had embraced and even kissed me. I raised my hand and rubbed the spot on the right cheek where the ashes of his Judas kiss still burned a bit.

"How is Brendan?" I asked her.

She pulled her head away and looked up into my eyes.

"Charles said he is going to be all right. The wound had festered and his fever was high, but Jim gave him some penicillin stuff and said he would pull out of it. Brendan's been through a lot the past week, the dear boy."

The dear boy? The dear boy! What the hell did she mean by *the dear boy?*

"Brendan and Sean?" I asked tentatively. "What do they all think about Brendan and Sean?"

She looked puzzled, her head cocked to one side as she weighed the question.

"Well," she said finally, "we're all happy that Aunt Meg hasn't lost a second son."

She hadn't understood. Catherine hadn't understood what Brendan was saying. Maybe none of them understood, the way his voice was slurred with the drink and the pain. They were all pretty drunk themselves. The priest had understood. Father Delavar had understood. You could see it in his eyes and hear it in his voice. But not Catherine; and not Uncle William; and not the rest of them. The priest wouldn't talk; he wouldn't tell anybody. So only the three of us really knew—me, Brendan and the priest. Brendan wouldn't make a confession like that twice. Without the fever and the booze, he wouldn't have the guts to do it again. He had gotten it out and now it wouldn't fester inside him. The only way he could be made to pay would be if I personally presented the bill. Was I my cousin's keeper? Was I the world's keeper? A weariness so heavy set over me that my knees felt like they were going to buckle. But I didn't bend. Let others bear the burden. Let the priest bear the burden. That's what priests were for, wasn't it?

"Come on," I said to Catherine. "Ride with me out to the airport."

"How would I get back?" she asked.

"I'll give you money for the taxi," I told her, taking her arm and leading her over to the desk where I paid my bill.

We were stopped once on the way to the airport, but the inspection was cursory and the soldier didn't even ask to see my papers. We rode in silence all the way. She probably was constrained by the presence of the driver, and I had too many things whirling in my mind.

The security at the airport was even tighter than when I had come over. The riots, as the newspapers had put it, still made their mark on everything in the aftermath. They'd happened before; they'd happen again no matter how much security was laid on.

"I assume that you haven't had breakfast either," I said to Catherine, and led her over to the restaurant where we secured pale tan coffees and stale raisin buns, and sat down in an isolated corner.

"Do you really have to go?" she asked, after taking a huge bite of her bun. "Father Delavar said I shouldn't have been plaguing you about joining the church and marrying you. If that's why you're leaving, I'll stop. I swear on my mother that I'll stop. I don't want you to go. Stay awhile longer."

"I have to go," I told her. "I have to get back to my job."

"Will you be coming again soon?"

"Maybe you could visit me in California, just as I said at the farewell banquet," I told her. "I meant every word of that. Anytime you want to come, I'll send you the tickets and traveling money, and we'll tour the States and show you the sights."

She shivered a bit as she thought on that.

"That sounds exciting," she said, "and maybe Brendan could come with me."

My heart sank as I realized that neither she nor Brendan would ever come to visit me, that their lives would sink back into the bog that held them so firmly. Did I want to see Brendan again? What would I do if I saw Brendan again? No, I didn't ever want to see Brendan again. Never.

"Maybe," I said brightly. "Maybe. But remember, if you ever need anything, anything at all, you let me know." I handed her my card, which she stuck into her pocket.

The flight was called.

"Why were you waiting for me at the hotel this morning?" I asked her.

"I don't know," she said. "I was so upset about Brendan and I had such a strange feeling at the party that I couldn't sleep afterward. I had to talk to someone. And when I thought about it, I realized you were the only one I wanted to talk to."

I put my arms around her and kissed her full on the lips. It was by no means a cousinly kiss, and even went beyond any we had done during our night of necking. She gave as good as she got, and when I finally pulled away, I saw that her eyes were filled with tears again.

"Oh, Cousin Benny," she said again, "what am I going to do without you? I'll never be the same."

I took out my long wallet from the inside pocket of my jacket, separated ten pounds from the stack and pushed the rest at her. There must have been a thousand pounds there, but she had no idea of the amount as she stuffed the wad into her catchall bag. I thought of her carrying the guns in her sister's sack, and it almost made me smile.

"Go get your taxi," I told her, pushing on her shoulders with the tips of my fingers, and she turned and walked briskly away without looking at my face again. If she had, I don't know what would have happened. Deep down she had to sense as well as I did that our worlds were too far apart.

I waited until everyone had checked through before I started for the gate. The young man tore the strip off my boarding pass and wished me a pleasant flight. The passageway was empty except for a man in a raincoat standing by the side. Somehow I wasn't surprised to see Inspector Simmons there. It was inevitable. Just as was the pipe he clutched in his right hand.

"So nice of you to see me off," I said.

He nodded as though that was to be the end of it, but then he spoke.

"Just wanted to make sure you got out safely," he said. "Professional courtesy to another police officer."

"You owe me nothing," I told him. "As you noted, that ride you gave me balanced out my saving your life."

"That's the very point, isn't it?" he said. "I wanted to thank you and shake your hand."

He slipped the pipe in his pocket and stuck out his right hand. I looked at it for a long moment, then took it and we shook, acknowledging all that had happened between us and the fact that we had both dedicated our lives to the same purpose. Each in his own way, of course, but basically for the same purpose.

But he couldn't let it go at that; he couldn't let it end on that formal note. We may have been in the same business, but we were definitely not the same people.

"You'll be better off when you're home again," he said. "You were out of your depth here. You told me you were going to find the killer of your cousin Sean."

"*And* I did," I told him. "I certainly did."

Lifting my flight bag to my shoulder, I started down the runway again, my ears ready for the yell or the feet pounding after me. He knew I was telling him the truth, he knew it as well as he knew the feel of that damned pipe.

But there was nothing, nothing at all. I didn't look back but continued on right through the door of the plane, where the stewardess looked at my ticket, gave me a smile, took my coat and settled me into my first-class seat. I was the only one in first class. I was all alone.

ABOUT THE AUTHOR

MILTON BASS is the author of three other Benny Freedman novels, *The Moving Finger, Dirty Money,* and *The Bandini Affair,* available in Signet editions. He has written seven other hardcover books, including *Jory,* which was also a movie. He lives in Pittsfield, Massachusetts.

⓪ SIGNET MYSTERY (0451)

MASTERS OF MYSTERY

☐ **MURDER MOVES IN by A.M. Pyle.** When gentrification comes to a Cincinnati slum, death starts making housecalls and a two-legged rat gets exterminated. But with the Mayor warning him not to step on any toes ... it is going to be a long walk along the dark side of revenge and murder for Cesar Franck, the city cop who has to put the pieces together. "Intriguing!"—*Booklist* (148894—$3.50)

☐ **A BODY SURROUNDED BY WATER by Eric Wright.** Inspector Charlie Salter travels to Prince Edward Island for a peaceful vacation. But instead of tranquility he finds a hotbed of crime and murder. "The Charlie Salter series is not to be missed."—*Washington Post* (163850—$3.95)

☐ **FADEAWAY by Richard Rosen.** From the Edgar Award-winning author of *Strike Three You're Dead.* A few months ago Harvey Blissberg was a major league outfielder. Now he's a private investigator trying to find out if there's life after baseball. There is. It's called basketball. "Blends sports and crime in a novel full of snap, crackle, and grace."—Robert Parker, author of "Spencer" novels. (400461—$3.95)

☐ **MORTAL SINS—A Judith Hayes Mystery by Anna Porter.** When a reclusive Canadian tycoon dies suddenly at his own dinner party, freelance reporter Judith Hayes is cheated out of a much-sought-after interview. But when a shoeless corpse also turns up, Judith begins to suspect that there's more to the story than meets the eye. "Splendid ... a compelling mystery—*Arthur Hailey* (401530—$4.50)

☐ **SATURDAY NIGHT DEAD by Richard Rosen.** In Rosen's third novel starring Harvey Blissberg, major-league baseball player turned detective, the suspicious suicide of a late-night TV show producer puts Harvey in the game. What he finds is a production company full of suspects ... and motives. "It's three hits in three at-bats for Harvey Blissberg ... An unusually satisfying mystery."—*ALA Booklist* (401344—$3.95)

☐ **JACK THE RIPPER by Mark Daniel.** The greatest manhunt—the most chilling mystery—is about to be solved, but first it will take you from the lowest depths of evil to the glittering heights of English society ... then at last you will be face to face with the man we now know only as Jack the Ripper. A bloody mystery with four different endings—watch the CBS TV Superspecial to discover the 'right' one! (160185—$3.95)

Buy them at your local bookstore or use this convenient coupon for ordering.
NEW AMERICAN LIBRARY
P.O. Box 999, Bergenfield, New Jersey 07621

Please send me the books I have checked above. I am enclosing $_____
(please add $1.00 to this cover postage and handling). Send check or money order—no cash or C.O.D.'s.

Name_____
Address_____
City _____ State _____ Zip Code _____

Allow 4-6 weeks for delivery.
This offer, prices and numbers are subject to change without notice.

ⓘ SIGNET (0451)

LIVES IN THE BALANCE

- [ ] **HARD RAIN by Peter Abrahams.** Once Jessie had been a free-spirited flower child. Now she was a divorced mother whose child was missing. The cops couldn't help her, and someone was trying to kill her, as she followed a trail of violence and treachery so far and yet so near to the lost Woodstock generation of peace and love ... "A nightmarish thriller that has it all."—*The New York Times Book Review*   (401131—$4.50)

- [ ] **TOUGH ENOUGH by W.R. Philbrick.** In this third T.D. Stash adventure, deadly greed and a terrified child stir part-time sleuth into the marshes of the Florida Everglades in search of a savage secret laying below the surface. "One of the best since Travis McGee!"—*Orlando Sentinal*   (159985—$3.50)

- [ ] **PATTERN CRIMES by William Bayer.** First the prostitute, then the nun, then the transvestite—all three corpses with the same hideous mutilations. The list of victims led Detective David Bar-Lev through Jerusalem on a trail of sex and savegery to reach a shocking secret and the hardest choice he had ever faced ...   (152816—$4.95)

- [ ] **WHITE SLAVE by Richard Owen.** A kidnapped girl. A Caribbean cocaine connection. And two tough cops caught up in a caper so hot it burns ...! "A plot that is well-handled and interesting ... well-drawn tropical locations ... arresting images and provocative questions."—*Publishers Weekly*   (153952—$4.50)

*Prices slightly higher in Canada

Buy them at your local bookstore or use this convenient coupon for ordering.

NEW AMERICAN LIBRARY
P.O. Box 999, Bergenfield, New Jersey 07621

Please send me the books I have checked above. I am enclosing $_____
(please add $1.00 to this order to cover postage and handling). Send check or money order—no cash or C.O.D.'s. Prices and numbers are subject to change without notice.

Name_____

Address_____

City _____ State _____ Zip Code _____

Allow 4-6 weeks for delivery.
This offer is subject to withdrawal without notice.

SIGNET MYSTERY (0451)

DEADLY DEALINGS

- ☐ **BINO by A.W. Gray.** Bino, is a white-haired, longhorn lawyer with the inside scoop on everything from hookers to Dallas high society. When his seediest client turns up dead, Bino suspects a whitewash of the dirtiest kind and goes on the offensive. What he finds links his client's demise to a political assassination, and the bodies start piling up. Politics has always been the dirtiest game in town—and it's about to become the deadliest. (401298—$3.95)

- ☐ **MURDER by Parnell Hall.** "A gem of a novel ... real fear and a strong sense of justice."—*Rave Reviews* Stanley Hastings never looks for trouble, but it finds him when bored housewife Pamela Barringer is trapped in a call-girl racket with blackmail and murder hot on her trail! "By turns hair-raising and hilarious!"—*Publishers Weekly* (401107—$3.95)

- ☐ **A CLUBBABLE WOMAN by Reginald Hill.** Sam Connon stood pale-faced and trembling in the darkened hall of his house, the telephone in his hand. Behind him, in the living room was his wife. She was quite, quite dead. And as even a distraught husband could tell, she must have known her killer very, very well.... (155165—$3.50)

- ☐ **DEATH SPIRAL by Bill Kelly and Dolph Le Moult.** Stunning young Lisa Thorpe was lying dead in a pool of her own blood. It's up to Detective Vince Crowly of the NYPD to uncover the ugliest secrets a beautiful girl ever left behind! (401395—$3.95)

Prices slightly higher in Canada

Buy them at your local bookstore or use coupon on next page for ordering.